Edith Pargeter has gained world-wide praise and recognition for her imaginative reconstructions of monastic life in the twelfth century in the Brother Cadfael series of novels, which are now in their twentieth volume.

By Firelight

Edith Pargeter

First published in 1948
by William Heinemann Ltd

First published in paperback in 1994
by HEADLINE BOOK PUBLISHING

A HEADLINE REVIEW paperback

10 9 8 7 6 5 4 3 2

ISBN 0 7472 4561 4

Typeset by
Avon Dataset Ltd., Bidford-on-Avon, B50 4JH
Printed and bound in Great Britain by
Cox & Wyman Ltd, Reading, Berks

HEADLINE BOOK PUBLISHING
A division of Hodder Headline PLC
338 Euston Road, London NW1 3BH

CONTENTS

I	Claire in Mourning	1
II	The House in School Lane	21
III	The Fire Begins to Burn	43
IV	Record of a Witch-Trial	65
V	Claire in the Garden	83
VI	The True Story of Salathiel Drury	103
VII	The True Story of Salathiel Drury (Contd.)	135
VIII	The True Story of Salathiel Drury (Contd.)	147
IX	The True Story of Salathiel Drury (Contd.)	171
X	'The Hour is About to Be—'	195
XI	The Others	199
XII	The Trial of Salathiel Drury	219
XIII	A Witch-Burning	251
XIV	'It Is—'	279
XV	'It Passes Away'	295

'The hour is about to be, it is, it passes away.'

I

CLAIRE IN MOURNING

On the second day after the funeral Claire observed a considerable drop in the number of sympathetic letters and telephone calls she found it necessary to answer. She had not, it seemed, so many friends that the list could not exhaust itself in a few days. She was not disposed to quarrel with this circumstance; she had done all the proper things, uttered all the proper phrases over and over with her usual chilly competence, and she was tired of them all. Not, as yet, tired with any vehemence or impatience; she merely found herself listening with wonder and almost amusement to her own voice, so limpid and cool, suitably acknowledging condolences which left no single ripple upon the flat, glazed surface of her mind. It surprised her that she should be looked upon as in need of sympathy and consideration, and yet she found it even more surprising that she should feel surprised. All the rules were laid down; she knew them all, had known them since she was a child and kept them, and her life had presented in consequence an austere symmetrical pattern which had its beauty. Naturally her world would continue to conform to that ideal of order. Stephen's death had merely set in motion a ritual to which she was less accustomed than to most, but her response had been mechanical and appropriate. In herself, now that the slight shock had passed, she felt no great change; there was no reminder even when she passed before a mirror, for black became her, and she had worn it for years. Nevertheless, a phase had ended; if she forgot it, the last of her friends would remind her.

Leonora had missed the funeral, being absent upon one of

her reluctant visits to her family in the Midlands, but she was back in town that morning, by Breck's report, and would certainly turn up before the day was out. Most of the others had already been, murmured their regrets for Stephen's early death and her widowhood, and gone thankfully away again with their duty done. Sincere regrets enough, for probably they had liked the dead man as well as need be. And yet, she had thought as she listened, how hard it must be for them to care very much, how hard it is at best for one living creature to yield up to another even such a small part of its individuality as will lie in one gesture of regret. The human heart is an enclosed place, a tower without window or door. Stephen had never entered hers, and never left it.

Leonora came after lunch, which was tactful of her, for Anne had not yet packed her cases and gone back to her new husband in Somerset, and to sit at table with these two would have been less than restful. They disliked each other with all the natural violence of Anne's twenty-one conventional years and Leonora's middle-aged, spiced bitterness. Better by far to have no such meetings; Claire had enjoyed them once, and some day, no doubt, would recapture that perverse pleasure, but for this time there must be quietness. She had no energy left in her, and malice requires plentiful energy. Leonora, who had spent her life being malicious, sometimes for money but oftener for love, perfectly understood that.

She sat in Claire's lounge, facing the light and looking her full age, which was forty-nine; and she said very much what had been said by all the rest, but with a certain perfunctory grace, almost absent-mindedly, so that Claire knew she was presenting for inspection an aspect of the bereavement with which she herself was not in the least preoccupied. Last she said, staring sidelong through her own ageing reflection with grey eyes whose look was like a flaying knife:

'All the same, you can't complain. You've had everything. Some people keep things longer, but at least you've had them, for as long as you could expect.'

'Have I?' said Claire.

'Haven't you? A career, a husband, and a child.'

'Is that everything?' asked Claire in the same considering voice, watching with some pleasure the dappling of leafy light over the smooth lines of her hands as they lay empty in her lap.

'There are decorations, but no more major experiences that I know of. The thing could have been improved. Your books might have been more important, though of their kind they could hardly be better. Your husband might have been more exciting, but if he had been you would have had no use for him. As for Anne, she's maddening but she is young, she was even a baby once, I suppose, and got herself born like all the rest.'

'Is that the main thing, then?'

'I think it must be,' said Leonora. 'The best and the worst of them hurt when they arrive; it seems to be the only thing they all have in common, besides being adored for it. There must be a connection.'

'You talk as if you were reaching the stage,' said Claire, faintly smiling, 'when even blessedness becomes only biological. Are you?'

'There are only three real ends in life that I can see. I've touched only one of them; you've had all three. I don't grudge them to you, Claire, but I grudge it that I've missed so much. I can't care that you've lost something I would have liked and have never had. How can I?'

'I don't ask you to, I don't want you to.'

'No,' said Leonora with her sudden blinding smile, 'after so much sympathy my egotism must be very refreshing. Your last few days must have been rather like slow suffocation under a succession of feather beds. Half one's life seems to be spent in trying to establish contact with people, and the other half in trying to escape from them. Have they driven you mad?'

The cool smile, the long eyes under their levelled brows, had never been so sane, the folded hands so serene. 'Everyone has been very kind,' said Claire indifferently.

'You sound like Anne!'

'I know. I often do. It took me a long time to recognise the likeness.'

Leonora turned and looked at her for some minutes without words, studying with her handsome, incisive eyes every feature of the pale face which fronted her faintly smiling, and would not change under her gaze. They had known each other for many years; there was no curiosity left in either of them concerning the other, but only an intelligent interest such as they might have felt in the contemplation of developing characters in their own half-written books. They waited upon revelation, respectfully, no emotion caught up into the exchange.

'Would you really have liked a daughter like Anne?'

'I would have liked a daughter of any kind, or a son of any kind. I shall never have either. How is Anne?'

'Very well. I think very happy. She goes home tomorrow.'

'I suppose you'll miss her,' said Leonora.

'I suppose so.' Claire's brown brows drew together, as if she saw only distantly any future in which Anne could be expected to leave a gap.

'What are you going to do? I suppose he left you well provided for?'

'Very much as we expected. A little less than my guess, and a little more than Breck's. It will keep me in a fashion.'

'But not this fashion?'

'Not for long.'

'I see. So you'll be writing again, I suppose. Have you anything in mind?'

'No, nothing.' It sounded to her like the literal truth. There was nothing within her but an emptiness, without even an echo to people it; and this not because Stephen was gone from there, not because Anne had married and taken her bright youth away out of it. It was an old emptiness, in which nothing had ever more than seemed to exist; all that had prevented her from seeing long ago how void it was, was that she had never paused to look until now. Things she had seemed to have, had seemed to go away out of her reach; and the very fact that their loss made so small a ripple upon her frigid content had driven her to search her life for the first time, and see with wonder how slight their presence had been.

Leonora, it appeared, found her in some way enviable. Leonora had never married, and thought now, at forty-nine, that she would have liked, after all, to be a wife and mother. Claire had been both, and exemplary in both characters in a negative sort of way; the marriage had been lasting, faithful and convenient, and Anne's careful upbringing had produced a graceful, sensible and accomplished young woman who had made in time an admirable marriage. This was what Leonora wanted now that it was too late. Or perhaps what Claire had had was only an illusion of the things Leonora wanted, and they had both been cheated.

'You'll stay on here, I suppose?'

'I don't know yet. I haven't had time to think about it.'

'No, of course not. I'm not good at this. I never lost a husband myself.' By her voice, easy though it was, she would have been glad to have one if only for the experience of loss. She stroked back her sleek, greying hair, and gave a short, sharp sigh. 'I'll go away and leave you in what peace you can find. If you have Anne in the flat and Breck hovering around with documents it won't be much.' She rose; she was still a slender and shapely woman, and with the light behind her could have been no more than thirty years old.

'If there should be anything I can do for you, you'll call upon me, won't you, Claire?'

'Thank you, but everything seems to be done.'

Afterwards, when she was alone, before Anne came in with her arms full of purchases and Breck with what scraps of business remained to be tidied away, Claire stood in the centre of her fawn-and-green lounge quite still, suddenly caught and frozen by the silence which came about her. Traffic noises came in only faintly, for her windows faced the court, and a green lace of birch trees, lavish with summer, made the light entering there shimmer between emerald and gold. It was hot and still and bright outside; black was no wear for such weather. She stood with her head raised, her senses like tentacles feeling outward into this soft, bright, indifferent quietness in which nothing was vehement but the memory of Leonora stating her grudge against the world, and nothing was articulate but her own voice saying, with double meaning:

'Thank you, but everything seems to be done.'

These were parallel, and could never meet. They pursued their own separated grievances, produced into infinity. Where was the good of that? And yet how could Leonora care that Claire was a widow, or Claire that Leonora should live and die a frustrated spinster, hankering after imaginary blessings? There is only one really immediate trouble, and that is one's own. All the rest can be considered, deferred, even enjoyed, all the rest take on a shadowy sentimental beauty one may well be reluctant to dispel or deface by touch; but this one hurts, not with a poignant delight but in ugly, disconcerting reality. Or should do so. Stephen Falchion's widow found it curious that her bereavement should, after all, have been performed so painlessly, for she had been a dutiful wife, and certainly a happy one. Happy might, perhaps, have been considered too exuberant a word; a comfortable wife, then, at least, a fortunate wife, one who should have been happy. Why did she feel so little sense of loss? She was sorry Stephen was dead, of course, but a remote business acquaintance of his could have said as much as that and told no lie. She suspected that some of them were sorrier than she was, for his business virtues had been large and positive, but as a husband his goodness had consisted chiefly in having no vices. It puzzled and disquieted her that he should be able, when it came to the point, to slip away out of life and leave so slight a gap. Could she do as much? Could she take away her familiar bodily presence and the influence of her mind from Anne, and Anne's husband, and Breck, and Leonora and the rest of them, and deprive them of nothing? Every morning now at breakfast, across the table from her, she was conscious of the exact shape of Stephen sitting opposite, a space of air stamped out from the rest by the lost outline of his head and shoulders; and at first it had startled and worried her that she could see through that space to the green brocade corner of the curtain, and the polished edge of the window-frame, and the little amber clock with its bluntly-rounded glass face tapered in the morning sun to an eye of reflected light. But every morning the outline became less distinct, the abrupt point of light less unexpected, as the habit of vision which was all that survived of Stephen dwindled away into the limbo of outworn things. If she tried to call his face to mind now she knew she would achieve only an uncertain picture. So she could pass, and be as little time in remembrance. Was that enough to have gained in a lifetime?

She liked the silence; she liked the unexpected loneliness, suspended here in the heart of the hot whirl which was London. It was pleasant to be absolved from both speech and thought, to be able to sit with her hands folded and watch the high, bright blaze of the afternoon burn down into the clear oblique light of evening, and never have to say one word, or elaborate a single wandering reflection. Even when Mrs. Preedy brought her tea she had only to let the few necessary habitual words slip out of her lips without effort, and the quietness was not shaken.

'Will Mrs. Coudray be in to tea later, Mrs. Falchion?'

'No, I think not. But we shall be three to dinner. Mr. Connard is coming in.'

'Yes, Mrs. Falchion, you told me this morning.'

'Did I? I couldn't remember.'

There were things the tongue could say unordered, the mind still half-drugged in a lethargy which was almost sleep. But when Anne's key crisped in the hall door a shiver seemed to swim through the hot, leaf-shadowed air, and every weariness and reluctance within hid itself in a corner. She came in like a breath of freshness, but nothing in this dreaming room welcomed her. The silence which had seemed so grateful and undemanding erected its hackles and withdrew from the click of her heels. She was radiant, cool and discreet,

7

her soft lavender-grey suit the zenith of sophisticated mourning for the young matron, her little black hat admirably modulated from a particularly sprightly model never designed to have to do with death. Traffic noises, heat and haste seemed to come in with her, though she was fragrant as the dawn. She had even some claim to beauty, which Claire had never had; a lively, vigorous colouring, corn-tinted hair and gentian eyes had made capture of Christopher Coudray before his hand was well free of the first touch of hers, and would hold him as long as need might be, for he was a simple soul who lived in his senses. He would not grudge it that she ran him; in all probability he would never notice.

'Mother!' cried Anne, sliding parcels out of her long left arm upon the table, and gazing over them with a kind of gay exasperation such as an enthusiastic nurse might employ upon a difficult patient. 'Is that what you've been doing all afternoon?'

'I suppose so, ever since Leonora left.'

'I wish you had come out with me. It would have been so much better for you than sitting here alone.'

'Would it?' said Claire, smiling. It reassured her to find her daughter still so young, so competent and so limited.

'Of course it would! Darling, you know it does you nothing but harm to sit here and mope by yourself. You can't just cut your life off short simply because father's dead.'

'What should I do?' asked Claire, still with the same wry smile.

'Come into town with me, and buy yourself a new frock, or theatre tickets, or a puppy, or whatever you fancy. You've got to emerge some time, you know, and pick up the threads again; you may as well begin at once.'

'She will talk to herself like this,' thought Claire, 'if she outlives poor Kit; and she'll believe every word of it, and put the treatment into effect, too. She'll be well able to, for she no more loves him than I loved her father. But I never thought or pretended I loved Stephen, and she – either believes or pretends, I don't know which – she married Kit for love.'

And abruptly she felt fonder of her son-in-law, for of his motives there had never been any doubt.

Aloud she said calmly: 'There's really no need to worry about me.'

'But I do, you know. I want to be quite sure you won't retire too far into yourself when I've gone back to Westow. After all, you're only forty-one; that's hardly even middle-aged. You've half your life still to come.'

Claire laughed. 'Don't be afraid, I shall insist on every moment.' She lay back in her chair and went on laughing, so clearly did she see herself just now as Anne was seeing her. A middle-aged woman, almost old, quite negligible as far as the true current of life was concerned, a piece of jetsam cast up by a lost tide, and doomed now to rot gently and helplessly until she died. All the choice that remained to her was to accept the inevitable with or without grace; and to accept it with grace meant to pretend that it was not there, to dress herself as if people still cared greatly how she looked, to go about as if she still expected pleasure and diversion to meet her in the street, to maintain contacts with her acquaintances as if it still mattered that she should like or dislike them, and be liked or disliked in return. It was necessary, of course, that Anne should pretend, too, but she could do that to such perfection as to deceive even herself. It discommoded her that Claire should laugh, but perhaps that was merely an unexpected nervous reaction, and in any case Anne could easily pretend that she had not noticed that, either.

She slipped off the little black hat and ran her fingers through her hair, waiting until the unseemly laughter should end; and then she came back to her duty conscientiously, her face assuming that look, at once serious and bright, which she had adopted only since Claire had become at one stroke a widow and a back-number.

'You know, mother, we really ought to consider the future. I shall be terribly worried until I know that you've made some sensible plans. You'll keep the flat on, of course. After all, you must have a place in London, mustn't you?'

'Must I?' said Claire. 'Why?'

'Well, there's your agent and publishers; and you always have had a place in town.'

'True,' she said thoughtfully. 'I might try a change. Perhaps, after all, I was really born to be a countrywoman.'

Watching her daughter, she saw the gentian eyes sharpen and lighten for a moment, and linger upon her warily even while the rounded lips uttered a little laugh of disbelief.

'Mother! You've the very picture of the urban woman. I can't even imagine you on a farm. You don't really feel tempted to disappear into the west country, or anything like that, do you?'

Poor Anne! She was thinking, of course, of the horror of having Claire at Westow for the rest of her life. Mother always about the place. Mother's books would have to be fished out of hiding and given a prominent place on the shelves; mother would watch her running the house, and raise her eyebrows just as she was raising them now, and make no comment. Worst of all, mother would get on much too well with Kit, as she always had. The engagement had been cut short solely because mother and Kit had achieved too great a degree of intimacy, though mother didn't realise that, of course! But if she came to live with them at Westow things would be unbearable. He would always be looking round for her, sitting at her feet, inviting her to join him in those teasing moods which were disturbing enough even when he had no ally. No, she must not come to Westow. And yet it was impossible, of course, to refuse her a home in so many words; it had to be done obliquely.

Claire saw the cool, small thoughts arranging themselves apprehensively behind the blue eyes. She felt a momentary idle temptation to prolong the issue and the disquiet, but the spark of energy which might have sustained her died out soon. 'I am a detestable woman,' she thought; 'why should she be otherwise?'

'Not the west country, at any rate. It's lovely, no doubt, when you're newly married into it, but it never charmed me particularly.' She did not make the mistake of watching Anne too closely, but she was aware of the inrush of relief and pleasure, and she would have liked to laugh again, though more gently.

'You know, darling,' said Anne, 'that you can always come to us.'

'Yes,' said Claire, smiling at the levelling light through the birch trees, 'I know that I *can*.' It was diverting, up to a point, to comply with Anne's designs so far as to put herself in the wrong; it was amusing to be reassured, with increasing confidence as it became clear that she had no intention of accepting it, that there was and always would be a home and a welcome waiting for her at Westow. She played the game until it sickened her, and suddenly she wanted the silence back again. After dinner there would be Breck Connard talking business, and at least she would not have to arrange her words for him, or play kitten tricks to cover up decently a cat's designs; but the silence in which she had almost lost herself for a while would have no chance of return. She supposed it existed somewhere, not by man's grace, but by right; it would be well worth a search to find that place.

After dinner Anne went out, and without her if it was not quieter at least it seemed so, for the disturbing brightness and gaiety went out with her. As for Breck, Claire had known him fairly intimately for twelve years, had entrusted her business affairs to him for ten, and still found herself able to like him. He was a small, careworn cynic, grey and spare, who brought no violence of feeling or thought or movement into the room, but sank into the despondent twilight until she became almost unconscious of his presence. Even his voice answering her was little and dry and cool, and could pass for an echo from the back of her own mind. He was no trouble.

'That's all?' she said, when she had signed her name for the last time.

'That's all. Well, Claire? So you're a widow, and about eight thousand pounds richer than you were. Feel any different?'

'I hardly know yet. How should I feel?'

'Bereaved, I suppose – however that may feel. But you know no more about it than I do.'

'No,' she admitted thoughtfully, 'whatever it may be, it isn't that.'

'It's the natural loss of equilibrium that results when a large lump is taken out of one side of your life, that's all. Everything will settle down again if you let it.'

'Perhaps – if I let it. How if I don't?'

'Then anything can happen. It's up to you. What do you think of doing?'

Claire got up and crossed to the window, where she stood looking out into the foliage silvered by the slant light of evening. A ghost of her own face, faint and transparent, looked back at her from within the glass with large, light eyes, and lifted brown, thin brows at her arrogantly. She smiled, but the reflected lips were too shadowy for the change to be seen clearly, and the eyes did not smile.

'I think I shall go away from here, Breck. I think I shall sell the flat, or let it, and clear out of London.'

'And what? Turn shepherdess?'

'Not quite. Find myself a cottage somewhere that will cost me a great deal less than this place does, preferably within easy reach of town, but anyhow, somewhere. And continue to make a living by the only means I know. I need a retired spot to pick up the threads; and anyhow, I can't afford to keep on the flat.'

'I see!' said Breck, watching her through the smoke of his cigarette. 'Well, that's all sane and sound enough.'

'Yes, isn't it?' She turned and looked at him with the sharp, oblique smile he had half expected. 'And all lies, every bit. I could write here, I daresay, if I wanted to. I'm running away, Breck. This is a panic, or something like it. I'm running away to hide.'

'So I thought,' he said, unmoved. 'From whom? Me? Or your friends? Or Anne?'

Claire looked at him for a moment more in silence, with a

distant unsurprised interest. 'You don't like her, either,' she said then. 'Isn't it extraordinary? She's young, pretty, sensible and virtuous; and nobody likes her.'

'Don't change the subject. From whom do you propose to hide? Or at least, why?'

'From a vacuum. I've been living in a bubble of nothing all my life, and never realised it until now. No, it wasn't losing Stephen that made me look behind. It may have started with him. After all, it forces you to take stock when you lose something that ought to be valuable, and find it really makes no great difference. But it was Leonora who drove me to investigate the thing properly. She envies me, Breck. I hadn't realised it was possible. She was here this afternoon, and it all came out. She envies me because I've contrived to be a wife and mother, as well as an author. She tells me I daren't complain of bereavement, I've already had everything that can be got out of life. Those few books on the shelf there, and Stephen, and Anne: that's all there is to hope for, Breck.'

'So you took stock. And now you want to go away and shake the dust of this life off your feet, and see if there isn't something else to be had in another.'

'Or get used to the idea that I've left it too late, and there isn't. Which is by far the more likely thing.'

He smoked and said nothing, watching her with narrowed, shrewd eyes across the room grown shadowy with dusk; until she asked reasonably: 'Well, why don't you say something?'

'I'm still listening. What have you got to complain of? Haven't you, by Leonora's standards, had everything? I think I'm on her side. I presume you married Stephen because you wanted to?'

'My marriage was made quite coldly,' said Claire, 'like everything else I've ever done.'

'Why not? You're a cold person.'

'Am I?' she said, suddenly rearing her head to look at him full. 'How do I know that? Nothing's ever happened to warm me.'

'You're cold, neat-minded and aloof. Stephen suited you

13

very well. There never was any discomfort between you. I believe you were even fond of him.'

'I'm fond of that clock; it's been there a long time, but if it were broken I shouldn't care very much. I should be what Mrs. Preedy calls vexed. And even that not for long.'

'In short,' said Breck, as mildly as if he had been drawing up a chemical formula, 'you think that in marrying as you did you missed marriage.'

'I suited Stephen's purposes, I suppose. I was decorative, gently fashionable, faithful, tedious and indifferent. I didn't bother him, and I filled the eye and made decent conversation, even added just the right sort of unobtrusive minor lustre to his name. I suppose he suited my purposes equally well – then.'

'So you want something more now!'

'I want what I know nothing about; whatever it is that people like Leonora see fit to envy. She thought it had been here; I can testify that was never true, but I suppose it must exist somewhere.'

'And is that all?' he asked, seeing that she paused.

'No, that's only the beginning. Even a marriage like ours might at least produce a child one could love. I was a model mother by the book, you know. I did everything one should do, and avoided everything one shouldn't. Probably there was a time when I had a satisfaction in it that wasn't altogether cold, but I can't remember it now. I looked at Anne this afternoon almost as if I'd never seen her before, because of what Leonora seemed to think I ought to see in her. It never occurred to me before to – to measure the feelings she roused in me. Breck, it's all wrong. Anne's my carefully-reared only daughter, and I don't even like her.'

She said this carefully, frowning over the words, considering rather their significance to herself than their effect upon him. He had been a kind of chorus to her life for years, he could bear the rôle a little longer, even though a weight of confidence was laid upon him this evening which he had never carried before. Whatever she said would not surprise him; he would still gaze back at her with the same impenetrable calm eyes, and assimilate every new facet of human folly as placidly as the old.

'Why don't you try reading your own books again?' he suggested with a wry smile. 'There seems to be nothing else left. Wallow in your own genius; there's a great deal of satisfaction to be got that way, I believe.'

'So I might, if I had any genius. But I don't have to take them down from the shelf to know the whole ten of them together don't matter a tinker's damn to me or to anyone else.'

'That's going farther than I care to follow,' said Breck. 'As an informed amateur I stick to my opinion – though I'm sorry to seem to be offering you comfort, and I suppose that makes everything I say suspect – that of their kind two at least of your books are perfect, one more very nearly so, and all deserve to be called good. You may be forty-one, frigid, and acting like a newly-converted fool, but nothing will persuade me you can't write a highly-specialised kind of prose better than anyone else. You've got a small but faithful public; they consider you've got a very discriminating public. What more do you want?'

Claire laughed. 'It has been fun, in a way. I liked being a lioness, even a very miniature and well-manicured one. I liked concocting little acid sweetmeats like *Rapunzel* and precious bits of enamelled extravagance like *Floral Tribute*, and pruning and polishing them until they were like pieces of jewellery. I liked making enthusiasm ridiculous – it almost always is from outside, but from inside I shouldn't think one would care – and emotion unbalanced, and simplicity as clumsy as affectation. I liked finishing off my little jokes so well that other people would take them seriously. But don't ask *me* to imagine they could ever *satisfy*. Why, you could eat the lot, and you'd still be empty. You might as well give me a handful of marrons glacés for dinner, and try to convince me I'd been fed.'

Breck leaned forward and offered his cigarette-case. 'Come

and sit down quietly for a few minutes. You make me restless, writhing about there by the window.' And as she came obediently he suggested: 'Shall we have some light? I am one person left alive who takes pleasure in looking at you, and it seems I'm to have the chance less often from now on.'

'Do you, Breck? That's nice of you. You never got much good by it, did you?'

'No harm that I know of, at any rate. There, that's better. Now keep still.' She narrowed her eyes at him above the glow of her cigarette, and smiled into the soft orange-coloured light of the lamp, and was still. Her eyes were light hazel, a summery, leafy, well-water colour, or like the shimmer of a brook over variegated pebbles and the green of young bright weed. As soon as the daylight was gone they lost their full, drowsy noonlight look, and became the cooler, greener colour of twilight under speckled woods. Her lashes were reddish-brown, like her hair, and long. The rest of her irregular, narrow face might belong to a woman of forty, but her eyes were young, wild and wary as a faun's. He wondered if she had often looked so, and he had never noticed. 'So you've suddenly acquired a human appetite,' he said, 'and sweets are no more use.'

'I could, of course, write a long, earthy novel about the struggle for existence on the land. We should then have a balanced diet.'

'Your sales would die of it first, and you after. Besides, your characters would still talk like Rapunzel. The graft would never take.'

'You admit it. So you see, I must starve after all. There's nothing left intact, Breck. I've been done out of everything.'

'It was entirely your own doing, Claire,' he said frankly.

'I know. Is it too late, do you suppose, for me to get something out of life yet? I know you could answer that I've never put anything in, but you won't be so obvious. What we put in is only seed, and we expect a crop from it. Even the joy of giving is only one more thing one sets out to get. My concern's all for myself. I've been done out of everything, and I've only just realised it. *Is* it too late, Breck?'

'Why ask me? If I knew the answer I might make an effort on my own account. In any case, you don't want an answer from me; you've already made up your mind.'

'Yes; so far it's easy. I shall write again because I must live; but I won't begin here. So I must go.'

'When do you propose to start?'

'As soon as I can. In a few days.'

'You want me to sell the flat?'

'Or let it. But sell it if you can.'

'I can, ten times over. Where do you think of going? Or am I not supposed to ask that?'

'I would tell you if I knew. It doesn't seem to matter much where. But I'll keep in touch, Breck; the hiding part of it shan't be too apparent, I promise you. I know you'll look after everything here for me.'

'For a consideration, as always, eh? Which is another reason you must go on earning money, of course.' He met her eyes and she smiled. 'Does Anne know what's in your mind? Have you talked to her about your plans?'

'She talked to me about them. She offered me a home and a welcome at Westow the moment she was sure I wouldn't go near it.' She laughed, a shade ruefully. 'I know what you're thinking. Why didn't I stagger her by accepting? It would have kept me amused for the rest of my life, wouldn't it? But I'm just not vicious enough for that, Breck, after all. I've done enough to Anne by giving her my nature. Oh, I know better than anyone how horribly like we are. No, if Kit Coudray can turn her into something different, God forbid I should ever get in the way and spoil his aim. I'm leaving them alone, Breck. I'm giving them at least whatever chance they have in the nature of things. Who knows? He may mellow her into a real live human being yet.'

'Which,' said Breck, 'is a thing no one ever did for you?'

'No one ever did. It's rather late to hope for it now. But Stephen wasn't a Christopher, and Anne may be luckier. At any rate, I won't hinder.' She rose restlessly, and crossed to the door. 'Let's have a drink, shall we? You must need one, after all this, and I know I do.'

'Sit down, and let me go. I know where to find everything.'

'No, I'll get it.' She brought back a loaded tray, and gave him his usual whisky and soda, and sat down and nursed her own glass in the fingertips of both hands, moodily watching how the warmer light softened the thin, astringent gold. She looked suddenly tired, and when the deep eyelids hid her eyes her age was heavy upon her. Breck found here, after all, no great likeness to Anne; but he did not say so. The thin, narrow face with its clear, almost translucent skin, powdered closely with fine gold freckles and lit by those bracken and well-water eyes, was like no other face he knew. Sharp, high cheek-bones she had, and a thin, arched nose, and her chin was too pointed for even the most modest beauty; but at least she was no copy of any other woman. And this in itself was strange, for she had been brought up to look as women of her class were expected to look, and behave as they were expected to behave; and coldly, as she confessed, she had conformed to that ideal in every particular, and yet she was not as they. Even now, in the discovery of the emptiness of her life, she remained very surely Claire, and no other woman. But it was not the time to say so; she would only lift her eyebrows at him, and flash through him the derisive green and amber glance bitter as gall, and say nothing in reply. He would not be believed.

'What is it you're looking for?' he asked. 'What is it you hope to find?'

Her lips twitched in the hint of a smile. 'You make it sound like a romantic quest. I'm not looking for anything, I'm not hoping for anything. Only waiting, perhaps. I shall never find anything, but perhaps something will find me. Probably seven devils worse than the first. There's plenty of room for them.' She shook her head. 'Oh, no, this is a retreat, not an advance. I'm getting out to do my readjustments in decent privacy, that's all. Something will fill this blankness in the end, I suppose, if it's only Siamese cats or first editions; nature abhors a vacuum. But with the well-disposed my disappearance will pass for grief. Very becoming, in the circumstances. And where I go they won't know I'm quite empty inside, and always have been. Someone may even be misguided enough to come in.'

'Someone you might be better without,' said Breck dryly.

'That's like warning a starving man not to touch stale bread. I know what you're thinking of; at forty-one a woman suffering from a sense of wrong against the world is liable to all sorts of follies. Well, so I am, but I don't ask you to rush to the rescue. It would be something new even to make a fool of myself. Failing humankind, a stray dog would be welcome, if he could just manage to matter to me a little.'

'As bad as that!' he said quite gravely.

'As bad as that.'

'In a month or so,' he prophesied, 'you'll be back in town, 'phoning up all your friends and arranging just the right-sized party at one of the old places.'

'I think you're being generous,' said Claire without indignation, 'but you'll find you're wrong. Slight emotional shock is one thing, and waking up to find your toes over the edge of a precipice is quite another, even if they look much alike from where you're sitting.'

She knew that he was not convinced, but that did not matter greatly. But neither was he curious. He would do what was required of him, and shrug his shoulders over whatever followed; and perhaps if she came to harm he would be sorry, as she was sorry that Stephen was dead. But beyond that she had no power to trouble him.

'You're tired,' he said. 'I'll leave you to wrestle with your problems in peace and quietness for tonight, but you'll see me before you make any move, won't you?'

'Oh, yes, of course, I'll keep you informed. Thanks for listening, at any rate. Wait, I'll come to the door with you.'

'No, don't bother, I'll let myself out. Good night, Claire!'

'Good night, Breck!'

Almost as soon as he was gone she felt the quietness again;

the silence shut within the room settled upon her like drifting silk, cool upon her bare arms and long throat. Amazing how instant it was and how complete. And how precarious and shy! If Anne's step crossed the hall it would shiver away from her and take to wild flight; if she came quietly and spoke suddenly it would die. Yet Claire could move through it and never shake it. When she crossed to the mirror and stood looking at her own face, smoothing out with her fingertips the little lines of her neck and the faint crow's-feet round her eyes, the silence clung to her step for step and hung upon her arms like a lover. She thrust her hands deep into the thick short mass of her brown hair, and spreading it between braced fingers looked at the threads of grey in it with a detached surprise, as if she wondered that a woman who had only recently come to life should so soon grow old.

II

THE HOUSE IN SCHOOL LANE

When she came to consider her actual departure, Claire found it impossible to go away without first having a clear idea where she was going. Her mind retained its habits of sanity and tidiness as if they had been an end in themselves, and would not let her stir a step until she had settled upon her destination; therefore she looked somewhat listlessly through her more remote memories of places seen and approved, and picked a small country town where she had once visited an elderly relative, now safely dead. The visit tasted of dust and ashes, like most other things, but she remembered the place as pleasant after its fashion, drowsy in a self-contained indifference, with no greater excitement in its week than Wednesday's market, and not one soul among its inhabitants who could ever conceivably have heard of Claire Falchion. That was virtue enough.

She went to Friary Shalford, and took a room at one of its four respectable hotels; but from the hour of her arrival she felt that she would not stay there long. She had not bargained for the changes a war could make even in this lost place. The neighbourhood had been alive with R.A.F. and American troops, all gone now, but their camps, empty and dilapidated, made the approaches to the town ugly on every side. The roads had been brought up to date, and the overhanging Tudor houses knit their brows over a white concrete dazzle and an explosive haste of traffic. The level meadows by the river carried a regular series of corrugated iron storage dumps. The race-course was marched and counter-marched into gaunt bare patches of clay-coloured soil. The black-and-white beauties of old Shalford bore a lost look among so many changes; the two spires of the older parish churches remained, and the castellated frontage of the disused gaol, patched with decay, but below these lofty antiquities the street seemed to have burst into a rash of minor bomb-damage, temporary shop-fronts, boarded windows, and dust. The world had reached this place. It was inevitable, and she should have foreseen it, but the importance of the world had receded from her, and she had overlooked the probability.

She spent a week roaming about the country from this defaced centre, and by chance she found Sunderne.

It was no prettier than a dozen other villages in the district, but it was more remote, buried in a cleft of hills once wooded, but long since deforested for the use of a primitive iron industry to a rolling wilderness of scrub, heath and sparse trees, leaning gradually southward to the sun. There was only a narrow second-class road running down the valley and through the single street, and of the village there was little to see in this street but the church and a lush triangular green and a half-dozen cottages, besides two inns that leaned upon the church-yard wall, one at either end. The rest lay out of sight along farm-tracks running off from the road, and had to be searched for, and even so came to light only by reluctant degrees, every bend of the lanes, every tall hedge concealing what it could. From no spot in this village could you see any human habitation which was not itself a part of Sunderne. The tattered groves of Sunderne Forest rose from it every way, and there were brackeny slopes to see, and airy tall birch trees, and open places of heather and grass, but no men except the natives or those who had business with the natives. No car would voluntarily take that bad road down the cleft, and no walker looking over the ridge would think that unkempt, surly place worth his while to visit. The village had by no means a welcoming look, nor the tidy inviting beauty which warms the chance comer to so many English hamlets, and makes him wish to linger. It was rich, weedy and decayed, from the squat-towered church with its defaced Norman door to the last low cottage with its wavy-backed roof mottled with housegreen, and the scutch-grass growing coarse and long between the broken stones of its pathway. No one would ever look for Claire Falchion here, and no one here would ever take any notice of her.

One of the two inns, the Black Bull, gave her a meal but nothing besides, no attention, no conversation, scarcely even a look. Requested to give her in addition a bed for the night, it consented without surprise, certainly with neither reluctance nor pleasure. No one in Sunderne cared whether she stayed or went. When she walked through the street the few people she met went by her with looks aloof and incurious; those to whom she spoke in passing answered her readily, but with an opaque gaze which belonged rather to the unsurprise of dreams than to a village in which she was well aware she fitted about as well as Carmen Miranda into a Sussex haymaking. Not good manners, but indifference, preserved her from any intent examination on their part; they did not stare because they did not desire to know. If they had conferred over her, whispered, turned to look again, there might have been some fear of her eventually being accepted and absorbed; but here where they went invulnerable in their own immemorial concerns she would always be an alien. Only the children looked directly at her, and seemed to see her clearly; and even they were neutral, their eyes neither friendly nor inimical but only keenly aware as the eyes of animals. They might have been young foxes staring at her out of the brakes of the draggled forest, secure in their own fleet wildness rather than in her goodwill.

There was an old man, lean and stringy and teak-coloured with a life lived outdoors in all weathers, clipping ivy away from the churchyard wall. Under the strokes of his shears the stones emerged reluctantly from a coating over six inches thick, and gave to the light uneven and unclean surfaces mottled with spiders' webs and mortar-rubbish, and veined with thread-thin, tenacious roots. The old man had eyes of a piercing Viking blue in his weathered face, the eyes of a man who has never had to wrestle with more subtleties than soil and sky between them thrust upon him. That was the look they all had, Claire thought, the self-contained, troubleless look of people living in an uncomplicated world and never glancing inward upon their own complications.

She stopped and spoke to him, and he returned her 'Good afternoon!' without a smile, looked through her with the observing but uncaring look to which she was becoming accustomed, and turned back to his half-naked wall.

'Your church looks interesting,' she said, 'and very old.'

''Tis powerful old,' he agreed, but volunteered nothing more.

'I should like to have a look inside. Can I get in?'

''Tis never locked but at night. Be open for hours yet.'

'I see. Thanks. Do you see many strangers hereabouts?'

'Not many,' he said. 'Now and again they pass through.'

But never stay, evidently, she thought. Possibly she had already made up her mind to be the exception. However, she did not, after all, go into the church. The sun shone, and stones, even Norman stones, could wait. Instead, she wandered away past a crooked lych-gate and down one of the farm tracks, where rose-briars and bramble trailers cascaded down tall hedge-banks, and leggy hawthorns streaked the dust with shade. It was not a lovely lane. Every grosser kind of weed seemed to thrive so well there that the hawthorns of the hedges had struggled four or five feet high to find the light, and grown thin and wasted in the effort. The track was good but narrow, and on either margin the grass was encroaching as if little wheeled traffic passed that way. A farm-track she had called it in her own mind, but looking at the almost unrutted surface she was not now so sure. She looked back, and the village had disappeared from sight beyond a double fold of hedge and a slight surging rise of the meadows. There was no sound; even the wind, which on the higher reaches stirred the leaves enough to dispel the silence, here failed in the sheltering fold of the ground, and let fall upon the meadows a hush as fine and soft as gauze, and greener than the evening. At the going away of the outer world Claire knew in a moment a loneliness iridescent and enclosed and airless, like the inside of a glass vessel tightly shut; yet the air was cool, and the lengthening sun lay sweetly down the valley, and over the green rim the world was not so far from her.

She went on, and the lane unwound coil upon coil downhill at a very gentle gradient, every curve giving to her vision only a few yards more of the way ahead, and gathering up at the same time as many yards of the way behind, so that she moved still in her hushed bubble of space, walled in from the century and her own kind. The lane under her feet began to grow green and shaggy with bird's-foot trefoil, and yellow clover, and short grass, until the two encroaching margins crept together in the middle, and from then on only a thin track half-veiled and half-naked reassured her that living creatures, human or wild, still occasionally passed that way.

She turned the last corner, and emerged upon a triangle of grass, across which the ghost of the trodden track moved away and lost itself in a small, flat copse beyond, and again beyond that in russet scrubland. The plot of grass was larger by much than the village green in Sunderne, and at this season was grown rank and tall and powdery with fruit, amber and purple heads, big with pollen, lolling above the blanching green; but as she waded through it she found the middle trodden bare in a large, irregular patch, as if children played there. She could not imagine that they did, or ever had within living memory, in so remote and silent a place; and when she stepped upon the bald lozenge of ground it rang harder under her feet, and she saw that splayed hands of dandelion and daisy clutched fierce hold of life there, and a few dwarfish docks persisted, but apart from these all green things dwindled away in discouragement. The soil was barren, not from activity above, but from dearth below; a whitish clay, baked like concrete, islanded in a softer, darker loam. It made curious, dull echoes as she crossed it, and the swish of the rising grasses along her skirt was welcome again after it.

Then she saw that at the edge of the triangle, on the left of the path, there were standing fragments of wall grey among the green, licheny stones half-submerged in nettles, fallen timbers embedded in the ground, their exposed parts eaten by the weather of centuries into a rotting, dry brown lace. Every rank richness of convolvulus, ground-ivy, rest-harrow and ragwort screened the shell of what had once been a large building, and made it into a mound of gross, sprawling bloom tangled with cobwebs and slimed by snails; but she saw clearly upon the few sound timbers and the mottled blocks of stone the marks of fire. How many centuries old was that burning she had no means of guessing, but the whole place seemed to have been deserted for generations, so completely had every echo and trace of humankind been effaced even from their own ruined handiwork.

But to the right, almost in the striped shadow of the copse, stood a brick house within the stone wall of its garden, coloured with mosses and creepers so nearly the grey-green of the tree-shade and the early evening that at first she had not observed it. Nothing ever fitted its background better. It was small but sprawling, a disproportionate but pleasing length of roof, a very plain frontage weathered to dullest buff between the creepers, and two clusters of fluted chimneys soaring. That part of it which did not echo the birches echoed the bracken. Here there was no stain of fire, no ruinous flowering; she walked round the house and found hardly a window wanting glass, or a gate-hinge broken. The place had been occupied no long time since, though it was deserted now.

There was a low iron gate piercing the garden wall; she pushed it open and went forward into a wilderness of feverfew daisies and willow-herb, under the blind eyes of the front rooms of the house. The garden here was small, and seemed once to have been laid out in flower-beds of intricate shape, separated by Lilliputian hedges of box; but beyond the house, when she turned a corner blunted by great weights of ivy, she found more space than the hollow square of the coppice had seemed able to contain. Upon the same level as the house there was a terrace of grass grown waist-high and russet with sorrel, and below that, down a shelving slope which had clearly been shaped by man, the garden extended away from her to the distant veiled wall in a confusion of tangled sweetness heaped in cushions of a dozen different greens about two intersecting paths. The tall grass thrust fruit and blade everywhere, casting a light gold glamour over the rich greens, and mosses like encrustations of mould tarnished the paths, but the design remained clear, and its content took the air with a spiced sweetness of pomander and sachets, lulling to the senses, insistent and yet aloof as a dream. Only in dreams, thought Claire, one is never conscious of perfumes; this sense, of all the five, sleeps the soundest. Here all the savour of life, all the silence, more beauty than the scene held, was distilled in the scent of herbs warmed all day in the summer sun. She walked down the path between overgrown mounds of thyme and sage, bushes of rosemary, rue and lavender, unkempt beds of mint, and the gentle brushing of her skirt caught and set in motion wave upon wave of warm and drowsy fragrance. She came to the intersection of the paths, and there was a sundial upon a square pedestal, taller than common, so that she had to climb its two wide steps to look at the face, which was of bronze, sunk flush with the stone. The figures were roughly cut, but deeply, for use and not for beauty, in Roman numerals. There was the sketchy outline of a face for decoration, with rays radiating from it, and a scrawl of letters round the outer edge of the dial. She rubbed away emerald green moss with her finger and made out the words: 'The hour is about to be, it is, it passes away'.

That was all, that and the profound and motionless silence which reached from the top branches of the overhanging trees to the spot where she stood; as if, indeed, the house and the garden and her heart all hung upon the expected hour with held breath and alert eyes. Only away beyond the ivied wall, where the ascending ridge of Sunderne Forest lifted its trees out of the shelter of the folded ground, did any breath of wind stir or leaf flutter; and never until that prevailing wind turned upon itself and came labouring up the valley would any tremor shake this lost, lush place, or blow away the heavy accumulations of sweetness and sleep from within the enclosing wall. Claire regarded the words which promised and threatened the impervious movement of time, and felt that time had ceased here, and the poised finger of the sundial waited for what would never come.

It was the quietness which drew her. It was so empty and so negative, even its warmth, even its indolence, rather of indifference than content. Feeling how her blood leaned to that emotionless ease, she turned and looked at the house again. It was easy to see why it should stand empty; Sunderne itself was far aside from any main road, and this spot was lost even from Sunderne by almost a mile of lane and footpath. No one would want to come here except, perhaps, for rest and solitude, and even so the inconveniences might outweigh the prospective peace. Why should she not have it? It seemed to be in very fair repair, the necessary work on it would not amount to much. The green stem which joined this shaggy flower to the village would not trouble her. She was not afraid of loneliness; it was what she needed and must have, at the taste of it she felt coolness upon her thirst. The more miles she could set between herself and people, the more hope she had of returning to them at last whole and alive. Why not here? She would go back to the Black Bull, and take her hired car, and bring away her luggage from Friary Shalford; there was no haste, she could ask about the house tomorrow, and take her time about the negotiations.

So she did, and for three days the Black Bull was her home, while she grew used to the eyes that looked through her in the street, and the sense that two centuries had slipped by and left no mark. She supposed that the year was 1947, here as in London, but it was hard to believe it always, when she could walk from end to end of the village and see nothing, no face, no dwelling, which need have belonged to the twentieth century. Occasionally there would be some little delivery van from Shalford at work in the street, or a plane passing overhead, or a young man in uniform strolling the lanes with a girl on his arm; and she would observe these, and be at once pleased and startled, as at memories rather than realities; but usually time withdrew itself, perhaps into the outer edges of this circle of lost land, perhaps into the lifted, intent, listening finger of the sundial in the herb-garden, poised over its endless sentence of expectation and loss: 'The hour is about to be, it is, it passes away'.

It was not difficult to find out about the house. Asked, they told her willingly who owned it, and what was its name, for they were not secretive, but only silent. Description located it at once. That must be old Fox's place, the old school-house; Long Coppice they called it now, but the lane that led to it was still known as School Lane. That ruinous place beside it used to be a school, so they said, but that was before the memories of the oldest living began, or the reported memories of their parents and grandparents. The school now was the usual little nineteenth-century box in two-coloured brick, with one cracked bell in a tiny steeple, the whole mercifully hidden a hundred yards off the street behind cottages and trees. Old Fox had died in the Long Coppice, four years ago, and left the place to his nephew up at the Ridge Farm, Mr. Kenton; but what with the war, and one thing and another, Mr. Kenton had never been able to do anything yet about letting or selling it. More accommodation wasn't needed here, seemingly; folks were leaving, not coming in, and the roads frightened away the people with cars, who might otherwise have been taken with the place.

This she could readily believe, and for her own sake she felt grateful to the second-class roads. More and more she wanted to stay, for the quietness, the sense of remoteness, grew into her heart day by day like a tender plant striking root, and for the moment filled her, though only with an illusion of fullness. She went to the Ridge Farm to seek out Mr. Kenton, who owned, it seemed, Long Coppice with all its herbs, and fluted chimneys, and loneliness.

The farm was large, and appeared prosperous, and the house, she thought, was at any rate partially Elizabethan, and kept in excellent preservation. In the yard there was an unexpected young man, sitting upon a mounting-block by the open half-door of a stable and gazing moodily upon his dusty boots; unexpected because he wore a khaki battle-dress blouse over his open-necked shirt, and for no other good reason seemed to belong more nearly to the outside world than to Sunderne. His face was not calm as the village faces were calm, had none of their unmoved strength or calculating resignation, but was violent and vulnerable and troubled from heavy-browed eyes to lean long jaw; yet his cast of features was exactly that which she had learned to associate with this antique land, narrow, swarthy, high-boned, with a great beak of nose jutting in the midst. A face that seemed to lean out unchanged from the dim recesses of the past, out of a long, obscure, tenacious ancestry; an ancient British face, a travelled, secret, Phoenician face. With its repose broken it seemed to her both moving and disturbing, the more so since he looked at her first as if he did not believe in her, and then as if he recognised her, and even had something to hope from her. Somewhere between this place and the more ephemeral world there was a magic circle drawn; she was from beyond it, he was from within but had been forced by circumstances beyond it, and now he belonged to neither life, or to both. It is not often, she thought as he jumped to his feet and moved towards her half-sullen and half-eager, that so much of a person is apparent upon a first touch, without a word spoken. But it was not by his will that she knew; and an impulse of kindness was tangled into the thread of reasoning which ran through her unaccustomed clairvoyance, and she took care to look at him as if she did not know.

'Mr. Kenton?' she asked, smiling at him with her adequate, accomplished smile, which also she saw that he recognised and welcomed.

'Yes,' he said in the deep voice of Sunderne, but refined or complicated by echoes from the outer world, 'my name's Kenton, but I expect it's my Uncle Charles you want. I'm only Jonathan. He's up the fields somewhere. I'll go and get him.'

'Oh, I shouldn't,' she said, 'I can easily come back later. He isn't expecting me, so perhaps we'd better not disturb him.' But because of the way the young man looked at her she did not immediately go away. He wanted her to stay; surprised but acquiescent, she lingered.

'Am I any good? Is there anything I can do?'

'Well, all I wanted was to ask about a house. But it will do another time.'

'About a house? You don't mean the old schoolhouse – Long Coppice? Are you thinking of – I mean, it's a dilapidated sort of hole, and damned lonely.'

'Oh, but I liked the look of it. I don't mind the loneliness, I assure you.'

He did not express his astonishment, but it was plain to read in his face that even here, in this higher, opener spot so much nearer to the rim of the charmed circle, he minded his own isolation very bitterly.

'I'm sorry, I don't have anything to do with the property,' he said, 'so I can't help. But if you don't mind walking we could go up the fields to him. It's not so very far, and the paths aren't bad, considering.' He made excuses for the country, she thought with amusement, as if it had been some shabby relation of his, of whom he was secretly ashamed. He was too young to feel as yet how little it cared for any reaction of his.

'But I shall be taking you away from your job, shan't I?'

'Not a bit of it. I was going up soon, in any case.'

They went up the farmyard together, watched all the way by the cold chrysolite eyes of a black tomcat which lay curled by the house door. A new-swung gate let them into rising meadows, and from these into the stubble of recently-carried hay, sweet as pot-pourri and embroidered with convolvulus and scarlet pimpernel. Looking back at the farm, she found in it none of the aloof singleness of Long Coppice, for it stood

31

much higher, and wind and sun and weather from beyond the bowl of Sunderne made it alive and dependent, certainly joined, however tenuously, to the sum of the forward-looking world; yet this changeling by her side found it oppressive. It needed no sympathy or generosity in her to feel his discontent, but more than she possessed to entertain and comfort it.

'Are you staying in the village?' asked Jonathan.

'Yes, at the Black Bull.'

'You haven't been here long? I couldn't have missed you if you had.'

'This is my third day in Sunderne,' she said.

'And you've already decided you want to stay?' he asked incredulously. 'Maybe it's *because* you've been here such a short time. I shouldn't do anything drastic for a week or so, just in case you change your mind. Not that I want you to go away again, goodness knows, but it wouldn't be fair to let you settle here in the first enthusiasm, and then wish yourself anywhere out of it.'

'I don't think you need worry. I know what I want.'

'I'm sure you do, but— It's odd you should *like* this place. And you seem to have picked out the most desolate bit of the lot.'

'It is very quiet, of course, but that's why I like it. Why, what's your objection to Sunderne? I see you've got a grievance against it.'

'I'm just not keen on being buried alive,' he said with suppressed violence.

'You belong here, though? I mean, you were brought up here?'

'Oh, lord, yes, I'm a native growth. You can't mistake the type.'

'Have you always felt so badly about living here, then?'

'Well, it hardly matters when you're a kid, does it? The place can be good enough fun during school holidays, and all that. I suppose it never occurred to me to wonder how it would feel to settle into it for life – not at that age. I'm making up for lost time now.'

By Firelight

He had not struck her at first glance as quite such a communicative young man; she supposed it was because she bore about her the marks of what he would certainly consider sophistication, and therefore was looked upon as a natural ally against Sunderne. She judged time must have brought him nearly to eighteen years or just over when war broke out, for among the ribbons on his battle-dress blouse she recognised the 1939-1945 Star, and by its dullness it was no new acquisition. Which would make him about twenty-six now. He was the kind of man who from twenty to fifty or later continues undateable and very little changed.

She looked at him and smiled, feeling momentarily touched by his restlessness, and unaccountably kind. Her life had not often been deflected by such impulses.

'How long have you been out?'

'Only four months,' he admitted shortly.

'It isn't comfortable, is it?'

'Oh, I don't know. Might be worse.'

'I think you're blaming Sunderne for difficulties of adjustment that belong to the times. It isn't any easier in London.'

She knew he did not believe her, and considering that she spoke from nothing better-founded than intuition, while he endured the experience, she had little right to expect to be believed. Still he gave her a quick, shy look which hesitated upon a smile, and his voice warmed into sudden staccato confidences.

'I was with the same push, barring one or two changes, for nearly four years. You miss them a good deal after that. We moved around, too, saw plenty of action. It does feel like hell when you come back to this. I'm expected to strike roots again on a day's notice, you see. I'm expected to know that good harvest weather down this valley is the most important thing on God's earth, and a wind from the right quarter in the lambing season a good second. They heard about Falaise, but it didn't matter, any more than I suppose Agincourt mattered.

33

Only I doubt if they even heard about that: we *have* made progress.'

To all of this she listened with her slight, grave, respectful smile, but noted very little of its meaning; she was accomplished in appearing to sympathise, and he was as satisfied as if she had wrung her heart for him, for, after all, his situation was none of her making, and far beyond her power to alter.

'It will pass,' she said abstractedly. 'Everything passes. In a few years you may find you have the better world of the two.'

'But you feel that way about it now, don't you?' he asked curiously.

'For myself, yes. Maybe not for life, but certainly for now. But I don't pretend to be able to persuade anybody else.'

'Still, you might be a pretty powerful argument,' said the young man, lapsing into frank impudence, 'if you stay here.' But to this she was giving, as before, only a part of her attention, and the look that went with it she did not notice at all. She was gazing ahead, her eyes fixed upon a figure which was tramping briskly down the slope of the field towards them.

'That's Charles. I thought he'd be on his way home.'

He was of his nephew's dark colouring, but built upon stockier, more obviously strong lines; a man of perhaps almost fifty, who moved with the casual power of a bull-terrier, and had something of a brindled bull-terrier's looks about him, a smooth, weathered, large-boned, handsome face, brown hair slightly grizzled at the temples, a body hard and springy as whalebone. Double the bulk of young Jonathan was packed into somewhat less than his height, and trod long and light down the fields. He looked upon her, she thought, with the direct, incurious observation she met everywhere in Sunderne, and upon Jonathan with nothing better than the patient intolerance a contented man erects against what he does not understand. It was resented, perhaps, that Sunderne flesh should not be grateful upon returning to its own.

34

'This lady wanted to see you,' said Jonathan, 'so I brought her up.' He looked at her and cocked an eyebrow. 'I don't think you mentioned your name?'

'My name's Falchion – Mrs. Falchion. You don't know me, Mr. Kenton, but there's a matter of business I want to discuss with you. If it isn't convenient now—'

'But it is, Mrs. Falchion. Why not? Walk down to the house again with me, and we'll have some tea. Are you coming yet, Jonty?'

'No, I'll be along in ten minutes or so. You go ahead.'

In fact, all he wanted, she thought, was not to have to walk back silently and tamely with them while they talked together about business or anything else, and he took a back seat against his will. Not, she supposed, for her bright eyes, but because he was at daggers drawn with his uncle, and would not remain in any situation which put him at even so slight a disadvantage with him. He went off up the fields, and left them to the short walk home.

'It's about Long Coppice I wanted to see you,' said Claire directly. 'They tell me it's yours.'

'Yes, it's mine all right. How in the world did you find your way to that place?'

'Oh, quite by chance, two days ago. I like it. I want a quiet house somewhere, and that one would suit me admirably. Is it to let? Or would you consider selling it?'

'It is, and I would. The fact is, I've had no chance to do anything about it so far. Nothing got dispersed into Sunderne during the war, you see; our population went down instead of up. This is one of the few places where you'll find quite presentable property standing empty. But Long Coppice is more remote even than most. It needs someone in special circumstances, with special needs, to find a use for a house like that.'

'Yes, I agree it does. But I am in rather special circumstances, and I have special needs. Quietness and loneliness are assets, to my present way of thinking; so, you see, Long Coppice is just what I want.'

He smiled at her; he had a very pleasant and assured smile. 'Dare I ask what your special circumstances are? You don't coin, by any chance? I'd hate to get into trouble over you with Frynne, you know.'

'Oh, I've no guilty secrets. Unless it's a guilty secret that I write.'

'Oh, I see.' He looked at her this time, she thought, with a new respect, but with no less self-confidence. 'Yes, I see it could suit you very well. But the disadvantages will still be there. School Lane becomes rather worse than a bore when you find yourself forced to walk it three or four times a day.'

'I shall take care to remember everything I need the first time.'

'But you haven't yet seen it in winter. We get rather a lot of snow here off a north-east wind; I've known that lane solid from hedge to hedge, six feet under.'

'In that case I must get some snowshoes.'

'I always thought,' he said as he held open the gate for her, 'that the best way to sell anything was to do your best to put 'em off it. Now I know.'

'I hope that means you want me to have Long Coppice,' said Claire.

'I do want you to have it. It's a legacy I never expected, and anyhow I can't live in two places at once. You want it, and I want to get rid of it. I daresay we shan't quarrel over details.'

They did not quarrel; their minds, indeed, marched together excellently. He saw nothing strange in her instant liking for the quiet house, or her desire to shut herself voluntarily into the enchanted ground of Sunderne. To him nothing could be more natural and laudable than to wish to purchase this quietness for all the haste and arrogance of the world. Yet he himself, she understood, had been out of the circle in his day. His voice, no less than Jonathan's, had more suggestions than the native qualities of depth, resonance and power which were common to all the local stock. He had been educated, if not expensively, certainly well, probably at some minor boarding school blossomed from an ancient royal grammar school foundation somewhere within his own county; the same school, it might be, to which Jonathan had been sent in his turn. On the walls of the wide, black-beamed room into which he brought her there were one or two unmistakable school groups of gravely proud young creatures in sports kit; her host doubtless among them, though she did not look closely enough at them to single him out. It came naturally to her to draw information from the background of a new acquaintance, and she sensed that here the blood was old and strong as the house, and held itself as high. The latest generation had been flung off its course by stress of circumstances, but Charles Kenton was on his own land, and he was as well satisfied with it as his first ancestors had been in their day. She suspected that she had under-estimated when she put him down as merely prosperous, for the house had every appearance of being a wealthy man's pride; a bachelor establishment, and apparently without even a sister, or any other female kin, for no hostess appeared, only a grave young maidservant and a middle-aged housekeeper. Charles poured tea with the nonchalance of one who has performed the office all his life, and she was confirmed in her guess; there was no wife in the background, dead or alive.

'I suppose the place is furnished?' she said thoughtfully, over her tea-cup. 'Long Coppice, I mean?'

'Overfurnished, if anything. My ancient uncle collected all manner of junk. But we can easily clear it all out for you, if you want to bring your own stuff in. It fetches prodigious prices just now. You might care for some of it, though; he occasionally picked up a good piece, and there are certain bits that came with the house. We could go down and have a look over it whenever you choose. This evening, if you'd care to.'

'Thanks, I should, very much. But are you sure I'm not disrupting your day altogether?'

'Not at all. I shall be doing something of importance for a change.' He stretched his compact, muscular body back into the depths of the high-backed armchair, and surveyed her with warming interest. 'You know, you're an unexpected person to take so strongly to Long Coppice. One would have said your spiritual home was — well, somewhere far removed from Sunderne, at any rate.'

'So it has been, though I doubt if it was very spiritual. Or, for that matter, very much of a home. But I'm pleasing myself now.'

She saw him speculating on this, and debating behind the broad-set eyes and wide, weathered brow if it did not mean she had now no one else to please.

'Well, I hope you'll like it as much on closer acquaintance. It's been in the family, passed backwards and forwards between Kentons and Foxes, for a couple of hundred years now. I got it through being old John Fox's last surviving nephew. We seem to run to nephews, for some reason. What do you think of mine?'

She laughed, rather out of sheer surprise than from any other cause. 'It's rather early to ask me that, isn't it? I've seen him once, for about ten minutes.'

'Oh, I daresay you've formed a judgement, just the same. In these parts we're definite enough to be seen the first time.'

'Very well, then. I think he's finding it hard to settle down here again after all he's seen and done in the last few years. He wasn't rooted firmly enough before he went to return easily now. And you, I should say, since you ask me for my opinion, are deliberately refraining from giving him any help.'

He received this calmly, even with an amused smile. 'You're probably right. I'm capable of seeing another man's point of view, provided he can see it himself, but Jonty's suffering from double vision. Doesn't know what he wants. I've no patience with people who don't know what they want.'

Jonathan came in at that moment, with an abrupt, hard step which argued no great indecision in his character. He dropped into a chair, looked from one to the other of them, and asked as he accepted his cup: 'Well, have you got it all settled?' He looked last and longest at Claire, so it was she who answered.

'We're going down to have a look at the house this evening. That's as far as we've got, but there seems to be no difficulty.'

'Well, rather you than me, I'm afraid. I'd as soon live in a dry well, myself.'

Claire looked at Charles, and smiled. 'You seem to share your uncle's views on salesmanship.'

'That must be pleasant hearing for him,' said Jonathan. 'I so seldom share his views on anything.'

She saw that there could be difficulties so long as these two remained together; better by far to meet them only separately, if she must henceforward have certain dealings with them. The very way they looked at each other reminded her of two dogs with their hackles erected, walking stiff-legged about each other looking for a hold. Anything, she thought, would serve them for a bone, even the attention of a not very young and not very attractive woman whom neither of them had ever seen before. She had no wish to see an artificial regard for herself kindled in either of these men simply by reason of an enmity already in being toward the other. Why couldn't some normal old farmer, without complications, own Long Coppice?

'I'll come down with you,' said Jonathan. 'It's a long time since I even saw the place; maybe I shall be able to spot what you saw in it to like so much if I come on it fresh.'

'Better complete the parallel,' said Charles, 'and come on it alone.'

'I'll try that later, if the first experiment fails. But I think Mrs. Falchion's company might be a lot more effective than solitude, thanks. After all, you want me to acquire a proper satisfaction with this sort of life, or so you say.'

'You'll not come with us tonight, however,' said Charles, tiring first of indirect battle.

Claire began to be irritated, and to fear that this ridiculous occasion of conflict would end in a shameless scene. But the large, ruthless assurance of Charles proved more effective than she had expected, and the composed antagonism of Jonathan more suave. Evidently they could go on like this for hours, even for days, and never come to the undignified shouting-match which seemed always imminent. The boy only smiled along his shoulder at her, a thin, dark, impudent smile, and remarked: 'You see? I'm too dangerous a rival, he won't risk it.' And he slid into easy talk about less troublesome subjects, the situation of Long Coppice, the walks close at hand, the harvest weather. It was in character that he should turn about in the middle of it and stare straightly at his uncle, as if he had said aloud: 'Well, am I behaving myself now? Is this good enough?' She supposed he could build up quite an illusion of submission like this, only to push it all down again in ruin with just such a look. What is particularly ridiculous, she thought, is that they're so very much alike.

'The school seems to have come to a bad end,' she remarked. 'Was it burned down by accident, or what happened to it?'

'I don't remember,' admitted Charles. 'I suppose there are records, but I doubt if they're very complete, and anyhow no one ever looks at them. We don't dwell on the past very much. All I know is, there was a school there, and it was burned. I don't even know when. Some time in the seventeenth century, I believe.'

'We were a queer lot, even then,' said Jonathan. 'Maybe it's just as well the records aren't very complete. Maybe the youth of the village didn't care a lot about school.'

'There's no special story attached to it, evidently,' said Claire.

'None that I know of. But as I say, we don't take over-much notice of our past here.'

He could say that and mean it, she reflected, without irony, though the memory and influence of the past ran like a cord through all the deeds and thoughts of Sunderne, and held them firmly together; upon the surface of it, it was even true. But the boy saw through it, by his derisive smile, and his eyes sought hers boldly in search of understanding and agreement. To him, because she seemed a woman of the world, she was in league with him against this blind, arrogant creature who could not feel or appreciate anything more than wind and weather; to the other, she supposed, because she wanted Long Coppice she was a witness for him against this unstable, restless boy who actually hankered after something other than Sunderne. And her mind was with neither of them; they were merely two small, rattling complications in the vast, simple fact of her need, and she rejected them both with impatience. She was glad when tea was safely over, and she was able to set out on the short walk through the village with only Charles to trouble her peace. And, alone, he did not trouble it; the contention was at once over and forgotten.

The scent of the herb-garden met them in School Lane, warmed and drowsy from the sun. It was earlier than on her first visit, and the high, gold light lay full upon it, gilding the licheny greenness of the house with a shining glaze. Under the trees of the copse the dappled shadows lay round and cool, and the garden was all a gloss and glimmer of drowning sweetness, almost palpable, almost radiant, through which they waded waist-deep as through a warm and fragrant sea. They stood beside the sundial and looked long at the house in silence, while the disturbed essences settled again about their stillness with a languorous slow, declining flight. And yet the place was not beautiful, thought Claire; it had no clear or pleasing form, only a jumble of old walls and the long, low crest of a faded roof, and the unshakable quietness.

'There used to be a dove-cote,' said Charles. 'It should have doves.'

'No,' she said jealously. 'They would make a noise.'

'You want the silence entire, it seems.'

'Yes, just as it is. Can we go in?'

'Of course. It's all dust-sheets and cobwebs, though. Watch your step on the slope here, the grass is polished up badly.'

He let her in by the long glass doors that opened from the garden, and led her through a hotch-potch of rooms full of shapeless sheeted ghosts of furniture, peeling off coverings in fine seethes of dust as he passed, and laying bare as motley a collection of treasure and trash as she had ever seen under one roof. All the downstairs rooms had once been panelled, and in some the panelling survived in excellent preservation, though it was plain enough in style, and darkened almost to black by age. The floors ran queerly on two levels, the rooms rambled round corners in an incoherent fashion; so that there appeared to be more floor-space than actually there was, and yet even a moderate amount of furniture made the place look overfurnished. The windows were good, and from the upper rooms gave upon a long vista of the valley, shut in by the embracing arm of Sunderne Forest. Claire wrestled with the hasp of the landing casement until it gave, and thrust open the window upon this soaring expanse of clear air. From this angle no trees close at hand broke the view, and low as the house lay she might have been looking out from the upper room of some watch-tower. So she felt against the world, walled in by her own will, safe for a while in this perfect isolation. She forgot even Charles Kenton, so quietly did he watch her. I must have it, she thought, leaning upon the sill over a world empty of men, I must have it. Everything will be resolved here, everything will become significant and simple here, even I, even Claire Falchion.

Charles watched her with his broad-set eyes, and did not say a word. She must have it, he thought. Her eyes, which had seemed green in the shadows, were a clear, sombre gold in the sun, and her thin face was dusted with the same gold upon its whiteness. Her short hair curled upon the nape of her neck in close, rounded brown curls. She carried her head as if it wore an invisible crown. Her hands were narrow, passionate hands, and her mouth was a virgin's mouth. I can be here when I please, he thought, and I shall find her here. Yes, she must have it.

III

THE FIRE BEGINS TO BURN

Claire had been in Long Coppice nearly three weeks when she began to write.

The house was hers by then, at a third of the price it would have fetched had it been in a more accessible township. The few broken windows had been repaired, the guttering cleaned out, and much of the surplus furniture removed into store pending its sale by auction. In the garden an old man from the village was scything the grass in leisurely, broad strokes, as if he had all time in his pocket. It was late August, and the world had flowered into ripeness and soft, pillowy heat, near to the oppression of thunder. And Claire, who had sat often at her table in the coign of the window with pen and book before her and her hands folded empty and still, suddenly began to write.

Within the house the initial upheaval was over, the curtains up, the freshly cleaned panelling and floors gleaming, and a capable middle-aged woman going about her business as if she had been there for years. Even the unrest generated by so much unwonted activity was already settling again like disturbed dust, or the floating odours of the garden after a passing step. It was possible now to sit still in the polished rooms, and accept their curious proportions and unfamiliar angles as things no longer strange. Claire sat so for two hours and more at a time on some evenings, after her daily woman had gone, and with all her relaxed senses took in the wonderful quietness, in a state of empty, patient, receptive content. Physically she had energy enough, but often it seemed pointless, even foolish, to move from her chair at all, or look

43

anywhere but directly before her. Besides, she could not always be so still. Too frequently Charles came down with some offer of a loaned man, or an hour of his own labour upon some invented job within the house or obvious one without; and then she must stir herself to talk to him and offer him refreshment and attention, even though she saw him only through a palpable veil of self-absorption. And if it was not Charles it was Jonathan, wanting to sit at her feet rather than trim hedges, to pour out his grievances against life rather than rig bookshelves; and he demanded more even of her mind than the other one, and did more violence to her charmed quiet with his uneasy thoughts than all his uncle's purposeful approaches could do. All the more must she cling to the silent evenings as they came, and prolong them far into the night in stillness, waiting for the stirring of her heart and never feeling it, and waiting still. Not in consciousness of waiting, certainly, but somewhere at the centre of her tranquil lethargy there was a small, clear conviction always of being incomplete.

She knew that she must write, and early began to make idle notes which never came to anything. She had spent a lot of money in one month upon Long Coppice, and it had to be replaced by the only means she knew. Yet her mind had never been so empty, or so content with emptiness. She sat over the blank pages until the light died, and the green of the trees leaned inward and shut upon the windows like a cool, tideless wave; and she would come to life again at last because of the cold and cramp of night, and find the clock past midnight and the silence full of the relaxing, secret sounds of old furniture, old floorboards, old walls stirring in their sleep. She came as near to loving the house then as she had ever come to loving anything. The hush was indifferent to her; she could move about through its breathing meshes and never break a thread; she could speak aloud, and move no startled echo in the recesses of the darkness to cry out upon her. There were no living things but wild ones within a mile of her on every side; she was free to do as she would, to feel as she would, and influence no one. But she was not lonely; she was merely alone.

Charles, familiar though he was with isolation for himself, had not approved of it for her; and as for Jonathan, the thought of spending one such night in Long Coppice would have filled him with horror. The boy had not spoken his protests, though she understood them very well; the man had, not once but repeatedly, with the flat decisive frankness which stopped just short of becoming proprietary. He had urged her to bring into the household a servant who would remain with her at night, as much for a calculated measure of physical safety as for a precaution against the nervous effect of loneliness; and she had simply refused, listening to no argument and putting no argument forward. The possibility of being murdered in her bed for the sake of what valuables she had in the house seemed to her so remote as to be quite trivial, and in any case she was incapable of becoming excited about that risk or any other. As for Jonathan's aversion to being buried alive, she acknowledged but could not comprehend it; to her this remoteness from her kind was comfortable and safe and serene, by night as by day. She feared only the too frequent invasions of it.

On this night, when she had sat idle for half an hour and written not a word, it was strange that lines should begin to string themselves together in her head just as Jonathan let himself in by the long windows from the garden. Any step then might have shaken the words out of coherence and frightened them away from her, yet they did not, after all, leave her even when his positive and constant trouble came in. He paused on the threshold, as always, but it was only a pretence of hesitation.

'Am I interrupting you?' He knew he was, but he had also already found out that she would not say so.

'I'm not doing anything.' The paper was still blank before her, but the words were coming to life in her mind, by no apparent motion of her will, and out of an infinite distance, listlessly moving into her consciousness as if blown by an unregarding wind. 'Yes, come in!' she said.

He came in and shut the window. Behind him the evening was grown cloudy and heavy, and all the odours of the garden hung low to the ground in an oppressive stillness. Uneasy as flame, the heat-haze had shivered all day along the distant ridges of hill upon the skyline, and now the horizon where it had played was coloured a lurid coppery gold, as if the earth had caught fire from it and burned sullenly.

'Going to be a storm,' said Jonathan, looking back at it. 'Pretty soon, by the look of it.'

'I don't mind storms.'

'You don't seem to mind anything very much. But I shall, if I get caught in it. I haven't a coat. Can I hang around for a while and see if it goes over?'

'You know quite well you can,' she said indifferently. 'Sit down and make yourself comfortable. If the worst comes to the worst there's a raincoat of my husband's that might fit you; at least it would be better than nothing.'

He sat down in the angle of the window, with the hot, heavy light making an angry nimbus about him; from this position he could watch her as intently as he pleased, and give her no cause for complaint.

'You don't often speak of your husband,' he said.

'No, I suppose I don't,' agreed Claire.

'Is he dead?'

'Yes, he died in May.'

He did not say that he was sorry; she hardly noticed the omission, for the conventional part of her mind was becoming submerged more surely every day in this place where the conventions hardly reached. Moreover, she was seeing him only as a lean black shape, narrow and sullen, outlined in slow fire, and the drifting words in her mind began to gather about him and take on form, shaping themselves into lines of verse. Something would certainly happen if he would just sit still like that, and let her look at him as fixedly as she wished to look at her. What pleasure he could get out of gazing at her by this sombre light she would give him and welcome in exchange for this first impulse of creation, if he could only keep it alive.

'Is that why you wanted to leave London and run away and hide here?' he asked dubiously.

'It was the occasion, but not the cause.'

'Then what was the cause?' he persisted.

'I'm not sure. Maybe I'd exhausted London.'

'Impossible!'

'From your point of view, perhaps, but not from mine. Or maybe I just felt like a change. Keep still!'

'Why?' he asked, obediently sitting still upon the instant.

'You're supplying me with ideas, and at the moment they're few and far between, so don't disturb them.'

'Oh! Can I talk?'

'As far as I know, nothing will stop you. Yes, talk as much as you like.'

Inevitably he was silent after that for some minutes, and still to an almost strained extent. She watched the set of his head, erect and stiff against the light, and could not choose but smile at him, though abstractedly. The first drops of the storm flattened themselves against the window behind him with a shattering suddenness, and did not deflect his attention from her. She saw the earliest lightning slash the darkness and set the panes blazing at his back for the fraction of a second, and at its passing the night seemed to topple upon them in full measure, like a curtain falling.

'You looked like Mephistophiles,' she said into their mutual blindness.

'You looked like Undine.' And so she had, with all the brilliant colour of her eyes, fern-green and pebble-brown, caught into the sudden light, and the quivering reflections of rain upon the window staining the whiteness of her face with greenish gleams; but she was startled because she had not expected him to retort so aptly or so promptly, and she answered between amusement and anger.

'Rubbish! Do you realise that I'm forty-one?'

47

'They don't have any age,' he said unabashed. 'And you did look like one.'

'It was quite involuntary, then, believe me, and will never happen again.'

'Then I'm glad I was here to see it.'

She realised that he was trying his tongue in an unfamiliar language, and revelling in the experience. It had occurred to her before that with her he spoke as he would not speak with anyone else; as if she had been an alien whose native tongue he knew and rejoiced to use after long enforced silence in it. Whatever she said he would turn to gallantry, so she might spare herself the effort of hunting a sensible subject. There was no harm in it, surely; he sought her out only because her company flattered him, made him feel a man of the world again, with a far wider horizon than the bowl of Sunderne. That was all he wanted of her; it could surely do no harm to let him have it, and it was less trouble by far than it would have been to deny him.

'Claire—' he said, and hesitated.

'Well?' She had never noticed how or when she became Claire to him, for her senses accepted the familiar name more readily than any other. It had always been Claire, and dear, and darling indiscriminately, from people who detested her among the rest.

'I should like to read your books, Claire. Will you lend them to me? I'd take great care of them.'

She laughed in sheer astonishment, but with the consciousness of his intent eyes upon her quickly halted the laugh. 'I'm sure you would, better than I ever do. But why should you want to read them? A month ago you'd never heard of me or them, and believe me, you weren't losing anything. They're not for you. They were none of them aimed at you, and you won't like them. I warn you, you won't like them at all.'

'Why not? What makes you think I shan't?'

'It would be like expecting you to take kindly to wearing ear-rings, or using expensive scent. You'll find them precious and rather nasty, I expect. Still, you can take them, of course. You've as much right to read them as anyone else, and you'll only be penalising yourself.'

'If you're trying to discourage me,' he said, 'better forget it.'

'I'm not. The books will do that. Go on, help yourself from the bookcase, they're all there. Better light the gas.'

He did so, and the lightning grew pale and the clouds darker outside the window. The storm was already passing, though the rain streamed greenly down the panes, showing them only a sleek underwater world. In her mind fire and rain gleamed and dimmed fitfully, and the words strung themselves like hasting drops and spurted up like sudden ardent flames. All the time that she watched him foraging along the shelves of the bookcase, and thought of him struggling doggedly and bewilderedly through the two hundred and fifty delicate bitter pages of *Rapunzel* or the sugared malice of *Floral Tribute*, all the time the words went on arranging themselves within her mind. When he goes away, she thought, I shall be able to write; the thaw has set in.

He chose *Rapunzel*. Well, it was the best of them, and would baffle him no worse than the rest. Probably he would never get so far as attempting the others, for he was no great reader, and would suffer agonies of unacknowledged boredom before he finished this first attempt to learn more about his recluse authoress.

'Can I really take it?' he asked, cocking an eye at her over his shoulder.

'Of course. I've warned you, I can't do more.'

'And now do you want me to go away?'

'You've got what you came for, I suppose. But it's still raining.'

'All right, I'll wait until it stops, and then I'll go.' And he came back and sat upon the corner of her desk, the book tucked under his arm. His eyes dwelt closely upon her face, of whose clear, angular lines, even with much staring, he did not seem to tire. She was aware of him more deeply and personally than she liked, for what had she to do with him? She wanted nothing from him, not even casual friendship; nor from Charles, either, for that matter, nor from anyone else in the world.

'I *have* interrupted you,' he said. 'I'm sorry.'

'No, it's all right. You see I'd written nothing.'

'I've been wanting to ask you – I mean for the books – all along. I suppose everyone who meets you works round to it in the end. Or do all the others know them already? Everything's out of print, you know, so it's borrow or nothing.'

'Do you mean you've tried to buy them?' she demanded.

He nodded, somewhat taken aback by her tone.

'Ridiculous! I'm glad you couldn't get them. The idea of throwing away money upon things that will never be any use to you, just out of a particularly foolish kind of vanity!'

'Why vanity? Curiosity, now, you could have said.' He laughed. 'You're funny, Claire. Why shouldn't I want to own your books? I should have thought you ought to be glad.'

'I should, if I had any affection for them, or if you wanted them for any of the right reasons. But you don't, and never will. And I haven't, you know.' She looked past him, where the clouds were breaking. 'Still, read them. You'll hate them, and be none the wiser, but that's for you to find out. It's stopped raining now, look.'

Jonathan slid off the desk. 'That means I'm in the way. All right, I'll go quietly. You won't mind if I pass this on to Charles afterwards, will you?'

'He's far too sane to want it, I should imagine.'

'That shows how well you know our Charles. The only reason he's refrained from asking you the same thing himself is because he knew I should do it if he waited long enough. Maybe after his fashion he suffers from the same brand of vanity as I do.' He flashed her an acid grin as he opened the long window, and cooler, softer air blew in upon them, and rumblings of thunder growing tired in the distance. 'Thanks, anyhow, from both of us. Good night, Claire!'

'Good night, Jonathan!'

She watched him go, and was glad to be alone again. There was no safety except in loneliness. Already she was being drawn into small, insidious, inescapable relationships, against her will, against her judgement, against all her instincts. Here as in London there were artificialities and subtleties waiting like marsh-ground for her first unthinking step. Do what she would, go where she would, as long as one human thing remained about her the troublous, tireless business would begin again. She had done foolishly in allowing even so slight an acquaintance to grow up between the Kentons and herself, but the purchase of the house had necessarily thrown them together, and now, before she knew it, the old gambits, once so flattering, now so wearisome, were opening before her the old sterile paths. Even here, unless she watched every step, she would find herself going round and round upon her own stale tracks, still empty of all promise or significance. It was not for this she had seen her life dwindle to ash, and compelled herself away shadow-like to look elsewhere for her own substance. But who would have thought that the complexities here, even if any existed, would prove to be the old complexities? Was there no human creature in the world whom she could approach without disguise and without fear, towards whom she could walk straightly, without this oblique fantasy, this forward and back and aside of grotesque, humiliating dance?

She went out into the wet garden, in the gathering twilight that dropped from the trees and sighed like the earth drawing breath. The drowning sweetness flooded over her, and swept the uneasiness out of her mind, smoothing aside the thought of Jonathan. His features faded from her until he became again the lean black shadow between her and the fire, then dwindled, then was nothing. In the half-cleared paths her feet left darker green prints, and the overgrown bushes shook scented rain over her skirt as she waded between them. She lost the occasion of her impatience, and felt pleased and expectant without the restless necessity of looking forward for the completion of her pleasure. She went back into the house, and wrote down what remained of the words the fiery sky had put into her mind. She felt they were obscure, she knew they were imperfectly realised, but there was no haste at all. When she was tired she went to bed, and slept without dreams.

The next day she cared so little about what she had written, and was so far from being troubled about its inadequacy, that she left it lying upon the desk all day, under the eyes of Mrs. Greenleaf or old Whitton or anyone who might choose to come in; and it was still lying there when Charles came down in mid-afternoon with a basket of plums for her, and found her busy polishing two carved oak panels they had found among the junk of the attic, relics, she supposed, of old Fox's mania for acquisition. She showed the one she had cleaned, a foot-square panel almost black with time, bearing a portrait head in profile, and what appeared to be the subject's coat-of-arms upon a small shield placed, for lack of space, directly under his long and heavy chin. The artist had begun in a grand generosity, making head and features too large for their frame, and had ended by having to cramp the shoulders into a space far too narrow, and curl the bonnet plume right out of the picture. Still, the thing was plainly a portrait, for the brutal but honest face had a direct power of appeal which never came from anything but life.

'Who's your friend?' asked Charles, studying it with his head on one side.

'I was hoping you could tell me that. He really belongs to you, you know. We found him and his good lady here in the attic. Look, there's his arms, if you can make anything of them. He's bound to be a local worthy.'

'Oh, I see! You're right, it is his arms. From any distance one would say he had a bad goitre.' He leaned over to examine it more closely. 'I'm no hand at these things, but I know those three birds – martlets, are they? In any case, there's only one family it could belong to; we had singularly few gentlemen of coat-armour in these parts. He's one of the Shenstones of Sunderne Friars. A queer crew, by their faces, but their reputation was not bad as those people go. They arrived during the Plantagenet days, and died out last century.' He spoke tolerantly, as became blood which was known to be older by many centuries, and had proved itself more durable. Beside these Kentons and Foxes and Groats and Chittams and Ferrises the house of Shenstone was but a minor comet passing among the unshaken planets. 'I suppose that's his wife.'

'Yes, but I haven't cleaned her up yet. For all we know she may prove to be a beauty, though, poor woman, she doesn't look it at the moment. Who were the Shenstones?'

'The only landed gentry around here. The rest of the ground stayed with us yeomen, but while they were in favour at court they had the bulk of the power; and they were curiously inoffensive for men with jaws like that, and stayed in favour longer than most.'

She smiled, stepping back to the length of her arms to see him the better. 'It's almost a Hapsburg chin, isn't it? Reminds me of Philip IV in the Velazquez portraits. Sit down for a while, Charles, and I'll presently show you Madam Shenstone, too.'

Instead of obeying her, he chose to walk about the room, examining all the latest small changes she had made now that some of her favourite possessions were arriving from London. In his wanderings he came to her desk, and the spread sheets scrawled with her sharp handwriting drew his eyes. He paused, instinctively smoothing them together.

'I see you've been working.'

She looked up. 'Oh, yes, but it doesn't amount to much.'

'May I see it?'

'Yes, if you care to.'

'You don't mind people being inquisitive about your work, then?'

'Oh, no, I'm not hypersensitive, unless it's something that

matters. That thing doesn't, not a tinker's curse. By all means read it if you want to.'

He took it up and read in silence for a few minutes; then, turning casually from her labours, she found his eyes fixed not upon the pages of discarded verse, but upon her.

'Well?'

'Queer stuff to get from you, Claire.'

'Is it? To tell the truth, I haven't looked at it since I wrote it, which was last night. I remember it as being pretty poor stuff, and not at all what I intended, but apart from that I've almost lost the sense of it. Read it aloud to me – some of it, at any rate. I know what it says; tell me how it says it.'

He twitched back to the beginning of it, and began, in a low, careful voice which made no pretence to understanding:

' "The embers crack; my calcined bones divide
In dissolution at the pikel's thrust,
An acrid-tasted, ashen-tinted dust
Snowing upon the fire of which I died.
Charred fronds of rope drip downward flake by flake
From all the blackened staples of the stake
Into the pyre whereon at eventide,
I burned, a candle for a candle's sake.

"Some in our seven lifted from the sea
Swallowed the candles and the Mass-book whole,
Deeming a body more than worth a soul.
Such also urged reversion upon me:
'These are conventions; God will give us shrift
Who cares not for observance nor for rift.'
I stood the firmer in my heresy;
Not worth the keeping is not worth the gift.

"For my soul's sake they gave me fire to purge,
Deeming the life well-lost that bought from hell
A soul which had endured so long and well
The red-hot pincers and the nine-fold scourge;

By Firelight

A ceremonial death also they gave,
Graceful with music and with banners brave,
Legions of priests to sound my funeral dirge
And all the winds of heaven to be my grave.

"Here lie the remnants of the stake and pyre.
Where is the hate which girded me to die?
Is it among the ashes where they lie,
The fragments of me reeking from the fire?
Or is it in the white-hot air which waves
Heavenward from this most reverenced of graves,
Like shaken locks of all the fiends that fly,
Dispersing from their terrible conclaves?" '

He paused, for she had suddenly drawn her hands together
in her lap and reared her head from the long-dead Shenstone
woman as if an abrupt and dazzling light had shone upon
her.
'What's the matter? Is anything wrong?'
'Nothing was right until then, but that's righter than I knew
when I put it down. Never mind! Go on!'
Charles went on reading:

' "Blown inward with my breast, burned with my heart,
The hate is perished with the purging fire;
Vengeance no more is part of my desire
As pain no more of my free mind is part.
Lord God my refuge, in the judgement hour
Be to my foes a stronghold and a tower.
The seed of love in me, long set apart,
Fed on my flesh, comes now at last to flower.

"Across the square all ways the white walls loom,
Their scattered casements closed against the smoke.
The night, receding, draws away her cloak,
Cold curtain of my theatre of doom.
No foe compassionate remains to pray

Into the shining onslaught of the day.
All, all have fled the sacrificial gloom;
Priests, penitent, and faithful, where are they?

"Here, where the shadow and the light divide
Dawn climbs the mild mid-heaven golden-shod.
In that marmoreal masterpiece of God
The winds for ever speed unsatisfied.
The setting moon and rising sun contend
A silver battle-field, world without end,
Neither triumphant, neither to abide.
Falling to rise, ascending to descend.

"Only the smoke of my destruction blown
Affronts the singing birds that seek the sun;
They wheel, and on spread wings, affrighted, shun
The stench of my still smouldering flesh and bone.
But to the lifted eye no other sign
Recalls this fiery battle-field of mine;
Above the gilding of the cornice-stone
The blanched blue sky soars tranquil and benign.

"Between the ramparts of the night and day,
Where time stays pendent heavily in heaven
And song-birds hymn their seventy joys and seven,
God sets the last great battle in array.
There all our differences He shall decide
For which so duteously we killed and died,
And in His army we shall take our pay,
The Don and I together, side by side.

"The unbelieving cities shall we sack,
Not as on earth, with butchery and chain;
Upon that battlefield shall none be slain,
None mutilate, none stretched upon the rack.
There shall be left behind at eventide
Only the votaries of suicide,

Who like dumb beasts that look not fore nor back,
Clasping the moment, with the moment died.

"Such as have closed their eyes and stopped their ears
To all that might have troubled their repose,
And plucked life delicately like a rose,
And sipped it like red wine grown rich with years.
They shall not see the dawn of heaven glow,
The bursting from the grave they shall not know,
Nor hear, when Gabriel at the gate appears,
The trumpet of the resurrection blow.

"We looked within; as in a polished glass
In our own souls dimly we learned to trace
The sweet and terrible creator's face.
Who then dared say to us, all flesh is grass?"'

She said sharply: 'It's folly, isn't it? After a horrible death, would you feel like that, I wonder?'

'After a death of any sort I very much doubt whether I shall feel anything at all,' said Charles blithely.

'I very much doubt if he did, either. But even if he did, would he be likely to find himself in such a forgiving frame of mind? Not if he came of this Sunderne breed, surely. They – you – bear grudges, don't you?'

'By the century rather than the year.'

'But after death? Supposing it's true that the passions are physical and die with the body?'

'Then there'd be no angry ghosts.'

'But of course there are none!'

He was silent, watching her with a non-committal half-smile. She looked at him in steady, almost pleased astonishment, her eyes clear green in the direct light. She looked like a sleek gold cat pondering in its ancestral memory the days of its godhood, with excitement, with secret delight.

'You believe there are! You believe in ghosts the moment after you've said you don't believe in survival! Oh, Charles, your world must operate in layers, with a good sensible crust of acquired rationalism on top, and all the native hells and heavens crowded with spirits underneath. What happens if it breaks through?'

His smile deepened, but remained absent from his eyes. 'It isn't nearly so simple or so neat. I keep an open mind. I'll wait and see; but I suspect it proves to be a dead end. Still, everything is possible.'

'The trouble with an open mind,' said Claire, 'is that you have no means of knowing what may not come in. Go on reading, Charles.'

He read:

' "The latticed windows in the white walls shake
Through the hot, ashen, smoke-polluted air.
I look upon Madrid and find it fair
From the exalted watch-tower of the stake.
Behind drawn curtains stir the priests who late
Destroyed me, and the flock who watched my fate;
Dawn troubles their strange dreams, and they arise
Freed of my life and death, my love and hate.

"The dawn, ascending, leans upon the day.
They shall arise absolved, but they shall know
Little of that far land to which I go;
Nor shall they understand as yet my way.
The day begins, and all my days are done.
Lost is the moon, and splendid rides the sun:
So did I set on Spain but yesterday,
So am I risen, but there beholds me none.

"None but my God that held me in His palm
While the young faggots half-defied the flame,
While the sad priests prayed pity in His name
With many a passionless, imploring psalm;
My God that saw my burning heart divide
Out of the glowing cavern of my side,

> That shared alike the anguish and the calm,
> The hunger, and the hunger satisfied."'

'Yes,' she said, 'I remember that nonsensical heaven of his. Leave out that part, it won't read aloud.'

'I read very badly, so don't accept this as the last word on it.'

'Oh, I've heard enough. Don't trouble to try and understand it, Charles, it isn't worth the effort.'

'Not even your "nonsensical heaven"?' He smiled at her, and read again:

> ' "Thither I go, follow and find me there.
> No flame shall blow between us at that feast;
> North shall not savage south, nor west rend east;
> No stench of burning flesh shall soil the air.
> The pallid paring of the moon, sunk low,
> Points me my hour, and with the hour I go,
> Freed of the body I was wont to wear,
> Known of my God, and soon my God to know."'

'No, it's served its purpose. I can remember every line of it that still means anything. Here, give it to me.' And she took the sheets from him, crumpled them in her hands and threw them into the empty fireplace.

'Oh, but why? It seemed perfectly all right to me.'

'No, it's of no value whatever. It's all wrong.'

'How – wrong? Artistically wrong?'

'Historically wrong,' she said. 'That isn't how it happened. It wasn't Spain, it wasn't for a religious scruple he was burned to death, and he didn't die in any forgiving spirit.' She got up and went to the window, and stood looking out toward the herb-garden with a small, thoughtful frown. 'Does that line remind you of anything? – "Points me my hour, and with the hour I go." It sounds like the echo of something.'

'It sounds like the posy on the sundial,' said Charles. 'You haven't forgotten it? "The hour is about to be, it is, it passes away." '

'Yes,' she said upon a gentle breath, 'yes, that's it. I knew it belonged to this house. No Inquisition, no religion, no pious reflections before or after death, and almost certainly no heaven. And yet the fire was right. I'm quite sure about the fire. And one other thing was accidentally right, too.' She repeated in a soft, pondering voice:

' "Like shaken locks of all the fiends that fly,
Dispersing from their terrible conclaves."

I recognised something about that, but as yet I'm not sure what it was. The only thing it really brings to mind is something I read once in translation, out of the trial of Joan of Arc. "Those who come in the air"! What is there so sinister about that phrase? "Those who come in the air"! Do you suppose, Charles, that they came here once? Do you suppose they still come? In the quiet of the evening, perhaps, when no one is here to bear witness?' She turned her head and looked at him, her eyes wide and bright. 'Do they come in the air over my garden, I wonder? I can well believe they do. Shall I meet them one day, do you think?' She laughed at the look he bent upon her. 'Don't worry, Charles, I'm not really as mad as I seem. After all, it's as well to be ready for any eventuality, isn't it? Why look at me like that? What are you thinking?'

He was thinking, though he did not say so, that it is strange to condemn an imaginative production as not being historically right, and still stranger to be able to say of it so flatly: 'That isn't how it happened.' She had written, surely, of the things which had never, except in her imagination, happened at all, and yet in settling those phrases in them which were right she had rejected the suggestion that she meant artistically right. He looked at her, and could discover in her nothing changed, except that there was a kind of shining through the glaze of her assured calm, as if from a core of excitement within. Whatever it was that possessed her she was perfectly in command of it.

'I don't pretend to understand what you're talking about,' he said frankly, 'but if you're content I suppose that's the main thing. Are you?'

'As near content as I've ever been,' said Claire upon consideration, but so indifferently that it did not seem to guarantee any great degree of satisfaction. 'Long Coppice suits me every bit as well as I supposed it would; you needn't worry about that. As for *Auto-da-Fé*, you've seen and heard the last of it, and it's just as well, for it was very bad. Next time you come you may find me working on something at least worth finishing.'

'I'm no judge, but this seemed perfectly all right to me. Are you always as capricious about what you write?'

She shrugged. 'I destroy a great deal, if that's what you mean.'

'From a conviction that it's historically wrong?' he asked curiously.

'Not that exactly, not until this case. It may be because of the quietness here that things come into mind so— I was going to say clearly, but I think what I really mean is something different. Nothing is very clear, but everything is very insistent. People may leave me alone from now on, but ideas won't. No, it's all right, I don't want them to, I should be sorry if they did. That's why I came here, to get rid of distractions.'

'Yes, but nothing so far has explained why you talk about how this thing happened, as if it really did happen, and could be verified one way or the other. Surely it's simply an idea that came into your mind, and you can settle the details just how you please?'

'Ideas come from all sorts of places,' said Claire. 'How do I know where this one came from?'

'Wherever it came from, it's still your own, isn't it? You can do what you like with it, shift it to Spain or Goa or

New Mexico if you choose. Your imaginary victim won't care.'

She looked at him thoughtfully for a moment, and for the first time seemed to realise that he possessed an intelligence of his own which was working curiously upon this problem, and not simply standing at gaze to watch the workings of hers. It was only too easy to let him slip into the background of her mind and forget that he might be less indifferent to her. She stirred herself to come back into his world, for it was by no means desirable for the peace of either of them that he should follow her into the queer, distorted emptiness of hers.

'Look, this isn't helping me to clean up Madam Shenstone, and I want, if you'll let me, to turn those two into a jointed fire-screen. Whitton's going to do the job for me. Would you like to go on polishing her while I get you some tea?'

'I ought really to get back,' said Charles, but making no move to go.

'I wouldn't be long. But it's up to you.'

He stayed, and she fed him; but partly because it was true that he ought to get back, true, indeed, that he ought never to have come, and partly because she made it so clear, without word or look amiss, that she wanted him to go, he did not stay long. He was not discouraged. For almost a quarter of an hour she had thought aloud in front of him, which was more than he had expected; and he was accustomed to waiting for things.

When he was gone she did not write any more. She went out along the rise of the hanging woods to the mysterious point where the winds sprang into life, and lay among the bracken and the spongy turf distant above her house; and the breath of lavender and thyme and mint came up against the wind in drifts of incense, but she was so accustomed to it now that she was hardly aware of it. Last night's rain was gone without trace, but as she walked home another brief, thundery shower passed over, a small black scud of clouds, swift and ominous, stinging her cheeks with a cold, slanting rain. Again she thought of 'those who come in the air', for these came and passed like shadows across the evening sun; and after their passing heat blazed again over the world, and from the garden of Long Coppice a scented steam went up visibly blue, like the smoke of a sacrificial fire.

IV

RECORD OF A WITCH-TRIAL

When Jonathan and Charles met in the late evenings, after one or the other of them had been at Long Coppice, the silent ill-feeling between them was more marked than at other times. Claire's recent visitor carried at such times a sort of satisfied excitement about him, which in Charles showed itself only in a thoughtful inward brightness in his eyes, and an added edge of robust intolerance in his voice when he spoke to his nephew, but in Jonathan produced a ripe and devilish aptitude for mischief undisguised. Whichever of the two had not been with her became jealous in watching for the signs, and hasty in imagining them even before they began. At such times they fell out over anything which came handy, from the day's work and the morrow's commitments to the points of spaniels or the quality and proof of beer; but never over Claire Falchion. Her name was protected by as exact a taboo as Rumpelstiltskin's.

Yet at these times it was that they were most disturbingly aware of her, as if each of them saw her better through the vision of the other. When Jonathan had brought home *Rapunzel* and embedded himself in an easy chair with it before his uncle's eyes, Charles had felt so instant a consciousness of her physical and mental attributes, so acute a perception of her indifference to himself, that it became doubly maddening to him that she should stoop to any intimacy with another man, particularly with one of his own blood, and one he despised. But now that he himself could sit and ponder over again those curious exchanges with her, it was Jonathan who sat watching him narrowly and coldly, and groping after

65

the very words and thoughts which had passed between them, and making more of them by far than they had been. For that was the main quality of this vicarious vision, that it magnified things beyond their size and coloured them brighter than nature. If Charles remembered her just now as attractive, Jonathan imagined her as lovely, which she was not, and fascinating, which she sometimes could be when she was not trying. If Charles recalled her careless sentences of self-revelation with pleasure, Jonathan imagined them as confidences seriously shared, the like of which would never be given to him. And after the manner of jealous children he immediately wanted them, for he had already lost his way in *Rapunzel*.

Jonathan was in no amenable temper tonight. He had spent a day no worse than most, and whiled away the evening in the Pearl of Price, where the beer was admittedly better by much than the Black Bull provided; but on his way home he had encountered a girl he was not anxious to see, and had been more or less compelled to walk up the fields with her as far as the gate of her home. She was a nice girl, practical, pretty and fond, besides being slightly under his own age. She had, in fact, every quality necessary to a wife; but she bored him most of the time, and irritated him for the remainder, which were exaggerated crimes in one who had pleased him well enough a few years ago. He knew he was, by her standards, behaving badly in altering his opinion of her, for she had enjoyed for several years, perhaps not without early encouragement from him, visions of herself as mistress of Ridge Farm in the time to come. But for the war she might by now have been in a fair way of staking her claim. Charles's bachelorhood was of such standing as to be taken for granted, and Sunderne people, whatever their quarrels with their own flesh and blood, did not leave their property out of the family. Jonathan thought, though his memories were hazy because of all the other happenings in between, that he had once come perilously near to marrying Joan Frennet. Well, that was all over; she might find it hard to realise, but she would come round to it in time. And now, after this uneasy stirring of old things, he came home to find Charles sitting smoking contentedly over pleasanter memories of a very different woman. He saw this contentment expressed in the very set of the big shoulders, and the solid ease of the hand that held the pipe, and the slow, rhythmic spirals of smoke ascending. He found it, too, in the way the broad-spaced eyes looked him over lengthily and quitted him again with indifference. Yet it was strange that he could not quarrel with him that night. He tried several goads, and they were merely brushed aside without more notice than a shortened version of the same detached glance, and a grunt, and a phrase of preoccupied impatience. He gave up the attempted mischief soon, and sat down to watch, from behind the pages of *Rapunzel*, the minute modulations which were all the indication he could get of the processes of mind behind that impassive countenance.

He could make nothing of it when Charles looked directly at him for the first time, and with less dislike than normally passed between them, and asked abruptly: 'Do you believe in second sight, Jonty?'

'No! Why, have you been seeing things?'

A taut but calm smile acknowledged the sourness of his tone. 'More in your line at the moment, I should say. No, without reference to anyone in particular – do you?'

'No. It's obvious rubbish.'

'And yet your grandmother was supposed to have it. She was Cornish, not local, but it was the locals who decided she had it. We had a white witch on the place then, too; the old cowman's wife she was.'

'We have now, for that matter,' said Jonathan scornfully. 'Old lady Ferris is noted for her cures among the cottagers' pigs. What about it? All you need is a bit of common sense and a working knowledge of herbs, and you can be a full-blown wizard in these parts. Anyhow, what about it? What started you on this? Not much in your line, is it?'

'Not in my line at all. Still, you never know what you may

run into. I wonder,' he said thoughtfully, 'if this district had much of a reputation in witch-hunting days? It wouldn't be surprising if it did.'

'Ask the postmaster, if you really want to know. He's supposed to be compiling a history of Sunderne Forest, or so Jim Whitton tells me. The old boy's a bit of a scholar in his way, you know; that's acknowledged. He did a bunch of articles once for the *Shalford News*, on the churches of the district, and somebody or other described 'em to me as being pretty hot. I never read 'em myself, though.'

'I remember,' said Charles. 'I did. They were over my head by miles, but that's not remarkable.' The arrogance of the unintellectual man made his voice complacent in self-depreciation, as if it was virtue to have lost all his Latin and most of what else he had picked up at school. 'Yes, I must have a word with Scholefield some time,' he said. 'He could be very useful.'

'Useful for what? What's it all about?'

But these were questions Charles would have found it difficult to answer even had he been willing to let Jonathan into his mind. He put them by him without a word or gesture, staring them away into limbo with his aggressive eyes; and Jonathan shrugged off the indignity and the mystery together, and went disgruntled to bed. The last person he would have associated with this sudden antiquarian interest was Claire Falchion. Certainly it did occur to him to wonder why a day partly spent in her company should cast up at the end of it so curious and irrelevant a conversation; but Charles was a cold-blooded stock at best, and the irregularity of his reactions was not matter for fretting. He could and did work himself into a very practical passion over a lamed horse next morning, as if no Claire existed for him, and certainly no prospective history of Sunderne Forest; and when Jonathan advised him maliciously to call in a charmer to treat the casualty he turned on him and damned his eyes with a vigour which struck Jonathan as altogether modern and realistic. Maybe, after all, this sudden interest in the occult history of the village had originated in some momentary enthusiasm of Claire's, and was hardly likely to be met with again.

He under-estimated Charles in this, however; everyone was liable to this mistake, except Charles himself. He was slow and sceptical in adopting a theory, but held fast to it once it was examined and credited; and of this one he was not yet sure. Accordingly he sought out the postmaster after hours, in the unpruned, spidery old orchard where he was busy picking streaky summer apples.

House and garden were placed upon an eastward slope, so that all the trees leaned, and the evening sun slanted vividly through their topmost branches while all beneath, grass and leaves and air, slumbered in a peaceful olive gloom. A certain threshing of leaves where no wind was led Charles straight to the tree in which Mr. Scholefield was sitting. A basket was wedged into the crotch, and a pair of large, nail-studded boot-soles depending from a mass of overgrown foliage beside it were all that was immediately visible of the postmaster; but as soon as Charles hailed him from below he thrust forth a wrinkled brown hand and a fresh-coloured round face after it, and blinked down short-sightedly from under immense snowy brows like pieces of overdone theatrical make-up.

'Oh, hullo, Charlie! You after my apples?'

'I remember the time when I was,' admitted Charles. 'This time I'd rather pick your brains, if you don't mind. Are you busy?'

'I am, but not incurably. If, that is, you make it worth my while to come down.'

'I want to dig up the past of Sunderne, and you're the man to help me. How do you feel about it?'

The improbable eyebrows bunched themselves together quizzically. The robust voice which might have belonged to a man in his early prime asked bluntly: 'What brought this on? It's very sudden. The one place I don't expect to have any sale is here in Sunderne.'

'Come down, and I'll tell you. But it's genuine; I really want information.'

'A very proper spirit. Here, take this basket from me, will you?' He heaved himself lower, and dropped the full basket down to Charles's hand, following it as neatly himself at the full swing of disproportionately long arms. A shower of leaves rustled dryly into the grass after him, and the boughs settled back into place with a series of diminuendo crashes, and shrank at last into stillness. Mr Scholefield stood revealed as a medium-sized, square man in the late sixties, with a patriarch's head upon a bruiser's body, deep-chested, wide-shouldered and in excellent condition to judge by his descent. He brushed leaves out of the white mane of his hair, removed a smear of very dirty gossamer from his left cheek upon his sleeve, and shook his loose clothes into comparative neatness with a series of vigorous agitations, as a sheep-dog on leaving the water settles his fleece. Then he set off abruptly for the house, and drew Charles after him into a low-ceilinged room opening directly upon the garden, where all the multitudinous jetsam of his seventy or so inquisitive years seemed to have washed up and come to rest.

To know this room well, as Charles knew it, was no guarantee of an unimpeded passage on any fresh visit. There was some sort of tide here that moved everything in a regular and yet incalculable fluctuation, one which had never yet been calendared. The actual furniture was hidden under layers of books, scattered sheets of manuscript, brass rubbings, newspaper cuttings, fossils, samples of stone, fragments of carved wood from discarded bench-ends, worm-eaten panels of oak, a lawn-mower in an advanced state of decomposition, two rolls of old stair-carpet and a rocking-chair jettisoned from the house, the cast-off toys of two generations of Scholefield children, three stuffed birds in sad dilapidation, and a case of wax fruit, besides other debris temporarily lost to sight. At every return this bewildering apartment presented fresh perils in unexpected places, for always the collection appeared to have been recently stirred with a large ladle, so that the hardest item cropped up in dark corners ready to be fallen over, and the missing parts of the mower, which had been about to be mended for over a year, inevitably rolled about the floor at every step and came to rest under the next descending foot. The approved method of clearing chairs here was to excavate until the back or arm of one came to hand, and tip it forward until everything fell off; and this done, it was expedient to claim squatter's rights at once, before some other stratum of the shifting collection was deposited and the opportunity lost. There were, however, comfortable chairs to be found by the experienced searcher, and there was good tobacco, and even, on some occasions, decent bottled beer from the Pearl of Price; this last, when available, being kept ranged like a row of soldiers within the pigeonholes of Mr. Scholefield's enormous desk, cheek by jowl with the manuscript and notes of his history of Sunderne. It was noticeable that the most precious items of his collection were carried upon the old man's person; he never had to hunt for the bottle-opener.

'Well, Charlie,' he said as he operated it with dexterity, 'what's your trouble? I've never known you to want to look further back than one harvest before. What's aroused your interest in the past?'

Charles lay back among rustling paper, and fixed his frowning eyes upon the bowl of the pipe in which he was stubbing down tobacco. 'Well, chiefly the new owner of Long Coppice, to tell the truth.'

'You might ask her for the answers,' suggested Mr. Scholefield dryly. 'Incomers usually have the history and antiquities of the place at their finger-ends inside a month, but I don't mind betting you'll hardly find a native, apart from me, who knows so many as five facts from two generations back. It's always the way. Well, go on. Your lady was interested in the village, I suppose?'

'It seems to be Long Coppice more than the village itself. I'm not surprised. To one who hasn't grown up with it that green must be an astonishing sight. And the house and the garden, side by side with the relics of the school, could easily catch the imagination. She found two portrait panels in the attic, of some dead and gone Shenstone pair. No date, but they looked Tudor or thereabouts. The coat of arms was clear enough. Naturally she feels curious. I thought I might with advantage learn a little more myself; it looks bad not to have any of the answers ready.'

Mr Scholefield leaned his snowy mane back upon the draggled feathers of the larger stuffed owl, and drank beer with a leisurely, meditative gusto. 'It's a bit of a death-bed repentance,' he said weightily, 'but I can understand it. She's a curious fine woman, that.'

'Oh, you've noticed her, have you?'

'She comes in now and again to the office or the shop. Every soul in the place has noticed her, but as you know, no stranger ever notices when and how much Sunderne folk are noticing. We're past grand masters at the art of not being seen to see. Well, what is it you want to know?'

'What there is to know about the house. Has it a history?'

'It's nearly four hundred years old. Few houses can get to that age without having something in their record worth remembering. On the whole, though, a quiet sort of house. The Shenstones built it, some time in the fifteen-fifties; the only record I ever found of the date was illegible after the second five, but the decade's all right.'

'What did the Shenstones want with another house? They already had Sunderne Friars, and they made a packet out of the Dissolution. Why build themselves a little shooting-box affair like Long Coppice?'

'Oh, it wasn't for themselves. They were going through a phase of being very public-spirited at the time; probably a revulsion from the orgy they had in Henry's time, selling up the Friary stone and building Sunderne Friars. Anyhow, the heir had married into a pious family, and wanted to keep in with his in-laws. They instituted a row of almshouses that used to stand along where the Black Bull is now; and they endowed a school.'

'*The* school?'

'*The* school, the one that was burned out in seventeen-some-

72

odd; the one by the old green at Long Coppice.'

'I see,' said Charles. 'So the old schoolhouse was literally built as a schoolhouse.'

'From the start. They maintained the school for the sons of their tenants – hardly anyone within five miles wasn't their tenant, except you yeoman farmers, of course – and they kept a permanent schoolmaster in house and ground and salary. How well, there doesn't seem to be any record, but I think not badly, not too badly. They weren't a bad bunch, as their kind go. The records are thin, though, very thin. Nobody here kept things for any length of time.' At this reflection upon the sense of values of his forefathers he looked vaguely sad, and felt moved to open the third bottle of beer. Thus recharged, and looking round him upon his own magnificent single effort at the preservation of old things, he seemed reassured, and content came back to his benign countenance.

'Well?' said Charles. 'What happened to the school?'

'Oh, I believe it flourished. You only hear of it here and there in the fragments of Shenstone family papers, but by about 1600 I gather it had quite a local reputation. The next mention I could find of it was a very precise one of 1636. It was the tombstone of one of the Shenstones that led me to it. I don't know if you ever noticed what the gravers said about Nicholas? The stone was cleaned a few years back, or I might never have happened on it myself. It said he "died by the secret evil of a false servant". The Latin uses the word "veneficio". Now that could mean poison, or it could mean witchcraft; and either of them needs to be secret, you'll allow. Anyhow, either of them would mean a trial; so I got my cousin in London to tackle the Public Record Office for me, and go through the files of the Oxford Circuit for all the 1630s. He found two indictments of the Summer Assizes of this county for 1636, held at Friary Shalford, and took abstracts for me. I've got them here somewhere, among my tranclements.'

He turned to the mass of paper upon his desk, and began to dig like a badger, finally emerging with two small sheets of paper clipped together.

'Here we are! Take a look at these, young Charles, and see what you make of 'em.'

Charles, bending his head in grave bewilderment over these shortened samples of antique legalese, made more of them than he had expected, though the Latin abbreviations meant nothing at all to him. The first read:

'Summer Sessions and general gaol delivery holden at Friary Shalford on 25 July, 12 Chas. I Commission dated 6 June, 12 Chas. I.

Salathiel Drury of Sunderne, clerk, on 20 Jan. II Chas. I at Sunderne bewitched Nicholas Shenstone, gentleman, who languished until II March, II Chas. I, when he died at Sunderne Friars.

Endorsed: Mary Butterworth, Thom. Scholefield, Francis Fox, clericus, Matthew Chittam, Beavis Frennet, Isabel Ferris, Francis Cates, & c.

Billa Vera.

Po se cul ca null. Judm modo.'

The second, from which the preliminaries were omitted, went straight to the charge:

'Salathiel Drewry of Sunderne, clerk, on 20 Jan. II Chas I at Sunderne did entertain, &c., an evil spirit in the likeness of a white hare to the end that he might practise witchcraft.

Endorsed Same witnesses as first charge, less Francis Fox, clericus.

Billa Vera.

Ponit se cul ca null. Judm modo.'

'Can you follow it?'

'The charge is plain enough, and I suppose the names on the back would be of the witnesses. Billa vera – I take it that means the grand jury found a true bill on both indictments? But after that I've shot my bolt. What's all the rest?'

' "Po se – ponit se", it's all the same, means he pleaded not guilty, and placed himself upon the judgement of the court, "Cul" means he was nevertheless found guilty. "Ca null" is abbreviated clap-trap for has no goods to be disposed of. Not much more than a habit, that, for it often goes side by side with an inventory of goods as long as your arm. And "Judm modo" is one of the shortened forms for "Judicium secundum formam statuti". "Judgement according to the form of the statute in this case made and provided".'

'Which means what?'

'It means he was hanged by the neck until he was dead.'

'Not burned? I thought they burned witches?'

'Not in England, no; the sentence was death by hanging. In Scotland they burned 'em; in Europe they burned 'em wholesale, besides what was done to 'em beforehand. But in England they were hanged.'

'And yet,' said Charles, harking back to some very distant reading in fields not touched for years, 'surely there were some burnings. There was a woman called the Witch of Eye—'

'Oh, yes, it did happen, but only, you'll find, in cases where the charge took on the suggestion of heresy or treason. For attacks by witchcraft on property or life the penalty was death by hanging. Not that I take it for virtue in us, but so it was. And another noticeable thing: in English prosecutions you find that the stress is always on malice rather than on heresy. We seem to have tolerated a lot of queerish behaviour without taking action, but any attempt on life or property produced an indictment like these. Oh, there was always method in English madness. Even outbreaks of fright couldn't drive us to extremes for long. Yet a large number of people died,' he said, shaking his head over the crumpled abstracts, 'Salathiel Drury among them. Notice the varied spelling? They were never over-particular, as long as they knew who was meant. Does the name mean anything to you?'

'Not a thing! Should it?'

'Oh, it was just possible you might have heard of him. The name does crop up in a few of the Shenstone records. He was schoolmaster here from 1620 to 1636; quite a long spell to end as it did, though of course there's no evidence of his reputation in between. He may have been considered pretty queer even before old Nicholas died of something the doctors couldn't diagnose, or it may all have happened in one fit of hysteria. Nobody'll ever know now, I suppose. That's all we have, two indictments and about three earlier mentions of his name in family letters. The rest is silence.'

'And he was hanged?'

'He was certainly hanged.'

'I suppose they all were,' said Charles, 'once they came to trial.'

'Ah, that's another common fallacy. Everybody thinks the judges just crossed themselves and gabbled prayers and ordered the jury to find 'em guilty. In reality they were most of 'em acquitted; over sixty per cent, I should say. There were panics now and then that made the local records pretty bad reading, but over all, most of 'em got off. No, those old justices and jurors weren't so credulous by many a mile as they're supposed to have been.'

'But the whole thing was moonshine, after all,' insisted Charles with his large scorn of all intangible things. 'There was nothing in it but a grand delusion and a lot of hysteria of a religious kind. There never were any witches, and there never was any such thing as witchcraft.'

'I don't know, Charles, I don't know!' The old man squinted at the light through his glass, and shook his head. 'Every fairy-tale has some sort of a fact behind it, if you keep your mind open enough. I've read all the theories. I could talk intelligently about the grisly business as a double illusion, a mass hallucination, the suspects dreaming they were witches and the accusers dreaming they suffered by it. I could preach the old sermon about the covens springing up as a perverted counter-blast to Christianity, with a very real devil and a live consciousness of rebellion. I could take the anthropologist's attitude, and explain that the witch-practices were survivals from a fertility cult older by far than Christianity and every bit as respectable, allowing for the customs of the day. Or I could go all the way to lunacy and assert that they existed, that they flew, and that they cast spells on those who offended them, spells that worked because they had power in themselves, not because of any such subtleties as auto-suggestion. But I won't. I can never quite make up my mind about anything but the cold facts. There were thousands of people tried for "veneficio" in England, and hundreds were hanged. There were scores on scores of confessions, some under brutal treatment, some given freely. It's odds against all of them being either lies or delusions; therefore some people certainly did believe they were witches and had powers and privileges other people couldn't match. Naturally the lunatic fringe joined on behind; aren't they doing it still? But we can leave them out of it. Free statements were made about the covens and their leaders and maidens; therefore it's long odds there did exist an organised cult, whatever its nature was originally. And there are records of undoubted attempts at crime – yes, and successes – by the members of the cult, though not always by supernatural methods. "Veneficio" doesn't mix poison and witchcraft for nothing. Therefore it's reasonable to assume that quite a number of the people hanged for murder by witchcraft were guilty, whether the thing was done in the end by spells or pills. You can be as sceptical as you like about the wax figures, but people died all right, and not all from unidentified diseases like peritonitis, and not all from auto-suggestion, either. But when I've said I believe so far, there I stop. I don't necessarily stop believing; I just wonder, and decide I'll never get it settled beyond that point. So I let it alone. How's your glass?'

'Still provided, thanks. But—'

'You're a slow drinker,' said Mr. Scholefield, rather reprovingly.

'Only when my attention is held. Go on! Do you think this fellow Drury really killed his patron?'

'Oh, there's no means of knowing that. I wish there were. No, there's no fresh evidence likely to turn up now. I'm afraid it will have to remain a secret.'

'But what about the other angle? The Shenstones left lavish family records, if not much besides. Isn't there anything about the cause of old Nicholas's death?'

'Not that I've ever discovered. But if you like to waste your leisure looking for information, let me in on anything you find, won't you?'

Charles frowned into his glass, turning it about and about in his fingers. 'What happened to the house and the school after that?'

'Oh, nothing very much. We have the names of two or three more schoolmasters after Salathiel, and they seem to have lived at the schoolhouse just the same. And then in 1709 or 1710, nobody knows which, the school caught fire and burned out. And that was all. The house passed into the hands of the Foxes some time before 1739, and it's been going back and forth between Foxes and Kentons ever since. None of them ever let go of it until now; and now you've let an incongruous London woman into it, and I doubt if the surviving Foxes will ever forgive you.'

'They can please themselves. Claire fits in there better than any of 'em, if she is a London woman. And Jonty didn't and doesn't want it, or I might have held on. What he wants, or what he thinks he wants, is to get clean away from here once for all. So it looks as if the Foxes will come in for Ridge Farm some day, and if that happens they're hardly likely to complain at being done out of Long Coppice. Talking of Long Coppice, by the way – it hasn't got any sort of bad record, has it? Bad occult record, I mean. It's surely never been known as a disturbed house?'

'Ghosts?' said Mr. Scholefield, narrowing his bright old eyes. 'Come, now, you know you don't believe in such things. Do you, Charlie?'

'I don't know. I've never even had to consider it, so how should I know? I'm ready to believe in anything I run my head against.'

'And have you? Against a ghost in Long Coppice? More likely one of those rafters you failed to duck properly. No, there's no occult dossier for that house, my boy, it's still the way it always has been, sweet as a nut. It's been occupied all along, and not even an adolescent housemaid has ever complained of so much as a queer noise in the night. No, if you're trying to keep your Claire happy by providing the place with a ghostly record you've got all your work cut out, you'll find. Has she got that sort of mind?'

Charles smiled, and was not drawn. 'Who said she entered into it at all? No, I'm not in flight from any psychic experience. Parting with a possession makes you look at it again, I suppose. But I don't anticipate any queer activities, thanks; and as for Mrs. Falchion, she would only laugh at the idea. And yet,' he said reflectively, 'Salathiel Drury seems to have had plenty of excuse for haunting the place, if he'd been given that way.'

'Plenty of excuse, but no opportunity. Here, fill up again and let's finish the lot. One bottle is a shameful leaving.'

They finished it, and the conversation turned to other fields. There was obviously nothing more to be drawn from him upon the subject of Long Coppice, or it would have come forth freely. He was a man who enjoyed imparting information almost as much as he enjoyed accumulating it. But as he was leaving at last Charles did hark back to the house for a moment. They had emerged from the smoky fug of the old man's museum into the evening dimness of the orchard, over which the last shafts of light passed out of reach, like a flight of golden arrows; and he remembered how these same arrows would shower upon the herb-garden to the last moment of the sun's life, and paused to frown back at the problem to which he had found no answer.

'It's queer, isn't it, that these tragedies from not so long back can disappear from view so completely? You would have thought a tale like that would be handed down by word of mouth, even if it changed a good deal in the process. As it is, no one seems to know or care a tinker's damn.'

'Oh, I don't know about queer,' said Mr. Scholefield comfortably. 'When you come to consider, it's all in keeping. We're looked upon as a dark, primitive, secret people keeping our own counsel and biding our time; how we got the reputation, unless it was partly on our looks and partly on our silence, I don't know. But what I said is true; we don't keep anything after it ceases to be useful. Even our memories only function for use, or else so deep within that only an earthquake can bring things to the surface. We may contain history, we may embody it, but we don't dwell on it or keep hold of it. What won't break soil or raise stock is no use to us, and what's no use to us we discard. Between you and me, Charlie, you could go from here to Shalford and never find a trace of a single native folk-tune or a nursery tale, much less a ghost. Incomers of the scholarly sort think we hide 'em; we haven't any to hide, my boy, they've all been thrown away as they wore out. Tragedies go the same way once they're passed. We don't know and we don't care. What interests us is the weather and the wind and the time of year *now*, and not much besides. There never was a more practical race on this earth, and we get taken for survivals from the prehistoric mysteries!' He shook his head over the gullibility of sophisticated man and chuckled. 'And *you* don't believe me, either!'

Charles did not say yes or no to that, nor, indeed, stop to investigate his own opinions and state of mind upon the subject, until he was walking through the village towards home. Then the origin of his search for knowledge came back into his mind, the few seconds which had set him, who never questioned or wondered, questioning and wondering: the silver pane of the window at Long Coppice, and Claire's head reared against it, in an attitude of watching and listening, while she repeated so intently, so softly: 'And yet the fire was right. I'm quite sure about the fire.' And again: ' "Those who come in the air!" "Those who come in the air!" Her very serenity troubled him in recollection, so unnatural should her mood have seemed to herself, and so unquestioningly did she accept it. He began to go over the ground again, and found himself to some degree at odds with Mr. Scholefield. Perhaps the people of Sunderne were unaware of half the memories they possessed, but that did not mean they were not there, and could not be evoked again, given the right circumstances. The key might be there, ready to turn, the door ready to open upon old darkness and confusion better left alone.

And yet there had been no death by burning, it seemed. After all she was not presumptuous and in danger, but imaginative and in error, nothing more. Yet when he remembered the pleased excitement of her eyes, their green, delighted expectancy, he knew that he must go back to her, for he was not satisfied; he did not admit or realise as yet that he was beginning to be afraid.

V

CLAIRE IN THE GARDEN

Claire Falchion wrote:

'There was at this time, when they brought him forth of the gaol and set him in the cart, some small wind blowing, but not so much as to cause any fear of storms, and it was said among those of the people who were come from Sunderne to accompany the cart that at home there would not be wind above what was needed to make the fire burn, the faggots being not well dried. But as they went by the way, being some two hours about the journey, a modest rain began to fall, that caused them to make all haste, by reason of which untoward weather they stopped but once upon the way, at the Falcon Inn at East Manningholt, there to refresh themselves; and at this place there was a woman that worked about the house, and was generally held to be a natural, or as some say an innocent, not having her mind fully about her. This wench drinking with them, and seeing that the convicted man sat all this time in the cart between the constables with his hands tied according to custom, began to ask in her silly poor fashion why they did not bring him in and give him drink. Perceiving that she was not with sense to understand the case, they would not tell her the truth, but made game of her by urging she should show him some kindness, whereupon the natural took a pot of beer in her hand, and went up to the cart to offer it to him; which he rejected, cursing her so extremely that she ran from him in bitter fright, and spilled the beer upon her coats, to the greater mirth of all who were watching. After which pleasant diversion the constables urged they should again set forth, which was done, and they came within the second hour to the village of Sunderne, and the green therein before the school, where his villainies were done, and where it was ordered his execution should be accomplished also.

'The pyre and stake were already prepared against the occasion, and having stood all night in a soft rain were now but indifferent dry; nevertheless the executioner determined upon examination that the matter might very properly proceed in accordance with the order, and so he advised those two Justices who were come to see the sentence carried out. So it was done according to the form of the statute.'

She stopped, as a waft of wind blew thyme-scented dust over the page. There was no other reason for her to halt, for the pen flowed of itself, without will or direction from her, and it scarcely mattered even that the light was failing. She blew the dust away, and saw as it flew that half of it was gold of pollen, soiled yellow now that the sun was gone. It was growing almost cold in the garden, and the sundial looked tall and flat, two-dimensional now that no shadows folded half about its pedestal, and no long shadow braced it from the ground. Distance was folded up and put away until morning, and only differing shades of blue singled hill from hill beyond the indefinite green and iris haze of the twilit trees. Having looked up, she did not want to return to the greying page, or work any longer tonight. It was not as if there was any haste. What was to come would come as it would, as it must, without the need of any effort upon her part, and she could wait as the channel of the dwindling brook waits for the next rain, sure of her function, secure of her destiny.

From the low, backless stone bench on which she sat, close under the sundial, she could just see old Whitton at the corner of the house, wiping down his scythe with steady sweeps of his long arm, as measured as the strokes with which he had cut down the tangled grass. He worked as he saw fit, and if it pleased him to go on all the evening one day, and perhaps not come at all the next, she could not see that she was in any way the loser. She never interfered with him, and it was seldom that they even spoke to each other. She knew nothing about gardening, and had no mind to learn, because it pleased her better to sit quietly and accept what the tended earth provided her of beauty and fragrance than to attempt to impose any wish of hers upon it. She preferred that he should decide whatever must be decided, for he seemed to her very near kin to his own earth, and she suspected that there was a shared language between them more lucid than any she spoke for the old man to understand. All the same, she had achieved an intimacy with him which did not express itself in speech. It had come about very gradually, and was not, she thought, perfect yet, but it was substantial and good. At first he had not looked at her as she went about the garden, but only beyond or through her, as if she had been a ghost invisible to him; but after seven or eight days had passed he had begun to see her, and she to be aware of his silent acceptance of her. It had never become more than that, never interest or curiosity or admiration; but no more was needed. To be accepted was everything. She had judged in the beginning that the change was in him, but one night upon going into her room and lighting the gas she had come upon her own reflection suddenly in the long mirror, and been startled as at seeing a stranger.

The changes in her were largely physical, she had thought, and unimportant, yet here there faced her a new person, a younger person. She had taken to wearing her oldest and simplest clothes and going without stockings, and her legs and arms were burned to a clear, speckled brown which made them seem smoother and rounder than before, and so younger. Her hair had grown down into heavy curls upon her neck, and its weight had drawn out the rigidity of her permanent wave into soft, wide swathes like a young girl's around the softened creamy oval of her gold-freckled face. She had given up using cosmetics because she no longer cared, with no eyes upon her expecting or demanding anything, to seem other than she was. But there was more than this to startle her. Her eyes against her darkened skin looked lighter, brighter, more of gold than of brown in their greenness; their well-water colouring was grown warm not with a reflected but with an innate light, as if the sun shone from below the leafy surface. Her mouth, no longer persuaded into a straighter shape than nature had given it, was large and full and smiling, the lips folded together as glossily as the petals of an opening rose. It reminded her of the mouths of children before they have learned to dissemble what they feel; and its candour had a fierceness about it, and a vigour, which at once charmed and repelled her. Her spare, high cheek-bones, her smooth temples, the bridge of her nose, all were polished to a clear sheen like ivory; everywhere that bone came near to skin was this summer glaze, sheer and bright. Out of her lightness, out of her emptiness, she had become transparent for this inexplicable radiance to shine through. She thought as she gazed that Anne would not have known this woman; she scarcely knew herself.

Had she always been like this behind her sophistication? Was this what she had been brought up not to see, to confine within the bounds of convention and fashion, to distort into conformity with customs, never to understand, or acknowledge, or express? Or was this the shining fruit of something new within her, a late growing-up into youth? She could only stand a moment still, and marvel, watching the strange, sudden girl who so candidly watched her; and the lightness and emptiness within her made her feel for a moment as if the floor reeled away under her feet, and she was uplifted toward flight. For she knew now how she seemed to old Whitton as he scythed the grass and trimmed the bushes; and it was as if she had found a faun in her own garden.

The old man shouldered the scythe and walked away down the cleared path to the shed under the wall. All things conspired to remind her in one moment of the evanescence of time; the sundial showing its ominous posy to the sky, the backward shedding of her own unfruited years, and the old man with the scythe pacing so leisurely and covering the ground so fast away from her. And above all, the few pages covered with her sharp handwriting, wherein was nothing she had deliberately set out to write, but only something which had flowed out of her as irresistibly as blood from a wound. She hardly knew as yet what it was; she knew little about it, not even the name of the man about whom she had written it. All she knew was that it was true, that this was how it had happened. No great show of piety, none of forgiveness; no faith, no hope, no pity, and very surely no consciousness of heaven upon either side. She smiled to think of her first hazard, and how awry it had fallen. But this sudden narrative without beginning or end, this record of death upon her very doorstep, she knew this was the truth.

She got up from her seat, leaving the few sheets of paper where they lay, and went slowly through the garden towards the wicket gate in the far wall. In the still of the evening the odours had settled heavily to earth, and stirred before her feet in waves, richness upon richness, drowning the senses. Though she walked towards the hanging wood and the ridges of bracken, what she saw clearly in her mind was the overgrown triangle of grass before the house, and the bare place in the centre, where the stake had been. She was seeing it still as she passed through the gate and climbed the rising path between the trees. The stake in the midst, taller than a man's height though he should be more than common tall, roughly lopped and peeled, looking raw and new even by this mournful light of a moist day; and about its foot the tied faggots piled in a pyre two feet high, with a segment cut clean out of it to the stake, and enough brushings beside to close up this path when the condemned man had been fastened into his chains. Around the edges of the green, quiet and watchful, the people of Sunderne, waiting for the cart to appear along School Lane; all of the people, from the ancients to the schoolboys who had sweated at their Cæsar under the dying man not many months previously. And over everything the soft, grudging breath of the rain. So it had been, the climax of this ferocious tragedy in which no one had had pity for anyone or anything. So it was still, for time had shouldered his scythe and turned his back upon the school green, time who was the mercy of eternity.

By the time she reached the barrier the wind could not pass, and leaned out eagerly to the troubled air beyond, she knew more of it; she knew the man's name, and the woman's. She knew the names of the three women, for the women had been three who would have answered for this barren business if there had been any justice. Best and worst of all, she knew what he had looked like even when he was not chained to a stake. It came to her as she stood in the brackeny clearing in the twilight, drinking the wind; and she went down the path again very slowly, contemplating him steadily and without wonder. A very tall man was Salathiel Drury, with broad, high shoulders and a long, tapered, narrow-flanked body; yet upon first sight a bulky-seeming creature, for he was well-fleshed about his large frame, and habitually moved over-fast and over-suddenly, as if his mind was in petulant haste to be where his body was not. He was not young; she recognised him for one of her own generation, and judged him to be perhaps forty-four or forty-five. He had a face which caused her instantly to reflect that she had seen it before, that in a sense it was well-known to her; and only gradually, because of the intensity of her perception of the whole, did she become aware of those features which she recognised in his face, and know them familiar only because they were the commonest of common coin among the people of Sunderne. The lean, bony cheeks, the high forehead distended into plateaux like the nubbles of horns beginning to grow, the high-bridged, great narrow hawk-nose were the ordinary markings of this race; she had seen them in young Jonathan and a dozen others since she came into the village. But the rest of this man she had never seen before. He had short, bushy chestnut hair streaked with grey and untidily kept, that fell forward in gaunt locks upon his forehead because of his forward-hastening gait. He had large, hollow eyes of an indistinguishable dark colour, some blue or brown very near to black, set wide from his beak of a nose, and made at once scornful and eager by the lofty arching of the strongly-marked brows over them. They conveyed a gaze to which certain contradictory words seemed equally applicable; angry she found it, and yet cold, insolent and yet calculating, wild yet aloof, shrewd yet doubting, self-contained and yet insatiably hungry. Like a wild animal with an intellect above that of most men; she could think of nothing nearer to his look than this. He had also an unexpected mouth, full and tender and softly-shaped as a woman's above a short, jutting chin stubborn like steel; and indeed the whole structure of the lower part of his face jutted, so that the very gentleness of his lips had a look of satire and even of cruelty upon so formidable a jaw, as if someone had baited a toothed iron trap with a brightly-coloured flower. The habitual expression of this mouth of his was a grave, sweet and dreadful smile, and of his eyes a bright, blistering antagonism. Some of Lucifer's companions, she supposed, might have looked like that when they remembered heaven.

She saw him with a dreamlike closeness and clarity, and was conscious of neither revulsion nor pity, neither liking nor hate, only an intent conviction within herself of some intimate cord binding up her intelligence with his experience. And as if that sexless connection set her apart from his emotions as he from hers, she looked back at him openly and curiously, with a glittering green stare, at the man who did not exist, at the man in her mind. There was no detail of him she could doubt, though the whole of him was only imagined; nor did she feel any fear that he might grow too significant, any desire to turn her mind away from him. She slackened her walk with watching him, pacing slow through the gathering dark between the birch trees, her eyes wide and fixed in that strange, alert stare. Observing, she began to wonder, though knowledge was pouring into her heart as fast as she could bear it or house it. She wondered if some demand was not, after all, being made of her. There had been in this story so much of savagery, and no pity at all; and where time had withdrawn its limitations nothing could ever come too late. Pity separated from indignation or deserving is a strange growth, solitary, monstrous and self-propagating, waiting upon no gardener's will.

Slowly she went down the declining path, and slowly let herself into the garden, and before her eyes the very darkness was coloured and shaped into the semblance of a stake, and a big man chained to it, knee-keep in faggots and brushwood, and hip-deep in damp and grudging fire, with a writhen, horrible face, and a great voice of malediction bellowing for death against a shocked and terrified silence of many people. She was aware of blood running from the bright, bitten lips and the breast torn by the chains, and of a slow, smoky blackening of flesh once strangely fair. She was aware of loneliness so absolute that it became an outrage done upon the spirit; and this before the fire, and during it, and after it, the first enormity and the last, out-enduring death.

In the garden all was grown shadowy, and outlines were lost in the encroaching dusk; but the stone bench and the pedestal of the sundial made faint, shapeless passages of pallor, and helped her to see that someone, a nameless dark figure, was seated in the place she had left, with the few abandoned sheets of her revelation spread upon his knee. He was motionless, his head bent, his face hidden from her; she saw only a deeper shadow among the shadows, and she approached him slowly but confidently along the path muffled with moss, where her feet made no sound. She did not feel excitement, only satisfaction that he was here in the garden with her, and in the semblance of flesh at least. She went close to him, and advanced her hand towards his arm, but did not touch, for the nearness of her fingers seemed to reach him, and he trembled and suddenly looked up. They stared at each other, and the night could not hide the abrupt and definite lines of Charles Kenton's face; nor did it soften, for him, the vision of her face lucid and smoothly moulded, like alabaster lit from within, with great eyes fixed and calm, and yet tears upon her cheeks. These she did not regard, but to him the sight of them, and her indifference to them, were curiously shocking. It was as if he had waited for the urban woman he knew, and been confronted with a salamander.

He jumped to his feet, the sheets of paper still in his hand.

'Claire! My God, Claire, what's the matter?'

She looked at him with recognition cooling the fire of her eyes, and the tears still shimmered unconsidered upon her face.

'Nothing. What should be the matter?'

He believed for a moment that she was daring him to notice that she had wept, sweeping over the inconvenient circumstance with her customary conventional poise, and ordering him to do the same; but then he saw that she did not know she had anything to hide. 'What should be the matter?' she asked in detached surprise, and laughed at the concern of his face.

'You came up so quietly,' he said, turning to the first excuse he could find. 'I never noticed you until you were at my elbow. Why in the world are you creeping about like that?'

'I'll wear a bell round my neck if you'd like me to,' she said, with a malicious playfulness which he saw came from only half her mind, and impatiently at that. She looked beyond him now, but no longer with clear and focused eyes, rather with a glance turned inward upon something remembered or imagined. 'I'm sorry I startled you. I didn't expect you tonight.'

'Or want me,' said Charles without resentment. 'I'll go. It was late to come worrying you.'

'No, stay now you're here. It's all right, you see I'm not working.'

'I see you have been.' He held out the pages, watching her face. She was still a long way from him, and he knew it now, and the anxiety which had not quite reached him advanced its hand a little nearer to his heart. He was not even so important that he need be shut out, it seemed.

'You've read it?' she asked.

'Yes. You don't mind, do you? I was curious, that's all.'

'That's frank, at any rate.'

'I couldn't help it, after seeing the beginning; and it was you who let me in on that, you know.'

'I haven't complained, have I? Don't become hypersensitive, Charles, it doesn't suit you. Why are you looking at me like that? Is there anything so very wrong with me?'

He said: 'Of course not!' from the old conventional motives, and as quickly forced himself back upon his true course. Where was the use of covering up what was strange, where it was obvious that they were far past any such shifts? Here in the dark only what was strange was real at all. 'I don't believe you know it, but you've been crying,' he said deliberately.

She did something then which frightened him more than the tears themselves had done. She put up her hands incredulously, and felt at her cheeks, and then held her wet fingertips spread before her eyes and stared at them in silence for some minutes. She was certainly surprised, but as certainly not distressed; rather she seemed pleased, if anything, to find she could weep and not know it. She looked at him through her fingers and smiled at him with a prepossessed gentleness. 'I have! You're right, I didn't even know. Don't look so serious, Charles, there's nothing the matter with me, not even melancholia.'

'But something must have upset you,' he insisted.

'I'm not in the least upset, thanks, Charles. I never felt more firmly upright in my life.'

Nor looked it, either, he thought upon reflection; tears were a phenomenon, no doubt, but in spite of them she was as aloof and self-contained as any half-wild cat, and would be about as easy and rewarding to any fool who conceived he ought to attempt comfort. No, privilege with her, however carelessly given, extended only so far, and if he stepped over the line he would be damned altogether and never admitted again. And yet he must venture a little, however cautiously; there was no caution in her venturing, and who knew into what unchancy land she might not be walking open-eyed?

'I suppose you know what you're doing,' he said dubiously.

'I'm doing nothing that isn't perfectly apparent. What is it you're worrying about, Charles? Do you think I can write without feeling anything?' He saw by her slight frown that he was in danger of becoming tedious, which he suspected would be fatal.

'Then your concern is all on his account, I suppose,' he said.

'I don't know. There were others not much more fortunate. I simply don't know. Don't ask me about it yet, for I can't answer.'

'But there are things you can answer. Who are these others you speak of? Who is "he" for that matter?'

'His name was Salathiel Drury,' she said.

'Have you been reading it up somewhere, that you're so sure? Or asking someone about him? Claire, have you?'

'Of course not! There's no one to ask. There's nowhere to read it up.'

'You haven't even mentioned it to anyone?'

'No one except you,' she assured him.

'Then how *can* you know this name? How did it come to you that he was Salathiel Drury more than another name? You must have some idea of how it happened, Claire; you're used to observing intellectual experiences.'

'Oh, leave me alone, Charles! I haven't investigated it; there's been no time, even if I'd wanted to. I wrote without having to think, and I knew without having to wonder. I'm satisfied that it should go on; I don't want to question it, and you can't.'

'Oh, yes, I can. I know who Salathiel Drury was. I know what he was charged with, and when and where he was tried. I know all that's yet been traced about him, or almost all, though the whole of it isn't much. Do you, Claire?'

'Not yet,' she said simply, 'but I shall. There's plenty of time.'

'Then suppose I tell you that your revelation so far is quite unreliable? You've already made one mistake, the greatest one possible. Suppose I prove that to you? Would you give up thinking about it then? Would you stop encouraging it? It's nothing but a sympathetic illusion you've deliberately created in your own mind. Will you break away from it if I show you it's no more?'

'You can't show anything of the kind,' she said with a flashing smile. 'But try, if you like. I'll listen to you. There's all the time in the world for arguing about it, if that's what you want. What was my great mistake?'

'Salathiel Drury wasn't burned; he was hanged. Death by burning was never the punishment for witchcraft in England.'

She laughed, quite softly and slowly. 'Yes, I know that, too. Oh, Charles, have I made *you* learned, of all people? Well, go on. You conclude I made the common error of thinking all witches were burned?'

'Most people think that. I did. Why shouldn't you?'

'Why, indeed? But I didn't. I merely knew this one was. I still know it. Is that all you have to say?'

.'Yes, that's all. Isn't it enough?'

'Then listen to me. I was worried about that same point myself, and I went to the trouble to find out a little more. I began from different ground, of course. You knew witches were hanged, and therefore he could not have been burned. I knew he was burned, and therefore his could not have been the ordinary case of witchcraft. There are always the exceptions that confirm rules. You knew, did you, that in some cases treason could be punished by burning?'

'I've been told so.'

'There are two kinds of treason. Grand treason you know. But do you know that murder of a husband by a wife, or a master by his servant, was ranked as petty treason? And do you know whom Salathiel Drury is said to have murdered? I see that you do. His patron, Nicholas Shenstone.'

He had nothing to say. She was so steady, so certain, that he felt for the first time convinced of her rightness; but what staggered him all the more for this conviction was her calm, her pleased acceptance of what was unnatural and disquieting to him. Could she so blandly swallow what would once have been suspect of witchcraft as surely as any deed of Salathiel Drury's? Whatever troubled or hurt her, it was not her own clairvoyance. She regarded him steadily, and laughed at his bewildered face.

'Now I should merely have been hanged. Or, of course, if I refused to plead, as I probably should, pressed to death by the "strong and hard pain". But he committed petty treason, or they said he did; and he burned, my good Charles, and what's more, he burned out there on the school green, near to the place where his crimes were supposed to have been committed – this house and this garden. Have I convinced you already?' she asked, as he was still silent. 'Wherever we differ on this one matter you'll find it the same. I tell you, Charles, I know. Not all of it yet, but I shall. And what part I do know is altogether true. Find me more discrepancies in it, and I shall still show you how they make perfect sense. I'm not guessing: this is knowledge. Do you believe me?'

'Yes,' said Charles, 'I believe you all right. I wish to hell I didn't.'

'Then let's be practical about it. There's nothing to worry about; why should there be? That was just something that happened; and this is something that's happening now. What more is there to say about it? What can there possibly be to do? You talk about breaking away from it, as if it could be a matter of choice, but I tell you it isn't.'

'If it was,' he said, 'you'd choose to go on with it.'

'Yes, I should. But it isn't, and I don't have to make any choice. I'm relieved of all responsibility. I'm only a channel, not an agent. I don't suppose you could stop it now, Charles, even if you forced me out of the house; and since you've sold it to me you can't even do that. So it's no use worrying, you see.'

95

She moved a little away from him, light and silent in her ivory frock, like a moth in the dark. Once out of reach of his hand she seemed so insubstantial that flight could not be far out of her scope. She stood with her head tilted back, watching something between herself and the stars, and listening to the stillness.

'Claire!' he said.

'Yes?' She turned instantly, responsive to the new note of gravity and resolve in his voice; she had not always, he thought, paid so much attention to him.

'Claire, have you been troubled by Long Coppice?'

'Troubled? In what way?'

'By the house. He lived in this house for sixteen years. I don't believe much in such things, but then, I don't believe much in visitations like yours, and yet I can't get away from it this time. I suppose it's just possible that a very unhappy man might leave some sort of a print behind, for the first hypersensitive person to find. I always thought it was moonshine, but somethings's happening here that I don't pretend to understand. Have you seen anything? Or heard anything? Is Long Coppice *haunted*? I suppose that's the way I should put it.'

Claire looked along her shoulder at him, and laughed, a clear, small, impersonal mockery aimed, he thought, at bigger stupidities than his, and only indirectly striking at him. 'No, Charles, the house isn't haunted. Not even for me! There's nothing here to trouble me, nothing to hear or see, no pale ghosts, no night terrors, no indoor winds, no traditional cold, not even fear of the dark, or discomfort at being alone. It's just a house like any other, only quieter than most. I give you my word there's never been anything in the least supernatural. Sometimes I wish there could be.'

'Then how *do* you account for this queer sort of knowledge you lay claim to? For it isn't natural, you can't say it is.'

'I don't feel any urge to account for it. I'm satisfied to have it. But how can you think the house has anything to do with it? Why should bricks and mortar hold impressions better than anything else, I wonder?'

'What other link is there between you and Salathiel Drury, except the house?'

She said in a soft voice: 'Ah, I've wondered that, too. What's the use of asking me that question? If I knew I could use it at will, but you see I can't do that. If I knew, there might be things to see, and things to hear, and no need to wait any longer to know everything; but you see I still have to wait. No, whatever it is, Charles, it isn't within reach of my senses, it isn't anything I can see, or hear, or touch.' She spread her hands. 'Empty, you see! No ghosts, no demons, no diabolical possession. What a fool you are!' she said, and laughed again. 'A pleasant enough fool, but still a fool!'

'That's as may be,' said Charles, unmoved. 'We weren't talking about me.'

'Let's stop talking about me, then, too,' she said. 'I tire very easily of being interesting. Forget I ever let you see *Auto-da-Fé*, and don't expect to see anything more.' She held out her hand. 'Please! You hold the pages as if they burned *you*.' He gave them up, nonetheless, with considerable reluctance, for it was plain now that he was banished, and these were his only hold on her.

'Have I offended you?'

'No. We're setting right something which was done wrong, that's all. I ought to have known I was only offering you a good deal of uneasiness. It never pays to share things too soon. If ever I come to print again, with this or anything else, I promise you shall be one of the first to know all about it; but until then, Charles, you'll forgive me if I become secretive. After all, you did expect me to be temperamental, remember.'

'Oh, damn it, Claire!' he protested, 'you know you've only got to warn me off once. I shall never bother you again. Unless, that is, I bother you just by coming here, for I won't promise not to come near you, even if you ask me to. But since there's no more privilege, I shan't trespass.'

'You know you'll always be welcome,' she said, so lightly, so sweetly that he knew she was not regarding the words or him. She was looking beyond him into the dark, and he felt her impatience that he should go. There was not room in the scented garden for him. Her mind had peopled it already, and he was only the unwelcome guest who kept her from her private pleasure. The touch of her hand as she took the papers from him was cold but vital, with the live cold of the wind; but as unaware of him as was her look, and the distant excitement of her eyes. He could vibrate to her near presence, and she would not know. He could love her, and she would not be moved.

He knew then that it was hopeless, all the more hopeless because he knew also that there had been a time when he had been within call of her, almost within touch. At their first meeting he believed he could have taken hold of her and she would have become his quite easily; but one does not readily recognise the moment of nearest approach, and he had let it go by as the conventional do who draw closer together by decorous slow degrees, hoping to creep more intimately into her grace tomorrow, and tomorrow's morrow. He had lost her for want of understanding the one moment when he might have had her, for ever since then she had receded from him steadily, and now she was far out of reach. Never again would she come within touch of him. Perhaps he deceived himself in thinking there had ever been an opportunity, but it was no error that there would never be another. Miles from him, her mind sealed against him, she went her way unpursuable. That was over before it began.

It was then that he began to want her without reserve, without restraint or moderation or unselfishness. He was as perverse in the end as young Jonathan; he wanted because he could not have, and the mere action of removing the creature he wanted to an ever remoter distance increased his desire to a point where it suddenly became unbearable to him. How if he should snatch now at what hope he had, and at her? There was nothing to lose, at any rate, since every moment increased their strangeness to each other. He took a couple of quick paces towards her, and took her by the wrists, drawing her round to face him. His suddenness, his ungentleness, did not seem to surprise or trouble her in the least, and whatever it was she saw she could see just as clearly with his face close in front of her own, for the expression of her eyes did not change. Only her brows drew together in a slight, preoccupied frown, as if his touch recalled to her something she had almost forgotten.

'Claire,' he said in a low, rapid voice, 'listen to me. You're turning your back on what's real for something that's only fantasy, and morbid fantasy at best. I don't ask you to come back for your own sake, though, since I've been warned off. But I've got a right to ask you to come back for mine, haven't I? That's my affair, very much my affair, and I can put both hands into it without meddling. You've got a just mind, you'll allow me my rights, even if you're jealous of your own. All right, now I've done being anxious about you, I'm only worrying about myself. I want you to look at me, and talk to me, and think about me, instead of running after a chimera.'

Claire said coolly: 'I'm not running after anything; nor away from anything, either.'

'Then try and remember I exist, will you, in the intervals of psychic experience? Try and look at me as if I'm really here, and even hear what I say. And if you could manage to notice some difference between the times when I'm here and the times when I'm not here – well, I should be glad.'

'I do,' said Claire. 'When you're not here it's quieter.'

'I can be silent if you value it so much.'

'If no reward was forthcoming,' she said indifferently, 'you wouldn't keep quiet for long.'

'My lord, you've a pretty poor opinion of me!' he exploded, tightening his hold of her.

'I don't think so. What's so poor about that? You do like to be paid your dues. You do like a proper value to be put on you. Why not? I should think less of you if you didn't. But not asking nor taking will get you anything here, Charles, except what you already have. There's nothing else to be had, that's all about it.'

He drew her close to him by the wrists, and shutting both of them into one big hand against his breast, held her body tightly pressed to his with the other arm. Pliant and undisconcerted, she gave to his hands without resistance or surrender, as a young tree bends but no otherwise; and with the warmth of him struggling to infect her blood she was still cold as a lake-lily. She even smiled at him, half in regret, half in derision, not troubling to be gentle nor caring to be cruel.

'Nothing, you see. It isn't in me to satisfy you, even if I wanted to, even if I seriously believed that you wanted me to. But I don't believe in this at all, Charles, and I won't be made to feel guilty about it. It's you who seem to be running after a chimera, not I. But if you expect me to get excited about your arm being round my waist, my dear man, you must think me as big a fool as you are.'

'And yet you can't get away from me,' he said, marvelling how slight she was to his touch, as if the true content of her still eluded him. 'I could do what I liked with you, and you couldn't help yourself.'

'What you like isn't likely to be so grim that I should need help, from myself or anyone else. Really, Charles, I know you too well to be in the least worried about this fictitious passion of yours. When you're sick of it you'll let me go.'

'You may tire first,' said Charles.

She laughed. 'It may become tedious. But I'm well trained; social contacts are often very tedious. I can support it all the better because I shan't have to pretend to enjoy it.'

He said on an incredulous breath: 'You're as cold as the devil!'

The eyes so near his own looked back at him with detached mockery. She said: 'So I have often been told, but I still think it must be a mistake.' And in a bitter light voice she quoted: ' "Ye have sought them and lain with them in spite of their freezing coldness".'

'What's that?'

'More witchcraft, but not mine.' Her hands lay placidly where he held them; she was not even trying to provoke him, only waiting patiently but sadly for him to come to his senses and let her alone; and in the meantime allaying the eagerness of her mind with silent promises of what should follow his going. He simply did not matter; not even as Whitton mattered, who was silent and old and calm, and fitted into the background as if he had grown there. Charles would never matter, unless he became too great a distraction; for she would not always be so acquiescent. He could torment her, and she would bear it; but only so long as he did not stand too clamorously between her and the secrets she desired. Besides, he thought, who knows if she may not fail of what she wants? There may come another time. Even if it's disappointment that brings her down to my level again, there may be something salvable; but if I vex her too far now it may be to someone else she turns then. He was careful, because of the instant heat about his heart, not to consider too nearly who the someone else might be; but for one instant he had been visited by the bitter vision of young Jonathan standing breast to breast with her as he stood now. Better by far to rein in now, and not throw her into the company of any other person, least of all Jonty.

It was painful to him to take his hands from her wrists, but he did it, reluctantly and slowly.

'Forgive me, Claire!'

'It's all right, Charles. Blame the twilight and the garden. Only don't blame me. Perhaps, after all, you and Breck are right, and I am a cold woman. Don't blame me for that, either.'

'You won't hold this against me, will you? I want to come again. If you try to keep me out I *will* be a nuisance. I'll drive you mad.'

Smiling remotely, eagerly through him, only the faintest warmth shed into him in passing, she said: 'I told you, it's all right. Come when you like. If it isn't what you want, I'm sorry, but at any rate I trust you, Charles.'

'I'll go now. Good night, Claire!'

'Good night, Charles!'

'So you trust me!' he thought as he walked up School Lane.

'The more fool you! The more fool you!' Yet if a dozen betrayals could not, after all, get him what he wanted she might be justified; for he would not hurt her wantonly, but only for excellent reason shown. Would he hesitate then? He doubted it. Nor the boy, either; he was the same blood. Nor, for that matter, would Claire withhold her hand if by destroying either or both of them she could get what she wanted. What it was he did not at all comprehend; but he had seen in her eyes what she would do to secure it, and there wasn't much she wouldn't.

When he was gone, she sat down again for a moment upon the stone bench, the papers still in her hands. It was grown cold suddenly, now that she had time to notice it; and the curious comfort of this peopled quietness was within the house as surely as without. Yet she sat there soothed and content, waiting until the silence was unbroken about her before she went in. By the time Charles's foot was off the green she had forgotten him; in her thoughts he had never been more than a trespasser. Tears sprang to her eyes again, and ran down her still face. She did not know why. They did not belong, it seemed, to her.

VI

THE TRUE STORY OF SALATHIEL DRURY

This is the story that Claire Falchion wrote during late August and September in Long Coppice:

In the year of our Lord 1620 there came to Sunderne as schoolmaster in the pay of Master Nicholas Shenstone one Salathiel Drury, a young man some twenty-eight years old, born in the village and son of a former clerk of the parish, but grown up in London, where his father obtained a cure and was advanced under the favour of a certain nobleman. This same Salathiel was for his years full of scholarship, and came back to his place of birth in good odour with all his neighbours by reason of the reputation and virtue of his father, who was well remembered. He was seen also to be well enough favoured, though somewhat heavy of countenance, and was known to have to his credit certain minor writings not all unfamiliar to such as read widely. Therefore his coming was welcomed, all the more as he came after a man old and forgetful, who had so little Latin he could not well bestow any; and upon his taking up residence in the Schoolhouse he was greeted gladly by his scholars and by the village, as one come to restore the reputation of Master Shenstone's foundation in its old quality. Which, moreover, he did, and soon, for he had notable parts. He continued sixteen years in this employ, and to good profit with those who sat under him; but by reason of some peculiarities of temper he was a man even more feared than respected, and the village did not meddle with him.

At the time of his coming and for a few years afterwards

Master Shenstone's bailiff, the incumbent of the parish, the clerk, and certain other worthies were at some pains to show him civility, but he was at none to welcome or respond to their gentilities, and made it but too plain that he was pleased with none but his own company, whereupon they drew off from him and let him be. It was soon said of him that he was a recluse, but it was truer that they were afraid of his tongue, which was bitter, and his manners, which were ungentle. He lived alone in the Schoolhouse, and was troubled no more with civil attentions, whereof he was clearly glad, but what had caused him to be thus set against his neighbours, or whether it was not some defect of nature in him, they could not well judge, nor did not venture to inquire. It was better to have no ado with him but as they must, and to make no complaint of his solitude, as he made none of their dislike. He gave their sons good schooling, which was chiefly required of him, and he troubled no one who did not first trouble him by crossing his path. So after their fashion he and they lived at peace, and having been for some short time an object of curiosity he became at last with all his waywardness but a piece of the village, as it might be a wall or a tree known to be of such a stone, or to grow in such a fashion. He had no other desire.

There were not wanting among the boys some who reported him as violent and severe, but this was the common repute of all schoolmasters, and the reproach was not put upon him with more bitterness than upon others; insomuch that many who had by ill-luck touched and tried his temper were amazed he was no worse spoke of, and allowed it was well worth the odd blow or two and the sarcastic word that their sons should be better-read than any who passed through that school before them. It was not denied that he made the dullest learn, but they said also that he never praised nor rewarded the most scholarly, and one or two who took pains to creep into his favour were so put down before the rest as never to use those arts again. Wise men did not venture to brush his patience once, nor fools twice. He was just, for he treated all his boys with equal scorn and harshness, whether they did well or ill. Yet for the most part he was a silent man, not as one having no words, rather as one finding no person worthy to have them spent on him.

This Salathiel took a housekeeper, a middle-aged widow of good character, the sister of Elias Weelkes, a small farmer in the village. She had one daughter, Mary, a young woman well thought of and well conducted in all her ways, who also remained with her mother and served as maid; and in some years, Jane Butterworth being grown infirm, the young woman Mary took upon her more and more the managing of the house. Last her mother, having been some two years blind, died and was buried in the winter months of 1630, leaving Mary, who was then about twenty-eight years old, to the care of Elias Weelkes her good uncle. Folk then supposed that the young woman would marry, and give up her labours for the schoolmaster, since there were young men who would gladly have had her to wife; but she continued in her old way, only removing to her uncle's house with all her gear, but day by day serving still as faithfully as while her mother lived. In ill weather, by winter snows and freezing winds, she did not fail to reach the house in good time, and was never known to leave Salathiel her master a single day unprovided. Nor did she listen to the young men who would have won her away for their own sakes, but only cast down her eyes modestly at their entreaties, and made haste away from them; but ever with a humble kindliness, as unwilling to hurt them, and unable to give them any satisfaction.

One there was who found favour in the eyes of her Uncle and Aunt Weelkes, for he had some land, and stood in a fair way to get cattle enough; they would not seek to enforce her, but only temperately urged on her that she should consider if she did well to let such an opportunity pass. Still she meekly replied that she could not in duty take him or any while she had a task laid upon her at her mother's hands, to do her proper service to her master. When they asked her if he was not already served better than well by her, having had ten years of her labour, she replied that he had been a just master to her, and she had no complaint to make of the hardness of his ways, for doubtless God had seen fit to lay this cursed temper upon him; howbeit he had been ever forbearing and generous with an old, unprofitable, blind woman and a faulty, inexperienced girl. So they let her alone, for a saint will not be meddled with.

At this time Mary Butterworth was not uncomely, being of the middle figure, very neat and light-handed, with a modest glance and a sober dress. Her hair, which was light brown, she wore plainly braided back under a starched white cap, and her lashes were of a colour yet lighter, as pale as amber, and her eyes of a greyish blue. She was of a pale complexion, but healthy and strong and hard-working. She walked in a manner unlike the countrywomen of Sunderne, with small, rapid steps, and quietly; and her voice was low and meek as becomes a serving-maid, having a very sweet submissive tone. With all this she was an excellent cook and a frugal housekeeper, and kept the house a shining place in spite of the bookish and untidy habit of her master. She could read a little, but had never in childhood learned to write; and by times she would borrow of the books that were about the house to try her knowledge, and would make out the greater part of the words therein; and by times Salathiel would spend an hour upon her to improve her in this kind, in which labour he was not gentler with her than with his boys, but she made no complaint. So in time she came to read as well as need be, but in writing her hand was still as a child's.

Such was the outward manner of the establishment these two kept at the Schoolhouse during those five years after the death of Jane Butterworth, until a day in the first month of 1636, when Master Nicholas Shenstone the patron came riding down from Sunderne Friars and was closeted long with Master Drury. Upon this day also, while they were together, came a messenger from Friary Shalford, bearing a letter brought in, as he said, from London by a gentleman who was conveying his wife and children to Bristol, and had been prayed of his kindness, by one little known to him, to make safe delivery of the same. The roads being then but barely passable by reason of an exceeding sudden thaw, this gentleman had been long upon the journey, and bade his courier between town and village make all haste, for it had been made plain to him the matter was of great urgency. Which he did, and gave the letter, which was well sealed, into the hand of Mary Butterworth, her master being then within in talk with his patron, and the woman enjoined upon no account to trouble him. She put the letter into the pocket of her stuff gown, and dismissed the messenger with thanks and commendations to the gentleman who sent him; and when he was gone she drew forth the letter again, and read over the superscription, observing also the seal, but it was strange to her. She supposed the hand to be a woman's, because of its excessive smallness and delicacy, and by holding up the packet to the light she hoped to have deciphered somewhat of the matter within, but the paper was so thick that nowhere did any word show through. While she was thus employed she heard Master Nicholas and Master Drury come forth from the library, and hid herself within the kitchen, but with the door ajar, to hear what should pass.

This Master Nicholas Shenstone was a man of middle age, ruddy of face and choleric, having the long jaw and high temper of his blood and family, but as quick to forget offence as to take it, and habitually on as good terms with his schoolmaster as human man could well keep. Yet on this afternoon he was ill pleased, for he had a mind to bark by turns for all his dogs, and was disposed, when he remembered the foundation, to order what should and should not be done, what subjects taught and what left untouched, besides directing the hours the boys should keep, and the rewards which should be made them. This Salathiel Drury would in no way endure, having set his face these fifteen years against all rewards, and being stout to maintain his own responsibilities without interference from any man. On this day it fell that Master Nicholas, being at odds with him, and knowing him to be of all things a classical scholar, more tender to Astyanax than to any boy of his years in Sunderne, ordered him to cease teaching these children their Latin and let them dwell only upon a good live English tongue; whereupon Master Drury as roundly told him no boy should ever pass through his hands and come from them ignorant in that delectable learning, though he were a fool and an innocent. Master Nicholas could not bear to be crossed, and upon this flung out with his clerk grim after him, and Mary Butterworth in the kitchen heard him cry: 'Then, sir, if you cannot do my work as I want it done I will find another who can.' Also she heard Salathiel Drury reply: 'Do so and be damned, sir, as before long I think you may.'

There was not in this more significance than in any of a dozen clashes long since past, and such high words were not unknown between them; nevertheless, Mary Butterworth put away these sayings within her mind, and recalled them afterwards at need. When Master Nicholas was gone, she opened the kitchen door and went out to her master, who was stalking back to his library in a black temper; and she gave him the letter, telling him by what messenger it was come. Seeing her come so softly, he was displeased, supposing she had been listening to what had passed, and gave her to know what was in his mind.

'You do ill,' she says, 'to be angry with me because I have your good at heart. If I creep soft-footed in this house to listen at doors, is it ever for any other man's advantage?'

'It is for your own purposes, snake,' says he, 'and so I well know. But I am not angry; I expect but claws of a cat, and God forbid I should ever complain if they scratch me. Do after your nature.'

'They never will,' says she, 'unless you tread on your cat. But I tell you roundly, you do foolishly to fall out with the old man. He has wit to know you do him good service whenever you do not madden him beyond remembering it; but when all's said he's a Shenstone, and if you go too far with him he will remember it to your cost.'

'He will be welcome,' said Salathiel, 'to order all as he chooses that is his to order; and so, by your leave, I will do with mine. What, are you to read my thoughts as well as my letters? Never look through your pale eyelashes at me, I am none of your witless worshippers. I dare swear you know the writer before the seal is broken.' Yet as he said, he was not angry with her, but spoke only as he was used, even laughing at her after his own dark fashion.

'I know nothing of it,' she said as roundly, 'but what I have told you. Come, you know better my ways with you than to suppose I am treasonous. Have I not borne with your moods these ten years, when I could have been a wife, and to good substance, too? Is it to your damage that I have kept my body faithful to your bed all this time, without your name or even your kindness? Do you think I meant any evil against you when I let you caress me before my mother's blind face? And now you do not trust me!' She went close to him so, and inclined herself upon him in such fashion that her two small breasts were pressed against his arm, and he being man, and having long known her, might not but be stirred by that touch.

'Neither now nor ever,' he says. 'I'll have you, never fear, but I am no such fool as to trust you.' As he said so he took her body between his hands and crushed her together as he would break her through, but she only smiled and leaned the more heavily upon him, caressing him with her bosom until he embraced her closely. At this she was satisfied, for though he should destroy her, she desired him to desire her still. Under his pressing mouth she sighed for content.

'Out!' said he, holding her away from him. 'I know you! You go about your own designs, and but that you have as much need of me as I of you I might run my head into the noose and be done with it whenever I would. What you have given up for me, mistress, I well know you gave up to purchase what was more to your liking; and if ever you cease to fancy me I warrant you I shall fear you.'

'You had better fear me, rather,' said Mary Butterworth very soft and meek, 'if ever you cease to fancy me. You know so little of women, I marvel you must in the nature of things have been born of one.'

'It is my most cursed regret,' replied Salathiel, 'that I must believe so. I wish from my heart it could have been done by other means, or never need have been done at all.'

'And yet,' she said, of her own will leaning and kissing him after he had said this bitter thing, 'I see you receive letters from women, for this, I am sure, is a woman's hand.'

'Ah!' said he, twisting her away from him, 'you are fixed to know more of her, are you? You will be in her secrets, will you? Be at ease, this is one I have not seen nor heard of for over seventeen years, nor never thought to be troubled with again.'

Smiling and looking through her light lashes she says: 'And one you despise with all the rest, I dare swear.'

'Worse than all the rest,' says he upon a voice she commonly thought well to leave unprovoked.

'And yet,' she says, smiling still, 'I see you remember her hand very well, for you have not broke the seal to find a name.'

Upon this he laughed when she had thought likely he would curse her; and: 'Remember!' says he. 'Have you found me quick to forget injury? She has not, by God, nor never shall.' Whereupon he flung away from her and shut himself in his library with the letter, and there secluded read it; and in a while he came forth very dark of face, and bade her put clothes and wherewithal for a journey in his saddle-bags, for he must ride to London.

'How, this night?' says Mary Butterworth, startled. 'What, do you run to her first call, and you so long-memoried for evil? Besides, it is freezing again, and tonight's ride may be a man's last by such roads. Wait until morning at least.'

However, he paid her no heed, nor gave any hearing to her entreaties, but would certainly go. She from old acquaintance knew well the moments when she might with safety presume upon his bodily intimacy with her, and knew that this was none; but she put herself in his path none-theless, being without fear, and taking him by the breast held him so against her even when he would have thrown her off.

'What do you fear?' said Salathiel, taking her by the wrists. 'She has no such call to make upon me as you suppose, fool. She is about a small matter of dying.'

'Very well,' says she, 'if I did but believe you!'

'Disbelieve me, then, fool,' he says, 'and torment yourself half to death with your own imaginings for aught I care. Look, now,' he says more kindly, 'I have no use for any woman but one use, and so I told you plainly when first I took you; and by God I have no use even in that kind now for any woman but one, and you are she. What more would you have?'

'What I cannot get out of you,' she says.

'What is not in me, not for you nor another to get. Be content, no one will ever have more of me than you have.'

'Yet you are a hard, bitter, irreligious man,' she says, 'why should you not also be a traitor? I bid you remember I have given up much for your sake, have crept to your bed early and late by stealth, and made myself a nameless abomination but to have you. I have gone about before my mother's blind face a shame to her in your house, and lied to her roundly a hundred times or more, and all to have you.'

'Yes, and by your own choice and nature, too, you mock virgin,' he said, and laughed. 'I'll have no creature unwilling, and well you know it. You, what, you devious thing, your natural movement is roundabout and by the backside of matters, and ever will be while you live. Was it I who would have lies told, and respectability for ever arranged about us? All to have me! Do you make it a reproach to me now that you chose to spend what you had to get what you wanted?'

'Not so, neither!' she said. 'I do but make things plain between us. It is very well that I have spent so heavily, while I continue to have the thing I bought; but if ever you take it back from me to give to another you may think well to beware of me, for I have then no more to lose.'

'What, do you threaten me?' says Salathiel Drury, taking her by the chin and staring upon her so fiercely that she thought for a moment he would have thrown her down and trampled over her. But in a moment he put her by without ungentleness, saying only: 'Have no fear, it is but right that two savage beasts should bed together and let the rest of the world alone.'

With this saying she must be content, for he would go; but before he left the house at last he came to her with a pair of leathern riding gloves in his hand, and: 'Look,' said he, 'if Nick has not gone off without these in his rage. Take them back to him when you have shut up the house, and tell him how I am called away upon immediate business. When I return I will send you word.'

'He will not be pleased,' she said.

'Let him choke himself with gall, then, and be done with it,' says he, and forthwith sets out upon his journey. And this same evening Mary Butterworth, having shut up the Schoolhouse, went to Sunderne Friars, and there she learned that since his return from the school Master Nicholas was taken with a seizure, and had been carried to his bed. The physician had made good report of him, but there was confusion and disquiet enough about the house for a dozen deathbeds, and Mary stood among the scurry unnoticed for a while before young Master Harry Shenstone, the eldest son and a sprig of the thorny kind, came up and asked her sharply what she did there. Whereupon she, who had the gloves under her cloak, did not show them, but cast down her eyes submissive and soft, and whispered her master's message, which was not much regarded; and being dismissed, she took the gloves home to her uncle's house, and hid them under her linen in a drawer. This she did as having yet no clear use for them, but being of a kind which keeps all that may in some unsure future have its use; being, as was said of her by the only man she let see her whole, in all things sidelong and devious.

Now Salathiel Drury slept a part of that night at Friary

Shalford, and rising betimes passed on in all haste towards London, which he reached late in the evening, having ridden a good-weather pace upon roads glazed with ice for much of the way. Without waiting for rest or food he stabled his horse at an inn which was near the house he sought, and went thither to inquire for his correspondent. It was but a poor place, and the woman that opened the door to him very mean and soiled. Upon his asking for Mistress Flint she made no more ado but beckoned him in, and pointing him the room where he should find her he sought, left him to climb the stairs alone and let himself in. Which he did, yet walking ever slower and slower now as to his own death, not another's, and when his hand was upon the door he stayed, and looked upon the ground a long time before he went in.

This room into which he came was a bedchamber, dark but for two candles that burned upon a table, and the curtains drawn close over the window. There were but two chairs in the room, and the said table with its candles and mirror and few bits of china and ornament, besides the bed and its draperies, which had been good but were now worn and threadbare. Upon one of the chairs were thrown down lightly some silken skirts and coats of a woman's apparel, and upon the other, which was low like a child's chair and had a seat and back of rushes, a young girl sat beside the bed, holding in her lap a handkerchief and a china cup of drink, and a vinaigrette and a fan, ready with these to answer whatever call should be next made upon her. But when the woman in the bed heard the door open, and looking up perceived Salathiel standing within the room, she lifted her hand and her eyes and said in a firm voice: 'Go now, Elizabeth, and remain below until he or I shall call you.'

The girl said: 'It is he then?' and the woman replied: 'It is he.'

Upon this the girl went out at once, closing the door after her, and the two were left alone. The canopy of the bed was deep and heavily curtained, and little light survived beneath it, so that he saw only the long, thin shape of her under the covers, making but a slight and rigid rise in the linen, as do the bodies of the dead. Yet he stood back from her, and was silent.

'Draw near,' said the woman, 'there is nothing here you would not wish to see, no beauty, no virtue, no hope, only ruin and death. Come and take comfort: I have my due.' And when he drew near and stood beside her she said: 'You have wished me this many and many a time, have you not?'

'Many and many a time,' he said harshly, 'but now I find I am not satisfied.'

'There is yet hell,' she said.

'And nothing beyond for him?' said he. 'I do not believe it. God will see to it better than you think, madam, for you shall never see hell. There are enough saints of my father's kind to fill it, and never room therein for you, or even, I doubt, for me.'

'Well, well!' she said with a weary sigh, 'I see you have not yet forgiven him.'

He said: 'Did you conceive I should, now or ever?'

'No,' she admitted, 'I did not conceive it. Yet seventeen years is a long time to go on loving or hating, and if I had ceased to fawn on him, why not you to curse him? It may be that hate is the more durable thing, after all. And have you, then,' she says, 'never forgiven me, neither?'

He being silent, and looking upon her long, she let this question go by heavily without an answer, and after asked him: 'What is it you see? Sit here beside me, and for this last time do not be angry. Sit here upon the bed; the chair is too low for you. Now, tell me what I am. They give me no mirror, for fear I should die of spleen, since I am so long adying of this indifference of heart.'

Still looking upon her, he said: 'I see the end of beauty. A pale, sullen face, greying hair, a dead-white mouth, eyes hollow and dull as the holes the thawing trees drop in the drifts. I see disease and grief and emptiness, emaciated hands and withered breasts and shoulders shrunken to the bone.

And you? What do you find in me, Alison Flint, now I am come?'

'You are as I supposed you to be,' she said. 'I look at you, and I see him.'

He cried below his breath, in a great gusty cry: 'Never say so! He has nothing in me, nothing!'

'He has more than you know. It is not possible, Salathiel Drury, to draw out that part of your blood which is from him, nor cut away his share in your nature, though you hate him to your own hurt. I look at you and I see him, like you but having that beauty you have not. Yes, he had great beauty, that saintly man. I think he went so often with my lord his patron hanging upon his arm that that ape face might be seen close beside his own, and the beholder might be the more dazzled, and I, like any raw parishioner of his, might forsake the world and follow him.' Low in her pillows, she laughed, and half-choked upon the laugh. 'Oh, never think, Salathiel,' she said, 'that you shall see him come to this pass. He will grow old with grace and good sense. He will grow silver and clear of the spirit, and shine like a lamp before the eyes of his flock, and die in good comradeship with himself and other men. You shall not see time avenge you on him as on me, never in this world.'

'You have reminded me,' said Salathiel, 'that there is yet hell.'

'Even there,' she said, 'even there I doubt the wicked flourish. And yet you were to blame in that matter, you who all but thrust your love into his arms, and he still no more than a youngish man, and widowed, and with that face of an angel upon him. You brought me to him like a stole to wear, or a pin for his scarf, or a tassel for his glove; and you knew how gracefully he could accept gifts even from a son.'

'Yet I did not kill him,' said Salathiel, as one marvelling.

'I have wondered often why we lived through that night,' she said. 'There are times when I so greatly wonder at it that it seems to me indeed I died then, and this long while since is only a dream the dead and damned do have.'

'Yet you loved him,' he said.

'Truly, I suppose I did love him.'

'And love him still?'

She smiled upon him with her blanched lips meagre and dry as meal. 'I have said, hate is more durable. But even hate is limited. What is he to me now? Or to you, I suppose? Only tell me, you, with all the strength there was in you, and all the passion, why did you never so much as reproach us? Why did you only look at us, and turn and go away from us? Why have I seen no more of you from that day to this, not even in anger?'

He looked at her and his face was cold as ever since he came in. 'To wish to kill,' he said, 'is only possible where there is still some love. Mine, for you as for him, was not so pliable. After the look you say I gave you, I cared no more for either of you, and the only hate I felt for you after was for my lasting injury, not for your false person nor his. He was as welcome to you as you to him. Then also, was I to forget you were born as free as I was? Free to make of yourself even that thing I perceived you had made.'

'Are you come all this way to reproach me at last?' she asked.

'I am come because you sent for me. I do not yet know why.'

The woman sighed, and fumbled with her thin hands along the coverlet, saying: 'The kerchief! Give me the kerchief!' And when he had put it into her hands she wiped her face, and lay quiet for a moment, and then she said: 'It is as it always was. I have sent word where I hoped for help. If I did wrong to hope, tell me so now. Of your life I have asked you nothing, nor will I tell you more of mine but this: I have a child, Salathiel, to leave behind me in a world in which the innocent fare very ill, to my notion. I would as lief she went to you as to any. Will you have her? Ah,' she said as he lifted his head and stared upon her awfully, 'you wonder that I should ask this of you, while he lives. It is not from care of his saintly name, nor because I have so great regard for you. There is but one concern with me, that she should be looked after well. Will you have her?'

After a moment's silence he replied in a harsh voice: 'You have not said as yet if she is his or no. Bear in mind I have asked you nothing; am I to know out of my faith in you that he has been your only lover?'

'She is his,' said the woman, and made no other answer.

Having received this reply, he got up from her bed, and began to walk the room in great agitation, yet keeping silence, and his face so set that she could not judge what was in his mind to do; but at length he turned and stood still before her, and: 'Where is my sister?' he said.

'You have seen her once already this evening,' said she. 'Her name is Elizabeth. Open the door and call her up. But remember that she knows nothing of her father, nor ever shall with my will. Sister is a name by which you must never call her.'

He said with bitterness: 'What do you think that I am?'

'Well I know what you are,' replied she in a whisper. 'You are the heaven I was offered, and gave in exchange for hell.'

'Another has bought me since for her hell, and at a price as high. Does that change your mind for your daughter?'

'Not so!' she said as lowly. 'I know what I do. Go and call her.'

So directed, he went out to the top of the staircase, and called for the girl Elizabeth, and presently she came up and stood before them. Upon his coming in he had paid her no heed, supposing her to be a neighbour's daughter or a girl of the house who had come in of her kindness to sit with the sick woman. Now he looked very narrowly at her, and observed that she was fully seventeen years of age, and like her mother somewhat above the middle height, and slender. He supposed her to have been conceived in the furtive time before his eyes were opened to the treason committed against him, yet her glance was wide and plaintive and innocent as day when she looked at him, so that she seemed a creature born in all virtue and gentle affection. In colouring she was dark, as her mother had been in the days of her beauty, but grave of mien and less handsome than she, and of a more robust rosiness. She stood silent and submissive, in a plain wool gown, her ringlets tied in blue ribbons under a small lace cap, but no other ornament upon her. He saw her demure and wholesome, no way touched nor smirched by the bitterness which had wound about and about her life. Also he saw in her young soft lips and round forehead some mirror image of his own days of innocence, and he was moved toward her.

'This is my daughter,' said the woman, 'and Elizabeth Flint is her name. She has been taught her duty to her elders, and you will find her perfect in it. Child, this is a good friend to me and to you, who will take care of you and be as a father to you until you come to the time of marriage. His name is Salathiel Drury. Make your reverence to him, for he will be your lawful guardian when I am gone.'

Now at this plain speaking he looked for some distress in the young girl's face, but found none, and she did but drop her eyes and make him an obedient curtsey to the ground, with no word said. Whereupon he went to her and took her by the hand, and raised her, saying: 'Well, Elizabeth, are you not willing to look at me? It is a grave matter to take a guardian upon another's recommendation, and I would have you satisfied with your mother's choice. Come, say if you will have me.'

She therefore raised her head and looked at him firmly, as he bade her, and in a small, sweet voice without tremor made answer that she wished to be in all things a dutiful daughter, and had in this no will but her mother's will. And this she said with so much address, for all her modest quietness, that he would gladly have heard her use the same tone upon matter more to his liking; for the longer that he looked upon her, the more did he see in her the image of his own youth, and the less of mother or father.

'This is not well,' said he, 'for I would have you lean upon no mind but your own, since I see it may bear a heavier weight than yours and take no hurt. Look well at me, and speak out what is in your heart. I am no easy nor patient man, I warrant you, but what I undertake I will perform as faithfully as a man may. If you will trust to me and bear with me I will not fail to do my part by you, Elizabeth, nor be hard with you, I trust, though overmuch experience has made me hard with most. I do not think you will be one to judge me for the first hasty or harsh word. Indeed I think better of you already than to be less than honest with you. Will you go with me of your own will, Elizabeth?'

Upon this she was silent a moment, and looked from him to her mother and again to him, her countenance being grave and tranquil, and receiving no sign she said in the same earnest tone: 'I have not been taught, sir, to choose for myself, and therefore in this matter you must hold me excused if I express myself ill. I am content that all should be as my mother pleases; but since you ask more of me than submission, I shall answer you as best I may. I take it as most kind in you that you should so freely set open your hearth to me, and I will with all duty and pleasure go with you so soon as it shall be time.'

'Do you say so from your heart?' asked Salathiel Drury, looking hard upon her.

'From my heart, sir, truly,' she replied. Even so it came to him that as yet she did not so much as know if indeed she possessed a heart, by no pricking nor aching, nor by no warmth of any man's touch upon it. Yet she spoke in good faith, believing this thing to be true, though all within her was limpid and cool as lake water.

'You shall not regret that you favoured me,' says he gently. 'As God sees me I will deal honourably with you in all affection, child, as a true father should. Go now and rest, for I will remain a while with your mother. There is yet somewhat we have to say.' And when she had made him once more her low reverence, and gone silently from the room, he shut the door between and went back to the foot of the bed. The

119

woman watching from her pillows saw his face very grim, quiet and dark, by no means as he had showed it to the girl.

'It is of no profit to frown upon me,' she said, unmoved. 'Much has been ill-done, by design or default, but not all done ill by me. There is yet a cure for all, once I am gone, but in me there is no cure, never think it. You have said you will have her; I have not asked for more.'

Looking upon her still as before he asked her: 'Madam, have you loved your daughter?'

'All my life,' she said, 'I have given her cause to believe so.'

'You give me no such cause,' said Salathiel.

'You are too shrewd. Indeed, there is no love in me for any, and for his daughter and the signal remembrancer of my ruin very surely none. Be content that I have not hated her,' she said very low.

'Are you content with what you have done?'

'I am content. Many times I have marvelled at my own faithfulness. Ah, you do well to reproach me, perhaps; yet love itself could not have served her and trained her better. What she has not had she has never yet missed, for she believes she possesses it. If she finds it somewhat colder than men say it is, I have not known her to complain. And look well to it,' she said, fixing her hollow eyes upon him, 'that you do not too rashly show her what affection can be, for as I live I believe her nature has no use for it, and what she will do with it only God knows. Moreover she knows you only as one who will stand to her as a father, and affection from you will not seem to her as brotherly.' Seeing the look he gave her for her words she smiled, with a white, fallen weariness. 'Well, you see I have thought of all. The worst happens ever, Salathiel Drury. Mark me well, and hope for no other. Truly the world is very ill, and I shall not be sorry to leave it. Only say again to me that you will take her.'

'I will take her,' he said, 'not for love of you nor in spite of hate of you, but because she is my flesh and blood, and the only atomy of it I ever saw without sickening.'

'Do you sicken, then, at your own?' she asked, gazing upon him.

'Should I love it? No other has but you, and in you did it last so long? Do you think I do not retch to remember that this flesh and this blood was moved once with obscene longings toward carrion the double of itself? Do you suppose you are comfortable to look upon now? Shall I be proud of having once desired you as the hound moans after the bitch? I loathe my body, and all its works stink of corruption to me. Out of your mud no doubt but mine seems no great matter, yet do not name me with what is clean.'

She clutched herself together under her flat breasts, as if she had great pain there, and said in a whisper: 'I have only my due.'

'And I also,' he said. 'Let us speak of your daughter. What would you have me to do?'

'Take her away with you. Do not wait. Take her away tomorrow, and let her forget me when she will, for I shall not care. Death is not for the young, I would wish her away from me now, and safe out of reach.'

'Yet she will not so softly consent to leave her mother at such a pass,' he said.

'But I say that she will. She knows no tenderness, but she knows her duty, and if I bid her go she will go. Service upon the sick is hideous, and watching by the dead a heavy thing. She will go with gladness, though not as one seeming glad. Between escape and self-sacrifice, trust me, she will seek escape. I know her, she is the bud of my body. Tomorrow come for her, and all will be ready.'

'And you? How will you fare alone?'

'I shall die, but not a whit more surely for her departure. My lodging is provided, there is money yet for my grave. I have asked you for one thing only; make no inquiry after the rest.'

'So be it,' said Salathiel Drury. And thereafter he took his leave of her, for she was so sunk and grey within the bed that death seemed indeed close upon her. Yet when his hand was upon the door he turned his head and looked back, and saw that her eyes followed him. Neither then nor at any other moment of this meeting did he feel any softening of his heart toward her, nor did her wailing voice pierce him, crying after him:

'Wait but a moment more, only one moment for a word of kindness. I shall be dead in a very little time. You will be troubled no more. Have you heart even at this pass to leave me unforgiven?'

He said: 'What would you have me to say? I am not God, to forgive sins. Yet if you do desire it, I forgive you.'

She looked at him long, and wept, seeing his face yet unshaken, and his eyes bitter as wormwood, though he spoke her soft and evenly.

'I marvel, madam,' said he, 'that you should yet strain at this old offence, though it went unforgiven to the grave. Is the power of a word so great? You have it freely. Or the touch of a hand? Has it grace to sweeten your bed now if I give you my hand? Take it then with my goodwill. What more there may be I have not done, before God I do not know, and therefore I can do no more for you.'

And upon his parting thus, she said only: 'Yet I can wait. In His own time doubtless God will bring you to heel.'

Then he left her, and went back to his inn, and the night through lay sleepless for thinking of those ended things which she had brought to life in him. But in the morning, being softer weather yet cold and still, he went about to procure a carriage because of the girl Elizabeth, knowing well she could not keep so hard a way upon horseback. When all was ready and it was almost noon he went back to the house, and the young girl let him in. She was already cloaked and hooded, and her small possessions roped together in a little leathern trunk at the foot of the stairs. She curtseyed to him as steadily as before, and looked upon him as he thought expectantly, not as he had feared in distress or anxiety. As he was silent long she folded her hands and waited innocently with her eyes very intent upon him.

'How is this, Elizabeth?' says he. 'Will they hustle you out of door with so much haste?'

Upon this she coloured like a rose, but not in displeasure, and said: 'It was my mother's wish, sir, that I should be in all points ready for you, since the way, she says, is long, and you know, sir, the days are very short. I have waited here almost an hour and I am ready to go.'

'And is there to be no leave-taking, then?' he says. 'Are you to step into the coach and so away, without a word at this latter end?'

She repeated only: 'It was my mother's wish.'

'And your own wish also, Elizabeth?'

'Yes, sir,' she says very low, 'mine also. Oh, sir, I am not insensible how unnatural I must seem to you, but indeed, indeed she bade me go even thus, and I have had no will but her will since I was born. If it is better for her that I should go I will not listen to my own heart, though it bid me stay a thousand times over.'

Now hearing her speak so he frowned, and taking her ungently by the wrist drew her to the light that he might the better study her face.

'By God, child,' says he grimly, 'they have made your tongue a very studied hypocrite, but your eyes tell another tale. No matter, for the moment pay me no heed. We will speak of it another opportunity. What said your mother of me? Would she see me?'

'She did not say so,' replied Elizabeth, in some dread at his darkened visage. 'She desired that we should leave her in quietness.'

'Why, so we will, then, since you are as willing as I. Come,' said he, 'let us be moving, for we have far to go.' Which said, he put her into the coach, and had her gear brought in also, and in this manner they set forth from London for Friary Shalford; nor did either of them see Mistress Flint again after that day. Some few days after came to them word of her death, and in a week following certain papers concerning her slight having, whereby a trinket or two of no worth and a letter in her hand came into the hold of her daughter; but the woman herself they saw no more, nor after this ride even spoke of her but as one passed clean out of sight, and but little grudged to the dark.

Now as they went it was very cold, and seeing that the girl's cloak was thin and but poorly lined, he asked if she had not some better covering to put about her, and she owning she had not, he took her within the folds of his own cloak, which was ample enough for two, and so they travelled close together. He felt that she held off somewhat from him, but did not refuse the shelter, and as he seemed but little aware of her, and that silently and coldly, she was the less disposed to be wary of him, and becoming forgetful of his strangeness let herself lean upon him when she was weary. This was to him a pleasing thing, for he considered that she was young, and he unknown to her, and confidence a tree of shy and delicate growth. Nor did he trouble her with talk until of her own will she began to speak of the journey, how tedious it was and hard, and to ask him of the home to which he led her. He told her all she desired to know, or such detail as he could remember, for he was one who took but little note of his surroundings; and she for her part appeared every minute more eager and young, so that he saw she was in no sorrow for the past, but pleased at the change which was come upon her.

'And shall I, sir,' says she, 'have the advantage of your instruction? For my mother told me you are a teacher, and not to deceive you, I am very ignorant of much that I should know.'

'I suppose,' said he, 'you have been taught as all your sex are, in all manner of foolishness belonging to the stillroom and the broidery frame, without a word of Latin or Greek. Come, tell me what you can do. We must pass the time somehow.'

'I have my letters,' she said, flushing, 'and can write a good hand and a pleasant enough period, or so I have been told; but indeed my reading has been narrow and poor, and I have no Latin. For the rest, I have learned something of the keeping of a house, I can sew and cook and brew, and distil herbs, and it has fallen to me to keep the purse this last year, and therefore I have learned management in spending.'

'And your accomplishments?' says he somewhat tartly. 'Doubtless you play upon the virginals, and sing a little, and perhaps paint a little, too? All of your sex, I believe, do so?'

She hung her head and looked sadly. 'I fear I fall short, sir, for I do not play nor sing, and as for painting, I never was taught it, nor have no aptitude. In all my life there was not time to learn the elegances I would have acquired, and it is my sorrow that I shall certainly be no ornament nor grace to your house, though indeed I promise you I shall be a very willing servant in it.'

'Come, you are too modest in your claims,' said he, 'for recollect that you are my ward, and have greater responsibilities than a servant's in my house. You shall be mistress there, Elizabeth, and keep the keys, as is your due. And as for ornament, why, I want none but youth and honesty in you, and we shall do very well, I daresay.'

'Shall I indeed keep your house?' she asked, looking up at him with astonishment and delight.

'That you shall, and certainly, Elizabeth. It is fitting that you should take your true place, and we must at all costs do things fittingly. I have lived but a bachelor's life hitherto, and you will find my house lacking in the small comforts a woman likes to have about her, I daresay, but it will be for you to order all things as you please now, so you do not meddle among my own quarters. For I will not have my books dusted out of their places, I give you warning, nor my papers rearranged for me when I am not by, and it is more than your life's value to lay a finger even by way of kindness upon my pens, for I will have them cut but one way, and a touch astray undoes all my work.' Seeing she understood the unaccustomed lightening of his mood so well as to laugh at him, he asked her: 'Do you find this prospect before you a grim one, Elizabeth? Are you not afraid to take upon you so bleak a life?'

'Oh, no, indeed you do not at all frighten me,' she said, 'but I am a little afraid of doing my part but poorly. I have no fear for your part, I promise you, sir, for I find you kind and gentle with me more than I deserve.'

'And if I am not always so,' he said, fixing his eyes upon her sombrely, 'will you consider that I am a man of ill moods, unused to having young girls about him, or tuning his words to a lady's ear? For it will be great wonder if I do not forget myself and you before a week is out, and have out upon you as if you were the crassest natural among my pupils.'

'As it will be greater wonder,' she replied as gravely, 'if I am not.'

'I do not think it, yet were it true it would but make my sin the more. Would you then make allowance, and still bear with me?'

She said that she would, and so freely that he could not but marvel they were already come so nearly together. It was strange and moving to him that he should sit beside her marking the clear flow of blood in the veins of her temples and her wrists, and reflect within himself in what monstrous treason this pure flesh was got, and in what dear, detestable relation she stood to him; insomuch that by moments he was in horror of her as the supernatural offspring of rottenness born into a white flower, and after and before these moments his mind was moved to her only as to a young child both sister and daughter to him, and having in all the world no other kin. More than he abhorred her did he then compassionate her, forgetting her horrid conception. Therefore he asked her with gentleness: 'Has your life heretofore been happy, Elizabeth? For I think you have been a lonely child.'

'In truth,' she said, as one observing it with surprise, 'I have been much apart from all other children, and if you find me grave and staid you must ascribe it to my training; but quietness will not displease you. Yet I do not think I have been unhappy. It is hard for me to say, who have so little experience of the world.' Yet she coloured and turned aside from him, unwilling that he should be the judge, and he was the more assured of his right judgement.

'I called your tongue a hypocrite,' he said, yet not unkindly, 'but I see it is only a liar. Well, I do not know but you have exchanged the spit for the fire, for mine has been a life no less secluded; yet I doubt not we shall do very well. I promise you you shall not be without companions at Sunderne. Tell me but one thing more, and show me if you have the truth in you. Did you love your mother, Elizabeth?'

She opened her lips in astonishment, and made as if to answer yes, but feeling his eyes heavy upon her she was dismayed, and hid her face, saying no word.

'Be at ease,' said he, 'for this is not mortal sin, but a notion of the heart as wilful as sap rising. You cannot help though you should deny, but let me say for you that which I believe in my soul. You did not love her, for she never gave you leave. And you are as glad to be free of her shadow as the flowers are to bid good-bye to the night. And wherefore not? Your place is not forever with sickness and disappointment. If she was a widow, need you put on weeds at a child's years? Trust me, as you live! It is not evil but good that you should rejoice to make your escape from so piteous a prison. Therefore look up, and look cheerily. Are you ashamed to find yourself alive and gay?'

Now when he had thus soothed her she looked up, and said to him: 'Sir, you make it seem as if I had done no wrong, and yet this long while I have been grieved because I could not cherish for my mother such an affection as seemed her due. It has been as you have said; she would not let me be fond.' This she said, and thereafter took heart from his calm, and no more covered her thoughts from him, but spoke openly. 'I have been at pains to do my whole duty,' she said, 'and have thought shame many a time that I took no joy in it. For she was ever just, and careful, and patient, deserving of service; only she never touched me nor spoke to me in any warmth of heart that ever I could discover. Often in my own despite I have longed to be but as other children were, kissed and fondled and scolded, but it was not in my mother to scold or kiss. As for this parting from her, my presence never gave her any pleasure, nor my going will not cost her any pain. Truly I was taught to believe there is love between mother and daughter, and therefore I have tried to hide from myself that I looked forward to this journey with curiosity and eagerness, but so I did, and now I see it is unworthy not to own it. Sir, if I have a true understanding of what love is, she never loved me, and indeed I think no creature living ever did, for my father, as I am sure you know, died before I was born.'

'Ay, so I have heard,' said he without a tremor, though he knew that her father and his yet flourished holy and reverenced in a parish of the City, and was like to come by a crozier before he died, and a pious memorial thereafter. 'Yet,' said he, 'for even this it may well be time has a remedy.'

So as they travelled together he had some pleasure in her, but also he pondered in his mind what troubles she might yet cost him; and at night, very late, they came into Friary Shalford, and there lay at the inn until next day, when Salathiel Drury rose early, and hired a messenger to carry letters before them to Sunderne. First he wrote with unaccustomed civility to Master Shenstone, acquainting him with the cause of his absence, and commending to Mistress Shenstone's kindness his new care, Elizabeth Flint; and after to Mary Butterworth, and shortly, bidding her make ready to receive his ward at the Schoolhouse. This he wrote, not observing that he had not made clear if the child were maid or boy, and nothing thinking nor caring what more fearful matter his words might convey; for as for this woman Mary, except as a savour to his bed he did not at all regard her.

When they had breakfasted at the inn they went forth again in the frosty morning, which had an early bright mist about it, and having paid their coach, went about to hire a carriage in the town to take them to Sunderne, for there were no horses just then to put to at the inn. And having procured what they needed, they came to Sunderne close upon noon, and to the Schoolhouse by the very ill ruts of School Lane as the church clock was striking twelve.

Now Mary Butterworth, who had seen them descend from the carriage, stood at the window and watched them come along the path to the doorway; she saw that the girl, though very young and but simply dressed, was at all points a woman in body, and comely, with high breasts and well-shaped shoulders, her limbs long and rounded, her hips wide and ample though as yet but maidenly covered, and her height something above the common in women. All this did Mary make due note of, and of his hand possessive upon the girl's arm no less; and she quickly plucked out the ribbons with which she had decked out her own hair, and put on her white cap over the curls she had tricked out for his homecoming, and went down to meet them as they came into the house. There she curtseyed to the ground, and said her welcome softly with her modest meek eyes downcast and her hands folded demure in the skirts of her stuff gown, so that Elizabeth, who was in awe of her, thought after all she had not much to fear. And as for Salathiel Drury, he fixed his eyes upon her with intent, but could not get her gaze until she would permit, which in a moment she did. Nor could he then discover any part of her thoughts, though he was perilously wise in her; for her eyes were grey and polished like glass or polished stones, having no clear places behind, and looked through her lashes at him with a submissive secrecy very disquieting to see. Yet she spoke as with gentleness and pleasure, smiling her welcome most maidenly and full of duty.

He said to her shortly: 'This is my ward of whom I wrote to you, Mary. Her name is Elizabeth Flint. From this day on she will make her home here.'

'Mistress Flint is right welcome,' said Mary Butterworth.

'I have made all ready for her, but if anything has been forgotten she has but to ask for it, and it shall be brought.'

'That is well,' he said. 'Take pains to know her, Mary, for she will have such stature in this place as the keeping of my house can give her; and in the morning, when she is at ease with us, I would have you show her all the appointments of your kitchen, and give up to her your keys. From this time on she is your mistress, and whatever orders she shall give you are as my orders.'

'I shall look well to it,' she said, gazing at him mildly.

'Do so, Mary, and we shall remain in harmony. Elizabeth, go with her and see what lodging is offered you. This is now your home, and I bid you use it as a home.'

So the women went away together to the room which had been prepared, and Mary Butterworth with great assiduity combed the young lady's hair and took off her cloak and travelling dress, and attired her in a yellow gown, making much of her, so that Elizabeth was well content with her welcome. Also she brought into the room such female ornaments as the house possessed, and carried to her steaming hot water in a brass jug to bathe her face and hands, and in all ways made her comfortable, treating her with deference as a woman grown, to her greater delight. But when she had done all for her she excused herself upon pretence of leaving her to rest, and went down to seek her master. She said to him without conceal, for there was no other in the house but the girl, and she was safe out of sight:

'Well, what is now your will? For I must know it, or I cannot perform it. I have so far done all faithfully; do me this justice, to deal faithfully with me. What is this creature you have taken to you?'

Salathiel Drury made answer: 'She is what she seems to be, a charge from a dying woman. What part she plays in your life and in mine I have already told you, and to you, even before witnesses as innocent as she, I do not lie. She is my daughter and the mistress of my house by right.'

'And I am your serving-woman,' said Mary Butterworth,

looking through her lowered lashes as through a curtain.

'What you have been you know well, and that you have had no rival in your own kind with me. What my mind is toward you even now you may know by your own heart, but not I nor you may any longer do as we please. That is over. You are my serving-woman or not, as you choose, but by God I swear you are that or nothing to me.'

'So!' said she, and a long while looked at him without any change of face. Then she said: 'So, I see! Things which could pass before my mother's blind eyes must not chance about the house where this pure girl is, though she be spared sight or knowledge of them. What harm if you should yet clip me in a dark corner, or let me in to your bed at night? Is she to be any the wiser? Will my mouth mark you, that I must not touch any more? Will she see the prints of my arms about your body, do you think, or will my breasts leave their impress like a devil's mark on you, to cast her into dread? Come, it is too late to be immaculate, and I never thought you the man to wish to seem so. If your tale is true, as you swear it is, is it any wrong to one who stands as a daughter to you that you should still live as you have been wont? I think you are foolish to attempt any other, for it cannot last. Hold fast to this pleasure, or admit you have no pleasure in it.'

'You have too much to say,' he said. 'I tell you it is over!'

'You are resolved,' said she, and drew near to him soundlessly as was her wont, for she was eloquent with her body when she had no more words.

'I am resolved,' he said. 'Never come leaning upon me with your soft seeking bosom, for though I starve myself of meat and drink in you I swear I will not be moved. It is finished with, and there is no more to say. Am I plain, mistress? I say we have done with each other, and bid you part without rancour, for I will not have you longer.'

Yet she came nearer and set her body against him, not yet doubting her power, though she knew him hard to bend; and only when he suffered her touch and looked down upon her with a sour smile did she begin to fear.

'You waste your wiles,' he said, 'for I will no more of you. Must I say it yet again? It is enough for you that I have dealt fairly. You are not supplanted; I have only done with you as with the rest.'

'All but one,' she said, and smiled sidelong upon him a concealing smile, pale as milk.

'All, you slut! You suggest what even you do not believe; yet do not again say it in my hearing.' He took her by the chin, and jerked her face up that he might look her in the eyes and see how she hated him, but her eyes were again more blank than glass. 'Hear me! She is a human creature like others, and fallible, but not yet dirtied, nor shall be by any new act of mine, though I grow hypocrite and take to myself all the meanest and most trivial sins I have despised to my height, and though you, thing, turn chaste in your prime against your will. That is your damnation and mine, not hers, and I for my part will be damned with a good heart, and you for yours must fend as you may, and find yourself another fancy if you can. It is all one to me though we both burn, but there shall be no more slaking of thirst in this house as there has been. Mark me, I tell you, for we do not speak so again. It is done, I am resolved, nor you nor the storms of God cannot move me.'

'I am your serving-woman,' said she, 'and nothing more, then, since it must be so. Yet this is extreme fondness for a stranger daughter who was neither kin nor kind to you until yesterday.'

'Off, then,' says he, 'if you will still be talking! I am done with this dalliance. Take your arms from me, and do not make me do you a hurt.' And thereupon she stepped back from him, for she saw that at that time she could do no more, and in the future, if she angered him further now, he would put her away out of the house and so take all hope from her. Therefore she put on an appearance of tranquillity, as even for him she well knew how to do, and pretended resignation to his wishes, for the rest of that day and thereafter going about her business in quietness, very housewifely and gentle, yet ever keeping herself comely and ready in his sight, and biding her time to regain her own.

VII

THE TRUE STORY OF SALATHIEL DRURY (Contd.)

In this wise came Elizabeth Flint to the Schoolhouse of Sunderne, and was mistress of the household, keeping the keys and ordering the managing of linen and the kitchen and all matters relating; and in this she was most duteously schooled and seconded by Mary Butterworth, than whom was never more painstaking servant known, so that there was matter for gratitude and regard between these two women.

Now at this time, being about the end of January, Salathiel Drury took the girl Elizabeth and presented her at Sunderne Friars, where she was most kindly received by Mistress Shenstone. And there he learned with some regret, for in truth they had a perverse regard for each other, how Master Nicholas had not stirred from his bed since the day of his coming to the Schoolhouse, though his case was much improved and his spirits so far mending as to make confinement irksome to him. The physician was still and ever about the house, and there was great running with possets and cordials and greases in and out of the old man's chamber, where there burned a fire wide as any door, but as yet no skill had contrived to raise him to his feet again. Upon these tidings Salathiel delivered messages of condolence and respect, and the girl Elizabeth murmured her timid regrets, and so they parted.

Under the favour of this great lady, which for himself he had never courted for he despised all patronage, did Salathiel Drury ensure to Elizabeth Flint the grace of that part of Sunderne which esteemed such notice, and made it safe to her that she should never partake of his chosen

135

loneliness nor be shut in with only his company. Yet being something shy and grave she did not go about very widely, nor was she often from home, preferring to look after her own tasks, which she much valued; and so came more and more under the eyes of Mary Butterworth, who was ever watchful and ready to advise and help her, and ever sought to have more perfect influence with her. And one day as they were preparing sweetmeats together in the kitchen Elizabeth took heart to tell her a thing which had much weighed on her.

'You must know, Mary,' she said, 'it has been in my mind how like an angel you have borne with me. I can tell you so now, for I am no longer at all afraid of you. When first I came here I was in great dread that you would go away and leave me to fend for myself; for consider, I was come from nowhere and with no warning, to take your rights away from you which you had held so long, and to be put over you in your own place. It would not have been strange had you withdrawn yourself and looked for other employ, or perhaps have married, as I am sure so excellent a person as you might very well do, instead of enduring this deprivation with so much patience and goodness. For you have not only remained with me, but taught me much of your own wisdom, and in all ways behaved to me as a careful and kindly friend, and I must ever be grateful to you for it.'

'There is no need to talk of gratitude, ma'am,' said Mary Butterworth gravely. 'It is a hard heart that cannot give place to kindness a little, I say. Besides, I could never willingly go away, even had I been offended, to leave you here alone with Master Drury.'

Said Elizabeth, somewhat surprised yet believing she read overmuch into this saying: 'Yet I have been the cause of some uneasiness to you, as I think.'

'I am uneasy only that I must leave you here at night with no other creature near you,' said Mary in a low tone, and as if she but thought aloud.

'I do not understand you,' said Elizabeth. 'Surely while he

is here you cannot think me unprotected? Of what should I be afraid?'

'Indeed I beg you pay no heed to my folly,' replied Mary shaking her head. 'I know of nothing that can any way justify me, and yet I profess from my heart I am uneasy. It is only a sensation in the mind, and if you press me for a reason I must confess I can give none. Yet I would the house were not so lonely, nor you so alone.'

'Is it possible,' exclaimed Elizabeth, 'that you believe I have something to fear from him, from Master Drury himself?'

'Now may God forbid!' cried Mary. 'I never said nor thought so. Are you not the apple of his eye, and he a man never yet satisfied with himself nor with any other?'

'From what creature, then, should I look for any anxiety? You are grown fanciful, Mary, surely.'

'Yet I was never wont to be so,' said Mary, and as at that time said no more. But ever and again she made occasion to trouble these same deeps, but as lightly as the tremor of water under the patting of a kitten's paw; and while by these means she sought to plant in the young girl's mind distrust and suspicion of her guardian, dark and without form but ever clouding her vision of him, before the man she was all patience and duty, by great appearance of tenderness to the girl seeking to win renewal of his favour. For though it was plain to her, who well knew him, that anger and venom would but get her her final dismissal, yet she had many other weapons in her armoury; and true it is that for some four or five weeks he was much softened and calmed by the sight of these two women setting about the work of the household together in so much harmony, Mary ever watchful and ready to help, Elizabeth ever attentive and eager; and true also that he was most happy to have Mary about her when there came from London her mother's last letter and few poor bequests, and surprised her into fonder tears than he had supposed likely, though they lasted not long. Then indeed he conceived that Mary had done more than well by him, and avenged herself with kindness and forbearance for what she had received in rebellion and bitterness. Yet was he never fully deceived, but ever kept in his heart the certainty that flesh is evil, its emotions evil, its intent evil, and that in Mary beyond all people was no prodigy of virtuous forgiveness to be looked for. So he held aloof from all appearance of noticing their intimacy, but watched it all the more acutely, until on a day late in February he discovered by chance toward what end it was bent.

It was upon a day of new soft snow, when he came in by the garden from walking in the woods after his scholars were dismissed. Having his books yet under his arm he chose to enter by the garden doors which were near to his library, and the women in the kitchen did not hear him come, as had he crossed the hall they must have done; and as he put his hand to the door of the library he heard them talking, and the first voice was Mary's voice.

'I would I had not told you,' she said, 'and yet how could you go for ever in ignorance? For you have eyes, and can see how they do look upon him, and you have walked with him, and know how they get them aside out of his path. It is not in nature you should be innocent all your life of what these things mean. Oh, I know not how just or unjust it may be to judge him as they judge him, and you see I have not been swayed thereby to leave his service. Yet these half-whisperings without substance or proof can so stick about a man as to dirty him past cleaning, and whatever he touches is marked and clouded also, and no help for it. I would you had fallen into the care of any man but this man.'

'I do wrong to listen to you,' then answered Elizabeth's voice, very high with fear. 'I am sure it is false that he would harm me or anyone. This is some cruel folly of men, and has no truth in it.'

'I know he means you no harm. Do you think there is never harm done but by will? Is there no sickness but by sin? I tell you,' said Mary Butterworth, 'these things fall upon the innocent out of the void, and there is harm done by a touch, by a look, by a thought, where nothing was meant but affection. How can I tell if it was indeed as they said, and his eyes lighting upon this wretched boy turned him to the natural he is? Yet I know that they say it, and I know that the boy has not all his wits to this day. Ah, could the will perfectly command what he gives to others of good or evil, I promise you I should have no fear for *you*. But I swear I am not happy in my mind for either of you. Child, I charge you never leave your prayers unsaid at night.'

'I never do,' said Elizabeth.

'Be instant in petition that no evil may come nigh you.'

'I have long made it my most urgent prayer.'

'Then is the matter in safer hands than ours,' said Mary. 'There is no more we can loyally do, except that I shall be in less anxiety for you if you will wear this little cross of mine about your neck ever. Come, give me the happiness of seeing it in your breast.'

There was then a pause and a rustling of silk, and Elizabeth said thereafter: 'But what will you do if I let you give me your talisman? How can I rob you of its protection?'

'I am not the nearest creature to him,' said Mary Butterworth, 'as you are.'

Now upon this he put forth his hand and thrust wide the door of the kitchen, and went in upon them suddenly in a great cold anger, that they started apart before him in fear, and were thrown in such a confusion they had no words between them to say to him. He set down his books, and going forward to where Elizabeth stood, took hold upon the silver chain which sustained the cross upon her breast, and with a sharp pull broke it and threw it down upon the floor between them. At the pain it gave her as the chain tightened she gave a shriek of terror and shrank from him weeping.

'So, you feeble fool!' said he. 'There shall no man, no, and by God no God, be invoked between us two! The nearest creature to me, and I find there is a world of ice intervening.'

She made no answer nor defence, but only stood crouched with her face in her hands, weeping between her fingers, the thin weal upon her neck blue as iris.

139

'Go,' he said, 'get out of my sight! Go and make yourself new prayers to put between you and my affection, ask God to flatten His hand against my care and hold me off from you. Get to your room and pray, for by God you are fit for nothing else.'

Hearing these bitter words she ran blindly, and groped her way out from the room, leaving these two together. Then he turned and looked at Mary Butterworth, who all this time stood watching him narrowly, and her mouth half in a smile and half in still anger, not running nor hiding from him, nor weeping, nor giving back from him as he came breast to breast with her and took her by the throat. For a moment he could not speak for the poison of rage that boiled up out of his breast, but he held her in his hands as an egg he would shortly break, and lingered over her crushing.

'What hinders,' he says, very low and thick, 'that I would kill you?'

'Yes, kill me,' says she, panting like a hart over-run, 'kill me and die, and so be damned with me, and then shall I have you for ever.' And straining against his hand she leaned with pain and kissed him, though it was but a touch of her lips in his neck before he wrenched her away from him and threw her down upon her silver cross, there to lie breathless.

'Pick up your trash,' says he, 'and get out of my house, before I forget what you have been to me and trample the lies out of your mouth. You have your revenge. Never again can I look at her and not remember that even you had qualities she has not, that you were clever and she is a fool, that you were strong and she is feeble as flax, that you had depths far beyond her reach, even though your deeps were toward hell. You have ruined her for me and me for her, as you meant. Is it enough, snake? Are you satisfied?'

She lay along the floor at his feet, and slowly drawing herself forward by her hands, fastened her arms about his ankles and laid her cheek against his feet. 'Fool, fool!' she said. 'It was not revenge I wanted. I did but want my own again, and went about with whatever came to hand to unwind that weed, that nothing, from your neck. If I have made you frightful to her it was only that you might come back to me. As indeed you must and shall, though you kill me when you come. For she will not have you longer, that soft sweet emptiness, she fears you, she thinks you will drag her to the pit with you. I have made that certain. But as for me, I will go after you thus upon my knees to the pit and beyond, but I will have you at last. I am not afraid of you, but I am afraid of not having you, oh, of this I am afraid!' she moaned.

'Your fear has overtaken you,' he said, and kicked her off from him.

'Do not say so! Do not send me away! Let me remain, and I will undo all,' she cried, rearing herself up on her knees before him.

'It has been done too well. Go, for I have done with you.'

'Starve, then!' she said. 'Burn in your own barren body, then! Send me away and gorge yourself on imaginary riches till you surfeit! Take all hell-fire to warm your cold bed, for she will bring to it nothing kinder than horror of you.'

At this he struck her in the face, and she shrieked aloud, staring at him over her hands with light fierce eyes yet tearless and unafraid.

'She is a fool,' said Salathiel in a low voice, 'but she is clean. Do not name her with one who has wallowed with you in the muck. We have done with argument, you and I. Never again come in touch of me, nor speak a word in my hearing, or I will make an end of you for the poisonous thing I see you to be. Be gone within the hour, and let me not see you in the going. Take your trumpery and go!'

Thereupon he turned and left her, closing the door after him, and being alone she picked up the silver cross and stood holding it in her cupped hands and staring before her. 'You may have done with me,' she said softly, 'but I have not done with you. If I could not cut her off from you, now I will cut you off from life, for if I cannot have you, by God no other shall, no, not yourself for long.' Then she went forth, and took her cloak and such small possessions as she had about the Schoolhouse, and went out from that place; and on her way to the village she went very slowly in spite of the freezing cold, for she was debating within her mind in what manner she should present herself at her uncle's farm, and what account she should as yet make of her banishment. But by the time she reached the end of School Lane she saw her way clear, and exulted within herself at the justice and simplicity of her resolve, though her face was cold as the snow. Not then nor ever did she utter any more curses against Salathiel Drury, but only went quietly about her business, and he was accursed.

As for the man himself, from the library where he had shut himself up in darkness he heard the door open and close upon her going, and he conceived that he was rid of her though her work remained ever with him. Yet he had no pleasure of her going, for all within him was dark, and she did but illumine it with a flash of memory and desire before she was gone. A long time he sat alone, and the hour of the evening meal approached and passed and he did not stir; but at last came in Elizabeth silently, bearing a candle in her hand and pacing slowly and heavily as a woman with child, for she had added to her years in an hour. He raised his head as the light shone upon him, and looked at her, and she saw in his face no anger nor threatening, but only a dark, savage sadness too vast to be of her making. Yet she went forward steadily, and so confronted him.

'Sir,' she said, 'you have eaten nothing. I pray you let me bring you in something.'

He thanked her in a firm voice, but said he desired nothing. Still she lingered, and setting down the candle went upon her knees at his feet and earnestly besought him to look at her, which he did without any tremor of heart, though the mark of his violence was still upon her neck.

'I have been much to blame,' she said, 'to listen to evil, even though it whispered to me under the guise of good. Forgive me!'

'Do not kneel to me,' said Salathiel, 'for I am not God. Get up from your knees and sit with me if you will, but do not, in affection's name, so soon remind me of your prayers.' And as she cast down her eyes in disappointment at this reception he said: 'You are too easily abashed. Speak out for the blood that is in you, tell me roundly it is your right to listen to what you will, to pray for what you will, to trust or distrust me as God shall give you wit, and ask no leave of me. Do not recant what I have given you no grounds to disbelieve, for no better reason than that I am angered. Are not you as much a person as I?'

'I am without experience,' she said with hesitation, 'and I dare not rest upon my own judgement. I have been at fault, I do repeat it. If you will not hear me, nevertheless I must say it.'

'Yet I am ungracious,' he said for her. 'Well, so I am, and so I bade you be ready to find me, a man of ill moods, unused to having young girls about me; and I am not to be diverted by these trivial matters of forgiving and being forgiven, so we come the wiser out of it. Sit, child, there before me, and make no more ado about what is done. Let us see how we shall live now.'

Thereupon she obeyed him, sitting where the candle-light showed him her face; and after a while of silence she asked tremblingly: 'Where is Mary?'

'She is gone,' he said, 'and her cross with her. She at least cannot stand between you and my ill-wishing. What will you do for a patron saint now, Elizabeth?'

'Alas, I am ashamed,' said she, and gently wept. 'I have allowed even this poor ignorant woman, who surely meant neither of us aught but good, to come to grief through me. I am deeply ashamed.'

'Ay, and so am I,' says he groaning, 'to think I have gone against my very nature, and made myself chaste and abstemious and lean, all and only for this! God be my judge, I am already overpaid for a late folly!'

This she did not at all understand, excepting that he was again angry with her, and she could but endure it as well as she might, hiding her face from him with her hands; but seeing her so young and fresh in the dim light he was as suddenly possessed with sorrow over her, and repented that he had made even her innocence a reproach to her.

'Yet look up,' he said, 'for you swore you would bear with me. Come, we are in the coach again, you and I; again I give you warning of what I am, and ask that you will make due allowance for a curst temper. Again say yes, and we are as we were then. Come, there is now no false interpreter between us. Speak truly to me, as I have ever done to you, and we shall not fear each other, I promise you. There, take heart, I have remembered myself; there will be no more outcries upon you.'

Thus reassured, she did look up in wonder and doubt, the tears standing upon her cheeks, and found him calm and sad in his regard as at her coming in she had first seen his face.

'I acknowledge that I broke my word,' she said, 'from thoughtlessness though not from ill-will. I shall not again forget.'

'Nor I,' he said, 'as I trust. I shall not again forget that you are but young and gentle, and in my charge, nor again puzzle you by speaking to you as to one at a man's full stature, with your feet upon the rootholds of the mountains and your forehead in the stars. The equality man has with his fellow-man, soul for soul, is only before God, Elizabeth; here it is invisible to man and fellow-man both, and here there is no communion nor fellowship. To look for it is folly, and to find it is to penetrate death. No, this is not for you I call my text, though you may listen and welcome. I do but think aloud now, no way merrily. In all my life I have looked for one human creature who could meet me straightly, without fear or interest or conceal, or any least artifice of this artificial, mincing, manipulating world, and have never found none, no, not one. And shall I foist all this weight of knowledge and grandeur upon one that is yet a child, and hold it against her that she falls under it? Do not look so fearfully upon me, Elizabeth, for I have done. Now tell me simply, do you believe what you were told of me, that I have the ancient evil in my nature? Do you believe I have turned a boy no nearer idiocy than most into a vacant natural? You have a right to entertain the thought if you will, and I shall not blame you for it.'

'No,' she said, darkly flushing, 'I do not believe it now. It wants but the touch of you now to reassure me this was impossible.'

'Do you believe, then, my poor child, that she was in good faith who told it you?'

'I did think she was, but now I am in confusion, and know not what to think. Sure she would never so deceive me from malice? There can be none so wicked! She is herself deceived.'

'Well, well,' he said with a melancholy smile, 'let us say so. She is herself deceived. There is much fear and ignorance in these quiet places; scratch but the soil and ghosts do walk by daylight, and what shall not happen at eve? She was herself in darkness, and would have you also know that it is dark. So be it, and we forgive her.'

'Ah, now you are good!' cried Elizabeth, 'now you are as you have ever been to me, and I foolish and ungrateful. You are good, and I love you for it.'

'Kiss me, then, and make peace, for in truth I do startle at myself, and you are to answer for all my virtue,' he said, and she kissed him daughterly, greatly rejoiced to see him grown so gentle and playful with her who had seemed for a time so dark and wild. 'Go now,' said he, 'and make ready what we have, and you and I shall dine together. If we come to it late, yet we shall have the better appetite.'

But when she was gone in good spirits he stood upright in the dark room, and stretched himself to his full bitter height, and let a great groaning cry go out of him, and said: 'I am fallen into nets, I am taken among trammels. Oh, damned, damned contrivance! Was it in this fashion the devil was conjured into a hazel nut? For I never heard that the devil had either daughter or sister.' And he laughed, but with no merriment in it, that the candle-flame shook and shivered in the draught; and thereafter he went forth to her, and was all that she would have him be of comfortable and kind.

VIII

THE TRUE STORY OF SALATHIEL DRURY (Contd.)

Now it was thus with Mary Butterworth, that she went home in silence, and passing by her aunt and uncle at the table with no word said, went into her little bedroom and shut the door, and quietly put away her bits of gear. After a while, seeing she did not return, her aunt went up to her, and asked if she was in her usual health, for she sat upon her bed looking straight before her as in a waking dream. She replied that she was well, and let herself be prevailed upon to go down and eat a little, but ever falling away from them into this distraction of mind, so that they marvelled much to see her so withdrawn from them, and pressed her to reveal the trouble that was in her, but ever she instantly swore there was none. Only at last, being greatly beset with their solicitude, she owned she would go to the Schoolhouse no more, and had excused herself from all further service to Salathiel Drury. When it was naturally demanded of her why this was so, seeing she had been so faithful in her attendance, she replied that they must know Mistress Elizabeth was now well versed in the ways of the house, and had no further need of her, but this was said in such a tone that they were assured it did but cover a truer reason. This she would in no wise reveal, but being much vexed with importunities suddenly cried out upon them: 'Do not ask me! Do not question me, for I cannot tell you!' and so started up and fled away from them. After this they made it up between them that she must not be directly questioned, nor must they seem to note anything strange in her behaviour, but by degrees as they were about the house together her aunt should get her

147

confidence and have the truth out of her. Which this good woman earnestly sought to do, but could by no means accomplish, for Mary Butterworth was close as the rock, though ever and again as the days went by she seemed to wring at some strange distress within her that darkened all her going. Nor could they prevail upon her to show what it was, but still she hugged it to her heart. And so went the days in great wonder and doubt and care among them.

But on the first night of her homecoming Mary arose after midnight, and put on her clothes, and took from under her linen in the drawer the gloves which Master Nicholas had left behind at the Schoolhouse; and with these in her pocket she went silently down and let herself out from the house. There were two dogs in the yard, but they knew her, and at her voice they lay down again and made no sound, so that without hindrance she passed them by and went out by the gate. To Sunderne Friars she went, and creeping into the grounds walked about and about until by the gleam of his great fire lighting the window she found the old man's room, and under the wall at this place she dug a hole with her hands in the soil of the garden, and there thrust in deep and covered the gloves from sight, pressing down the mould again until it lay firm over them. Then she went homeward by the lanes in the dark, and as she stepped she danced, and as she danced she laughed, that her kin would not have known her for the same wasting creature they were troubled over by day. But of this going by night they never knew, neither then nor after, for by morning her shoes were cleaned of the mould, her cloak dried of the dew of the rainy bushes, and she in her bed and quiet and wan in waking, as ever now she seemed.

After this she made also other dispositions, for she was much about the school, though ever out of view from the windows of the house; and she took pains to single out from among the boys, though but passing among them as if by chance, three who were most at odds with their master, being idle and impudent of habit, three overgrown lads who made great brag of their deeds against him when he was not by, but were shrunken before his eyes and under his tongue to mere babes yet inarticulate and helpless. Upon these three, though separately always, she worked to such a tune that before long they were all in the one tale, though she did not use the same trick ever above once, nor suffer herself to be too conspicuous in the matter. For upon the first, which was a neighbour's boy by name Thomas Scholefield, one that was not dull at his books but careless and slovenly, thereby earning for himself many an ill moment, she laid this errand, that he should carry a letter for her to Mistress Elizabeth, at a time when Master Drury would be from home; this she said, indeed, but in truth she sent him with the letter at a time when she well knew Salathiel would be by, and set her own hand plain upon the wrapping, that he, who had formed it, might know it at a glance.

'Go,' said she, 'quickly, and return, and I will await you here where I may not be seen; for indeed he will not let me have any word with my dear young mistress.'

So he went, and in no long while came back to her muttering with a flea in his ear, and brought her the note again.

'How?' says she in great agitation. 'Did you not give it to her? What has befallen?'

'Small chance I had,' says Thomas, grumbling, 'to speak so much as a word to her. And the next time, for all your pennies, you may carry your own messages to that house, for I'll not be a beating-post out of school for you or any.'

'But did not my mistress come to the door?' asked Mary.

'She came well enough, but before I had more than got your name off my tongue out comes he from the house in a rage and plucks her within, and bids me be off about my business to her who sent me, and with a buffet to help me along. And there is your letter again, for I could get no good of it.'

'Does he indeed watch her so narrowly?' said Mary. 'Then I have small hope of any word with her. Yet you saw her?

How did she seem? Was she in good countenance? Come, tell me!'

'Well enough for all I could see,' he says, gaping. 'She was well enough, it was he that sent me off so sharp.'

'Fool, do I not know it? He will not let her have my company, the poor child. I fear things are not so well with her as they seem. Tell me straightly whatever else you saw, and you shall have your money though she has not her letter.'

So he cudgelled his wits, but could dredge up nothing of great import. 'Why, she did seem very tame to his calling,' he said, 'and I daresay he is as rough with his tongue to her as to us, for that matter. She ever seemed a very quiet lady.'

'Do you tell me she goes in fear of him?' says she. 'Alas, poor young mistress.'

'Truly you may say so,' he says, thus prompted.

'And did you see aught else? Were there any there but they two? Think well, did you see any other?'

'Why, no,' says Thomas, yet reluctant to have it so dull and plain since she looked for more, 'there was nothing but this, unless it be anything that there was a little, brownish, mouse-eared dog running about the bushes in the garden, one that I never saw before.'

At this intelligence she started, and had him repeat it, which he did, marking it deep upon his memory because of her intent face and urgent eyes. 'God have mercy!' she says then, as if to herself. 'Is it come to this, that the children see it also, and in plain daylight?' And when he questioned her of her meaning she bade him pray the protection of heaven against all evil spirits and imps, coming in whatsoever shape. Then she went from him hurriedly, and left him alone, that he might marvel and remember the more.

And the next one that she put her hand to was one Matthew Chittam, that was dull of wit yet imagined much of self-glory that never befell, a mere boy yet near man-size, and though without malice, able much for ill by reason of a gift he had for convincing himself and others upon grounds too slender for evidence. With this lad she fell in as he carried milk, and began to talk with him, and as it was dark she dwelt much upon the loneliness and strangeness of the way, never naming but only shadowing forth her uneasiness; whereupon this boy Matthew fell much in love with his own valour that did nightly walk this road alone, and began to enlarge it this way and that, adding an unchancy sound here and a curious shape there, until verily he did believe he had seen and heard about the Schoolhouse by night more than was in nature as God made it. So that as they went together, and she started and exclaimed aloud, pointing ahead, he was as ready as she to see whatever she would put into his eyes, and he was greatly frightened for all his bravo ways.

'Did you not see a flash of white,' she said, trembling, 'that passed down from the ridge into the herb-garden? There, at the very house door, see—Ah, it is gone!'

'I saw it indeed,' he swore. 'It was light as snow, and little.'

'Less than a dog, and ran lower,' she said, 'like a hare.'

'It was a hare,' says he, holding fast by her arm, 'and milk-white. White hares are not canny. Witches go in white hares. Where did it run?'

'It ran to the house door, and then I could not see it. But sure it did not go in, for the door is fast shut.'

'Let us hurry from here,' said the boy, shaking. 'Better not to stay where those hares run that pass through doors. You see yourself it is clean gone. Oh, come away past, before it crosses us again.'

'If I were not with you,' she said, 'I should run, but for all you are but a boy I know you are not afraid at anything.'

'I am not afeared at anything human,' he says, and his teeth chattering, 'but sure it is no worth to be strong nor bold where there's ancient evil to reckon with, and I'd as lief see no more such hares. Mark a cross with your fingers as we go by the house, and then let us run if you're affrighted. Be sure I'll not leave you.'

So they ran by and fled up the lane towards the village, and at the turn of the hedge young Matthew looked back and swore he saw again the white hare pass from the shut house and away into the ridge of the wood. So belike he did, for he was in such a condition from excitement and dread that what was not afore him his eyes supplied, and she was quick to prompt. And when she asked him if he had not seen the same on other occasions he swore he had seen the like, but not so clear, and at length it came to a tale that he had once pursued it, but got no certainty of it for it vanished among the bushes of the garden, there being still scattered snow at that time to cover it.

Now though he was in such awe of these imaginings as to be silent concerning them for some days, even to a week or more, he could not for his nature be thus continent for ever, and in a while he began to whisper to some intimates these terrible confidences; and chancing among others upon Thomas Scholefield, he found his white hare matched with a little dun dog with ears of a mouse, and they came in quick rivalry upon this head until they made agreement to go by night and watch for the visitation together. Which by day was well enough, but by moonlight was none so well, that a hunting cat and a drift of sudden rain sent them running in terror that they had seen both hare and dog, and neither of this world. Being afraid to tell their parents they kept silence upon this adventure, and yet their subdued demeanour thereafter, falling as it seemed almost into a sickness, caused their mothers to wonder and complain, and in time the tale came out by whispers, and ran wide as a tide through Sunderne, though never breaking surface nor being handed on aloud.

And the third of these boys was Beavis Frennet, and he was but eleven years old, clever and shrewish and full of malice, but of a fair face and well-spoken tongue; and he was a child that did not imagine, but knew only too well how to lie, and so did whenever his own acts were called in question. With his books this one was accomplished, but from his soul hated Master Drury because he conceived he was not given due praise for his work, nor sufficiently held up for an example among the rest. For there was nothing Salathiel so much loathed as a child that greatly approved his own works, and would have all others exclaim over him, and therefore he was ever cold and mocking with this boy, and the more embittered him by the slight regard in which he held his enmity. With this Beavis Mary Butterworth did but dally now and then when he fetched and carried about her uncle's farm, and led him on to boast of his works at school, and so to talk of Salathiel as he dared not at any other time or place; and by degrees she put into his mind measure upon measure of lies concerning the schoolmaster, which he for his part took to himself readily, and willingly improved upon. It needed no confidences between these two, for each readily understood the other's mind. Both the white hare and the little brownish dog this child gladly took for his own, and repeated the tale to others in secret.

One other was also directly troubled with these things, and that was a certain young widowed man who thought well of Mary Butterworth, and as at this time had it in mind to make her his second wife. This young man was a smith, and had his forge close by the green over against the churchyard wall, and he was of an old Sunderne family, by name Francis Cates, a worthy man and a good match. She had no thought of satisfying him, yet she so looked his way in those days that he was not discouraged, and pressed her sometimes to walk with him at night, for March was come in softly that year, and the spring promised to be early. Three times she did so, and the third time so contrived that they came by a little-used path down to the ridge-track which ran past the school. There she halted, and hanging upon his arm swore she had forgotten they must end here, and would rather for her life go back by the same way than pass by the Schoolhouse at night. He asking why, she half-owned she was afraid because of things seen there which terrified her to remember and which she would not upon any account describe. But to this man she said nothing of having seen any such matter as dogs or hares, for he had wits, and she thought well to let it seem that there was somewhat amiss with hers, yet not to let him judge what it was. So he was convinced of her distemper, and in great concern of mind took her home by the way they had come; and as she grew calmer he began to question her gently of her terrors.

'All the village knows, Mary lass,' he says, 'that you have been a right good servant to Master Drury, and done very faithfully by him these many years; and truth to tell there's many a one has wondered how you could endure to be about him so long, seeing he is so hard and ill-spoken a man. But sure you never made no complaint, but stood up for him roundly when we miscalled him. Yet now 'tis you who shrink from going anigh him, and will not even pass his house at night, no, not with me beside you. What ails you at the schoolmaster, Mary? Tell me, now, if ever he behaved ill to you, and I'll make it my own charge to pay him, and gladly.'

'No, no,' she says in agitation, hanging on his arm, 'never touch him, 'tis your life else, I warn you.'

'Why, girl,' says the smith, grinning, 'I do take a deal of killing, I warrant you. Your master may be a long lad, and fine in the reach, but never doubt I could mark him, I could make good account of him and never let blood in the doing of it, neither.'

'Fool!' she says, and sharp and sudden as one in desperation, 'do you suppose your big body could serve you there? If you fought with the devil himself I believe you would expect to outdo hell-fire with your fists. There be some that have done less than lay a hand on Salathiel Drury that have already good reason to repent it, and shall yet have better.'

At this he was much startled, and pressed her to tell her meaning more plainly, but she only hid her face and broke out in agitated evasions.

'Do not ask me more,' she said. 'Can I tell you what I do not understand? Let me alone, now, for if we do not meddle we can do no harm and bring no ill luck down upon us. Let me alone, and him too, for God's love.' Nor would she say more nor better than this, so that he went away from her in great unease of mind, only begging her to assure him at least that no wrong had been done to her in that ill house, which she did with returning calm, and so they parted.

While she made these dispositions came daily and dolorous news from Sunderne Friars, where the old man Master Nicholas grew worse of his illness, and having once so improved as to stand again upon his feet, again fell down in the like seizure as before, and rose no more, but after this most constantly faded until he held life or was held by no more than a thread; and Mary Butterworth waited upon this news, and not in vain, for on the eleventh day of March he died. Now she was carrying a pitcher of milk to table in her uncle's house when a neighbour came in with the news, and sudden at the words she stood still, and the pitcher fell from between her hands and was broken to atoms upon the floor of the kitchen. She put her hands to her face, and without a cry out of her fled instantly away out of the house, with so strange and wild a look that her uncle thought well to go after her, and followed her at last into the forest, and there she flagged and he overtook her. Her eyes were blank as those of one who walks in her sleep, and she never spoke word all that day, but let herself be led home gently, and a cloak put about her, for it was a day of new frost, and her arms were bare to the elbow. Day-long she sat drooping and never spoke, though they questioned her tenderly, and brought in Francis Cates the better to soften her; but ever she sat and stared and made no reply. And at evening she rose once again and caught her cloak about her, and rushed away out of the house, but this time she went not to the forest, but hasted through the village to the church, and there went in.

'This is an ill matter,' said her uncle when he had looked in and seen her lying prostrate with her hands clutching at the rails of the chancel. 'Let us go and fetch the priest to her, for it is plain what ails her is not for us to meddle with, nor for physicians either.'

So they did, and brought back the good old man, one Francis Fox, that was a native of the place; and when he had seen the woman lying spread upon the pavement and unmoving, he instructed that he should be left alone with her, for in truth he was greatly perplexed and in some fear at what she might do. When therefore they had gone out and shut the door between he went to her, and kneeling took her by the hand, and raised her with holy exhortations, bidding her speak out her grief and anxiety without fear, for in God was pardon and peace without measure. Thus sweetly encouraged, Mary at last looked up and besought him in a whisper: 'Oh, help me, sir, for I am a lost creature. There is a great wrong done here in this town, that God requires me to answer. Bitter signs were shown me, and I did not believe, but now I hear of the evil I might have prevented, and I shall get no rest until I have cleared my soul. Oh, help me and stay with me until I have eased my load. Sir, do not upon any urgency leave me, or I shall run mad. Remain with me, I beg, and give me courage to speak.'

'I will not leave you,' said the old man. 'Have no fear, my daughter, that God will let you fail of your intent, nor look hardly upon your offence.'

'Not mine,' she said, 'not mine except as from fear I shut my eyes to portents, and therefore have let murder be done among us.' And upon this word her voice was so low that the old man, being somewhat thick of hearing, did not at first understand what it was she would say.

'What is this sin,' he asked, 'which so much hangs upon you? For there is infinite mercy.'

'It is of murder I speak,' said Mary Butterworth. 'Is there mercy for murder?'

At this repetition he heard indeed, and was so took aback he could scarce keep upright or feel for a word, for he had never met with such a declaration in a long life.

'Do you shrink from me,' she said, clutching at the skirts of his gown. 'I swear the crime is not mine nor connived at by me. I did but doubt the signs, ah, wretched creature that I am, I doubted and so let it come to pass. Oh, listen to me, hear and believe me, for the devil is loose among us here in Sunderne.'

'Yet this is grave matter,' said the parson, swallowing his

speechlessness, though hardly. 'Sure you do not know what you say, for I know of no such thing chancing in our midst.'

'But I know it,' she cried, 'and the shadow of it has been like lead on me these four weeks and more, and I have shook it off. Nor is that all the matter, enough though it be. Oh, let me tell it all, let me assoil myself, and then ask me what you please, and I shall answer it, and you shall see if I lie. There are abominations,' she whispered, clutching her mouth, 'that I dread even here, for if God do not strike me, yet the old enemy may. Keep fast hold of me, and give me your strength.'

'Speak, then,' he said, 'and if your heart fail look up at the altar.'

Thither she looked, and smiling under her pale lashes, where the old man could not see the glittering, and God, she was assured, would not heed it, she told her story.

'Master Nicholas Shenstone is dead,' she said, 'and not, as you suppose, in the innocent ways of age, but by malice and murder, for Salathiel Drury has gone about with witchcraft and familiars to destroy him, his master the devil aiding him to this present success. Do not start. Bid me, and I will swear it, yes, here, and solemnly. Ah, now my lips are open, now it will forth, God aiding. You know me. I was his servant, I served him most truly until a day not long ago when the meaning of certain things came on me like lightening-stroke, and I went home afraid to serve him longer, afraid to cut myself off from him, afraid to speak or keep silent, and have been ever since in this same grey sickness of mind, from which I must break now or die. You must know there had been things which troubled me before this, and my mind was not easy in me for the young girl Elizabeth. I was ill-pleased when she came, for I remembered clearer then the things I shall tell you, and always I was afraid for her to come into a place so dark. But this day of which I speak I took upon me to warn her, and he came home before I was aware, and overheard. I had hung my little silver cross about her neck, and when he broke in upon us and saw it there it was as if he had the devil

in him. He took hold upon it and wrenched it from her neck
and threw it to the ground. I swear it! Do not believe me
only. Ask her, she will tell you the same. It was then I
understood those things I remembered and had ever
remembered with dread and unease, for I knew the cross
was his enemy, most hateful to him, most detested, and upon
this I could measure all his acts and words, and know most
surely what he was. There should no God, he said, be invoked
between them two. He drove her away, and threatened me,
and struck me, and said nothing hindered that he should kill
me, if I did not keep lifelong silence. Since then I have lived
in this oppression of fear in which you see me, stirring little
from home, and dreading to open my lips upon truth until
this moment; and after this, unless God stand by me, it shall
go ill with me for speaking out at last. Yet the good old man
is dead, and it is too late for me to save my soul or his
venerable body. What avails it to deliver myself thus a
sacrifice to truth when no one will believe me, and I must
answer for it alone?'

'Tell all your tale,' said Master Fox, 'and it shall yet go
well with you in spite of all.'

'Do you then believe me?' she asked.

'I do believe you are honest, Mary. If you are deceived by
your fears, well, and if not deceived there is the more reason
you should speak out, that the evil thing may be uprooted
from among us.'

'I tell you, he tore the cross from her breast and cast it
down under his feet. Looks this like a dream of mine?'

'A grave charge,' he said. 'Yet tell all the tale. When began
this fear of yours? Can you remember surely the date and
time of any happening that lodged in your mind?'

'That can I,' said Mary Butterworth, 'and by very sure
token, for there was somewhat upon the day that Master
Shenstone first fell suddenly into this sickness of which he is
now dead, and I well remember the words I heard spoken
between them that day, and he cannot deny without he lies.
But afore this there was three times that I was in great

astonishment and wonder, but being young made no long nor steady account of it, and alas, I know no dates for these. The first was a long while since, when I was but twenty-two or twenty-three years old, and it was of a summer day when I rose very early and went to my work straight, for at that time I shared my mother's bedchamber at the Schoolhouse. The sun had woke me and I was up afore my time, and went along the gallery. And as I came near to my master's door some little creature broke out past me as it had come from within, and ran before me quick as light down the stairs, and so I lost sight of it for that time. Yet the door was fast shut, and I swear had never been opened to let it out.'

'God mend all!' said the old man, shivering. 'What manner of thing was it?'

'It was like the fashion of a little dog, but having ears round and close-set to its head like a mouse's ears, and its colour was brownish and dun. It ran quick and low, and I could see no more; but I tell you it was not canny. Also I thought, though I cannot now be so secure of this, that it was a bitch.'

'Powers of grace defend us all,' said he, 'from incubus and succubus and all the evil of the great dark!'

'Amen. But the enemy is strong and full of rage, and I am afraid for my soul's sake. Yet then I was not greatly afraid, for I was young and innocent, and my mother with me, and it did but quench my spirits for a day with misgiving, and then passed from me, and I forgot it for a while. But a few years later, I cannot tell how many but my mother was yet alive, I saw this same thing again. I met it in the garden as I came home from a late errand by moonlight, and there it sat as tame as any fireside cat and looked at me, and I well remembered the look of it. While I stared at it it turned about and ran towards the house. I watched it run out of the moonlight into the shadow, and as I live and breathe I never saw it come forth again. It melted into the shade. And the third time that I saw it was but two months ago, on a morning early in January, in the snow and dark when I was early about the Schoolhouse, and Master Drury was but newly up. I went into his bed-chamber to make his bed, and there upon the pillows was this she-dog reclining licking herself; and when she saw me she ran across the room and leaped out from the window, which had blown open and was swinging in the wind. I went after to see which way she would go, and she was running through the garden towards the forest, and beside her another thing running, too, less than she, and white, and long, that looked like a hare. They went out of sight in the trees. Did you ever see bitch and hare that ran together? I never did, neither before nor since, but that one time. And after, upon the pillow where she had lain, I found a long yellow hair that was sure none of hers, but came from a woman's head, or the head of something in the likeness of a woman.'

'In God's name, child,' says he, 'why did you not come to me then, while there was yet time to put chains upon the evil?'

'Ah, so I cry to myself,' she said, 'and have done since the thing befell. And yet bethink you, these three things came but singly, and some years between them, and the easy heart is not quick to think evil. I would half terrify myself into confession many a time by night, but daylight would make a mock of my fears until the creatures that started them seemed only a dream. When this was past, still I had never any true content, but I shrank from stirring a storm that might end deadly, when there was no utter conviction in me. I believed and did not believe. Only when Mistress Elizabeth came I grew truly afraid for her, and so came this business of the cross which I have told you.'

'Ay, so,' said the old man. 'And this is all?'

'This is but the half. I have said that there was somewhat upon the day that Master Nicholas was took ill, but I have not yet told you the way of it. It was thus. Master Nicholas came down in mid-afternoon, when the children were newly gone, and he upon horseback. He was within with my master for a long hour, and at the end of that time he came out of the room where they were, and he in great anger, and Master

Salathiel after him no calmer. And this passed, which I do
perfectly remember and will swear to with my life. Master
Nicholas cried: "Then sir, if you cannot do my work as I want
it done, I will find another who can"; and my master replied:
"Do so, and be damned, sir, as before long I think you may."
Right so the good old man rode away, but after he was gone
Master Salathiel came through the hall with a pair of gloves
in his hand, and seeing me look upon them he says: "Look, if
Nick has not gone off without these in his rage," and with
that he carried them off with him into his library, and he
being called away that night to London on the errand that
brought back Mistress Elizabeth, I conceived he had left them
in his haste for me to return, and looked for them, but could
not by any means find them. And when I locked up the house
that night I went up to Sunderne Friars as I had been bid, to
tell Master Nicholas that my master was called away upon
urgent business, and there I found I must do my errand to
his son, for the old man was already fallen in the first fit of
his sickness. Now has it been his death, and I have been silent
from want of wit and courage to see I must save him. And
where are the gloves? I have heard tell there is a power over
a man's life even in so light a thing from about his body as a
pin, or the paring of his nail. Would not a glove suffice? For
certainly this good old man is dead, and will you tell me
there is so much of pure chance in the world as to end him
after so glib a fashion as this?'

So she said, and fell to weeping and wringing her hands,
but Master Fox fell upon his knees beside her and began to
pour out urgent prayers to heaven for protection from evil
and for right guidance, even while she knelt by him and
sobbed amens at every close. And when he was well resolved
he rose up and ordered her that she should come with him
and tell her tale to the magistrate even as she had told it to
him, for there was certainly matter in it for grave thought.
She went with him unquestioningly, and she was quiet as
one spent by the effort that was gone out of her, but at this no
one wondered, and therefore she was at no pains to have it

seem otherwise. She went where he took her, hot-foot to the house of Master Philip Harding, who was the only magistrate resident so near to Sunderne as to be reached that night. This was an old gentleman who had been for most of his life a merchant of Shalford, but in middle age had bought himself estates, and farmed some thirty acres in the quiet of Sunderne valley, and become a Justice of the Peace, and whatsoever else he might well be that would add to his stature, besides making himself very busy about such country activities as were meant to lessen his girth. To his house, even in the late hours of a March evening, it was no great matter to walk, and thither went Master Fox bearing Mary Butterworth along with him, and Elias Weelkes and Francis Cates followed on their heels; also some others, seeing this sober procession go by, fetched their cloaks and went after. Upon their way they paused to call forth the Constable to bear them company, who went unwillingly at first, not knowing what was toward, but when he saw the village following like an army he was reconciled, and would not for his life have been out of the flood. When they were thus come in silence and awe to Master Harding's house, upon Master Fox's urgent plea he was admitted, with the girl and her menfolk and the Constable, while all those who followed remained without, and waited silent in the cold.

Now the Justice at their coming was snoring over a great fire with a bowl of punch beside him and a handkerchief spread upon his face, but seeing he was to have no more peace he roused himself and came forth to them in no good temper, yet civilly, for he was well-disposed toward Master Fox by reason of his family, who were not without influence in the valley, though they came nowhere greater than farming stock. So he came to them in the hall of his house, a great old man of a gross red countenance, rolling in his walk and propping himself with a thick staff. To him Mary Butterworth was bidden repeat her story, and so she did with more composure than she had hitherto shown, her confidence being now much greater because of the success she had already achieved. All this matter the Constable wrote down from her lips, and having read through the information thus lodged she put her name to it with right goodwill.

'This is aggravated offence,' then said the Justice, 'if all be as you say, Mary. What, are we to fall foul of Satan's works here in our very midst? Here is a very full case made, as I judge, why we should hold this man; and yet I would have the depositions of such others as may wish to testify, before I commit him. You, fellow, Elias Weelkes you say your name is? You say you are this woman's uncle, and she abides with you. Can you speak to this matter?'

'That can I,' said the farmer, 'but only to this purpose, that I dare swear Mary here has had no peace since that day she spoke of, when she left Master Drury's service. To the motions of the man himself I say nothing, for I have no special knowledge more than we all have, that he is very ill to deal with, worse to cross, and worst of all to anger, and I like no part of him or his works. But as to dogs and hares, I was never about the place by dark, and I never saw such.'

'Speak to the woman's part, then, good Elias,' says the old Justice, 'and a' God's name let us have your matter in black and white, too. Constable, do you set down his deposition.'

The Constable therefore had down from him this statement:

'On the last Tuesday of February it was, as I well remember, our girl Mary came home earlier than she was wont, as my wife and I were sat at meat, and she came in very pale and wild-looking, much as you see her now, sir, and went by us without a word said, and shut herself up in her bedchamber. She was never wont to behave so, I tell you truly, and my wife was concerned for her and presently went and brought her down, but she would not eat nor drink, nor spoke but when she was questioned, and would not tell us what ailed her. She owned at last she would go no more to the Schoolhouse, but would not for any persuasion tell us why, and when we pressed her she wept and paled and begged us to leave her be. And I can vouch for it, and my good wife can do as much also, that she had the cross she speaks of secure about her neck by a silver chain when she left us that morn, but when she came back she carried it in her pocket, and two links of the chain were stretched out of their shape and one was broken clean through. But the young mistress there at the Schoolhouse, Mistress Flint, she can better testify of how it came so. All I know is Mary has been like a creature crazed or bewitched from that day to this, and we have been able to do nothing with her. If this be the loosing of her trouble I say thank God for it!'

'Well said, Uncle!' says the Justice heartily. 'But I am a man of matters myself, and I do not meddle overmuch with God's business. Let us by all means stick to the case in hand. Have out the thanks to God, Constable, but keep the meat of the witness. And you, blacksmith, have you a word to add?'

'It is but to the same effect, sir, if I have,' said Francis Cates. 'I do not like Master Drury, but that is not evidence, for every man has his likes and dislikings. All I can say is that this same Mary has been out of herself, as Master Weelkes has testified, since that last Tuesday of February; and when she walked with me at evening once and we came upon the Schoolhouse by an unfamiliar way she would not pass the place, but entreated to go back by the way we had come, and owned she was afraid for her life to be about that spot. I asked her if the man had done her any wrong while she served him, and said I would make it my own charge to pay him his full coin on her part, but at this she grew agitated and bade me never think to lay hand on him, for that some had offended him in less manner than that and had cause already to be sorry for it, and should yet have better cause. But she would not say more, and I was in shame to pester her, she was in such distress. Only today, as you have heard, when the news of Master Shenstone's death came to her ears she was as one struck silent mad, and ran from us to the church, and Master Fox came out to her and so brought her here.'

'Here are two trusty men,' said the Justice, musing to himself, which he did aloud and in a thunderous voice, 'that tell one tale to prove you honest, Mary. And sure your pale face and your wild eyes speak for you also, and your name is known to me for clean, modest and virtuous. But there are deceptions can take in even the honest mind. I have a hankering in me for good solid fact can be held in the hand and looked over with the eye. Certainly we shall hear Mistress Flint's account of the matter, and make present inquiry if there be not others in the village here have seen these imps we hear of. But as for me, I would gladly have sight of those same gloves Master Shenstone left behind in his anger. Grave it is that they should be at odds together on the very day when the illness falls upon the one o' them, and no small matter it is to bid a man be damned and have him fall as dead within the hour. To have familiars about his house, if these be such – for by your leave I've seen fox cubs and spaniel pups that were raised together – the offence is certainly gross. And troth, my cubs did never run through shut doors that ever I heard of. Of all this we shall have more witness, I make no doubt. Yet I would fain have word of the gloves, for they have a smell of this material world about them that likes me better than all your imps and spells. Harkee, Mary, have you ever a fancy where these gloves should be?'

'I cannot tell, sir,' she said. 'It came to my mind they could be made ill use of, but how the ill is done I never learned, nor never wish to know.'

'You are a wise woman,' says he, 'and I am not ashamed to take warning of you. But it is laid upon me that I must be informed on a great many matters of which I would as soon go ignorant; and among many others I am made aware of this thing, this fact or fable or what you will, that to injure a man by his belongings or his clothing or something from about his body you must bury the prize, and as it rots so its master will rot. Moreover I am informed you may make a speedier and surer end of him if you do your burying as near as may be to his person. Constable, you shall leave Mistress Mary here with me, take these good fellows for your deputies, and get you to Sunderne Friars. There find me what is to be found about the grounds, and look to it that you seek well under the walls of the house, for if we have to do with so accomplished a wizard he will know the letters of his art better than do I.'

'Shall I acquaint Master Henry Shenstone with this matter?' asked the Constable.

'Ay, do so for your body, or he will be at you with his keepers,' said the Justice. 'But be moderate in your going, not to offend about a house where the master is dead.'

'I shall, sir, for my part; but at your door there stands half the village into the bargain, and would see the end of the matter, and I doubt I shall have more help than will be welcome to me or to my lady at Sunderne Friars. Speak you a word to them, your worship, and send them about their business.'

Thus appealed, Master Harding went forth upon the steps of his hall, and saw all those men and women of the village standing silent, waiting for his word. From among them he chose out a few who seemed to him strong and trusty fellows, and bade them put themselves under the Constable's orders to perform whatever he should require of them; and next he demanded if there were any among them that had aught to say in the matter, that they should come forth and make their depositions truthfully, whereupon came out Matthew Chittam and Thomas Scholefield in a terrible haste and eagerness to offer themselves, and after them a certain young woman that would not be out of anything, and one her envious fellow that would not be outdone by her, also a poor labourer's wife that was with child, and had unquiet dreams and fears in her sickness, and had long moped in a belief she was ill-wished by some wicked creature. These all swore they could speak to the purpose, and these he kept, but roared at the others that they should go quietly to their homes under fear of his anger. Upon hearing this they withdrew out of his sight, but no farther, and waited, and when the Constable set forth with his little company to Sunderne Friars this great company went upon their heels, and would be seeing all though they died for it. But the witnesses went in to Master Harding's library, where Mary Butterworth also was now taken, and there they made their statements before the clerk that kept the Justice's estate, and swore to all they told.

Thomas Scholefield and Matthew Chittam severally told of how they had seen the one the dun dog and the other the white hare, and how they had gone together by night and seen and fled from them both. They were in great excitement and most pleasurable terror, and told their stories with trembling and after-vision, as truly seeing again what they had once believed they saw. When they were done, the first young woman told a long tale of how she had once met the schoolmaster by night in the churchyard, and how the little brown dog had run before him; and the second young woman said she had once passed along the hillside path in darkness, and had seen strange lights and dancing in the garden of the Schoolhouse, and a man in the midst of the rout whom she knew by his bulk for Salathiel Drury, but she swore she was afraid to go so near as to know any other; and the labourer's wife said that all had gone well with her load until the day she met Master Drury in a narrow way, and he had looked upon her and bid her good day, when even at his greeting the child had leaped and shook in her womb, and ever since she had gone in sickness and despondency, dreading the fulfilment of her time, for she was sure some monstrosity should come forth of her at his over-looking. To all these several imagined horrors they swore with right vehement will. As for Beavis Frennet, though he was now asleep in his bed Mary Butterworth never doubted but that he would be forward with his complaint and perfect in his story before another day was out, and she was well content.

There was now but an hour wanting of midnight, and they waited but the half of that again before the Constable and his companions returned, bearing in hand the gloves of Master Nicholas, much stained and slimed with earth and rain, and bleached of a clay colour like dead flesh, besides being of that tender rottenness to part at a touch. They told where they had found them, under Master Nicholas's window, there buried to a foot of depth and covered over firm. At this the Justice sat back in his chair and received them very soberly.

'I see there is but one way of it,' he said. 'Not even I can complain of lack of witness, and here we are but begun. I would I might never have seen you, Mary, until the morrow, but what's done is done, and the King's justice has eaten my night's rest, and yours, every one. Constable, I bid you take these same good deputies of yours, and go bring me this man who stands accused. You shall have warrant enough, for he is already committed. As for the lady, present her my compliments and beg her to come to me here; say she shall be well cared for, and put to no annoy that I can spare her, but it is needful that she come. Say I have a wife and daughters who shall make it their charge to entertain her for the night, and after if she will have it so. Go, you have your warranty. Bring me Salathiel Drury.'

So they went out to do their errand, and while they were about this Mary Butterworth entered into a recognizance to appear at the gaol delivery, when and wheresoever it might be, when Salathiel Drury should come to his trial, there to make good upon him what she had sworn in her information upon oath. The witnesses also were bound in like manner, and after this the Justice dismissed them all.

'Get you home to your beds,' he said, 'and let me not hear of you running loose about the countryside, neither, or I will have you all committed upon suspicion of the same offence you charge upon the schoolmaster. Go, and be easy, for whether you have captured me a murderer or run your heads upon a folly I know not, but I know the trail is fired that your match was laid to. Go, I am weary of you.'

Then they went away as they were bidden; but Mary Butterworth separated herself from Master Fox in the darkness as they walked together, and turned down by School

Lane to behold the first pains of her vengeance take hold; and as she went she laughed and wept horribly in silence, shutting her hands over her mouth and drawing her hood close about her face, that not even the night might hear or see what joy and grief she had.

IX

THE TRUE STORY OF SALATHIEL DRURY (Contd.)

The word was gone about among the waiting people that the Constable was sent after Master Drury, and they waited no longer, for it was a rein loosed from them. There were not wanting some who were enemies of Salathiel, some who cared not for the man but much for the mischief, some who were ever ready to kindle to any flame, being but straw, or to rend any man upon the first breath of suspicion, being blown by every wind. Beyond this there was a great fear now upon them all, and a killing fear it·was like to be for whoever had brought it to birth. To Sunderne Friars they had followed the Constable, but to the Schoolhouse they went before him, and battered upon the door, shouting that they would drag out the wizard and swim him in the pool.

At the time of their coming it was past one in the morning, and Salathiel and Elizabeth had been more than two hours in their beds; yet he was fully awake, and heard the howling of many voices and the thundering of fists upon his door, for he slept little and then lightly since his bed was solitary. He rose and put on a gown and went to the window, and there stood looking down upon the crowd and listening to their crying upon his name as wizard, and murderer, and devil. The turmoil took him by the heart because of the night's silence, for he was weary in mind and would gladly have had quietness within him and without, but could get neither the one nor the other. When he was clear what terror was loose upon him he put off his night-clothes and dressed himself slowly and carefully by the dark and the thin moonlight, and went forth to Elizabeth's room, where she sat upright in her

171

bed, newly-awakened by the knocking and in sad fright.

'What is it?' she said in a whisper, seeing him come and fastening upon him eagerly. 'What has happened? What do they want?'

'They want my body,' said Salathiel, and a moment looked on her and smiled. 'Do not be alarmed, they mean you no harm. Do as I tell you. Remain here, dress yourself and be quiet, and they will not molest you. Only be patient and calm, and wait until I come to you. Or until another come, it is no great matter, for you will be safe enough.'

'But what is it?' she persisted, clinging to his hand. 'Listen to them! They are mad, like wild animals. They are saying mad things, awful things, only hear them! Why do they come here at this hour? What have we done to anger them? Oh, I am afraid, do not leave me alone.'

'I must,' he said, 'and that quickly. What brings them here howling under our windows I do not know, but go I must or they will batter in the shutters. Be bold for me now, and do not make me slow to answer though the devil himself call me. It is the best that I can do in this foolish pass. Let me go and hear them out and they will howl the less, I trust, and you may yet sleep.'

'But they mean murder,' she cried, 'for I heard them call you a wizard, a master of witches, and other worse names, too.'

'If you believe them, then,' he says smiling gently upon her still, though the cries for his blood rang steady and ominous in his ears, 'loose my hand and do not touch pitch. If you do not believe them, loose my hand in token that you would have me go down and cast their folly in their teeth. Either way loose my hand.'

She obeyed him then, and was somewhat calmed by his calm. 'Oh, take care,' she besought him as she let him go, 'for I am sure some awful calamity has made them leave their wits, and there is nothing they may not do, being mad. Are you not afraid?'

'That is for God to know,' he said, 'if God can see beyond

the nebulae. Now, child, do as I have bidden you, dress yourself and wait here for me, and remember me in your prayers if you will, for your kindness will be my blessing if God have none to spare.'

She promised to do his bidding faithfully, and then he kissed her forehead and went out from her, and taking a candle in his hand descended the stairs. When he was come to the foot, a lad who was looking though the keyhole saw the flickering of the candle and instantly reported his coming, whereupon such a hateful wolfish cry went up as caused him to halt and struggle for a moment as one breasting a heavy wave; but he recovered himself, and passing on into his library searched about among his papers until he found Mistress Flint's letter summoning him to London. There only was there matter he wished to hide, as he had hidden it many years. He lit it at the candle-flame, and casting it into the fireplace watched it burn out to black among the wood ashes. Then when it was all consumed he went forth again to the hall and unbolted the doors, setting them wide and passing out through them into the view of the pack that bayed him. They cried all together once with a weird harsh cry, and then fell silent before him a moment, for he was upon them before they were aware, and his face very black and boding as they had been rascally brawling boys under his thrall; yet well he knew the case was long past any such matter.

'Well?' he says, loud and imperious over their heads, and he above them by a tall step or two. 'Well, I am here! You can bay the moon, hounds. Can you speak with language also? Speak up, then, and despatch. What do you here? What do you want about this place with your midnight bellowing, you apes, you clods of forest clay? Swine, I see you can but grunt, and not articulate.' He took one great stride to the edge of the step upon which he stood, and they gave back before him as far, being still unrecovered from the suddenness of his coming out upon them; yet they gave not back an inch more than this one pace, and held their ground there with their eyes fixed upon him. He singled out one, the nearest and one

that had been loud among the leaders, a great young labourer
as tall as he and heavier, who had learned his letters under
him once, and that not without pain. 'You,' he says, 'you James
Childe, what have you to say to me? Come, you could screech
loud enough about my door when I was not by. Now speak
your fill to my face close. Speak and be damned! You at least
have not called me from my bed for love of beholding my
beauty. What do you want of me? I am here. State your
business or else get out of my sight, and take your moonstruck
gossips with you.'

The young man, amazed, could scarcely find words to his
tongue, and though he was wishful to hold his leadership he
missed his way and began between brag and stammer:

'Look you, now, Master Drury, sir—'

'No master of yours now, dolt,' says Salathiel, sharp as an
east wind. 'Your fat shanks are as safe from me as your thick
wits are from wisdom. Speak more to the purpose than your
sirs and your masters, or leave talking to the women who do
it better, and do you howl again, for after all said and done it
becomes you more. You, the rest of you, you worthless,
witless guts,' he said, sweeping the guttering candle round
about him, 'are you all fallen dumb? I ask you again what
you want with me.'

Then one cried out: 'We want no devil-worshipping
witches here in Sunderne.' And another: 'Where is your bitch?
Where is your succubus?' And a third: 'Master Shenstone's
blood cries after you.' And all together they began to scream
to those in front: 'Pull him down! Stop his mouth! He is but
one. His master is not with him. Cast him down to us!' With
all this there went up such a babel as made the moonlight
shake and shiver, but as yet no one durst lift a hand to do, for
he stood there curling his lips at them and retreating no inch,
and his anger now was above the measure of his discretion
even on Elizabeth's behalf, and he would make no compound
with them. When he could make himself heard he cried out
in a great withering voice:

'You crazed children, you lapses of God, get you to your

homes and leave peaceable people to sleep. You shame your manhood here and make me malcontent with mine. If any of you have complaint against me, as God knows I might well have against you, let him come to me by daylight like an honest man, and he shall certainly find me here waiting for him like another as honest as he. But if you must run in packs to prop one another, and so huddle together as to leave a man in doubt which of you snarled – no, by God, 'tis a dog's word, snarled, and dogs are honest creatures I will not offend by naming with you – which of you hissed, you creeping circuitous worms, you, I say may the curse of God light on you all and strike you with agues and itches enough to keep your hands occupied with scratching and your filthy tongues with whining, and so hold both off your neighbours. Now go, get out of my sight, for I sicken to look on you.'

Yet he knew, even in his rage, that he would not be rid of them so, for this thing was gone beyond what he could control. Nonetheless, he held them off still another minute with eyes and voice, marvelling that he was not already overrun, and still more that so sudden a hate should leap up at him unheralded out of the dark of a day much like any other day. Then young James Childe, grown desperate valorous in his despite at being so smartly put aside, struck at him with a cudgel and dashed the candle out of his hand, and instantly they were all upon him screaming and rending, and he went down under them trampled and half-suffocated, still cursing them until the breath was out of him. One saner than the rest cried out most urgently that they must not kill him, for the law was jealous of its possessions; and they took warning before it was too late, and pulled him to his feet, holding off from him the women who would have clawed him to death for savage fright. His lean face was marked now with mud, and bruised, and blood smeared his forehead and his hair, but he fought them so that half a dozen must get fast hold of him where they might and so still him by their united weight dragging upon him. Two hung upon either arm, one by the skirts of his coat, and others pressing in were as lead about his legs; and one caught him by the dabbled chestnut hair and pulled back his head so that his eyes stared madly at the moon as they had him forth in triumph out of the garden. But once having cursed his fill he shut his mouth upon complaint and let not a cry nor a word out of him to feed their little swollen, windy victory, but only raged within him and suffered what they willed, being helpless.

In this manner, shouting and singing for very ill joy, they brought him into Sunderne village, to the pool, and there thrust him in, that they might prove if he floated or no. This also he had supposed would be his usage, and this also he fought as well as he might, but to no purpose, for a dozen at once raised him and cast him in where the water was known to be deep, and having his coat upon him the skirts spread and held him upon the surface, so that they howled the more in their triumph and terror that he floated, and therefore he was damned. They ran about the margin of the pool, the better to be assured he should not wade out upon the farther side and escape them, but this he did not attempt, but only turned upon his side in the midst of the water and so lay for a moment gasping, while with one hand he clawed away weed and mud from his eyes and spat out green slime from his mouth. Then he thrust out with a fast, wild stroke towards where they stood thickest with their toes in the brink, and rose upon his feet and marched upon them through the long shallows, tossing off water from his shoulders like a dog; and his face streaked with mud and blood was dreadful to see, cold and vehement as lightning with rage and hate. He said never a word, but bit with his teeth at his bloody lips, and raised his clenched fists above his head, shaking and griping with them towards his enemies. Some among them, the women more particularly, wailed that his master the devil was with him again, and angered for his servant, and would blast them all; and some were so possessed with terror that they took to their heels and fled from him, nor ever turned to see who pursued. Even those who remained gave somewhat back from the margin of the pool, so that he came to shore alone in the midst of a circle of watchers, and none knew how to take hold on him again, but every man nudged his neighbour forward to the attempt, and himself sought to shrink behind.

In this pass the Constable came as kindly to these as to Master Drury, Elizabeth upon his arm half beside herself, and Master Fox and his fellows sturdy and solid at his back.

'What's this, you rogues?' they heard his voice cry at the hem of the shifting crowd. 'What are you about? Let me through, and be off with you to your beds as you were told, or some of you will see the inside of Shalford Gaol for this night's work. Get off, I say! Out of my way!' And more tamely than he had held likely they made way for him, and one by one slipped away, glad to go from that savage presence lest the devil truly smite them, yet not glad to have this gladness seen by those they had hallooed on to the sport; and in a while the Constable and his men, the girl with them, came face to face with the draggled wild creature storming in through the reeds, and there was no other man left beside. One woman there was that watched from a distance among trees, and fed herself full and smiled yet a hungry smile; but her they did not see.

Elizabeth, with tears made dumb for the while, loosed her hands from the Constable's arm and ran towards Salathiel, but at the look upon his face even she shrank and paused. Seeing which, with great agony he compelled his voice to its own level and his body to its proper gait, and was at pain to swallow the venom she had but glimpsed in him and must not see again.

'Take care, my heart,' he said, 'for I am not in a fit state to have you touch me. Do not spoil your cloak for me, nor your eyes neither. You see I am not dead nor greatly damaged.'

Yet he would have been warmed to the heart then if she had given no heed to his words but flung her arms round him indignant and piteous; but this he did not look for nor desire, for she had ever been to him submissive and pliant, as her mother had proclaimed her, and now as ever she obeyed him. She held off from him, but only by a little, and clasping her hands moaned over him most distressfully.

'There is blood on your head,' she said, weeping. 'Oh, they have hurt you, you are wounded.'

'It is no great matter,' he said, for indeed the hurt was to him the least of cares, and not from this proceeded that horror of hate which he had hidden away from her knowledge. 'There is no need for you to be anxious. Worse has befallen better men since time was.' Yet his voice was uncommonly low and slow, the labour of its quietness a weight upon her ears.

'No need!' she cried, breaking out afresh in terrible weeping. 'Ah, they would have killed you. I never saw men so bestial, never heard such words from them.'

'Say that it was an evil dream,' he said, 'and is over.' And he passed his cold hands over his soiled and spotty countenance, and cursed behind them with scalding curses upon the lie and the liar.

'Alas, it is not over!' cried Elizabeth. 'This man here is sent to you, sent to us both, to do an office I do not know how to name to you.' She turned towards the Constable as if she would have made some present appeal to him for relenting, or at the least for gentleness, but the sobs so stopped her throat that she could get out no word more; therefore Salathiel must needs follow her look and read there what he might, for the Constable, good man, was dumb with staring and had not yet summoned his wits.

'Sets the wind so?' said Salathiel. 'Well I knew the bite of it was not so keen for no reason. So, then, make an end. Do your errand and despatch, for I am chilled to the bone.'

'Salathiel Drury,' then said the Constable, 'I have warranty from the Justices to take you into hold, that you may be examined upon grave charges touching the death of Master Nicholas Shenstone, together with other matters concerning witchcraft and like black arts. And I charge you that you do deliver yourself to answer these informations against you as the law will have them answered. Make no doubt but we shall be able to keep you if you try to escape us, and therefore

178

do nothing so ill-judged, but come softly, like a wise man, and do yourself no more hurt.'

Now while he said this Master Drury stood stiff as stone before him, though the cold bit into his bones; and at the name of Master Nicholas he reared back his head as he had been galled in the face, and at the mention of witchcraft a brief laugh went out of him sudden as the flight of a bird.

'I am not like to do you any, at least,' he said. 'Well, so all is made plainer than day, is it? And you are come out to take me with half a dozen stout neighbours at your back, while a woman has committed me already with her little finger's least crook. No, be at ease, I shall not give you any trouble. I will go where I am summoned and I will answer what I am charged with, let it end as it will. I never turned my back yet upon an enemy that had a word to say to me.'

'You do well,' said the Constable. 'Let us be going forward, then, for half the night is gone, and the other half we are losing as we stand here. Come, Master Drury, and walk between us.'

'Put no hand on me,' said Salathiel, 'and I will go your pace to hell if you please. But if you or your playfellows touch or hold me I will not be answerable, and so I give you all the warning you will have of me. By God I have been pawed enough for one night, and I will stomach no more.'

They were wary, therefore, that they did not crowd him too close, though they made a secure circle about him. Seeing how he shivered in spite of his blinding rage, Elizabeth took heart to pray the Constable that they should return to the Schoolhouse, in order that her guardian might put on dry clothes, and so be rid of one death at least of the many that threatened him; for though she was frightened half out of her wits, and stupid with want of sleep and the suddenness of this shadow upon them, yet she had ever a well of good sense in her. The Constable, though in haste to have his errand over, was a kindly fellow, and in some dread, moreover, that some evil influence should overlook him did he too grossly affront the wizard; therefore he thought well to agree, and back to the Schoolhouse they went, where Salathiel changed his clothes and cleaned himself of blood and mire, and so made himself ready. Then they went forth again, and made all haste to Master Harding's house, nor did they speak often as they went, but walked buried in their several cares. But Elizabeth leaned now upon Salathiel's arm, and would not leave it though he was concerned for her to keep separate; he wished much to give her some warning, yet was unwilling to seem to have any urgent or secret speech with her lest they should suppose her a party to his imagined guilt. Only when they drew near to the magistrate's house at last did he venture to speak.

'Do not cause this man to suspect any evil of you,' he said. 'If he has so much against me, and you are too fond, certainly some crumbs of my infamy will cling about you also. I would not have you smirched, even so foolishly, therefore do you hold off from me when we are before him.'

'I do not care,' she said stoutly, 'what he may think of me. I would have him know, and all these men too, how truly I hold faith in you.'

'And if they prove my guilt upon me?' he said in a harsh voice, for already he knew in his heart a part at least of what would be said, and he stood in great dread of beholding her face when she also heard it. 'There were certain things said to you once, Elizabeth, concerning me. Do you remember? Was I angry then as the innocent are? Or as the guilty? Think well before you pledge me trust it is not in your power to command. I am what I am, and to you I can never be better nor worse than you behold me. I would have you see with your own true-reporting eyes and not as I bid you. Oh, my most dear,' he said, suddenly wringing at the heart of his distress, 'my only dear, to what extremity have I brought you? Curse me quickly that I fended not better for you than this, and take away your hand from my arm.'

'Do not bid me do so bitter a thing,' she entreated, 'or I must obey you. Let me be dutiful and faithful both for this one time!'

'God help me,' he said, groaning, 'I cannot send you from me.'

So they came into Master Harding's house, and into his presence; but upon the threshold Salathiel as with the tearing of his flesh broke aside from her, and went out of her reach; and then she was obedient to his desire, and made no more ado.

The old Justice, resigned to the loss of his night's rest, was settled down with the dregs of his bowl and exceeding comfortable, and having in the glow of the punch almost forgot upon how grim an occasion they came, greeted them at the first but as welcome company, and was at point of calling for more glasses when it came back upon him sadly what was his true part. Yet he consoled himself with making much of the lady, leading her to a seat beside the fire, and giving her many cushions to keep off the draughts; receiving which attentions she gave him a pale and startled smile which put him in a very good conceit of her. The Constable made quick occasion to whisper in his ear:

'By your leave, your worship, if I were you I would keep the lady by while you examine him. His tongue will wag fast enough for her sake when he might keep it stubborn-locked were it only for his own. You may have the whole story tumbling out of him if you do but let him suppose you are in doubt of her innocence in the matter.'

'Ay, so?' says the Justice, middling quiet for a sign of his displeasure. 'And are you?'

'Lord, no, sir, not truly so.'

'Neither am I,' says the Justice. 'As white a vessel of glass, by God, as ever I saw, and I'll have none of your traps laid for him around such a bait. Do you look to your part, fellow, and leave mine be, or your ears shall answer it. Yet stay she shall, and be reassured if he can do it, and at least know that he is not searched, nor walked, nor any way tormented for this one night, and in my house.'

'It is as well,' said the Constable, thinking well to change the subject, 'for he has been swum already.' And he told him

181

the way of it, whereat the stout old man was greatly vexed, and vowed he would arraign the whole village for such mischievous doings.

'What, Salathiel Drury,' says he, turning to the suspect, 'they tell me you have been ill-used already upon this untried count. I am right sorry for it, and will proceed against the ringleaders if you will but name them.'

'Had I been what they suppose me,' said Salathiel, 'you should have been spared the necessity of proceeding against dead men, for I would certainly have left not one living. Yet, sir, it seems to me there is trouble enough in Sunderne without looking for more. As for me, I hope still to have the pleasure of meeting those same exceeding busy persons again some day, and having certain speech with them. Our accounts will then be well settled without need of law, nor of magic neither.'

'Well, 'tis very well, if you are content,' said the Justice. 'Yet do you come to the fire, for it is a chilly night for such cantrips as I hear you have been indulging in, and I would not have you take any bodily hurt from it.' And when all was arranged as in the mellowness of his heart he wished, and the clerk ready at the table over his ink-horn and his papers, he asked Elizabeth if she would tell of her relations with Mary Butterworth at the Schoolhouse, and what had passed between them with regard to Master Drury. Elizabeth faltered, looking at Salathiel, who smiled at her and nodded that she should recount all the story. Which, though with hesitation and distress, she did, denouncing her own fears for folly and making vehement allowance for his anger; yet her tale was not without its effect, even upon herself, for since the day of these events she had not until now so clearly remembered them, and they were still frightening to her. When she could call to mind no more items to the purpose the Justice turned to Salathiel, and asked him if he had aught to add upon this incident.

'Nothing,' said Salathiel, 'but to confirm what Mistress Flint has said insofar as it falls within my knowledge. The rest I can well believe, though I have never asked her any question upon these passages. I am not a man of even temper, nor I will not have my ward prised away from me by a lever of pious lies. As for your cross, it was to me then but an odious sign of disbelief, and not the cross to which your Christian clings. I am not placid when I hear myself mouthed into a devil, sir, nor, I think, would you have been so in my shoes.'

'It is very like, I grant you,' said Master Harding, 'that I should have been in a tolerable rage, but let that by. There are yet other counts of evidence to be met, and you shall hear them all. The most grievous is the matter of Master Nicholas Shenstone lately dead.'

Then he told him honestly what was all the charge against him, but not the evidence, mentioning after the main charge those secondary horrors of the dog and the hare which had so set fire to Sunderne minds; and he adjured him that he should make as full a statement as he might upon these grave matters. This Salathiel did so well as his memory would serve him, but being in great weariness and some pain he made but a brusque business, and had to be often prompted. Nor did he look at Elizabeth as he spoke, but fixed his eyes upon the red of the fire, and so held still.

'In this affair,' said he, concluding, 'I can bring forth no other word nor act of mine or his or any other man's that can have any bearing, and all that I have brought seems to me to have little enough. It was my understanding that he died of the cyclic sickness for which we find no name but seizure or stroke, and if there were no natural witchcraft of that kind in the world we should be laden with old men and all the physicians would be out of business. But let that be. The kernel of all this is, that I am as innocent of procuring or causing or even desiring his death as you are, sir, and so I will maintain against all comers.'

The Justice pondered for a while, and then began to question him shrewdly.

'Upon the day,' he said, 'that you say you received a message from the mother of this lady calling you to London, Master Nicholas was with you upon some business of the school. Can you recollect what words passed between you then?'

'I cannot immediately recall,' said Salathiel frowning, 'that there was anything of any moment.'

'Did you quarrel with him that day?' pursued Master Harding.

'Very like. I do not recollect.'

'Very like you were at odds, yet you say there was nothing of any moment?'

'Why, that was none,' said Salathiel with a wry smile. 'It was ever a wonder did we meet and not quarrel, and more a wonder did the quarrel endure until we met again. He was a stubborn creature but without malice. As for me, if I had more than my share yet I bore none to him.'

'Yet hear what I have on sworn oath as passing between you when he took his leave,' said the Justice, and read from the statement of Mary Butterworth: ' "He came out of the room where they were, and he in great anger, and Master Salathiel after him no calmer. Master Nicholas cried: 'Then, sir, if you cannot do my work as I want it done, I will find another who can.' And my master replied: 'Do so, and be damned, sir, as before long I think you may.'" What have you to say to this account, Salathiel? Does it refresh your memory upon that dispute?'

'Ay, truly it does,' said Salathiel. 'Now I remember the cause we argued between us, and not for the first time, neither. It was a matter of honour with him to have ever the last word, and if he had it not he would spite me by the nearest way to hand, and put himself and me into a rage, and as thoroughly forget it before we met again. That day I was angry because he, somewhat put out over I know not what careless answer of mine, again threatened, as he had often done, that the classics should no longer be taught in the school. I was as resolved they should, and so arose those high words your witness overheard from behind the kitchen door.'

'But the words, then, were spoken?'

'Some such words were surely spoken. I do not know if

one here or there may not have been changed, but I do not quarrel with this arrangement. Let it stand that I damned him with my mouth; I did not so with my mind, and my hands have certainly never occupied themselves about the business.'

'Well, well!' said the Justice. 'Write his words in full, let us have no crabbing of meanings. Now as to the gloves he left behind him, Salathiel Drury, what did you with those gloves?'

'I sent them back to him by the hand of my servant, and have seen nor thought no more of them until now. What of those gloves? Are they a part of the fandango?'

Then the Justice showed him the gloves all slimed and rotting with earth and rain, and asked him if these were they.

'Ay, well I remember these red thongs at the wrist,' said Salathiel. 'These are the very same. But how came they in this case? They were well enough when I gave them to Mary Butterworth to carry to Sunderne Friars.' Then as he held them in his hands it came on him what frightful meaning was pinned upon these flimsy things, and in what danger he stood from them, and he looked up and found Elizabeth hiding her face and Master Harding regarding him with intent, as they also had perceived the full drift as soon as he. 'Well I see,' he said, 'that all has been done before me with care and prevision, and I am already in the pit. Listen, and I will tell you what was *her* story; you shall not need to recount it to me. This Mary Butterworth says that she observed the gloves in my possession, that I took them away out of her sight, and after I was gone from the house she could not find them. Yet she had wit enough to suggest to you, I dare wager, how they have been used and where they should now be found. Now hear mine. I say she lies, and has lied, and will lie and lie. I say I gave her these gloves to restore, with a message from me, since I had not time enough to do my own errand. I say that on her going up to the house she found the old man struck down, and none to say if he came home with or without his gloves, and therefore she did the message but kept the gloves that she might have a weapon to hand against

185

me. I say that she herself put them in the earth, and has built all this tower of lies upon them to destroy me.'

All this he said outright in very sober and black anger, not yet considering into what dark stratagems and silences it must lead him to make it good; yet already Elizabeth looked upon him through her fingers with stricken, doubting eyes, and he felt as one who would draw back his first steps out of a quagmire, and cannot for his life get loose again.

'Yet there was no witness by to uphold you,' said the Justice.

'Nor any to compound with her. It is my word for hers, and hers for mine, and you must balance them. But I am on oath, and have not yet been known for a liar.'

'Moreover,' said Master Harding, 'what cause could she have to wish to harm you so? It is not in nature to bear so much ill-will but for a great injury.'

'No doubt she bore me hate for cause enough to her mind.'

'For what cause? She had served you, as I understand, for many years and most faithfully. What could so move her to hate where she had been all service and duty?'

Then Salathiel saw to what an extremity he was brought, that he must either keep silence and leave his counter-charge without weight, or tell out fully all he had striven to keep hidden from Elizabeth, the years of alliance with Mary Butterworth and the suspicion she had of her as a rival for his bed, and matter enough to let loose half a dozen new and odious accusations, and to make him foul for ever in the eyes of his young secret sister, whom alone in the world he valued and cherished. For a while he hung upon this choice in torment, whether to throw away his life or her love, and whichever way he cast it seemed to him there was some danger he might yet lose both; for did he defend himself with every last morsel of the truth, leaving nothing hid but their blood kinship, she must certainly learn more of him than her heart could bear, and turn from him in loathing, for in the young and virgin there is no gentleness; and above all this he might still find the case go against him. And if he kept silence, by so much more would he seem guilty, and so might come by his death; and again above this, though silence would cover his nakedness from her, yet she might believe in his witchcrafts and sever her love from him as surely. Yet he reflected that by this way there might be the hope at least of keeping both Elizabeth and life, and time and fortune might settle all; he could but choose the lesser evil now, and let the rest bide. The pause he made was long, and would be marked for matter of suspicion; but he put a resolute face upon it, and answered at last:

'I cannot tell, for I do not understand what it is she bears against me, but certain it is that of late she has gone about to do me injury, for you see how again and again she laboured to turn my ward here against me. I do avouch it, she has been for years as true a servant as ever man had in all that appears in the act; but as for the heart, if in man it is a mystery, how much more is it so in woman? I do not know what ails her at me, but I see that to her it is enough, and I feel that to me it is like to be too much.'

'And upon this point,' said the Justice, gazing upon him in heavy doubt, 'you can say no better and no more than that?'

'I can say no more. I have declared I sent back the gloves by her, and see them again now for the first time. That is all I know of them.'

'Well, well!' said the old man, and looked once at the girl and ventured no more. 'Yet there is another count, and upon this there is more witness than one woman's word. It is set down that there have been seen about you in unnatural communion certain animals your familiars, in the shapes of a white hare and a small brownish dog. What have you to say to the hare and the dog, Salathiel Drury?'

'They are wind and no more. I know nothing of any such creatures.'

'How, then, should four several people testify that they have seen them?'

'One so testified first,' said Salathiel, 'and well you know which of the four was she.'

187

'Yet those who came after heard no word of her witness. How say you now? Are all these liars, too?'

'Liars or deluded, I know not. But I tell you I have no familiars, I know nothing of any such tomfoolery. I have to do with books, not with devils, and as for giving any credence to your imps and your witchcraft, I deny and defy them all, every imagined power in all the benighted minds that accuse me. There is no more I can or will say.'

'You have never used spells or incantations?' said the Justice.

'As God sees me, never any such folly.'

'Nor ever enjoyed a succubus?'

'God's curse!' he cried, patience and endurance cracking together. 'I will stand to be called every villain they please, but must I answer to such abject stupidity as this? I have been civil too long with lunacy, I will hold with you no more. Believe what you may of your succubus, set down against me what you will, I have done.'

'Yet you were well advised to answer fairly,' said Master Harding very gravely. 'I speak for your good, Salathiel, for should you fail to plead to this charge you will be pressed in another sense than this in which I now press you. Call this matter of belief whatever ignorance or folly you please, but on your life answer to it frankly.'

'It is your privilege, sir,' says Salathiel, raging, 'to threaten me, but it is mine to be stubborn, and one I will not let go for you nor all the Judges of Assize. I have said I deny and defy all the powers of darkness, and that is enough for you. Write it so, and have done with me.'

Then the old man, who was by no measure one to be lightly offended, was minded to grow grim in his turn, being so rebuffed, yet he answered mildly enough: 'You do ill to make me an enemy or say that I threaten you, for you shall find I have gone aside to consider you in this matter, and I doubt if you will be so used again until you are brought off clean, if such is your fortune, as I continue to hope it may be. Yet be it so. Write that the accused would make no answer.'

Now it was at this unhappy moment that Elizabeth put up her handkerchief and hid her face, and would look up no more. This Salathiel remarked in extremity of dread and chagrin, for he was now assured she could not stand against so much of treason and hate for his sake. Yet he watched her most urgently to take of her whatsoever sign of kindness she should be able to offer him.

'What more is there?' he asked. 'Let me hear all.'

'All is heard but the detail with which they accuse you. There are those, and so I warn you, who will swear to the uncanny beasts and their nearness to you, even to your bed-chamber and your very bed. Think once more if it would not be well to answer to this now, while it is warm, and so kill the lie if lie it be? For if it grow unchecked it will not be so easy to stamp upon it.'

'I deny the murder, the beasts, and the stranger in my bed,' said Salathiel. 'There is no more to say. If this kills, these lies are dead indeed, but you know as I know they are hardier meat, though in the beginning they are but breath. I am a man other men do not love, sir, and God forbid they should ever be blamed for that, for I do not greatly love myself, nor them neither; yet even honest hate takes kindly to calumnies, believing by instinct what will best serve its turn. It needed but one mind with malice in it to breed and bring forth the story, and there would be believers enough, ay, and witnesses too. I do steadfastly assert that though I be as faulty as most men, and worse than many, yet of all this evil charged against me I am innocent.' This he said vehemently and with great solemnity, fixing his bruised eyes upon Elizabeth, but she kept her face hidden, and gave no sign of having believed or even heard his avowal. The Justice, conceiving that his advice had availed to temper the rage of this passionate man, had his denial written fully, and felt the more kindly toward him.

Now all was completed that could this night be done, and the dawn was not above an hour away. It remained only that the accused should be either released upon his recognisance to appear at the next gaol delivery, or committed to prison to await the same, and it was plain to the Justice that here was due cause shown for committal, since the villagers clearly held there was no safety for them should Salathiel be released, and it needed not a second plunge into the pool to acquaint him there was no safety for Salathiel among these his neighbours. Therefore he took the only wise course, and authorised his committal to Friary Shalford Gaol to wait his trial; and so he told him plainly, justly believing he did all for the best.

'It is all one,' said Salathiel, and his voice was like a falling stone in a well-shaft, even so hollow and heavy.

'What, man,' says Master Harding, willing to cheer him, yet not understanding aright the cause of his darkness of spirit. 'How's this, are you tried already?'

'And judged also,' said Salathiel, ever watching Elizabeth.

Now though she had seemed but half-aware of all that had lately passed, at this she broke out weeping silently, and thereupon he knew that he had spoken what she felt to be true. He supposed that there was in her some fondness for him, but very surely it stood upon no foundation able to hold it upright against so searching a wind, and if it was not already fallen yet it shook as he gazed. Had she been any other that failed him so, as never to another had he so trusted, he must then have cursed her outright with whips of words, and scalded her from him beyond returning. But of her he said only:

'This lady my ward has been put to much distress and weariness for my sake. I pray you, sir, show her some care in the days when I cannot, and have some woman, as honest as can be found, help her to keep her house and her person honoured and safe while there is no man about her. Do so for her sake and not mine, yet I shall be grateful.'

'Rest assured,' said the Justice with goodwill, 'Mistress Flint shall be put to no annoy. My wife has been called this hour, and waits to lead her to a room prepared in some haste, but not, I trust, unworthily, and not, I well know, without a welcome in it. Nor must she go from us until all is arranged for her protection. There is no haste, and one more among my three daughters will come kindly to me.' And thereupon he approached her and raised her, saying: 'Come now, mistress, all will look better when you are rested. Think no more of it for this time, but come and shut your eyes upon it, and a long sleep will restore you.'

She rose submissively upon his arm, and so moved to the door; and at her going Salathiel had looked for some gesture of leave-taking though none of confidence, but she went by him like one blind and dumb. Nor did he reach after her nor speak a word to stay her, being absolute not to compel nor persuade what she could not give of her own will. Therefore she went from him unhindered, and was received by Mistress Harding with great kindness, albeit with some secret misgiving, she being concerned for her own daughters lest they should be brought too near to this unjudged case. Yet she obeyed her husband in this as in all things, for she was confident of her ability to control whatsoever confusions he might launch upon her, and keep the peace with him into the bargain.

But as for Salathiel, he was permitted to sit beside the fire in one of the great chairs until the morning came, when he should be taken under escort to Friary Shalford and there committed to the gaol. To him returned Master Harding, being set to watch out the night, and having found his second brew of punch not yet emptied nor cold, pressed both the Constable and his prisoner to join him in finishing it. So strangely they three drank together as the dawn came, and warmed themselves within and without, which came so gratefully to Salathiel as to cause him to doze in his chair, whereby he had by glimpses some present relief from pain, anger and humiliation. Yet was this his farewell of all kindness as in this life, which shall hereafter be shown, and even in this he had no steadfast comfort, for well he knew both these his companions believed him a lost creature. And had he not known this of his own wit, at his going forth it was made plain, for the sturdy old man took leave of him with these words:

'Yet, Salathiel, I would you had not been a warlock,' said he, 'I would liefer you had been an honest Christian like the rest of us.'

To this Salathiel made no reply, rightly supposing he could not get out any that should do him any credit or this well-meaning man any good. Only as the irons were put on his wrists he made shift to utter some words of thanks for his generous entertainment, well knowing it was but truth he should find no more such. Then he was taken forth and put into a hired coach, and so borne away by the early morning, but not so swiftly that word of his committal had not gone before him. There was no passable way from the Justice's house but through Sunderne, and therefore he was forced to endure once again the hostile eyes of all the villagers, who ran out to cry after him, so crowding the road that the coach must move but slowly between them. And while this was passing he saw one who stood a little apart, and silent, but watched him as hatefully as any; and upon her he fixed his eyes, as hoping she might come within reach of tooth and claw, but she made no move to close in upon him as did the crowd, and in a few short minutes she was lost to sight. Yet he thought by the greed of her eyes she would as readily as he have come to close communion could she have done so and no witness by, but she had put him as securely from her own neighbourhood as from that of other men, and must forgo the cream of her own jest, since by no trickery could she now taste it without imperilling all her laborious erection of calumny. Only the passing glimpse of his face in weariness and disgust fed her, and she was hungry yet for more when he was taken away, and she must go home insatiate.

Howbeit he believed she must have some content in telling over within her own mind the gross offences he had yet to endure. For on his being received into Friary Shalford Gaol it was inquired by the chief gaoler whether he had been searched yet, or walked to keep him wakeful as the custom was; and being given all the details of the examination this man made due report to the governor under whose authority he was, and received orders accordingly that the prisoner should be instantly and most rigorously searched for any devil's marks or teats whereat it might be found his familiars had suckled, and moreover should be kept wakeful as a means to bring him to confession. All this was done as commanded. Some four or five turnkeys laid hands on him and hailed him to a bare room, and there stripped him naked and handled him over inch by inch in most coarse and curious exploration, being practised in offending against all secrecies. A full half-hour they fingered him about, he being held helpless by two of their number upon a rough table, and turned this way and that under their hands at command; and though his bosom was full of gall and his mouth wry with curses he kept his lips shut and suffered all silently, being past even such relief as lies in anger; and when they were done with him, from swallowing his own venom he was direly sick, for he was not by nature a silent or a patient man under ill-usage. Yet they found his flesh clear and fair, without blemish but for one pale, small mole under his heart, not darker than yellowed ivory; and on this they seized and wrung it to discover if blood or other matter would come forth, nor left it until they got blood of him. This mark they then reported as showing signs of having suckled some small creature, as it might well be the white hare, and opened Salathiel's shirt that the chief gaoler might see the place for himself; and being by this time bruised and tender the mole ran blood and ichor at a touch, so that the chief gaoler made report in his turn that the prisoner had in his breast one more nipple than was natural, and further testified that he himself had examined it and found it to have been recently mouthed. Thus was set down a further evidence against Salathiel.

But as to the order that he should be kept from sleeping, he felt less ill of it than might be supposed, seeing sleep was in any case impossible to him, so was he poisoned with outrage and shame at the handling he had suffered, and with horror of his situation. Hourly the turnkey came and rattled at the grille of the cell where he was shut alone, but never

193

was there cause to enter and shake him by the shoulder, for never during that first night did he close his eyes. He had but one blanket and a palliasse of straw against the cold, and was much visited with vermin, yet these caused but a little easing smart upon the body of his anguish.

Now in the morning came the chief gaoler and asked him if he had not any word to say for the ease of his soul, whereat he laughed aloud and made answer: 'You waste your time and mine. I am not to be driven into confession as a beaten servant to drink, though you paw me over with your foul hands daily, and prise open my teeth to look down my throat for devils. Get from me, I have nothing to say to you, nor never shall have while I live and keep my mind entire.'

When they perceived that he was indeed fast set against speech they made no more direct advances, but on the third night sent in to him a poor, quiet, tamed young man who was waiting his trial for theft, and had no great hope of his life but in helping the gaolers in whatsoever ways they set forth to him. It was their hope that Salathiel might open his mind to a fellow-prisoner though he would not have any dealings with the gaolers; but to him it was as if he had still been alone, so little did he notice the man's presence or answer his questions, so they got no good of their stratagem.

Yet there was one in Sunderne who made discreet inquiry after all that befell in the gaol, making use for this purpose of a certain carter who plied to Shalford and had a brother among the turnkeys. Mary Butterworth was not left without word how Salathiel was searched, and what was found upon him, nor how he was kept from sleep and pestered for confession; nor did she fail to picture what was not told her. And often she shut herself in her chamber and laughed and wept in a silence and isolation not less extreme than his whom she had destroyed.

X

'THE HOUR IS ABOUT TO BE—'

During the day, while Mrs. Greenleaf was about the house, and old Whitton inhabited the garden, while delivery vans circled the triangle of green and occasional tattoos of baker and postman sounded at the back door, Claire made herself content with the world as it was. This was the time when she knew she was dreaming, and waited the return of reality without impatience, remembering that dreams are not really endlessly long, but only seem so. She was able, therefore, to amuse herself with the small illogical businesses of the dream without any feeling of irritation or ill-usage, to entertain her few visitors with a friendly if distant grace, to busy her hands about any number of household jobs and produce results which satisfied herself and apparently placated others, even to write to Anne in Somerset and Breck in London letters no colder nor more detached than had been her habit beforetime. By these means she passed the days and bought off the world from her evenings, that she might awake unhindered to the other world within her mind, where in contrast to this arrangement of toys and trivialities all was sharp and perilous and real.

But in the dwindling October evenings, when she was alone in Long Coppice and the awakening had been achieved, every step on the gravel, every hand at the door, every shadow between her hurrying pen and the declining light made her draw breath upon an expectancy more intense and arduous than any she had ever known. The rustle of a leaf which might almost have been a light foot in the drying grass would arrest her hand upon the paper and halt her breath in her lips to

195

listen the more sharply; and she would pause before she dared turn her head, for fear she should not be ready to meet him steadily, and lengthen the pause for greater fear that she should find only the blank space of the window fronting her still when at last she did adventure. Yet repeated disappointment seemed neither to diminish her hope nor to discomfort her spirit, as if the deferred moment was always there though never fully realised, only a step away from her and there suspended, in no haste to come but never withdrawing farther than the limit of her consciousness. After birth the next thing counted secure was death, yet she found death not more certain than this awaited moment.

While she waited, even while the words flowed out of her like blood and stained the paper, she could loose her mind upon the mysteries of her own conduct; and to her these were not those aspects of her possession which seemed mysterious to Charles, and which could not have come more naturally had she been born to them. The outward view of what she did no longer had power to trouble her, but perpetually she dwelt with interest and pleasure upon the contemplation of those problems no one else stood near enough to see.

Since every conviction in the human mind sprang, in her knowledge, from desire and not from proof, out of which of them proceeded this assurance of approaching revelation? Was it she who was urgent to draw him down out of the height and up from the depth to be touched and held upon the plane of her own flesh? Or was it he who had compressed his passion of necessity through three centuries for want of a fit vessel to receive the intolerable burden and give him relief? And having so endured every hell of constriction and suffocation and loneliness, did he now draw her to him as a cupping-glass, and let down into her heart the blood of his heart, and so lean over her as for breath, as for renewed life, in the first hope of ease from a pain far worse and far longer than mortal? She had come into Long Coppice a fit vessel for his hand in this, at least, that she was empty. Every emptiness aches to be filled, with a frenzy which cannot be resisted, but his ache, his frenzy, he had enclosed with the vehemence of adamant. The desire emanated from her, then? Or more violently from her? For there had been no haunting. That dark, erect and ferocious spirit had never come crawling and whining about the world looking for a heart to hide in or eyes to weep over him. It was she who had sought, and accident, or perhaps the same attraction of surfeit for starvation, which had led her where she could be satisfied. Knowledge and feeling had gushed into her and fed her full, but whether with or against his will she could not be sure, for the swollen freshet cannot but break through where its bank crumbles away over a dry meadow. She had taken, but had he given? She knew him because he was in her being, and her cold transparency was become a vase full of his fire, so that even strangers, even half-strangers like Charles, saw how she shone. But was there as acute a perception, as voluntary a fusion upon his part? 'There will be a meeting,' she told herself. 'To me it will be welcome. Will it be welcome to him?'

Yet by these reluctant twilights she felt no disquiet that this doubt could not reasonably be answered. There was no haste. Never before had she had all the time in the world at her disposal, and never had she felt herself rushing so directly upon her desire, as the metal to the magnet, secure of arrival and confident of union. What was not understood could be accepted. She felt no great anxiety even upon the score of her own preparedness, only these instinctive moments of pause to draw herself upright before she turned at a step which might be his. Her part was passive, when the hour came. She had only to be the needful creature; she had only to be enough for him, as he was enough for her. Not suspicion nor hate nor bitterness could quench her light, nor despair cool her heat, now that his fire was lit in her. All the poison of his wronged nature was miraculous fire in hers, an elixir white-hot and cleaner than innocence. He had leaned upon innocence, and it had proved too narrow and slight to support him. He had wallowed with experience in a mud at once warm and wearisome to him, and it had proved sour enough in the end.

'But I am a body he cannot desire,' she said, 'and he has no flesh for me to covet. I am a mind that knows him through and through and with no hankering after perfectness and no illusions to bind him even if he could still be bound. He is as he is, and I shall be satisfied. I have become what I have become, and he will recognise it. In the flesh we cannot limit, or exhaust, or disgust each other, and in the mind, or the heart, or the soul, whatever it is that keeps us from being people other than ourselves, we shall explain nothing, defend nothing, forgive nothing, only share and accept everything. He will meet me without going roundabout, and I shall go to him straightly and without artifice, like the creature he never found. I shall not be young, nor gentle, nor in his charge, and if my forehead is not in the stars it will be level with his; and I shall be enough.'

XI

THE OTHERS

She had stopped writing earlier than usual one night, or perhaps only paused to allow the words to array themselves ready to her hand, and she was sitting over a sluggish fire when someone came to the long windows quite slowly and heavily, and let himself in. She heard the quiet, long-pacing feet pass along the paved path, and the gentleness of the tread moved her; she heard the slight shifting of the latch as it was touched, the small metallic contact as it lifted, and then the shurring of shoes upon the carpet, so soft that her ears hardly caught it at all. The evening air blew in upon her coldly for a moment, and then fell still. She arrived at the moment of hesitation, not more hopeful than at every such occasion, not less confident; then she turned her head. Jonathan Kenton was just lowering the latch into place.

He said: 'You didn't expect me, did you?'

'No, I didn't expect you,' she said, repeating his words thoughtfully. She had forgotten the others; to this part of the day they did not belong, and when they intruded she was at a loss how to meet them. She sat looking at him gravely and letting her hands dwell upon the paper before her, as if she could take up again with her fingertips the latest words of those many which were not hers. '—in a silence and isolation not less extreme than his—' 'You came so soberly,' she said, 'not like yourself at all. What's the matter? Are you all right?' But it was hard to remember that she was expected to care, that to him it mattered if not to her.

'Perfectly all right, thanks!' he said composedly, and came forward to the fire, and uninvited began to goad and coax it

199

into a quick small flame. The daylight was gone past use; she lit the desk lamp, and saw him jerk his face away from the rim of its circle of light. That dark, narrow country face, with its intolerant eyes and hawk's nose, had need of a more intense darkness than its own if it had anything to hide. But she had looked for nothing there, and did not regard him more closely now. She felt a trouble and a tension, but they were so far distant from her that they could not make her pay attention to them. Her eyes and her mind were on other things.

'I don't suppose you've noticed,' he said abruptly, 'but it's over a week since I've been here.'

'I had noticed,' said Claire, but forbore to say how grateful she had been. Some, she reflected, you can placate only by telling the truth, others only by lying. Jonathan remained one of the others. 'I missed you,' she said. He would pretend not to believe her, she knew, without even realising that it was a pretence; but in his heart his desire that the words might be true would make them true. Could she but have fixed all her mind's burning energy upon him it would have been easy to satisfy him, and she would have liked to make him happy; but she could scarcely even see him, so steadily must she watch another man's fortunes. To divide her intelligence would be to waste it, and neither of them would be any the better off, and she infinitely the worse.

'I wish you meant that, Claire,' said Jonathan ruefully, 'but I know you don't want me here. I know I'm in the way. Well, I'll get out of it presently, but just now I really want to talk to you.'

'Something has happened,' she said. 'What is it?'

He poised the poker like a spear, and thrust it into the heart of the glow he had raised. She watched the red run darker around its blackness, and then whiten and steady as the heat began to gnaw at the metal. Iron whitens to translucence, flesh blackens and blisters; both consume at last, though by degrees so different that they seem to be going opposite ways.

'What is it, Jonathan?'

'Not much, at least on the surface of it. But I wonder! Our Charles,' he said, with a smile which was not his nicest, 'is a dark sort of horse. When he suddenly becomes very pleasant and thoughtful and accommodating you can bet your boots there's a reason for it. There's something in it for Charles, no matter who seems to be making the profit.'

'You're no more fair to him,' said Claire absently, 'than he is to you. I suppose you're far too much alike to do each other justice.'

'Alike?' The poker was wrenched out of the fire in a sputter of sparks. 'God forbid! If I thought I was like him I'd cut my throat. But listen, this is damned serious. You know how I've hated being back here in Sunderne, and nagged at him about getting away again; and you know what his attitude's always been. Sunderne's all anybody ought to want. It's good enough for me, and a damned sight too good for you, and if you haven't the sense or the guts to appreciate it you can just stay here and get your nose rubbed in it until you do! That's how he's always prescribed for me. You know it yourself.'

'Still,' she said, sighing, 'you're of age, Jonathan. If you wanted so desperately to go, why did you never just pack up and go? He couldn't have stopped you.'

'I know that. A few times I did come pretty near it. But after all, why should I go tamely away without a penny? He had everything, you know. Younger sons don't count for much in the Kenton family, you just kick 'em out and let 'em get on as best they can. The land's what matters, and the eldest gets that, and everything else goes with it, among the Kentons. No, if I go against his will I shall never touch a penny or a grain of soil, and I know it, and he knows I know it. I don't see my way to do that. I was determined to stick it out and have my rights out of him, but now – well, he's trying to face about, and I wish I knew why.' He looked up abruptly into her face. 'Has he talked about me to you?'

'No,' she said. 'Why should he?'

'Because you come into it somewhere, of course. At least, that's all I can see for it. Nothing but you could make him go back on his whole habit of life like this. I thought you might have said something that made him think – well, that it might be as well to get me out of his way.' He had withheld his gaze from her while he got through this curious sentence, but at this pause he looked up at her again, sullenly expectant of indignation in her face, or worse, amusement. He caught the white incandescence of her look fixed and bright, shining beyond him into a distance neither within nor without the parchment-coloured walls. He had greed and determination and a passionate self-centred optimism, but no conceit, and he knew he was not regarded, not even remembered. Only the insistence of his voice could reach her; only constant bludgeoning could keep his personality impressed ever so faintly upon the crystalline surface of hers. She had said that she had missed him, though he had accepted that only as an automatic reassurance such as is offered to fretful children; not wholly a lie, for he could not believe Claire would go to the trouble to lie for anyone living, but not very deeply true. How far dared he presume upon this motionless tolerance she practised towards him? Far enough to startle her? Far enough to shatter the crystal, or only to scratch at it from without? And what violence must he do to achieve even the lesser effect, when she could fix and glitter and whiten upon her own thoughts even as he pestered her with his, and offer him only a few tranquil words sloughed from the surface of her mind, while all was pale fire below? He had never had any hold upon her, never would have any; he could get of her only what she would give him, compel her as he might.

'Charles is in love with you,' he said suddenly. 'I daresay you know it, but let's have it said. If you don't want him, better begin to lay your own plans. He never stops short of what he wants.'

He got her notice, at any rate, for she turned her head sharply in astonishment and some displeasure, and sat gazing at him with her eyes greener than usual in the shaded light, and her brows drawn thin and straight. The fire within her, which he saw as if through alabaster, burned steadily and fiercely, but it was only the cut surface of the stone that frowned on him.

'Yes,' he said, as she was still silent, 'I know, and you're right. I'm insolent, and from your point of view behaving like a child, and a detestable child at that. I've no right whatever to meddle. What's between you and Charles is your business, and none of mine. I know all that. But go ahead and say it, I don't mind. Only at the end of it, still deal carefully with Charles if you ever want to be rid of him again.'

A voice more familiar than any she had yet used to him this night said deliberately: 'Jonathan, come and sit down, here beside me. And stop shouting; at that range it won't be necessary.' And when he had obeyed her, content to have wrested some part of her intelligence to himself, she leaned forward and sat looking into the fire for a moment, arranging her thoughts tidily before she opened them to him. Then she said: 'Well, let us have it, then, all of it. You haven't yet told me what has happened. Charles is trying to face about, you say. How? What has he done?'

Jonathan, watching her narrowly, thought for a moment that she looked very tired, the smooth veins of her lowered eyelids bluish-green like the threads of an anemone petal. He supposed she might sometimes look her age, but this was such a weariness as a young girl might wear after unaccustomed dissipation, beautiful and languid and sad about that core of flame which made her shine so.

'He's offered to set me up with a handsome capital in Australia. It's a scheme I put up to him myself six months ago, when I came out of the army. Four of us had planned to club together and go into cattle there in quite a moderate way. Well, he killed it on the spot as far as I was concerned. If I went I went, but it would be without a penny of his money. I wasn't going empty-handed to be a labourer for the others. That finished it. Well, a week ago he revived the idea off his own bat. Oh, very gingerly, of course, just putting it in front of me again and watching to see if I bit. I didn't. I acted dumb and stupid – yes, I know I can, too often for your liking or his

– and waited for him to come into the open.'

'And he did?' asked Claire.

'Not exactly. The twilight of the grove is his natural lighting. But he gradually pushed the old project into the open, bang in front of my nose. I can go when I like, and take what I like. He *means* me to go, Claire, and the farther the better. It's worth going back on all his own dearest prejudices to get rid of me.' His voice was hesitant between bitterness and triumph.

She said very carefully, holding her attention upon him with an effort: 'You see all the unessentials, but never the one thing that matters. He's offering you the thing you wanted most. Take it and be thankful. What is it to you if he also wants you to go? You complain of his prejudices, and yet it seems you're willing to consider throwing away your own chance in life just to avoid doing what it also happens to suit him you should do. And you complain that I call you alike!'

'But, you see, what I wanted most a few months ago may not be what I want most now,' said Jonathan deliberately.

'That is for you to decide,' she said, 'not for me.'

'But I'm asking for your advice,' he insisted. 'Shall I take the chance and go, even though that's playing into his hands? Or shall I stay and be a thorn in his flesh to the finish – whatever the finish may be? What would you do, Claire, if you were me? What do you think I ought to do?'

'How can I answer that for you? I won't be made responsible for your decision; you must settle it for yourself.'

'But it depends on you,' he burst out, 'and you know it. Don't be so damned dishonest as to pretend the whole thing's nothing to do with you. It's because of you, because he's clearing the ground around you, that he's kept me away all the week with some unnecessary job or other, anything to keep me out of your sight. It's because of you that he's willing and anxious to set me up in Australia. It's worth money and time and trouble to him to get rid of me, just in case I may get in his way with you. You can't wash your hands of it. You've got to tell me what to do.'

He might have said more, but her stillness and silence

daunted him, and in his turn he fell silent. She was sitting with her face between her hands, and the pressure of her palms had drawn close the gold-flecked skin over bright cheek-bones, and made her brows thin and oblique. He saw the glow of the firelight into which she stared reflected in her eyes. She did not look angry, if it mattered; he was not convinced that it did. She seemed intent, but not upon anything her eyes saw; rather she had the look of one listening. He wondered what would happen if he touched her, whether that brittle calm would shatter towards him or away, for she was and always had been to him as incalculable as some mysterious green and amber crystals in a laboratory bottle, and with the same implicit temptation. Even aside from his present greed for her notice he had always suffered an insatiable itch to meddle, to experiment with those untried lightnings, those white magnetic heats pent within her disguising coolness. But there was always a last caution in him which reflected how often the dazzle and venture had proved to end in nothing more than an evil smell, a little acrid mud and a burned finger. All incalculable things are liable to be disappointing when tried. Better to stand off for ever and watch her potential beauties wane and glow, and have no clue to what depths and heights or narrow emptinesses lay within. Or was it better to know? He was still unsure, still allured. Never to have her should upon this reasoning have been to have her for ever without satiety, but he knew it was no such matter.

'I won't be so naïve,' said Claire without moving out of her stillness, 'as to pretend to misunderstand you, then. You're trying to say that Charles is shipping you away from fear that you may appeal to me more than he does. It would be only exchanging one thorn for another, but neither of you can be expected to realise that.'

'You don't believe me.'

'It isn't a matter of believing or disbelieving,' she said. 'I can hardly *not* know that you've often been mistaken before.'

'I know. You regard me as an incapable adolescent,' he

said bitterly. 'My judgments are all suspect as far as you're concerned.'

'I regard you as a young man one generation behind me in experience, and perhaps a few years even in sense. As for judgement, it seems to me that it has no place in the make-up of the Kenton family, and no right to creep in sideways there, either. It isn't that you do not know, but that you take no notice of what you know. You say Charles would have seen to it that if you went against his will you went penniless. How little of what you know of him you'll consent to admit! He's a Kenton; the name and the blood and the land and the continuity of all three mean more to him than anything else ever has or ever will. Oh, and I don't mean he spends any time or pains on doting on them, or that the thought ever occurs to him at all. It doesn't have to, it's as much a part of him as his right hand. You know he would have passed everything on to you as inevitably as he breathes, and as naturally. It's only an example of the way you argue over and through every fact that stands in your way. Why not? He manages no better in his dealings with you. I don't accept it as any more true that he wants you out of his way now. Do I know it, simply because you tell me so?'

'Are you saying it isn't so? Dare you tell me nothing particular passed between you and him the last time he was here?'

She turned her head at the vehemence of his tone, and looked at him long and clearly. 'Nothing particular enough to make me remember it. What are you suggesting happened?'

'I can almost believe,' said Jonathan, marvelling, 'that it went clean by you, but I'm morally certain *he* thinks he – what would the phrase be in this case? They all sound equally silly – made love to you? For want of a better, let's make that do. He made love to you. And that you – well, it seems to be that you didn't even realise it, not enough to remember it, at any rate. Let's say, being considerately vague, that he got no forrarder. Well, Charles isn't put off like that. I've seen him wait his time to get a horse he wanted, or a sheep-dog. I know the process. You've lived a very retired life here, Claire. Not many people have access to you. After himself, I was the nearest and most intimate. After himself, I had most of your confidence. He made up his mind to remove me. After me, he'll turn his attention to any other man under sixty who comes near you. If you let him he'll strip the world round you so bare of people that if ever you do need company and look round for another human creature you'll find no one but him.'

He had found the way to convince her now, he was speaking quite levelly and dryly, and the words came to his tongue with a facility he seldom knew; yet she sat there smiling, and the gold of her eyes molten, paling the green to the whiteness of glass.

'It isn't so simple,' she said, 'to isolate me, even if that was all that's necessary. But I do believe that you think you're considering only me in this, Jonathan, and it isn't that I don't appreciate it.'

'I'm considering myself first. Do you think I should hesitate what to do if I'd nothing to gain here?' He leaned forward and took hold of her hand, folding it over his own with interlocked fingers as a child might do, or a lover. She let them lie upon her knees without demur, even adjusting her thin fingers to his. 'Whatever I could say, Claire, you would know before I said it, and it would seem pretty trivial and silly to you. Why should we talk any more? Let me just sit here and not say another word. Then we shan't quarrel.'

'No,' she said, 'you wouldn't be satisfied. Besides, you want words from me. You want me to tell you to stay. You want me to say that I need you, that I want you to be within reach, and to come and keep me company now and then. You want me to beg you not to go so far away. Above all, you want me to take sides with you against Charles, and to dislike him in my own mind because of what you've told me. You want me to be the coup de grâce in the feud you've been conducting against him for a long time, I suppose all the years you've lived with him.'

Breathless with astonishment and indignation he burst out: 'Do you think he loves me? Is it all on *my* side?'

'I didn't say so. Hush, Jonathan, don't! It isn't that I haven't seen your side of it all, and his, too. Let me go on, and you may catch a glimpse of mine. I like you, Jonathan. I like Charles, and I like you, and if that had been enough you'd both have been welcome to it for good. But neither of you was satisfied. I had to like one better than the other. Hasn't it been the same with anything that's ever touched you both? It didn't matter what I was, or what I felt. Another woman in my place would have done as well. What mattered was that I was one more thing you could fight over and beat each other with. You think you care for me, I know; that's part of the ritual. He thinks he loves me. But it isn't so. It's just that you happen to have been born incompatible, like two dogs from the same stock that can't come within a hundred yards of each other without putting up their hackles, or meet without flying at each other's throats. I am merely the bone that happened to fall between you.'

He began to say dully: 'If that's what you think—'

'No, that's what it seems to me that you think, consciously or unconsciously. My view is different.' Her voice was quite gentle, almost regretful, and she made no move to release her hand, rather deliberately kept her cool responsive grip upon him. 'I don't need you, Jonathan. I don't need you, or Charles either. I don't want you to be within reach, or to come and keep me company. It's only a very little more than nothing to me if you go away to the other side of the world, and no more if Charles goes with you. I was willing to like you both, but you're not willing to be liked. I shall live as tranquilly if you never come here again. You ask me what you ought to do. Take your chance while it offers. Get away from him, for his sake and your own. Get away from him for my sake. Get away while you can do it with his consent. Your only hope of continuing friends with him is to put a few seas between you. But,' she said in a voice curiously cold, 'I have a feeling that quite apart from any excuse I might afford you for wanting to stay, you'd never leave him. You're too much in love with hating him.'

He waited, watching her with a grim face. She felt a tension like the first freshening moment of wind at the blowing up of a storm.

'That's all I can say, and all I mean to say. Well?'

'You haven't left a hell of a lot for me to say, either,' he said in a low voice.

'You know you can say whatever you like to me.'

'Maybe I could, but I've had my answer.' He got up abruptly, and walked away from her to the window, and stood there drumming his fingers almost soundlessly upon the glass. The set of his back was rigid, but by moving her head only a little she could see the reflection of his face painted in thin luminous lines over the matt darkness of the garden; and though in this reversed image also all was still, yet the indirect stare of those bold, debating eyes moved her more than any appeal could have done. She understood what was going on in his mind, with how jealously nursed a desire he coveted her, to his own torment and hindrance and bitterly to hers; and she felt no impatience nor resentment against him, only regret that he must deliberately waste so positive a passion. He could help his nature perhaps rather less than most men, since more of him than in most men was instinct, and less was reason; and only within certain limits could the coldest of wills or most watchful of consciousness confine or extend any man's potentialities. Perhaps, she thought, there are people whose whole existence it is, once they have met, to combat and destroy each other, just as there are others who lose sight of all the rest in too vehement a love. Yet he was so young that it should have been possible to be amused by him, and it was not possible; so young that it should have been absurd to take him seriously, and she was assured he must be taken seriously, and had acted accordingly. He could have been her son, and she had let him continue to see himself as her unwanted lover.

'Well,' she thought, 'am I to forget he was born as free as I was? I have learned what is due to human dignity.' And suddenly and terribly she was visited by all the horror of physical humiliation in that other tormented creature upon whom her whole heart dwelt; and tears burst in her eyes as sharply as the breaking of sweat, but did not fall. The image of Jonathan's face glittered and blurred for a moment before she saw it clearly again.

'And if I go,' he burst out wildly, 'if I give up and go, how can I be sure I'm not leaving him a field he *can* occupy? – yes, in spite of you! How can I be sure he won't get his own way in the end?'

'You couldn't bear that,' she said, with no implied reproach.

'I couldn't. I'd kill him first, if there was no other way of making sure he should never have you.' He said this in a voice somewhat lower and milder than normal, as if only from an illusion of being alone did he utter the words at all.

'It's for me to make sure of that,' said Claire. 'I can give you no more assurances than you see in me now, or hear in my voice, and I give you those because I want you to be satisfied, not because you have any right to ask for them. If I wanted Charles you should not stop me from having him. But I don't. I never shall. You'll be as safe from that worry in Australia as you could be here. Go, Jonathan, you'll be glad after a few months to be free of me as well as Charles. It's only difficult to make the break; afterwards you'll find it worth the effort.'

His fingers halted their silent tattoo, splaying their tips gently against the window. 'Are you so anxious to get rid of me, then?'

'I can live with or without you. You asked me what you ought to do. It's for you to decide whether you'll do it.'

Something between a laugh and a groan came from Jonathan. She had hardly expected so much at such a moment, and her answering smile was instant and pleased. 'You're so *reasonable*!' he said. 'What's come over you? I expected to be handed all the usual gaff about being a young fool, and talking melodramatic rubbish. I thought you'd remind me that you were old enough to be my mother, and say – oh, all the things I ought to have known you wouldn't say. It's queer when things don't happen as you've rehearsed them. I don't know where I am. Wait a minute or two, let me think.'

'There's no hurry,' she said, 'take your time.' But now that he had laughed she was almost reassured that he would go, and in the following silence, always so close upon their most violent speech, she let her mind slip from him and rush back gratefully to its steady pole. The decision mattered much to him, the singleness with which he would make it mattered more; to her these were still no more than extraordinarily vivid dreams, to be put away out of regret or enjoyment at waking. She put her hands very gently upon the pages of her manuscript, her palms hiding the record of Salathiel's defiance, and under her fingertips the grossest stupidities of the humiliation his fellow-creatures had put upon him. 'Yet they found his flesh clear and fair, without a blemish but for one pale small mole under his heart, not darker than yellowed ivory; and on this they seized and wrung it to discover if blood or other matter would come forth, nor left it until they got blood of him.' Under her own breast there sprang to life a comparable pinpoint of heat, as if angry blood flowed; and a central clarity of daylight lit her mind and expanded against the unrealities of the dream which had bound her. This awakening was like bursting out of a small locked room into an infinite space of air and light. Never until now had she known how large a thing was pain, and how spacious was pity, that they should demand to move in something so much vaster than a world. What had happened to her, that she could not breathe but in this wider air, that she must lean down low to bring her senses within reach of human speech, and constrict her heart to bursting-point to comprehend Jonathan's trouble? In this other, this monstrous anguish there was room enough to stand upright and stretch her arms, and this wilder, harsher speech came to her ears like a fanfare of trumpets. She forgot the rest. It was difficult not to forget the rest, they were so wraithlike in their unimportance. What remained was an inexhaustible sorrow and joy to her, forever startling and brilliant with astonishment, even with beauty.

'I am alive,' she thought, 'I have proof of it. I am angry, and not for myself. I feel, and not by instinct, not for my own, but by choice and for a stranger.'

There was always, close upon the awakening, this outcry of delight as she drew again the deeper breath of realisation, and shut the door upon the world. And always thereafter the onset of pain, instant and breathless and always new. All fires burn out at last, but this fire never, for even time was fuel, and every renewed thought fed it with slow green wood. It was not only, not even chiefly, the pain of the body that mattered, though cold and wounds and confinement and a horrible death still marked against heaven a three-hundred-year-old account, still unpaid. These she could bear, even these, she who had never for her own sake had to endure a single considerable pain or a solitary privation. But how much more did her heart cry out under the loads of his humiliation, his self-disgust and his awful, his impenetrable loneliness. That he, who had held it against God that he must be shut within the limits of the human body and its appetites, must be dragged through the obscene comedy of severing himself from these appetites against his will for a helpless little sexless, unencouraged love, and beyond this must be stripped and pawed in search of the marks of familiars, fingered for fooleries he held in bitter contempt, and the single blemish upon his flesh made a brand to light his pyre, this was accumulation of horror. And last and most desolate of all, and least subject to the annealing of time, his loneliness fronted her wherever she turned her eyes, the extremest suffering of man, to be immured so deep from the touch of humankind that every companionship must fall off from him, every voice fail in his ears, every face be an alien face to his eyes, and never one single motion of understanding or compassion anchor him fast and safe in another creature's heart. This was the last cruelty, and this she could not bear.

'I never understood pity,' she thought, losing her footing in the flowing sea. 'No one understands pity. I thought it was a cold luxury, and I find it a molten necessity. I thought it could only touch, like dimpling a cushion, but now I know it can possess, and I feel it can kill, and perhaps it can even save. I thought it condescended, and now I know it fills and overflows and sweeps everything away.' And again she wondered with longing in what a tremor and frenzy his blood and hers would meet and merge. 'It's the only ease for me,' she thought, 'and the only rest for him, and it will happen because it must.'

To this hope she rode always now, as to an anchor, leaned forward eagerly into the wind of time that should blow the hour upon her. From how far it would come she dragged at her imagination to know, and with how irresistible an impetus, taking the breath from her lips; but in the heart of the whirlwind she foresaw always a cone of stillness which was the hour itself and the man, his deliverance from loneliness and hers from futility all in a touch, in a meeting of eyes and a measuring of hearts; and this would be peace, this would be fulfilment.

Strange, she thought, that they should all have lost him so utterly, strange that she had no rival. The woman who had loved him had lost him in time and driven him from her in eternity, making of herself his most dreadful enemy; the woman he had loved once for a short time had let herself be seduced from him into the most damaging union the world could offer her; and the girl her daughter, cursed perhaps with the same rootless pliability of mind, had committed the same sin, but against his spirit. All impermanent, they were fallen away even from his memory very long ago, sloughed off from him and left far behind. Nor had he helped one of them to hold fast or be more fixed than her nature, for fear he should offend against that demon of his, the liberty of the single spirit, the terrible integrity of man. Even at the door of the heart, she thought, unless a hand be offered freely and fearlessly to draw him over the threshold he will not come in. Not for ridicule, not for shame, not for death and torture all over again will he ask or persuade what does not come to meet him. He did not help them, and he will not help me. But I shall need no help.

'Get from me, I have nothing to say to you, nor never shall have while I live and keep my mind entire.' But he will not say any such thing to me, she thought with exultation; he will own my right to go forward to meet him as firmly as he owned theirs to fail and fall away from him. She remembered other words of his, spoken at another meeting. 'I would have you lean upon no mind but your own, since I see it may bear a heavier weight than yours and take no hurt. Look well at me, and speak out what is in your heart. I think better of you already than to be less than honest with you.' No formal dance-steps led him to his meetings, he carried no circumstances in his hand to wind about her; she went freely, her eyes expectant upon the way ahead, waiting for the lightnings. She had reached the time when even her companion in the room was gone clean out of mind, and only the small conventional glaze upon her senses continued to be aware of him; and she was very happy.

What was the sound that came to her ears then she never knew; there was no need for it to have been anything heavier than the brushing of a moth along the window. But there was something, at any rate, so light, so quickly lost that she could be sure only that she had not imagined it. It might have been a step; it might have been a hand feeling at the latch. She sat upright, rearing her head, and because Jonathan's movement as he turned to look at her made a small obscuring sound she said: 'Hush!' imperiously and aloud, without realising fully that there was anyone by to hear. But the step had gone by, or the hand had withdrawn, or the moth had beaten itself dazed against the glass and fallen to the ground; there was only the silence as she listened.

Very softly and levelly, avoiding every inflection of

suspicion or interest, Jonathan said behind her: 'You're expecting someone?'

'No,' she said, answering without thought, in the merest breath of sound, 'he won't come while you're here.'

It was not immediately borne in upon her what she had said; but the silence began instantly to be oppressive, and the exaggerated sensitivity which was so new in her felt the air shaken by a sudden hot and ugly wind of ill-feeling. She started back with a pang to the lower air, with its constriction iron about her, and the shock of surprise made her dizzy for a moment. She was aware of the island of lamp-light, and the arching of dim air over it inflamed by a straight, narrow and steely stare impaling her like a lance. She saw in those levelled and narrowed eyes as calculating and intense a distrust as she had ever dreamed a silent human glance could contain, and all directed against her. It was too late to call back one word, even if she could immediately grasp the meaning he had set upon her utterance. Nor would she go so far aside from her path to undo what damage an unwitting answer had done. He had set a trap, and he must abide by what he had caught in it, and so must she. Very softly he had insinuated that innocent-seeming question into the edge of her consciousness, and very softly had accepted the implications of her reply. That was his method, and she could not be responsible for this or any other act of his. He was a free agent.

She knew at once that he would not ask her anything more, would assure himself there was no more he needed to know, and her, if she was such a fool as to tax him, that he had never tried to surprise anything out of her, that she was imagining things. He would smile and put her in an impossible position with a gaiety and lightness he never had while he was sincere, his eyes all the while fixed in that raging, hating stare, calling her liar and cheat. He would drag her into the roundabout of deceit and complication and stifling cross-purpose of which she had sickened and rid herself, the witches'-dance which second-rate civilisation had made of enmity as surely as of love. No, she thought, I won't play your game, Jonathan; not even you shall find it possible to tangle me up in that kind of grand chain again.

'Why are you looking at me like that?' he asked, smiling at her from his narrowed eyes. 'Are you waiting for me to surrender gracefully? – sign it, maybe, and kiss your hand on it?'

'I am waiting for you to go,' said Claire.

He was startled, perhaps because she had said it at all, perhaps because she had said it so simply, without anger or anxiety that he could detect. But he continued to smile.

'Yes, I've been inconsiderate. I don't want to be in your way,' he said. 'I'll go now.' He turned from her with a long, laborious withdrawal, as if he drew out the spear with which he had thrust her through. She rose, and stood watching him until his hand was upon the door, and then she said steadily:

'You'll not go away – I mean out of the country – without coming here again to say good-bye?'

'It isn't done so quickly as all that by a long way – not these days. Besides,' he said, looking back at her over his shoulder, 'I haven't decided yet. It will bear a bit of consideration, won't it? You've given me a good deal to think about tonight.'

'It's your problem,' she agreed equably.

'Still, I can see all the sides of it now. It won't be hard to work out what to do, now I've got everything clear in my mind.' His eyes flashed wide for a moment, burning upon her. 'Good night, Claire!' He was gone.

'Well, go home,' she said aloud after him. 'Go and find him there, go and find him snoring over the fire, and know what a vicious little fool you are. And tomorrow come back and crawl to me.'

She was sick and angry and sad, but it was past. He would soon have to put aside his darling theory that she had lied to him about Charles, that she had an assignation which she had chosen to hide in order to induce him to go quietly away to Australia and stop making a nuisance of himself. As though her life must revolve about him at all costs, and if not for love, then for hate or fear! But he could stalk home by the shadows waiting to see the living proof go by, and never an uncle on the road, and never an uncle at all until he walked into the hall at Ridge Farm and found him with his old coat on and his feet in the hearth. He would be confounded, he might even, in a small way, be ashamed. The damage, at least, would be undone. She found herself tired. It was difficult to care very much, but at any rate he would know without any word or effort from her that he had made a fool of himself this time. It might even occur to him that it was not the first occasion.

She had not been alone longer than ten minutes when Charles Kenton let himself in by the front door and came to her through the hall. He wondered why she gave him so short and blank a stare as he entered, and then laid down her pen and began to laugh in so helpless and exasperated a fashion.

'What's the matter?' he asked. 'What's so funny?'

'Just that you're even more inopportune than usual. Have you seen Jonathan? He left here only a short while ago. Did you meet him?' She leaned back with a sigh. 'But you did. Of course you did. Oh, God, why can't we do better than this?'

Charles was staring at her, but he had learned to let her act strangely when she pleased, and think no more of it after her mood changed; for whatever puzzled him was bound to be a mood.

'We ran full tilt into each other in the lane,' he said. 'What's been happening. Claire? He looks as black as thunder. Has he been pestering you?'

She shook her head. 'Let him alone. Did he have anything to say to you just now?'

'He did, damn him! I gather he's also been having quite a lot to say to you. Good God, Claire—!' He halted, staring at her wide-eyed across the table. 'It wasn't from you he took the advice, was it?'

'What advice?' she asked, looking back at him wearily.

'Oh, if you don't know about it, never mind. I knew you wouldn't have put him up to it, anyhow. It's just an offer I made him, in the way of business—'

He saw the tremor of a smile shake her lips. 'A generous offer, Charles?'

'To both of us, I thought, but it was what he's been bleating for ever since he came home. I thought he'd have jumped at it, but instead he's been staving off answering all the week, and just now he brought up the offer himself in the middle of School Lane for the pleasure of turning it down cold in about ten words, and without thanks. What the devil's got into him?'

'A conviction that you and I are in a conspiracy against him,' said Claire. 'That's all, and that's more than enough. I hope you were suitably casual about it?'

'I was too surprised to be anything else. I just said: "All right, then, stay and be damned!" and came on.'

'That was all you could do,' said Claire, 'all anyone could have done.'

Yet she foresaw the damnation of more than one person emerging from this jungle of misunderstanding in which they floundered. How could they hope to come out of it unscarred? They had not even community of language; what the heart spoke the ears translated at best haltingly, and at worst treacherously. Every good intention grew to a winding briar of thorns, every affection to an encumbering narcotic vine. The truth is, she said to herself in her weariness, that I am the source of all this confusion and pain. I have schooled myself so willingly in the ways of approach to one creature that I've lost contact with all the rest. I am so content to be in sympathy with him that I am become a stranger among the others.

XII

THE TRIAL OF SALATHIEL DRURY

Here continues Claire Falchion's manuscript:

There was a Gaol Delivery holden at Friary Shalford that year for the county, upon a Commission of the 6th day of June, the Delivery beginning late in July, upon the 25th of the month, so that Salathiel Drury lay not so long awaiting trial as many have done. Yet though his time within the gaol had been but four months and a half it was observed of him by those curious persons who were present at his indictment that he was greatly changed, not less so than many after years of imprisonment. This was the more striking as no man had visited him during this time; for the girl Elizabeth Flint had taken counsel with Master Fox upon the peril of her soul if she should continue to respect and comfort one so deep in league with evil, and being advised she should not go to him, but exercise herself in prayer privately for her spiritual deliverance out of his affection, she had so done most assiduously, to her great calm and consolation. Nor had any other creature in Sunderne seen fit to go near him, for there was but one who would fain have done so, and she for her life dared not, lest she should upon some stray word overheard between them betray herself and deliver him. Therefore at his coming into the court there went up a great murmur and sigh, seeing how God had wrought hardly with His enemy. His hair which had been ever dark and profuse was now very ill clipped at his own hands, for it had been verminous, and there were in it certain streaks and flashes of white. He was much fallen from his goodly state of the flesh, very gaunt and pale, and marred by broken sores upon his neck and hands. His walk was halt upon the left foot by reason of an ankle gall, for he had been in ill repute with the gaolers because they complained that he despised them, and having him in their hold they had used him accordingly. These men were much offended at his arrogant bearing and silences, and his manner of reviling them foully before their charges when he could be provoked out of silence; for they knew his blood, that he was of no quality to warrant him the liberties of a gentleman. And therefore they had gone about with all the means at their dispose to make his captivity very evil to him, but grumbled among themselves that he had not been left longer among them, for they should have brought him to be civil had they had him for the leave of the year.

Such he was when he was indicted before the grand jury upon these two charges here following:

Indictment the first:
The Jurors for the Lord the King do present that Salathiel Drury, late of Sunderne in the county aforesaid, not having the fear of God before his eyes, but being moved and seduced by the instigation of the devil, by the devilish arts of witchcraft, on 20 Jan. II Chas. I and divers days and places as well before as afterwards at Sunderne aforesaid, a certain Nicholas Shenstone, gentleman, did bewitch and enchant, by reason of which the said Nicholas Shenstone did languish until II March, II Chas. I when he died at Sunderne aforesaid. Wherefore the Jurors aforesaid do affirm that the said Salathiel by enchantment and witchcraft aforesaid, the day, year and place aforesaid, feloniously did kill and murder the said Nicholas against the peace of the said lord the King, his crown and dignity, and against the form of the statute in this case made and provided, & c.

Indictment the second:
The Jurors for the lord the King do present that Salathiel Drury, late of Sunderne in the county aforesaid,

clerk, not having the fear of God before his eyes, but being moved and seduced by the instigation of the devil, on 20 Jan. II Chas. I and diverse days as well before as after at Sunderne aforesaid, feloniously and wickedly did entertain, govern and employ certain evil and wicked spirits in the likenesses the one of a white hare, the other of a female dog of a dun colour, with the intent and purpose that he, the said Salathiel, by the aid of the said spirits certain evil and devilish arts called witchcrafts might use and practise against the peace of the said lord the King, his crown and dignity, and against the form of the statute in this case made and provided, & c.

Upon both these the grand jury could not well do other than find a true bill, seeing the volume of depositions against him was then sufficient to bring a dozen men to trial. Wherefore he was duly arraigned upon the day following, and a day was fixed when the case should come on, which was but four days more he had to wait. And on the day fixed he came into court before one of the Judges of Common Bench, one Sir William Thurley, which was a small, shrivelled, dainty gentleman, very careful of his herbs and his pomander, being desperate afraid of fevers. He was scented all over with rosemary and lavender, and smelled very sweet, besides being delicate as a flower to look upon, for he was particular of his person and very elegantly clothed. It was known of him that he had hanged already a score of witches, though his care was ever to be at the truth in the case, and his record was not an ill one; for it was so with him, that he had himself been made the target of more than one attempted ill-wishing, and kept among his possessions a wax doll which had done secret duty for him at a rite it was not in nature he should forget. As bound in justice he had abjured all part in judging the witch who had so used him, but the shadow of danger was ever in his mind, so that he was grown something chary of believing the innocence of man or woman once so charged.

He was wont to instruct the petty juries that sat under him that they should look first for motive, and only upon unmistakable witness convict any suspected witch where there was not matter to be gained, either in goods or vengeance; for it was his maxim that your wizard or witch is a creature of shrewd reason, and must so be judged. Yet he believed that the disciples of the devil were many and with power, and was intent to stamp them out wheresoever they crossed his path.

This worthy judge had not been informed of the circumstances of the case, nor was he acquainted with more than the name of Master Shenstone; and upon his first examination of Salathiel as he came into the court he thought him but a surly creature, not of an intelligence to mark him out for a practitioner of parts, but ill-conditioned enough to have tried his hand at a matter past his skill. As for the prisoner's judgement of his judge, at a later hour it was made manifest.

Now when Salathiel was brought in before this Sir William he saw there all those witnesses who had laid depositions against him, Master Fox, Elias Weelkes, the boys Scholefield, Chittam and Frennet, the two young women whose names were not even known to him, the labourer's wife now delivered, and with all these Elizabeth sitting, and Mary Butterworth beside her. Nor was it any way unexpected to him to behold these two so close and kind, though it added gall to his wounds, for Mary leaned friendly towards the girl, and seemed to encourage her as well as she might to look up and endure the sight of him. Yet Elizabeth kept her eyes cast down, and when she must raise her lashes gazed but straight before her, careful for her own repute because it had been urged upon her from more than one quarter that she must not appear to be linked by any especial kindness to the evildoer. Such was his meeting with her after four months of separation and silence.

The form of the indictment being read, namely the former of the two, upon which was made the charge of murder, it was required of the prisoner how he would plead to it. He replied in a strong, harsh voice that he would plead not guilty, and would maintain it with his life; whereby they all perceived that his spirit was yet unbroken, and he would fight tooth and nail upon this charge. But at this stage he continued, except when thus addressed, silent and still in face of all the tales they made against him, being intent to waste no effort upon unneedful things, but save all his energies for such moments of struggle as might seem to him vital. Yet there was that quality in his voice which his looks had not upon immediate observance shown, so that the Judge was moved to more curiosity than hitherto, and put to him a few questions concerning his situation, not altogether unkindly.

'Well, it shall be my charge,' says he, 'that you shall be given every chance to uphold this proper plea. Are you a man of learning, Salathiel Drury, that are here, I see, set down as clerk?'

Says Salathiel: 'My lord, I am a schoolmaster to the village of Sunderne, under Shenstone patronage. I have been accounted fairly read, and of my record I am not ashamed.'

'That is well said,' replied the Judge, 'if your plea be made upon a good conscience. But no doubt it shall presently appear. I am the sorrier that a man of your wit should be here in this situation.'

'And I, having wit,' said Salathiel, grim, 'am the sorrier to be here.'

'And do you,' says he, 'place yourself upon your country and this court with confidence to have justice?'

'I place myself,' said Salathiel, 'upon this court with as much confidence to have justice as a man may well have who must needs lean upon other men. If it is not great it is all I can muster.'

At this the Judge was somewhat taken aback, and marked him the more narrowly thereafter. 'What, then,' says he, mildly still, 'have you not in your experience thought well of humanity?'

'Has any man of wit at five and forty got any better than

disappointment of his fellows? I know not if my weight be more than another's, but I have not yet known man or woman could continue upright with my hand upon his shoulder. If your lordship's fortune has been happier than mine I am glad of it.'

'Well, well!' said the Judge. 'Let us proceed. I will have the first witness sworn.'

Mary Butterworth therefore rose in her place meekly when she was called, and was sworn most piously to speak the truth as in God's sight. Her information was already put in as evidence, and the Judge had it before him, but he required of her that she should repeat the story in full, in order as it had befallen. This she did, being by this time perfect in it, even to the niceties of fear and distress, where to pause and where to heave a sigh, and where to falter upon Elizabeth's name. The Judge said but a word here and there to direct the flow of her words and encourage her, which he could not well perceive was very little needed; and there was silence among the hearers but for a shiver or a murmur now and again, when she came to matter for horror. When she was done, she let fall her lashes and stood as it were trembling, for indeed it was no light story to tell, having all the weight of her love and hatred in it.

'Well, Mary Butterworth,' said the Judge then, 'you make a good clear story as ever I heard told. Now answer me to this upon your oath, have you any malice in you against this man?'

She said: 'As God sees me, my lord, none.'

'Have you any private end or vengeance to serve by bringing his life into peril?'

She answered meekly: 'Sir, I can but swear upon my own part that I have none. Yet this is not to the purpose if it comes from no lips but mine. I entreat you, therefore, examine others and not me of this thing, and they shall say if I had ever complaint to make of him while I was his servant, or gave him less than my best.'

The Judge mused a moment, flicking his quill. 'There is

one other matter concerning your own conduct. You are a maid, and of good repute among your neighbours; yet you endured to remain in the prisoner's service after you confess you had seen sights not lightly to be supported. How was it you did not take yourself away with all speed out of the place of evil, for fear of your soul's cost if not of your body's? Were you threatened that you should keep silence and accept all under pain of some curious injury?'

Mary replied, but in some hesitation: 'No, sir. These times were far between, and he cannot have supposed I had observed anything strange, of that I am well assured.'

'Why, then, having confessed to superstitious fears however brief and rare, why did you remain?'

She drooped her head and answered him in a low voice: 'My lord, I had yet hopes to be stronger than he, if God would give me the victory. But my prayers did not avail to draw him back.'

At this there went over the prisoner's face a spasm as of a silent laugh, or it might have been an onset of pain, but it passed as it came, and few marked it, and none looked for a reason in it.

'There is a time for devotion, no doubt,' said the Judge, 'but when the soul approaches near to damnation, that is no such time.'

'My lord, I confess it, and thank God I am come whole out of it.'

'And now,' said he, having the rotting gloves of Master Nicholas in his hand, now stiff and blackened as though they had been tarred, 'for these gloves, are you absolute they are the same you saw in the prisoner's keep, the same Master Shenstone left behind him?'

'I am perfect, my lord, they are none other. There be others can speak to them even more surely than I.'

'They shall do so. How comes it you had knowledge these might be used against the owner, his life? It is not for a maid to be learned in such matters.'

'Nor was I, sir. I knew only that I had heard clothing could be so used, but never knew how the thing was done, nor wished to know. Recollect I thought no more of it at the time, but on the old man's death the quarrel and the gloves together came back into my mind.'

'It is well seen they might so come back,' allowed the Judge. 'And now, Salathiel Drury, have you any question to put to the witness before she stand down?'

Now all eyes turned upon the prisoner, and looked for some feeling in him, but he continued as iron, both grey and calm, saying only: 'My lord, with your goodwill I have.'

'You may proceed,' said the Judge, 'and do you, jurors, pay attention as well to these answers as those she made to me.'

Then Salathiel rose, and stood looking upon his meek mistress and terrible enemy across the heads of the people, and she let her lashes lie upon her cheeks under his look, and knit her hands as if she leaned upon prayer for her strength; but ever she fed her eyes upon him secretly, and his misery which he would show to no man was not hid from her. Nor was she at this moment more afraid than when first she tested her tale, though a word astray might undo all, and his wit was not so blunted that she could well afford to despise him yet.

'You have spoken,' he said slowly, 'of a quarrel, repeating Master Shenstone's words and mine. The court well remembers what those words were. Where stood we when they passed between us?'

She had looked for something more sudden and hot, but she replied, continuing wary: 'Master Shenstone came forth from the library, and you at his heels, and spoke these words in the hall.'

'And where were you at that time?' he pursued.

'In my kitchen, sir, and at work with my dishes.'

'And where stands the kitchen of my house from the hall? For bear in mind not all have seen it as we have.'

'There is a short passage off the hall, and the kitchen door is a yard or two within upon the right-hand side.'

'And a door also between the hall and the passage?'

'Yes, a heavy door.'

'Yet, with two doors between, and the clashing of your dishes atop, you are word-perfect in a conversation passing in the hall. How can this be?'

She said, looking at him fixedly through her lashes: 'Both of these doors were standing open. I could not choose but hear. I would I had never heard.'

'Yet if the doors stood open it was your hand set them so, madam. For what reason? Was it so hot upon a January day at the coming of the worst frost of the year, that you needed your door open to get your due of air?'

At this all the court murmured, but she only drooped her eyelids anew, and looked as one unjustly reproved; and when there was silence again and all watched her she was ready to reply. 'It was but a few minutes before the words passed,' she said, 'that I was called to the door to take in a letter brought for you from London, as well you remember, the same letter which sent you off hotfoot that very night to bring home Mistress Flint. Being warned this letter was urgent, and yet unwilling to break in upon your talk with Master Shenstone, I set both the doors open that I might hear when you came forth, and so put it in your hands as soon as he was gone. As you shall yourself bear witness I did.'

'Yet that was not your reason,' said Salathiel. 'Have you not spied on me and stored up my words against such a day as this? Have not doors stood open for you many a time that you might hear what was not meant for you?'

'Not so!' she said, breaking gently into tears. 'I have never done you any ill-service, nor wished you harm, but I am upon oath and must speak truly though I die for it.'

'It is not you will die for it,' said Salathiel, very grim.

Said the Judge: 'Is this to the purpose? What shall you show by it?'

'I trust, my lord, I shall make it plain this woman is full of that malice toward me which she has denied, and that from malice she has raised this evil wind against me. Also there are other things may appear. I shall not persist longer than you permit, sir.'

'I see no harm,' said the Judge. 'Continue.'

'Now for the words which were so overheard, have they not been made too much of? May not one angry man damn another, and escape suspicion of his death? Is this enough to build a charge upon, if this be all? Mary Butterworth, do you ask this court to believe in a hate to the point of murder, and the only outward sign of it a single bitter answer?'

'It was not the only sign,' she said, 'though it was the last.'

'What, you have heard us quarrel more than once, have you?'

'I have heard high words between you often enough, though I marked none so narrowly as this.'

'Yet enough to assure you I hated him to the death?'

'God forgive you,' she said, 'I believe you did so hate him.'

'And all this passed upon his frequent visits to me?'

'I do not know what may have passed between you abroad.'

'But you know what chanced at home. Yet the library has a well-set door, and I stake my life this door at least was shut, and ever shut, when we talked within. Was your ear so ready at the keyhole, Mary, that even so we had no privacy?'

'I have heard,' she said, breathing fast, 'only what has been so cried out that I could not but hear. Angry men do not speak low.'

'Well,' he said, 'let it pass at that. So you maintain, do you not, that we quarrelled as often as we met, and spared no wind to rend each other?'

'It is but true,' she answered. 'So it was you lived.'

'Yet we did live, ay, both of us, and bore with each other sixteen years without or death or anger parting us. Looks this like hatred? And would you have sane men believe one of us a murderer upon such a slight falling-out as you admit, upon your own witness, was the common coin of our exchange for sixteen years?'

She looked back unshaken, and answered him: 'How dare

I aver it cannot be so? I have told what I heard, and it is well known what followed it.'

Seeing she was not to be hurried into a rash answer, nor so driven as to be unable to answer at all, he left this point and went on to other matter, trying if by unexpected questions he might not draw her into a lie which might be seen to be a lie; but ever she held to her story and would add no new detail however he tempted her, so that she showed dull, patient and virtuous, by no means capable of so monstrous a fantasy as he strove to show in her. Yet there appeared in him as inexhaustible an endurance, so that those who watched and murmured at this struggle between them knew not what to believe. But as the time wore on the dark of weariness came on Salathiel, for he was weak and sick, and she showed but the stronger. And ever as their eyes met it was as if they two were in the room alone, so did they wrestle together. In the matter of the gloves he made her answer to the charge that they had been entrusted to her to redeliver; but this she denied so steadfastly that having her good repute before him the most honest of judges must needs have taken her word for it. As for the Sunderne people, they were come to hear no arguments but upon one side, and began to be angry that she should so be dragged back and forth through her own tale, and more than once there was brief but urgent outcry against the wizard that he went about to undo an innocent woman. All this the Judge made haste to quell ere it grew out of hand; but seeing how bitter was the feeling in them he adjured Salathiel to be brief if he might so serve his purpose.

Said Salathiel then: 'My lord, I have done.'

After Mary was seated came up one by one those women and boys who had sworn to seeing the familiars about him, and those other matters not good to be spoken of; and to the first such evidence which was offered, being that of Beavis Frennet, he objected, first, that the witness was not yet arrived at the age of discretion appointed by law, being fourteen years, but the Judge answered weightily that though in all other criminal trials whatsoever this was indeed so, in cases of witchcraft children of tenderer years might testify, having the permission of the Bench, which he here saw fit to grant. The child proceeding, and that with eagerness, upon his description of those grave things he had seen about the Schoolhouse, Salathiel again objected that this evidence was material only to the second indictment, which was not then before the court; but again it was held against him that the boy's tale was to the purpose, since it sought to show that he had the aid of uncanny creatures about him to help him to the means of magical murder whenever he should conceive the intention. By the same token did all the rest in turn swear their imagined terrors to be true, and Salathiel stood mute and let all this pass before him without question, well knowing there was nothing here he could turn to his favour better than by denying it when the time should come. Only when the labourer's wife, very rosy and fair, stood up to testify how he had bewitched her burden, he put certain questions to her.

'I see,' he said, 'you are happily delivered of this anxiety. What issue have you? A man child?'

She stared at him and flushed, hesitating to answer from fear of him, as if Satan had risen to question her face to face.

'Come!' said the Judge. 'You may answer without fear, and should not scruple to avow what is matter for just pride.'

Then she said, holding fast to the bench before her for awe: 'It is a boy.'

'Hard fate indeed to have an ugly, misshapen son, a monster,' he said. 'Do your neighbours mark crosses against their thighs as they go by him? In what shape did he come, crooked, or miscoloured, or having two noses?'

She cried: 'My boy is as straight as any ever I saw, and properly made, too.'

'Why, then,' says Salathiel, 'it seems you speak out of turn in saying I or any man ill-wished him in your womb. Confess it, you have been in grave error.'

'I know well it was by you I was troubled,' she said, now hot and triumphant, 'for the night we had the swimming of you in Sunderne Pool I made good sure I got my nails in your face, and from the same night I was easy in my mind, and knew the overlooking was took off. I never drew blood from any other, man or woman, but the child came fair and right from the time God led me to bleed you.'

Now at this, all the more seeing it came in good faith, he was secretly afraid, for he had thought to get at least one small seed of doubt out of her, knowing her honest. Yet to labour upon this was but to fix it more surely against him, therefore he said only: 'Yet, my lord, it cannot well be proved there was ever any such ill-wishing but in this woman's sick mind.' Having so said, he let her go, but by faces and eyes about him he well knew the moment had turned against him. Nor did he speak again until Elizabeth was called, when he raised his head and fixed her dreadfully and hopefully with his sunken wild eyes, though he knew she could not either kill or save him, and what he looked for from her was at once more and less than life. She rose slowly when her name was spoken, and took the oath in a voice so low they had to strain to hear her, and in the same tone went through her story. Her eyes she kept most resolutely cast down from the prisoner, and said not one word beyond what she must; and ever Salathiel fixed her as he would have the heart out of her for a salve against his anguish, so that he could not bear it that she gave him no look nor word, and still he must go in doubt how she thought of him. At the end she would gladly have slipped away and hid herself again, but it was more than he could endure to lose sight of her so with her eyes fallen before his and no touch nor communion between them.

'My lord,' he said, and his voice was shaken, 'I would question the witness.'

'It is your right,' said the Judge. 'Mistress Flint, we must keep you yet a moment, it seems.'

'It need not be longer,' said Salathiel.

She stood as one waiting to be slain, her hands knit under her breast and her face like marble, the lids hiding her eyes.

'I cannot speak with you,' said Salathiel, 'if you will not

231

look at me. Look up, and do not fear to show me whatever you hide in your lashes, for I shall abide it and make no complaint. Moreover it is not fitting you should avoid any man's eyes for fear, and I know no cause you have to do so for shame. Do me this justice, Elizabeth, to face me honourably.'

Hearing his voice so gentle and cold, the one thing in him which remained as she had remembered it, she was a little charmed to lean to him, and so looked up. Until this she had observed only so much of his misery and degradation as could be gleaned by sidelong glances, but now she stood face to face with the whole of it, and it swept over her like a wave of the sea, snatching the breath out of her. She pressed her hands tightly under her heart, and her eyes clung in horror upon his streaked hair and hollow face; nor could she release herself from his devouring stare once she had fixed upon it, but so hung as suffocating in the love and desire of his eyes. For so it was, that his flesh at this pass yet ached towards its own.

Then he asked her those questions no man had looked for, such as had lain in him without an answer four months and more, and could be put to her only here before the eyes of his enemies; nor for his life could he forbear.

'Elizabeth,' he said, 'since I was taken away, has all been well with you? Have they used you with gentleness now I am not by? Say to me that you are not companionless.'

She answered in a voice which came to him but as a frightened breath: 'I am well, and Mary is with me.'

He put his hands up suddenly and hid his face, crushing within his lips the laughter which arose in him at the name of her comforter; and on his wrists she saw the weals of irons raw and brown, and shivered at the sight.

'No man,' he said when he could again speak, 'has offered you insult? There is no enmity against you?'

'I thank God, no,' she said, faltering.

'Why, so do I, from my heart. Do not go from me, Elizabeth, I have yet a thing to say.' And as she stood before him shrinking and eager to be gone, yet held fast by the eyes and unable to release herself, he was silent, feeling for that thing he would say.

'It seems to me we are astray,' said the Judge. 'I will not hurry you, Salathiel Drury, but we must touch only the matter in hand.'

'Bear with me, my lord,' said Salathiel, groaning, 'for this child is dear to me, and I have not set eyes on her since this accursed business began. My tongue knows her speech less well than once, and this heat turns my brain to a running gall. Let me have but a minute more, and I have done.'

Said the Judge: 'Well, so be it.'

After a moment of stillness then he looked upon her again, and she was braced to sustain his gaze, though with labour and pain.

'Elizabeth,' he said, 'you have been in my care, and you were to me as a daughter or a young sister. Say now if of yourself, and not being prompted by another, you ever saw reason to believe there was any guilt of witchcraft in me.'

Now it was not for her word before the court he pleaded, but only for her firm assurance to him, but this she could not know; and being aware of Judge and jury waiting for her reply she was in great uneasiness lest by satisfying Salathiel she should arouse in others what she marvelled she had so far escaped, suspicion that she herself was not without taint of his disease. To be come from this household was in itself dangerous, and she was grown perceptive of danger. Yet it was out of her courage to stand face to face with him and denounce him outright. She looked about her wildly, and her eyes came back to his face, finding no other place to rest. She broke into tears, and cried out:

'The cross! I cannot forget the cross!'

'Nor can I,' he said with great heaviness, looking upon her steadfastly still though his hope in her was fast ebbing. 'Remember it, then, if you must, but remember also my words to you thereafter. Let there be what darkness there will upon me, but by God I have not been dark to you. Look at me but once more full, look into me and see if I have any secret from you. Or if you see only the devil's mark between my eyes, so tell me roundly, for you should speak out your mind as freely as any creature living. If I have no claim to any other gift of you I can at least make me a title to your truth, whether it heal or kill me. Answer me faithfully, and for pity at least do not let me see you fear me: do you believe this thing they bring against me?'

She said, shuddering: 'How can I answer? The case is not yet above half-heard.'

'With you it is judged,' he cried, 'and I will be answered. Do you believe it?'

There began to be a murmur and outcry around them, angry voices muttering first and shouting after that the wizard was about his devil's work even in their midst, and the maid would be stricken and wither before his eyes. The Judge raised his hands and his voice against the clamour, but not Elizabeth and not Salathiel cared for it or verily heard it. Against her will she was held and wrung by monstrous terror of him, and leaned back and cast herself about to be free of his eyes, but could not get any ease of him, only so wrenched at his barb in her as to turn it in the wound and rend her own heart. In extremity of fear she flung up her hands between them with fingers crossed and rigid to break the transfixing stare he set upon her. He saw the sign made against him that was to him beyond damnation, that if she had made her avowal loud and clear she could not have blasted him worse than by this motion of her flung hands. He gave a wailing cry, not loud but as the wind cries of a winter night in the cold and the loneliness of an open place; and shrinking together so that he seemed to dwindle and grow older in the slow passing of that lamentable sound, he covered his face, never again to see how she warded him off, nor hurt her with his basilisk looks which so destroyed all they dwelt upon. And from that moment there was broken the one strength in him which had warmth in it and could bleed, and all that sustained him after was as iron or stone.

As for the girl, it was Mary Butterworth who went to her

and assisted her, bringing her to sit quietly leaning upon her shoulder with shut eyes and fallen hair, in extreme weariness. There was no more passage between them, nor looks struggling in the mid of the air. After this time these two let each other be, and never crossed again but once, and that by malignant fortune.

So this trial went on, one testifying to the prisoner's witchmark and the finding of it, another to the exact hour of Master Nicholas's death and the course of the cycles of his sickness before he died; and only once more did Salathiel, until he himself was called, uncover his face and rise to do battle again for his life. The physician who had attended Master Nicholas swore so lightly against him that all the instinct remaining at this time alive in him was stung to guard itself, and he lifted up and showed them a ghastly face, the skin strained bone-white back from the pits of his eyes, and his mouth as the dry, healed scar of a knife-wound, thin and miscoloured. When he spoke all the court fell silent before the change in him, for even his voice was become as iron roughly rung, so that they whispered among themselves that the devil his master was strong in him again, and would yet show fight.

'My lord,' he said, 'this cannot pass. Yet once give me leave to examine.'

'Do so,' said the Judge, but with no great goodwill, for he was growing weary.

'Master doctor,' says Salathiel, turning upon him his fearsome visage, 'did you not in your wisdom report of Master Nicholas that he was fallen of a seizure three times, as is the nature of this evil, and at the third fit died?'

'Such was the apparent form of his death,' said the doctor in a loud and peremptory voice, for he was a man accustomed to reverence, and not to be questioned.

'Have you known many men die after the like fashion?'

'Enough,' said he.

'Is it not, then, a manner of dying out of the nature of man?'

'In the circumstances of life and age conducive to it,

certainly it is known and natural.'

'Why, then, look for this foolery and knavery of ill-wishing and rotting gloves behind a natural death? Do you dare say he could not so have died had we all been faithfully on our knees for him day and night, and no gloves in the ground, neither?'

'He could,' said the doctor, 'yet the gloves were in the ground, and there was ill-will, too, as it was the duty of others to show. My part is only to assert that it is within my experience, and is manifest here, that witchcraft may compel the processes of nature itself, even of death in form wholly natural; and so I do assert. Though Master Nicholas was a man to whom such a visitation might well have come at this very time and in the clear way of nature, yet that makes it but the more conceivable that this vile and accursed art has employed the self-same device to cover its guilt. So I read the signs.'

'It is well seen,' said Salathiel, 'that you do well to read them so when your patients die under your hands. Yet by the same charm, and even upon your own reasoning, this world is full of witches all bent upon murder, and more competent in their business than you in yours, for in the nature of things all men die. And it behoves you all, it seems, who find grey hairs coming upon you, to look about you for the miscreant who has bewitched you to old age. Be not put off by the consideration that wrinkles overtake us every one, but get blood of your neighbours, and see if you grow not young and fair again. And for you, sir,' he said to the doctor, who stood speechless for wrath, 'you will do well to look for the enemy who compelled the processes of nature and charmed you to so monstrous a stupidity.'

'Enough!' said the Judge. 'You exceed your rights and my patience. Have you further questions to put to the witness?'

'He has said all I trusted he would say, my lord, and I have done.'

It was but a short while after that he himself was called to testify, and taking the oath with violent quietness he began

236

to tell his own story. He told how little he knew of Master Nicholas's disease, and how unthinkingly his life had continued in its equal pattern while those events went forward which were to bring life and all in peril, how he had received the news of the old man's death as innocently as any man in the village, and thought no manner of evil until after midnight the mob came battering at his door. He stood stoutly upon his anger in the matter of the cross as a man's right rage who finds himself so misused in his own house, and would not abate the heat of it then nor make apology now for all the penalties known to the law. Moreover he made bold delivery how he was not only no witch himself, but no believer in witches, and so cried out against their credulity that many there present lowered their heads and durst not meet his eyes, for there was come back into him that quality which had ever made them afraid, and though he was gaunt and fallen from his lordliness he was yet their master.

'For this extremity in which I am set,' he said, 'it is the work of man, as I am, conceived in sin and brought to birth out of great pain. I have said malice has made it, and that guilt you may well leave, as I do, to God; but I bid you look to another guilt which lies very heavy against you all, without the human colour of malice about it, or the warmth of hatred, except as fear has made you to hate me. Look to it, for my life shall be required of you; and not mine only, but that of many another poor wretch done to death in this place before me. What, you are not ashamed to wear crosses against me, or make the same sign with your fingers secretly! Does it give you heart to invoke God for your mercenary, since you think so poorly of Him as to suppose He must be talked to in signs and through priests, and placated with humiliations wrought upon the sacredness of the body, His very image, dust and ashes emptied upon those temples He gave you to glorify with thought and crown with a crown? Do you think He will run to save you with the more diligence, the more you do insult His nature? As for me, for that in me which needs repentance I will repent upright, and with my eyes open; but as God sees me this sin of yours shall never be sin of mine. Does a cow die, or a crop fail, or a sickness come upon you, you cast about you for a scapegoat and kill him. You had far better set your mind to discover by what folly of your own or contendable stroke of nature comes the sickness or the death, or what failing of your care caused your sowing to go awry. It is the armour of littleness to cast the blame upon another creature. Do you suppose, you godly and virtuous, that God is flattered when you make him your ally in despoiling the manhood he gave you? I tell you roundly, we have indeed the making of heaven and of hell in us for other men, but not by these feeble devices of incantation and potion and spell, not by burying of garments nor piercing of waxen figures. Tell me again, it is proven, you have taken witches in the act, and they have confessed, still I tell you they as well as you are deceived. It is within their power to encompass the evil intent, to believe they do hurt, but it is not within their power to do the hurt itself, no, not to drop one hair nor raise one sigh of fever. Witchcraft is but a vapour in the mind, and nothing more. I do defy it; and if you will stand upon your faith, so will I on mine. Desire my death of whatsoever magical adept you will, bid every such creature loose his powers upon me, and see if I live or die. Can I stake more than my life?'

So saying, he cast his eyes over them all, and by that sole look made known to them all wordlessly how he despised them; for he was fallen, as he had said, by a sin which was not their sin.

'I am judged,' he said, 'and therefore I dare judge, and what crime I do commit in the judgment is out of your hands. Nor do I expect God to lean down out of His eminence and pluck me out of your hold, nor loose His thunders against you for my sake. What I am to Him He best knows, and as I suppose it is little enough, and not the least of His laws shall bend for it, nor the most passing moment of all His moments falter. But I shall keep my own soul though you hang my body, and if by all your ingenuity you ever wring any sound from me, be assured it is not of pleading nor regret, either to God or you. What I am I am, and I will abide it, it is the one load I cannot throw off; but never shall you get of me in the matter of this charge any withdrawing or any bending upon a false issue I do despise from my very marrow. What I am I am, but this I am not, and do most vehemently scorn to be. So deal with me as you think fit, it is yourselves you meddle with and spoil, for I am now and ever out of your reach. Now, my lord, you have borne with me long enough, and I am as weary of this rigmarole as you. So, make an end.'

At this the Judge looked upon him long and thoughtfully, divining as best he might what arrogance of Lucifer was this which could agonise publicly and yet so stand immovable upon defiance.

'Salathiel,' said he, 'I have but a few things, and brief, to ask of you, and you must bear with me as you say I have done with you. It is not for me to dispute with you as to the wisdom or folly of believing on witches. I am here to follow the law as it is laid down for me, even as you are here to abide it. Do you as absolutely deny the existence of incubus and succubus?'

'Sir,' said Salathiel, 'with my life.'

'And have never had knowledge of any such, neither in dreams nor waking?'

'Nor ever shall, even in Bedlam, my lord.'

'Well, so!' he said, and wrote slowly across the paper before him. 'Now as to this vexed matter of the gloves, you have seen and recognised them; you have said that you entrusted them to Mary Butterworth to return, and that you saw no more of them until they were shown to you in this their present state. How, then, do you suggest they came to be in the soil of Master Shenstone's garden, and for what purpose?'

'By what hand they were set there,' said Salathiel, 'I can no more safely hazard than can you, sir. As for the purpose, there can be but two to choose between. Either some enemy of his, as I swear I was none, was knave enough to design his death and fool enough to believe it could be brought about by these means; or some enemy of mine, as you see I have enough to spare one for the folly, planted them there to give weight to this whole case against me. It was in either event a malignant charm, and meant to procure a death.'

'And do you,' said the Judge, 'know of any such enemy, in his life or in yours?'

'In his, no, very surely none so hated him.'

'And you?'

'I am better hated than I knew, and I knew I was not loved.'

'Do you accuse any man by name?'

'I have said,' replied Salathiel firmly, 'that the chief witness against me is possessed with malice, and has lied to destroy me. Whether she has also gone to this added length she best knows. I can but make my own denial. I am not the keeper of her conscience.'

The Judge laid down his pen, and sitting back in his seat requested that Salathiel should say the Lord's prayer before them all.

'My prayers,' said Salathiel, 'are between God and me.'

'It is an acknowledged custom, of which you must know well, and the implication you must know as surely. I advise you should comply, in your own interest, for if you refuse it must be thought you fear the test.'

'So much I do perfectly understand,' replied Salathiel in the same tone, 'but until I have somewhat to say to heaven I will not pray, and when the time is right yet the words I use shall be of my choosing, and not you, my lord, nor any man or this company shall be by.'

'If you fear to be hurried,' said the Judge, 'and so to stumble even where you well know the way, rest assured you need not begin until you are ready. Only consent to attempt it, for recall your life may lean upon it.'

'I will not speak one word of it but in privacy and when my heart is moved to mean it, not for twenty lives.'

'Is your privilege with God so dear to you?' said the Judge, not without bitterness, for he believed this to be but a means of turning a danger to virtue and covering over a vulnerable place with a lie.

'Were I Moor or Jew and had the words by heart that meant nothing to me, I would not say them even then at your bidding. The end is the one thing sure after the beginning; my silence can but bring it a little sooner upon me. Will you, my lord, say me the same prayer backwards to avoid the magical death I may be moved to damn you with?'

Upon the uproar which then broke out upon him the Judge looked sternly, and with calm presence and lifted hand put it by at length. 'Do not think,' said he when he could again be heard, 'that I come unarmed to such an encounter as this. It is upon yourself you call down injury. But I see there is here, whatever be your condition, no penitence at all. Are you not afraid for your soul, since you do disavow the body? Remember the soul is eternal.'

'I have been reminded before this,' said Salathiel, 'that there is yet hell.' Nevertheless he set his hand against his heart, and there knotted it.

'How, have I troubled you?' said the Judge. 'It is not too late to consider on your soul, Salathiel.'

'God forbid,' cried the prisoner then in a great voice, 'that any part of me should survive that can be destroyed. Study how to end me, for I am sick of being.'

Thereafter, having uttered all his heart in this cry, he made for a long time no more sound, nor looked upon any man of them, but into the stones of the wall, and replied to direct question only when he must, and that with effort, as though he suffered pressing before their eyes and could but hardly draw breath to speak. And indeed he was in no case to endure readily so protracted a pain as was this day of heat and hatred to him, even though there had been some good hope at the end of it, and there was none.

There was now no more left to do but that the Judge should deliver his charge to the petty jury and require of them a verdict. He spoke long and equally, putting before them the substance of the case against Salathiel, but ever balancing it with the prisoner's denial and defence.

'In the matter of the chief material evidence,' said he, 'I

mean the gloves, you will take note it is not disputed they are the very same left behind at the Schoolhouse by Master Shenstone. Upon their ownership all are agreed, it is only on the point of how they came buried in the garden that there is dispute; and bear in mind, here there is no direct evidence to help you to decide. The witnesses confirm only that they were found in such circumstances as to show they had been used against the life of their owner. As to their last appearance before this discovery, there is conflict. The principal witness has sworn she last saw them in the keep of the prisoner; the prisoner states they were entrusted to her. You will weigh these sworn statements according to your judgement, and give credence as God shall direct your consciences. No man can do more.

'Now as for motive, there is certainly evidence of disagreement between these two men, and I am bound to say of a rebellious attitude in the prisoner not becoming in one owing service and allegiance, in particular toward a master against whom he can now allege no maltreatment nor abuse. He has said, as against this, that their relations were ever so, and it was well understood by both they should not be taken with overmuch gravity. This you will remember and weigh, as certainly the prisoner had been sixteen years in this employ, and with no very bad blood to show for it; yet consider also that upon this occasion there was a threat made, and the prisoner does not deny it, to be rid of him. What weight to set upon that you must settle in your own minds, but do so remembering all these considerations, and giving them their just share in your thoughts. Moreover, there is this very ill circumstance to be had in mind, that the dead man's first seizure followed within the hour upon the accused's threat of damnation loosed upon him as they parted. Of this illness you have heard it said the manner of it was natural to man, but it is for you to judge if the cause of it was beyond nature, and on this question you have heard the opinions of the physician who attended upon the sick man's bed.

'If you are satisfied upon all these counts that Master Shenstone was killed by witchcraft, of which his gloves were the agent; and if you hold that motive and means were ready to the accused's hand; yet you must consider if he had the knowledge to use that means. Was he, think you, proficient in the dark art, as one would need to be who planned so to make away with his patron? Here is the greatest and gravest weight of evidence. You have heard it sworn by seven separate witnesses that at the least he had sinister agreement with that deeper world into which God-fearing men do not dare to look. Five of these seven have sworn to beholding his familiars about him, one to personal danger from him which was relieved as soon as she drew blood of him, one to witnessing certain lights and dances in his garden, as of Sabbat or Esbat. One, and she his own servant, has taken her oath that he enjoyed a succubus which came to him, before putting on her loathly parody of woman, in the form others have seen in the more frequent of the two familiars. There has no cause been put forward why any of these should be discredited, though malice has been charged against one without reason or proof to back it. I do not say that a good repute may not cling about one who can, being human, hate and lie as roundly as another; that is a heavy part of your heavy duty to consider. Yet you cannot put that good repute out of your mind in assessing the right and wrong of this dispute.

'Again there is other matter, agreed by both sides, though with differing meaning. For my part, like one of these your witnesses, I cannot forget the cross. Anger is a livid thing, and steadfastly to be avoided, yet it is within the nature of man; and it may be, who shall say, that an innocent but violent man beholding himself so privily insulted to a dear member of his household, and she ignorantly consenting, might so act as this man says he acted, and so cry out, as he admits he cried: "There shall no God be invoked between us two." Do not reject his word upon this on the supposition that ordinary men neither say nor do so; for you have seen and heard him even here in passionate kind, and you must know that innocent or guilty he is a man of violence, whose deeds and words are his own, and wilful as he.

'You have, then, these points to answer within yourselves. Was the death of Master Shenstone brought about by ill arts, and if so, was the agency the gloves he had been wont to wear? Should you be satisfied upon this count, then what you are now considering is most surely murder, and in as rank a kind as ever was wrought. You must then examine the question, by whom were these gloves buried in that spot where they were found? As to this you have only evidence of ill-feeling, and the witness of time itself, the succession of events more mysterious than the march of season after season. It is for you, who have heard all that can be said, to decide whether there is evidence enough to bring home the deed to any man by name, and whether that man is he who here stands accused. As for his defence that witchcraft has no life but as a thing humankind has imagined to cover its weaknesses and loose its wickedness, I do not need to comment upon that deceitful belief, excepting only to point and say, these things have happened and men have seen them happen: the strong man has dwindled without disease, the corn has sickened without rust, the happy child has pined and the breed beast dried into barrenness, even in our own generation and within the knowledge of some here among us. If it be credulous to acknowledge what we have seen with our own eyes, I am credulous. Do not be led away into debate upon this bold challenge in doctrine, for it is not to the purpose here. You have as hard a thing to answer. Is this murder, and is this the murderer? If you conceive there is yet doubt, I charge you that you deliver him; but if you are sure that this is he who privily and treasonably killed his master, remember then upon your own lives the charge laid upon you: "Suffer not a witch to live."

'Go now, and consider and acquaint me with your verdict,' he said, ending, 'and may God be among your deliberations, and bring them to a right harbourage. Amen.'

244

Thereupon he arose and left the court, holding his
pomander to his nose as he passed among them, and wafting
of orange and cloves spiced the air after his going. The
jurymen also removed, and there was great stirring and
yawning of advocates and notaries and lawyers, likewise of
the crowd of the people, for they were much cramped with
so long stillness. The gaolers that kept Salathiel haled him
aside into a small chamber and let him sit upon a bench by
the wall until he should again be sent for; and the time being
wearily long and hot, the chief of them charged two
underlings that they should look to the prisoner, and himself
lay down and slept. Then these two, being young and
gamesome and not over-particular how they got their sport,
and soon tiring of their own company and his, for he was
silent, thought of a way to turn him to good account; and one
of them, passing among those of the crowd in court who had
money to pay for novelties, made known to them singly that
if they could be privy, and not grudge a consideration, they
might have sight of the witch more closely, and examine and
touch his devil's mark if they so desired, where the very
demons of his following had nursed. Nor were there wanting
some who ventured for the privilege, and boasted of it after.
These they brought in quietly by ones and twos to the cell
where he was, and holding him down against the wall with
his arms spread, cast open his shirt from his breast and made
an enforced show of him for every fool and knave who had a
groat to spare. So handled, he could not for weakness put
forth any great effort against them, but must suffer all, which
he did without word, shutting his mouth upon the extreme
of loathing and grief.

Now while this was toward, Elizabeth passed by going
towards the air, for she was faint, and the door being then
open, she saw him held so by the arms, and his head by the
hair thrust back to the wall, and his own blood smeared upon
his breast where the linen was drawn aside, and two or three
young gentlemen gaping, one of whom fingered the place.
Also his eyes, which alone he could then move, fell upon her

as she stood in horror and pity looking in upon him. There was but one moment they so held each other, and scarcely could he forbear to cry out on her with curses to get from him, for she had now cast him lower even than these his tormentors, when she so read his outraged silence and fled from him. Nor was there any bitterness for him that day so bitter as that pity of hers, for not less grievously would she have looked upon a fox torn by hounds, and it was like enough she would have remembered the fox longer. When she was returned in her distress to Mary Butterworth she told her what was come upon him, and with tears declared she could not but be sorry for him.

'That crime, at least,' said Mary Butterworth mildly, 'I have not committed.' But this reply Elizabeth did not mark, being so deep aghast in her own troubles.

So went the time until the jury, being in agreement, so signified to Sir William's clerk, and the court was again called. Then the two young gaolers rid themselves of their customers in such haste that the last got only a glimpse of bloody linen as it was drawn back and buttoned across Salathiel's breast, for with handling the mole was become a running wound. Yet they had him neat and ready enough by the time they must wake up the chief gaoler and lead him back into the court, and if he showed a little whiter and wilder than before, it was readily laid against the consideration that he was now come to a verdict nor he nor any man present could doubt. Therefore as he came limping back to the bar they eyed him one and all, and whispered together over him, but saw no more frenzy nor fear in him than before, and from the whitened bones of the jaws and his starting nostrils, that could not breathe in breath enough for cleanness or coolness, conceived him yet sullen and rebellious who struggled with principalities and powers they knew not of. They were right only in supposing that there was in him little of what they understood by fear, for he had been so used that he had nothing more to fear, and nothing to hope for, having experienced all the depth of pain which a man can compass in the mind, and had now only to discover the breadth and curiousness of man's endurance in the body.

When all were again in their places the Judge came in, stepping delicately but looking gravely and with a stern sadness, and settled himself in state, next inquiring of the petty jury if they were all in agreement upon their verdict, who replied that they were. He required thereupon that they should deliver it, and the court fell silent at that word, as they pronounced with solemnity that they found him guilty. Some attempt there was to signify gladness at such a verdict, as if God had given Sunderne the victory over an enemy, but the Judge cried out for silence in so dire a voice that they were subdued and made no more unseemly ado. Then at length he turned his sorrowful but severe regard upon Salathiel, who encountered that gaze upright and without a start, having received no blow he had not savoured long before.

'Salathiel Drury,' said the Judge, 'you have been given fair trial upon the charge brought against you, and have been held to be proven guilty. Have you anything more to say? It is allowed you to speak before a sentence, if you so desire, and you shall be heard with attention.'

Said Salathiel: 'What I have said is still what I would say, and there is but little to add. Have no fear, I shall utter no curses upon any who have part in destroying me. Time may avenge me, but heaven, I know, will not, and the course of the world is not likely to be deflected for me. If I were what I am judged to be you should all go sleepless and afraid from this on, looking for your own deaths to loose you; but well I know you will live on and flourish in virtue and stupidity and fat long after my neck is wrung, and I must swallow my gall and let you alone for want of that power you may smugly kill me for possessing. God knows you do affront His truth, but I believe He may not greatly care, and it is not inconceivable He is as helpless as I am to smear you into the ground and be relieved of you. Live, then, and time and circumstance may yet bring you into as raging a damnation as mine; for somewhere there may be a natural vengeance stored up that strikes with rottenness for lightnings, and comes about with the turn of the years and not momentarily upon a man's calling. To that hope I leave you all. And lastly,' he said, very low after this level speech, 'remember I said and say again that I am innocent. It is not a plea, it is a claim from which I will not retreat in life or death. I have not killed.'

Seeing that after this he was silent, the Judge said: 'You have finished?'

'My lord,' he said, 'I have and am finished.'

Then the Judge drew breath to give sentence, which was ever a dragging load to him, and came now upon the heels of more than ordinary weariness.

'Salathiel Drury,' he said, 'it is a very ill thing that a man of knowledge and scholarship, used honourably and trusted by a patron so noble as Master Shenstone, should after long years of duty so requite him as this court holds you have done; and all men must hold in the utmost detestation any man who does so. Unnatural servant, it is justice that death should be visited upon you for the death you visited upon him, and death you must undergo according to the form of the statute made and provided against such a case. Had the relationship from you to the murdered man been one of less honour and trust, or you an ignorant poor man favoured beyond your scope in his service, I might have been wrought upon to let pass that you were in his employ, and therefore doubly forbidden from all attempt against him. But you are the man you are, without plea of ignorance or lowness of spirit or misuse or enforcement, one so gifted by God as to owe more than most men in duty and faith. And so it is, that I may not forget he was through all your master. Your crime is therefore one of a gravity murder of itself does not bear. You have committed petty treason, and been convicted of it, and you must abide the penalty allotted. Salathiel Drury, I sentence you to be chained to a stake and burned alive until you be consumed and dead, according to the law relating to petty treason; and as is laid down by the particular law and custom of this county, I order that this be done in the public place nearest where the crime was committed of which you stand convicted, and under the jurisdiction of the Justices of that place. And may God Almighty show mercy on your soul in the day of His judgement.'

To this no man said Amen nor any other word, being in awe. And in silence and heavily the Judge went from the court with the load of the condemned man's face huge upon his mind, and so continued all that night with no more sleep than the prisoner himself had; for though he had no doubt in him the verdict was true and just, yet the coming death was but a second death to him, as wasteful as the first, and he had neither joy nor satisfaction from the contemplation of it.

Salathiel having received this awful pronouncement with unlowered head and mutely, looking full upon the Judge as he gave sentence, then submitted himself to the hands of his gaolers, and was led forth to return to prison. Yet his submission was such as he ever refuged in when he was past help for the mass and number of his enemies, and they were enraged at it still, for they knew it well, and having encountered it in every mean situation of ridicule and shame felt it still to be live and brimming and bitter with unbendable scorn of them. So also felt the people, and pressed upon him with gibes and triumphs to scourge where they were after given leave to kill, and his path to the doorway was between their joyous mockeries as between many whips. Beside the door, when he came there, was Mary Butterworth standing, and met him eye to eye. Her face was white half to translucency, as marble or pearl, and her mouth set as one who would weep if she had tears, but he saw her eyes under the modest lashes, how they triumphed over him to the death. Suddenly recoiling, he checked his limping walk an instant before her, and stared upon her as if he was minded to speak, but did not speak; and as silently passed by her close, their sleeves brushing lightly, and so was taken away. And then this trial was over.

XIII

A WITCH-BURNING

There was but one other death sentence passed at that Gaol
Delivery, and that upon a young man of Shalford for theft,
and therefore there was no reason for delaying execution
beyond the time needed for stake and pyre to be prepared,
and the faggots and resin well dried. So it was that Salathiel
was held but a day more before the day and hour of his death
was fixed and conveyed to him, and he had then but a week
of life left him. It was said of him after that he sat to receive
the news in a quietness as deep as if he had not understood,
or even heard, and then raised his eyes, which his gaoler ever
shunned to meet for they were sunk and far-looking and in
colour as coals burning out from red to black, and asked in a
commanding voice for ink and paper. Upon this they could
but gape upon him in surprise, supposing him to be a little
out of his wits for horror of his end; whereon the same vicious
impatience came on him which had made him terrible to fools
at the school in Sunderne, and he blazed forth:

'Dolts, what language is it I must speak to reach your
swinish understanding? If you are without power to grant,
have me to the governor who can, but do not cause me to
look down your gaping throats into your swilling bellies
because I ask you for so simple a thing. If you can neither
write nor read, you must credit me some of us can; and if
you desire to learn get me rods enough and, by God, in the
week left to me I will yet teach you.'

This fury at stupidity, or even at a slowness of response
born of fear or astonishment, he could never contain, and
had brought upon himself much evil he might have avoided

251

because his gorge so rose still at some who had absolute power over him. Yet since his condemnation they had been ordered to let him alone, for his doom was read, and had been willing to obey, for at bottom they were better-natured fellows than he; therefore being so raved against they forbore to wreak it upon him again, but went to the governor and confided what he would have. The governor being curious about him went himself to see him in the cell where he was held solitary, but got no dignity by it, for Salathiel remained seated at his coming in, and frowned upon him without welcome, as though his squalor had been an imperial solitude.

'Well, sir,' said the governor, somewhat offended by this black front, 'they tell me you are asking for the means of writing.'

'I did so ask,' says Salathiel, fixing him with a high, bright stare.

'What do you hope to do in this fashion?'

'Pass the time until I leave this place,' replied Salathiel no less briefly.

'How comes it then, sir,' said the governor smartly, 'that you make your request in such a fashion? You are more like to obtain if you ask with humility.'

'To obtain is certainly worth something,' said Salathiel, 'but it is not worth humility to me.'

Said the governor to the gaoler who was by him: 'How long has he been thus?'

'Sir, since yesterday when he was sentenced to death he has acted as one out of his mind, but always he was troublesome and very high of his bearing toward us. I did not think he would be so with you.'

'Do you not know, fellow,' said the governor again to Salathiel, 'that if you displease me I can make your life hideous to you?'

He wondered at the look that answered him, so did it wither his blood as a cold blast, utterly piercing through and beyond him without hindrance, as though he had been standing corn.

'I know, fellow,' said Salathiel, 'that you cannot make it more hideous to me than now it is. And well I know you cannot make it long.'

It was made plain by the bleak level of voice and eye that he had uttered not more nor less than truth, and therefore there was no means at hand to subdue or change him, and no profit in the attempt.

'Yet I marvel,' said the governor, 'that you do not make better friends with men in the week that is yet left you of your life, instead of going about to offend them more grossly against you.'

'To make better friends with men,' replied Salathiel, 'is to make better friends with life, and leave it the harder. Yet you are mistaken in me, for I do not go aside for you either to one hand or the other. Give or withhold, for that is in your power, but do not threaten me. What has a dead man to fear from you?'

So they let him alone, seeing him walled in from their spite or their compassion as in a tomb; but paper and ink and pens they gave him, thinking to have some record of a disordered mind after his execution, and it might even be a confession which should leave all beyond doubt. While the light in his cell sufficed he sat day by day constant with paper before him and pen in hand, and ever and again wrote a few lines in a flagging hand, as with infinite labour; and when the dark covered him he lay open-eyed all night long for an hour or it might be less of exhausted sleep toward the dawning. But as for confiding in any other living creature, or showing by speech or motion what passed within in his mind, there was none could claim he had ever done so; and it was the judgement of the chaplain who visited him upon his last night in Shalford Gaol that he was a soul utterly lost to the world, and no hand could hope to draw him back from the abyss. This worthy man had in his time received the last confidences and witnessed the penitent tears of many murderers, even within this same cell, and was well accustomed to dealing with all manner of fears and frenzies; but it was no way comprehended in his experience that he should be brought in and left standing before a frowning creature that pored upon a writing, and at last upon the piebald head being raised should meet a clouded and smouldering regard which gave him no better welcome than a shut purse does to a beggar. None the less for this inauspicious opening he did his devoir faithfully so long as he might, until Salathiel clapped to the book in his hands sudden as the spring of a cat, and bade him speak out of himself if he had aught within worth the utterance.

'Unhappy man,' said the chaplain, 'do you not know I am the mouthpiece of God?'

'From God's lips I will believe it,' said Salathiel, 'but not from yours.'

'You are surely possessed of demons,' said the chaplain in much sadness.

'Yet all is in God's hand, by your reasoning,' answered Salathiel wildly smiling, 'who possesses even the demons that do possess me. What need, then, have I of a go-between like you, who need only to commune with the seven devils that I have within me? Yet I will be pliant,' he said softly, 'and listen to my salvation. What is it you would have me do?'

Then the good man spoke to him of penitence and resignation, for neither of which was there room in his nature, and in especial begged him to ask forgiveness of such as he had offended against, beginning with the family of the dead man, and ending with Mary Butterworth, whom, said he, he had so unworthily abused in fear of his own life. Upon which suggestion Salathiel was taken with a horrible laughter, and held himself by the throat that he might the less ache and burn with it. The chaplain, believing this to be the wilfullest of blasphemies, and cast in the teeth of the Lord in the person of His proxy, cried out against him in wrath:

'Wretched man, I bid you beware of the pit of fire!'

'Only show me,' cried Salathiel, breasting his frightful mirth at this new irony as a tired swimmer the last wave that barely spares to drown, 'only show me how to avoid it, and I will so with all my heart. Is this God's message indeed, that I should beware of the pit of fire? Was it needful he should send you to me to urge me to shun burning? Go, fool, go to the Judge, the honest Judge who condemned me, go to the jury that convicted me, tell them I must not be cast into the pit of fire. Go, for by God I have been doomed to but one death, and you visit me with torments of fool's breath and sheep's virtue and humours I cannot bear. Get out of my sight and let me be in peace, for my demons are better company than your God.'

So very sorrowfully he went away from him; and Salathiel watched out the night after his going in an anguish unspeakable, no more touching pen nor uttering word, but moving back and forth in the dark of his cell to touch and feel at wall and bench and chain, and hear the rustle of his own steps, and gnaw upon his knuckles till they bled, who should presently touch and hear and taste no more. And in the morning came the executioner and his men to end his watch, in the early hours of a cloudy and unpleasing day.

There was at this time, when they brought him forth of the gaol and set him in the cart, some small wind blowing, but not so much as to cause any fear of storms, and it was said among those of the people who were come from Sunderne to accompany the cart that at home there would not be wind above what was needed to make the fire to burn, the faggots being not well dried. But as they went by the way, being some two hours about the journey, a modest rain began to fall, that caused them to make all haste, by reason of which untoward weather they stopped but once upon the way, at the Falcon Inn at East Manningholt, there to refresh themselves; and at this place there was a woman that worked about the house, and was generally held to be a natural, or as some say an innocent, not having her mind fully about her. This wench drinking with them, and seeing that the convicted man sat all this time in the cart between the constables with his hands tied according to custom, began to ask in her silly poor fashion why they did not bring him in and give him drink. Perceiving that she was not with sense to understand the case, they would not tell her the truth, but made game of her by urging she should show him some kindness, whereupon the natural took a pot of beer in her hand and went up to the cart to offer it to him; which he rejected, cursing her so extremely that she ran from him in fright, and spilled the beer upon her coats, to the greater mirth of all who were watching. After which pleasant diversion the constables urged they should again set forth, which was done, and they came within the second hour to the village of Sunderne, and the green therein before the school, where his villainies were done, and where it was ordered his execution should be accomplished also.

The pyre and stake were already prepared against the occasion, and having stood all night in a soft rain were now but indifferent dry; nevertheless the executioner determined upon examination that the matter might very properly proceed in accordance with the order, and so he advised those two Justices who were come to see the sentence carried out. So it was done according to the form of the statute. They thrust Salathiel from the cart, and brought him limping through the pressing people who cursed and spat upon him as he passed by, and so along the lane left open through the faggots to hale him to the stake. There they passed the chains about him, and making all fast about his breast, belly and arms, withdrew from him to confer with the Justices. Master Francis Fox, who was come to see the end, was desirous to make a last appeal to the condemned for his soul's welfare, and it was granted gladly, for none there wished to deny the dying man a hope of heaven. Therefore the good old man now advanced and stood between the fringes of the brushwood at the edge of the opening in the pyre, and there addressed Salathiel.

'You are now come to atonement, Salathiel Drury,' he said gravely, 'and if there be any matter left in your heart to cause you unease before your Maker, I adjure you rid yourself of it now. Repent, and it shall not be found too late. Is there any act of yours heavy upon your conscience against this dying hour?'

Salathiel looked straining over him and over them all, and said: 'I call to mind but one thing I am ashamed of and would have undone.'

'Utter it faithfully,' said Master Fox, 'and surely it shall be forgiven.'

'At the Falcon at East Manningholt,' said Salathiel, heavy and slow, 'there is a poor witless wench who offered me gentleness, and her I cursed very foully for her pains. If you are truly a man of God, go to her and get on your knees for me, and ask her pardon. Tell her the drink she offered is the only cool I have known for many a day, and though I refused it then I have drunk it now and found it sweet.'

People said: 'He raves, and is astray. What talk is this of a pothouse girl?'

'This is but trivial,' said Master Fox. 'Think upon higher things, while yet there is time.'

'I know of no higher thing than charity,' said Salathiel, 'and have found none upon earth so rare. Do my errand and have my thanks, or get back among the executioners where you belong, and let me alone.'

'Then I will do your errand,' said the old man, 'rather than let you go so. But is there no graver thing than this upon your conscience? Let me unwind from you the fetters of guilt, that your soul may pass in peace. Confess your ill deeds, and be free.'

Salathiel's lips made as if they would echo: 'Free!' but writhed and uttered no sound for monstrous laughter and awful tears that struggled in him. His breast swelled for a great gusty breath or two, filling and straining at the chains, and he got command of his voice to cry out loud and lamentably: 'Lay to the fire, and let me away to my end, for I am weary of living!' And again he said, groaning: 'Come, death, and quiet me!'

Seeing that the soft rain again began to come down, though

light as mist, the Justices ordered that all should be set in train without more delay, and accordingly they built up the lane with faggots and brushwood, and the executioner set the torches to his brazier until the smoke of their resin blew spicy over the green and broke apart upon a quick, hot flame. Then he thrust well in among the brushwood upon four several sides of the stake, and the constables moved back the watching people out of range of the fire, and so paraded about and about to restrain them, for there were young boys among them who would creep back at every opening to watch how the flames took hold. This, in fact, they did but slowly, the wood being so sullen that one of the torches went out, and must be rekindled and thrust in again and the remaining three made for the first half-hour only a strong green smoke not thick enough to strangle or stupefy. Master Fox fell upon his knees and so remained in the damp unmoving, in prayer for the soul of the murderer; but so early did he begin this intercession that his old bones could not abide the slow time, and long before the end he was helped away to the Schoolhouse to rest himself within doors.

But of dying, though it be but slow, there is no respite. Salathiel's face, made grey by the rising smoke, long looked out over the shifting clouds in continual and unchanging expectation of pain while the fire was yet reluctant to touch him; but after a while the heat began to prevail over the rain, and steam clung about him, and under his feet there were places where the faggots began to burn through at the heart from black to red. Then it was that the door of the Schoolhouse opened, and there came forth Mary Butterworth, in a light cloak flung loose about her, shadowing her face. She came slipping from one man's shelter to another's until she had reached a place where she might see him clearly and yet be unseen, and there she stood gazing upon him as he rolled back his head against the stake to get but a mouthful of clean air. She saw the pits of his eyes grow black with grime, and the sweat gather and roll down his face, and his breast labouring against the chains for breath; and presently after

she saw how his lips parted and drew back gasping for
drouth. But she never moved nor spoke; and some of the
boys who were running about the green and shouting at the
sight elbowed hard against her and were not noticed, until a
neighbour who held her child up to see better chanced to
peer into the shadow of her hood, and knew who stood among
them. Now Mary was with honour among them for laying
the information which had brought a witch to justice, and
they cried one to another to give place to her and let her
through, that she might stand near to see the end of her work;
and so they helped her forward whether she would or no
until she stood clear in face of him, and his eyes as they cast
about between heaven and earth could not fail to sweep over
her. He had as yet uttered no sound which could be heard
above the rustling of the fire in the slow brushwood, nor did
he now give utterance, that she could not know if he saw and
knew her or if he was in extremity beyond recognition. As
she had sought to avoid his look, so she now longed for it
though it must abhor her, but could not get it a moment to
herself, for it shifted and sought ceaselessly a refuge where it
might rest and be in darkness, but there was none.

Now there sprang up suddenly a gust of wind, and pulled
the smoke tautly about the stake as a grey winding-sheet,
and drew the sullen glow within the pyre into a roaring
rosiness that spat out sparks; and full before him, where most
the wind tugged, the surface of the faggots caved in upon the
heart of the fire, and there went up seven or eight feet high a
great sheet of flame, casting off white ash like down, and
forcing back those who stood nearest by reason of its heat.
The dimness of the day being thus lit, they were dazzled with
gazing upon it, and shut their eyes against the scorching pallor
while it endured, which it did diminishing for many minutes;
all but Mary Butterworth, who stood open-eyed through all,
only shielding her face with the edge of her hood. In the midst,
in the bending rose of the fire, there was a long, bellowing
cry that continued unbroken a long time, and might better
have been of beast or ghost than of man. Certain of the

children present began to scream and wail for fear of the roaring and this awful sound within it, and their mothers, who would for their own part have been willing to remain, thought better to take them away. Master Fox also here faltered in his prayers, and was helped to his feet and led apart, for he was old and pitiful. Upon those who stayed, and they were enough, the rain halted as it fell, drifting into steam upon the air; and after a while the fire levelled, burning steady and fierce upon all sides of the stake but declining from its excessive height upon this one side, so that they saw the clearer what went forward. And none looked more fixedly than Mary Butterworth.

The flames sinking and steadying upon the freshening wind, again by flickering glimpses they had sight of Salathiel Drury, the head of him only, and then the breast, and then the whole body, and again thereafter in the tower of smoke and wrappings of fire he was lost to view. The clothes were burned off him in that first blast of flame but for certain black rags of tinder that stood upright in the heat, and they saw his flesh as yet but lightly blistered, and white as ivory; but his face was hairless, blackening and demoniac, the long parti-coloured locks upon his head flaking into dust in the whirl of the draught. Out of him came a voice not known for his, howling upon death, and yet ever and again caught up into grimmest of silence as his mind had for an instant the mastery over his body. He cast himself about as the flames lanced at him, and the chains he strained against fetched blood upon his fairness, and the blood blackened and dried as it ran, until all his breast smoked darkly. Yet he continued a long time live and conscious with the crackling and hissing of the fire momently drawing in more lovingly to him, until no manner of writhing could anywhere draw him aside out of reach of it. His howling from extreme grew intermittent, and became at length but a moaning sound all but lost in the din of the flames; but still by convulsive movements they knew he lived. And this had now continued far into the afternoon, and some among the people went home, for they were wearied of the scene, and some, being hungry, went and came again when they had fed.

The executioner seeing the fire inclined to subside while the creature hanging in chains yet twitched and started, and little uneven sounds yet proceeded out of him, asked if there were not more fuel to be had. But such as they had proved to be green, and when his fellow Justice would have given leave to pile it on none the less Master Harding would by no means consent.

'Not so,' said he, all his ruddiness of face mottled and purple for what in another must have been pallor. 'For my part I would liefer put a ball through the poor wretch and done with it, and so I will if you are agreed.'

'That is against the law, sir,' said the executioner, 'and bear in mind I must render account what is here done. Burn he must until he be dead, according to his sentence.'

'In the name of God, then,' said Master Harding, 'cast on oil and resin and hasten him out of the world as best you may!'

Therefore they poured oil over the best of the wood they had left, and set it on with pikels close about the stake, and there went up a column of flame a second time, higher than the first, and so continued fully ten minutes before the roaring of it began to slacken. All the midst of the pyre, stake and chains and body, passed into a single, white-hot, shivering light, so fierce that all must give back before it. Only Mary Butterworth stood as she had been turned to stone, not marking her danger, until Master Harding went and plucked her back by the arm.

'What?' says he, perceiving who it was he held. 'Are you not she who laid information against this man?'

She gave him but a pale, demented look, and turned again to the fire.

'All is now accomplished,' he said, 'there is no more to do here. You had better go in to your mistress.'

She seemed as though she had not heard, and made no move; yet she continued so quiet that they let her be, content to suppose she would depart when she had seen the end. Already it was late afternoon stilling to evening, and many among the crowd were gone to their homes, and more were going. The Justices pronounced the sentence well carried out, and repaired to their own houses, and the executioner, seeing what lingered dark in the heart of the column of fire was but a half-consumed torch, deader than ashes, put up the tools of his trade and betook him to the village with the constables, to see what fashion of liquor they kept at the Pearl of Price to salve so sulphurous a thirst. A few boys lingered, but finding no change nor movement in the scene to excite them, and growing hungry at last, departed also. Yet so it was, that always came some new face to stare, one that had missed, perhaps, the events of the day, or left them but half-done, and never could Mary Butterworth be alone upon the green. None the less she waited until the clear flames burned low, and that which remained in one self-same pinnacle of heat with the stake, so burned clean through to the heart that light shone through it, began to show white edges of ash, and to fall apart in flakes into the bed of glowing wood-embers below. She saw driftings of ash caught upward by the hot wind even from the molten chains, and that which hung within them began to slip low and small out of the festoons as if consumed away, and lay at last spilled bone from bone in the rose-red bed of the pyre. She left her stillness, and went weaving and circling about the stake, seeking vainly to come at it closer whenever she was not observed, and even stretching out her hands to feel her way forward, but ever the heat blasted forth and drove her back. When she perceived that it was useless she drew off and stood again at distance; and when after a time certain curious stares drew about her from those who came to see, she went away into the Schoolhouse very lightly and quickly, and there remained all that evening hidden.

But at night when it was fully dark, there being but a wan moon, she crept forth again stealthily, and taking a pikel, raked out the midmost of the pile, where now but a few dull embers made a ruddiness among the black and white; and seeing from this that she might now with safety go about her search, and risk nothing but the scorching of her hands upon half-burned wood, she went upon her knees and sifted among the ashes, causing fine bitter dust and an acrid stench to rise in her face. Thus groping, for she dared bring no light to the work, she found the hanging chains yet very hot below, but grappled them none the less, and the ash of clothing fell to dust along them as she touched, and left her holding the calcined bone of an arm. This she wrapped in her cloak as in a nest, and setting it aside, again fell to the same search, and as she felt about among the hot bed of ashes she whispered and muttered to herself as mad people do, and said, moaning:

'Well, have I not brought you low enough, my love, my dear? Have I not undone you utterly, as I swore I would do? Have I not snatched you out of her arms for ever? What is there more I can do to you that I have not done? Answer me from where you are now, Salathiel, curse or forgive me, but answer, answer. Oh, have I silenced you?' she said, 'and what voice then can break this silence ever more for me?'

And when she had searched all the night through, by times waiting that the quaking furnace might cool further, she had got but a few poor bones laid in her cloak, the pyre was so fallen inextricably together as to engulf all beside past finding. Nor dared she wait longer, for the first hint of the light began, and she was so smeared with ash, and stank so of scorching, that she must not be seen by any man. Therefore she wrapped up her prizes, and taking them to her breast, fled hurriedly with them into the garden, for the churchyard was so far that she durst not venture it; and for want of tools she took her hands to the work, and dug madly in the soft soil until she had made a pit deep enough to hide her bundle. There she laid it, and covered it over, and pressed down the earth over it with her hands and after with the weight of her body lying upon it. Which done, and having ever present in her mind the onset of the day, she went in silently to her bedchamber, and there stripped off her clothes and washed herself, and put clean linen upon her body; that when the dawn was fully come she beheld herself in the mirror fit to appear before any eyes, not more wan and wild than would well pass muster for a woman's proper bearing after so distressful a day past. And silently and composedly she bore herself that day and many days about the soft person of Elizabeth, as though she had never broken neither her nails nor her heart making a grave where she might gently lay his bones.

As for Elizabeth Flint, she never spoke of what had been done, and from the windows which looked out upon the green she resolutely averted her eyes until the executioner's cart had carried away and dispersed all the ashes of the pyre, and the stake was torn up and taken away, and rain had washed clean the circle of bare ground from the taint and soiling of burned flesh. As she had sought neither to see nor hear, so she sought not to remember, such terror, danger and pain.

So ended the justice of our lord the King against Salathiel Drury. His goods all being forfeit, there was no portion left to Elizabeth, but by the clemency of the court it was provided that his books and personal property should be sold and the money devoted to trust for her; and until she should be come to her majority she wisely besought Mistress Shenstone to give her shelter and guard, herself making this delicate approach with modesty and grief so touching that the lady embraced and pitied her, and willingly undertook to have her in keep. And in her excellent care this poor troubled girl put by the short but dreadful memory of her former guardian, and so lived that her gentle patroness had great solace of her company, kept her small portion safe, and married her at length, not dowerless, to a gentleman of Berkshire who was esteemed her better in family, goods and gear, and not above double her years in age.

Yet was not all done that sprang out of Salathiel's passing; for before he was a week out of the world the child Beavis Frennet, having conceived an appetite for bearing witness, began to throw himself into curious fits, and foam at the mouth, and declare he was possessed. Ere he had been so three times publicly in the street and in the church, there was terror loose again, and every man accused his friend, and every woman her neighbour. Then the boy sprang one day upon that very labourer's wife who had borne witness against Salathiel, and so clawed her that he drew blood, and thereupon grew calm upon the instant, saying that he was healed of his infirmity. But though that woman was cast forthwith into gaol the clamour was by no means stayed, and there began to be talk of a coven at Sunderne, and names were whispered, so that before September was come in there were nine persons lying in durance awaiting the next delivery, upon suspicion of the like odious crime, and one had died under the ordeal by swimming, and so was held to have been innocent. There was no safety for man nor woman, so did fear raven abroad; and had not our lord the King upon progress lodged some few nights in the house of Sir George Martingale at Friary Shalford during this same month of September it is certain that some or all of these poor creatures must have gone to the gallows.

It fell thus. The King was pleased to make this visit the occasion of no ceremony, and therefore desired to hear the talk of the town privately through his host rather than by any other channel; and it so chanced that those papers which Salathiel had left behind him, being his last writings, had been delivered to Sir George by reason of the strangeness of their content, that he might advise upon their disposal. These, as matter of curious interest, he delivered in his turn to the King's Majesty, together with all the story of the supposed coven at Sunderne, and of Salathiel's conviction and death, which was news not yet held to be stale. The King with gravity heard all, and addressed himself next to the reading of those few pages which had sought to occupy the last days of Salathiel's life. Their purport was as follows: under a heading of the date and place of his labour, and without any other preamble, this:

'I am now come down full into the abyss and torment of

despair, beyond where hope lodges, and thrust out of the company of men, to which I was never prone, cannot but contemplate or myself or nothingness. My mind was not aforetime given to turning its looks inward, yet here there is nothing without but by night a darkness and by day the colour of a wall before my face wheresoever I turn; and therefore I am come to this, that I can endure to probe within myself better than to look upon a blankness, though for detestation of this ill-made and vilely-used body I am sick at the necessity of choice. Yet and at this extreme I cannot but loose my energies in thought as well as in sense, and am come by reasonable compulsion to meddle with such meat as I have, and search and examine into the true nature of pain.

'With this monster, or as some would have him, saint, the maker of martyrs and concocter of confessions, the atonement of sin and prover of truth, I am now well acquaint. He is in my confidence, and I am in his affection, all the more because he has made no martyr of me, drawn out of me no confession, proved no part of my faithfulness, and cleansed me of nothing but cleanness. And though he burn me, as before many days he will, no theorem will have been justified then, and no wrong avenged. I believe in his wantonness, not alone upon me; and in his uselessness, for in killing me he betters no other creature's lot. Yet have I sometime seen how there might be a kind of beauty and peace whereof he keeps the door, but cannot for my soul see any way to come at it either in the flesh or the spirit without passing through him unchanged; and behold how he changes me. I have heard him called a chastener, but I am not chastened. He pricks me, and I must rend in return, he goads me and I lust after the throats of his missionaries, he brings me sprawling in the dust, and I sicken with my own venom to murder his agents, though they be unshakably steadfast, sad and gentle as was my judge, and I without just complaint against them. Not for such a creature is that quietness I see or feel or know to be but just beyond his shoulders and forever out of my reach; for by these means he cannot be overcome.

'It is with him, I suppose, as with all other creatures, he must be friend or enemy; for though he be mixed of his nature as is man he must fall upon one side or the other of the line we draw between love and detestation, whose hearts know nothing of indifference. And as some can endure to receive guidance and enforcement from their fellow-men, so do some embrace pain humbly, and go to his arms without anger or reproach; and to them, it may be, he shows that kindness I have sometimes thought to see in him. But I can no more be so than I can suffer a fool gladly or return soft answers to an enemy who buffets me in the face. It was never in me to kiss the rod, nor can I learn the way of it at so late a time. I recollect it was once said of me that doubtless in His own time God would bring me to heel, yet the labour expended upon me has been all man's, and all unavailing. I learn to keep silence, yet cannot make my silence willing nor meek; doubtless before the end I shall also learn to cry, but so does the tiger, being maimed, and I never heard that any man went near to comfort him. Pain, I am your implacable enemy, and shall continue until I die as the tiger dies, snarling and unapproachable still. Yet by these means, as I have said, there is no triumph to be had over you, and the door you keep will never be opened to me.

'To those of us, then, who cannot love nor reverence him as he would have us to do, nor take his yoke upon our bent necks as gently as love's kisses upon the mouth, there is but the advance upon an enemy to be at last resorted to. He has then this bitter advantage of us, that every stripe he deals us our own venom causes to fester, that we become our own torturers, and put ourselves to the sword. Yet to perceive this folly is not to be rid of it, as I well know who have as it were stood aside and cursed myself while I contended madly for my silence and dignity under the extreme of choler and hate, my own poison swelling in my throat to burst me. By which means I am made weak before him who most need to be strong, as an enemy disarmed and brought down with wounds who lacks a tongue to wind about his conqueror with pleading and circumstance, and beg his life and liberty of him from whom he has failed to hold it by force. A stiff neck has been my undoing, as anger must be my death. I have fought as I might, but with double-edged weapons that cut my hands to the bone, and have bled me to death at last. To have the better of pain his resolute foe must have in him that calm which I have not, such a calm as keeps the mind content upon consciousness of victory, and makes wounds and humiliations of none account. By such a man heaven, I suppose, may be carried in the pocket, and all the fires of Smithfield will be to him as a lamp beside his bed. At his firm approach pain must fall down and be trodden underfoot, and so might the door of that treasure-house beyond be taken victoriously, and entered over his very body. But who is to know until the fire be lighted whether he is truly such an one or no? I know of none but one that came clean out of the death. And of this test there can be no second assay.

'As for me, I am better acquainted with the fate of him who attempts and falls short, and this is like to be all my knowledge. How gladly would I put myself above weakness and rage if I could, to be out of his reach through whatsoever pangs he could launch upon me, and keep my soul entire and inviolate though my body were shamed and rent in pieces. So indeed might a man be satisfied of his pride and hate, to have so signal and complete a triumph, but so it is, by the wisdom of heaven or the malignance of hell, I know not which, that none can get that laurel to himself unless pride and hate are clean gone out of him, and upon what thirst then falls the enchanted rain? As well be offered good wine with your throat slit.

'So have I shut against myself that islanded peace for which I yearn with my whole unquiet mind; for though I should resolve upon submission I could not keep my hands from struggle nor my tongue from defiance when the first stroke was laid on, and though I should study and determine to be as adamant unmoved through all without complaint or yielding, to overtop my judges and tread my adversary pain underfoot, I know I am flesh, and it is not in me to abide the doing. I know no third way to be at peace with him, nor is design able to be my salvation. I must do after my nature.

'Yet, and more strangely, he is not my master, neither as monster nor saint, accuser nor confessor. Something I have kept apart from him of which he cannot get possession, some tiny citadel walled from him still, I believe not in the mind but in the heart. Though he wring me to shrieking when the body's hurts grow too gross for the senses to endure, yet there he shall never come, for there resides whatsoever this thing may be which makes me in a little myself, and no other man; and whether it be ill or well, that is mine until I willingly render it up, and that I can keep. There also abides, as with my life I believe, my abused and neglected and inextinguishable godhead, against which only myself can deal the killing stroke. And these things are known to pain, my enemy, and he has respect to them, never attempting what it is out of his power to do. And perfectly do we understand each other, howsoever we are at odds.

'Yet how this thing shall be resolved I had better have asked of God than of him, but that God has more upon His mind than the nursing of my hurts. It is for me to find my way to Him if I can, and not with snivelling prayers assay to draw him down to me, as though the rest of the world were of no moment against my suffering, and the whole calendar of saints but a fistful of dust against my salvation. I have been held in my time for as arrogant a creature as ever despised his fellows out of hand, yet I have never reached that degree of conceit to suppose heaven would be any the worse off for the want of me, or God the lonelier. It is for me to undergo what falls upon me, and not to recrucify the crucified. Break or triumph, so I shall do, but to triumph is my most vehement and agonised desire, and my spirit would encounter hell for it, but how if my flesh cringe at even so much of hell as man has learned the trick of? Within this life I shall not find an answer; and after, there may be more yet to sustain than I have dared to suppose, though there my enemy must gnaw upon so much stouter a part of me that I shall not fear him as now I do. Whatsoever remains, I shall be free of this my body, which I have grown so to loathe, this which has been made a legend of evil, gross and obscene horror to me, a bedfellow of succubi and nourisher of imps and familiars, eaten with every foulness and folly the mind of ignorance can imagine into a clean and comely world. There, lacking of this ready instrument to play on, pain must claw me with other talons and burn me with other fires. What he can accomplish in this subtler kind I am not all inexperienced. I have learned to shut my mouth upon cursing; it may be that in one lifetime this progress is not so ill.

'I am halt of my words, and the time runs out fast. Even my pen is become labour to me, so does the heart turn even from what it loves to regard what it fears. To fear I have been much a stranger, but we grow familiar now, and he is ever with me beside the other. After the fall of night upon tomorrow's day will they be still with me? And shall I remember them and know them through whatever new form they may put on? Or is death the end of them? Well I know it is not the end of me. If there might but be quietness a little, and sleep, and a respite in that solitude of the mind which knows no loneliness, pain, I might have my will of you yet, for there is a constancy in me the fellow of your own.'

Here ended the writing, as he was goaded from it at the coming in of the chaplain upon the evening before his execution. All this the King read gravely, and setting it down at last out of his hand, mused frowning for a little space.

'You did not yourself meet with the man?' he said.

'No, sir, I never saw him. They say he had a rare mind when he pleased.'

'He wrote a rare hand,' said the King, 'for a man about to die. What do the men of law say of this writing?'

'Sir, I have not consulted. What would your Majesty say?'

But the King said only: 'You say there are others now in prison upon the same witness? Let me hear that tale again.'

And when it was told he sighed, and said: 'I would I had my father's skill in demonology. Let this boy be brought to me, this child who was afflicted.'

So they brought to him from Sunderne Beavis Frennet, in some terror when he knew by whom he was sent for, yet keeping his fears hidden; and when he was come into the presence he took heart, seeing only a slender gentleman in burnished satins and laces fine as cobweb, with hair and beard as soft as floss, and his face delicate, irresolute and subtle, with petulant mouth and plaintive eyes. Conceiving himself able to keep pace with such an one, he conducted himself modestly and boldly, answering many questions without slip, both concerning the labourer's wife who had afflicted him with fits, and also regarding the case of Salathiel Drury.

'Well,' said the King at length, and smiling, though something sadly, 'I see you are a fellow of excellent good sense, friend Beavis, and therefore I dare ask you to help me in some small matters. I am not without cunning myself in the recovery of poor souls bewitched, yet I never met with this falling, passionate sickness wherewith it seems you were visited. I would have more knowledge of it, and by your aid so I shall. There is a drink I can give you shall bring the simulacrum of your fit upon you again, in all respects the same. We shall be present to see you take no hurt, and I shall enrich my knowledge. Come, child, shall we make the test? It will but repeat in you the image of the thing you have suffered.'

Said the boy, trembling, for terribly he feared witchcrafts though having no fear of those he had himself invented. 'But, sir, how if this time I should never be restored?'

'Have no fear,' said the King. 'I can recover you in a word, or a mere pass of my hand.'

Beavis thereupon consented, being afraid to do other, and perfectly assured he could produce again every symptom of his assumed malady, supposed that his safety lay in pretending to the King that the potion had not failed of its effect. The King therefore called in Sir George and a trusted

271

servant, and in their presence administered to the child a harmless brew of milk and sweet herbs and spices; upon swallowing which, Beavis cast the cup from him, and stood a moment staring and running at the mouth, and after fell down and rolled about the floor foaming, and shrieked aloud, and rolled up his eyes to the whites, all as he had before done when he claimed the fit or possession was upon him.

'Do you observe,' said the King in the saddest of voices, 'the true purport of this performance?'

'I do, sir,' said Sir George, greatly astonished. 'Yet may it not be that fear and faith in your magic has induced the attack, though the drink was innocence itself? I have sometimes heard the like.'

'And have you ever,' sighed the King, 'seen any man in a true falling fit put out his hands so wittily to save himself the worst shock of the fall?'

'It is true,' said his host. 'I had not remarked it.'

Then the King looked long upon the boy as he threshed and screamed, and suddenly stretching out his hand, said gently: 'Enough! It is time I restored you, and I will do it. Infamous little liar, get up and stop your play-acting. Get up, I say, you have rolled and shrieked me dizzy and dumb. Now let us have the truth, or you shall have sorrow.'

In consternation then Beavis ceased his antics and sat upon the floor ludicrously staring, and made some effort to act as if he had been in good faith, but had not that brazen front to maintain it under the King's eye. Seeing himself discovered he fell to weeping with great noise, in terror lest his own life should pay the score; but being as sternly checked upon this course, found no way open to him but to confess all his fantasies and spites, as well against Salathiel as these newer victims. All which the King heard out in silence, his hand shading his face; and when all was heard he delivered him to the servant to be conveyed to the nearest Justice, and there repeat his recantation, assuring him with inexpressible detestation he should not be thrown into gaol nor tortured out of hand. After he was gone and his crying no longer heard the King wrung the fingers which had put him off from touching, and said with heaviness:

'Upon such testimony, then, life may hang. I charge you, see to it they are not kept waiting the processes of law longer than need be, for we are quicker to imprison than to let go.'

So ended the whirlwind of rumour concerning the coven at Sunderne, for after the King's intervention men hesitated for fear as well as shame to accuse one another, and the madness passed as it had come. But the King pondered much over the last writings of Salathiel Drury, and was unsatisfied.

'There is one more,' said he, 'I would speak with before I go. Bring to me this woman Mary Butterworth.'

Said Sir George: 'This case, sir, was not as the others. She spoke of facts which were not denied.'

'It is not in nature she should so sift as the child,' replied the King, 'besides that she may be honest. But I tell you, my mind is not easy. Let me be humoured in this, and I shall be content.'

Upon the following day she presented herself, therefore, as she had been instructed, very pale and quiet, with modest eyes downcast, and her face calm as marble. So she had been in the world's eyes since Salathiel's death, for she was ever the mistress of her appearing; and so she maintained now unfailingly her equable, blameless front, matching his thoughtful and melancholy eyes with a look as sorrowful. And for the King's Majesty, she thought him but a dainty puppet upon first seeing, but before he had said many words to her she drew her wits about her sharply and thought the better of him, knowing, too, that he had brought about the release of all the suspected persons and the undoing of the boy. Yet she was not in any fear, for it was thus with her, that there remained in the world nothing which could be done to her for which she would greatly care, and therefore fear was impossible to her. Only she maintained her stand from habit and a kind of pride in holding all other intelligence at bay, and so faced the King in a stony but watchful tranquillity, and answered him as it were willingly but slowly, thinking well upon her words. He led her, and she submissively went with him, through all the story she had before told, altering no detail nor being beguiled into adding any; nor could he anywhere descry a chink by which to come at the hidden truth of her, so that he ended as unsure as he began. For he was too shrewd in his judgement to suppose that she was of the boy's unstable mettle, or could be mauled by a little professed magic, as he. Knowing not how to have her if she should be other than she seemed, and being reluctant to torment her if all her nature was crystal, he continued to question her gently and pressingly, but at every turn she satisfied him.

'Mary,' said he at last, 'you know, do you not, that all those persons charged upon this same count have been found to be accused falsely, and are now set free? You know there have been terrible lies told?'

She said with her eyes downcast: 'Sir, they became afraid. Wild things are said and done in fear, and they had seen the devil break loose among them. What wonder if they laid about them blindly, and struck at poor souls who did them no hurt?'

'You say well,' said the King, 'and it might well be so. But do you know also that even in the case of this Salathiel Drury there was false evidence given? The child confessed it for his part. How if he should also have made it plain for yours?'

She looked up at him with a pale smile, and said: 'Your Majesty says this to try me. Well I know he cannot have disproved any testimony of mine, for all I have sworn I would swear again this hour, and all of it is truth. But indeed this Beavis is a strange child, and his mind ever dwelt unnaturally upon darkness. To make black blacker is ever his habit, and I believe he can scarcely help it. I grieve that it was I who put the seed in his mind, for I was distract with dread for my young mistress Elizabeth, and he was close at hand about my uncle's house, and quaint and old of his ways, that I talked to him of what I was bursting with, and never thought to doubt him when he met me half-way. He swore to me he had seen those demons as I had, and if he lied I am to blame for putting the thought into his mind; but what I have seen I cannot therefore unsee. I would to God I could!'

Then the King was silent for a long time, looking upon her, and by the clear look of his eyes she knew he accounted her justified. Yet there lingered a cloud upon him.

'You comprehend, Mary,' he said, as one musing to himself, 'there is a disposition in men to forejudge what is hard to understand. I am not unversed in the ways of witches. My father suffered abominable attacks upon his life and safety by the spells of certain of this terrible sort, and I myself have seen much evil that came of them; but it is not therefore true that every man against whom the cry is raised must be guilty. And I will go to all lengths to sift them, and have the guilty suffer and the innocent go free, as my father taught me in his lifetime.' Looking down upon the writings of Salathiel, which he held upon his knee, he here fetched a sudden sharp sigh, and asked her again: 'Mary, they asked you, I know, over and over, if you had cause to accuse him by reason of a private hate. But I put to you another and a last question. Had you cause to accuse him, not for hate, but for love?'

This she had not foreseen, and her heart was transfixed a moment, but outwardly she gave no sign, continuing grave and calm, and saying: 'No, sir, it was not so. He was a man no one greatly loved, though many may have hated. And alas, sir, who could so wrong a man for love? It is not in nature.'

Seeing how constant she was, the King acknowledged her honest, and so dismissed her, and she went from him with a shut heart and motionless face, as she had entered. But long after she was gone he sat reading in Salathiel's writings, and the cloud still upon his brow; and yet once more he spoke of the dead man before he left that town.

'Well I know,' he said, 'that there was all against him, and of the blackest ever I heard. Yet never but in him did I see this mind toward dying, to make no defence for himself, and no charge against any other, but only look pain and death and all the weakness of the flesh full in the face, and consider how to be equal to the sum of them. In this he had lost all his passion and indignation against men, and as I think this was so great it could not well be lost but in the contemplation of a thing infinitely greater. Guilt stands large before the guilty. I doubt if they see much beside. Alas,' he said, leaning his head upon his slender hand, 'I fear we have done a frightful wrong.'

'I beseech you, sir,' said Sir George, 'think no more of it. The evidence was heavy and grave, and the trial as fair as man ever had, and for my part I am content to believe he had his due and no whit over.'

'But your part is not mine,' said the King with his melancholy smile. 'As for me, I believe it, but still I am not content.'

There remained the issue of this matter, irresolute as it began between good and evil, the woman eaten alive of memories, the girl readily recoiling into her crystal innocence, the man dead and, as many conceived, damned past redemption. But which of these three received or deserved damnation it shall go hard for man to decide, and for all that His Majesty or his least subject could determine by thought or reflection it had better have been left, like the judgement upon all our judgements here, to the hereafter and to God. Sure it is that within some few years, less by far than a life's span, the name and repute of Salathiel Drury were as his body, consumed away to a few poor bones, and laid in earth in the rotting cloak of one woman's memory, and she his murderess. Yet there is no surety but that the Lord beholds both the beginning and the ending, which ending is not yet, nor until He please to be the Judge, when some esteemed children of virtue may be found lighter than ash, and some whose lives and deaths were darkened may stand forth into daybreak and be seen brighter than gold, and more yet may, after the lame manner for which this chronicler can alone hope, creep in holding by the tattered hems of good intention, and find a place among the blessed by Christ's marvellous goodness where their own must have cast them out. In which day shall be resolved all the guilt and all the innocence of this lamentable history, which we now leave who cannot bring to a full conclusion; trusting in the perfect wisdom of the same Lord who is both justice and mercy. Amen.

XIV

'IT IS—'

On the night when she completed the story of Salathiel Drury
Claire put the manuscript away without re-reading a sentence,
and went to bed, and slept long and without a dream; and on
the following day she rose and behaved herself like a decent,
ordinary housewife all day long, yet always some
infinitesimally small fragment of her mind, sharp and bright
as a diamond, stood off glittering in a windy void, watching
from great distance and marvelling at her own domestic
readiness, her neat paces about the kitchen, her brisk walking
and aptitude with cabbages and canned fruit as she shopped
through the village. The rest of her mind, and it was all but
complete and felt the loss of its part only as a very small
discomfort, slept curled like a dormouse in a warm content,
drowsy and relaxed, as if it had cast off a load and turned
back to a level and easy and known way; and only seldom
and briefly did some scintillating ray from the severed splinter
quivering in its zenith reach and trouble that false ease. Once
it happened when she walked full tilt into the flood of children
as they came out from afternoon school, and a thin, dark boy,
running with his chin on his shoulder and a mouthful of shrill
challenges streaming out behind him, dashed full into her
and embraced her thighs to steady himself from the shock.
She saw him for only a moment, but he turned up to her a
face so elderly and disingenuous that she might have been
looking at the child Beavis Frennet, a seed of the same plant,
bred in the same soil, and reaching his terrible peak at not
much above this boy's age. And again she was reminded when
she passed the time of day with the postmaster, and

remembered suddenly that his name was Scholefield. The consideration made her observe him carefully while he handed her stamps, and slid her change in a stream of small silver under the grille. For all she knew he was descended in the direct line from the William of 1636, and divided from him, after all, by only a dozen or so generations. She saw a sturdy elderly man, rosy-faced and white-haired, with exceedingly bright and active eyes under bushes of brow like the curled wool of traveller's joy. What he saw, that he should look at her as intently, she could not guess or greatly care; and all the surface of her mind felt toward him was a kind of bright, astonished benevolence such as happy lovers may feel toward an inquisitive stranger who envies their rapture. His smile was knowing and almost intimate, the exact antithesis of the looks she met always from the rest of the village, which admitted to no knowledge and withheld themselves from contact. Yet his name alone was warranty that he was bone of the bone of Sunderne, and for all that she had seen of him he might have been any one of the squat, sturdy oaks left solitary here and there in windy grandeur among the ruins of the forest. No one could disappear into the picture better than he, nor remain more alert and intact within himself at the same time. She allowed herself to return his smile as she stamped her letter to Anne; but she desired no conversation with him or anyone beyond the easy formulæ of greeting which could be exchanged without thought, and she did not linger. What he knew, of her as of Sunderne, she no longer needed to know; she had everything in her heart. Yet she wished him well as she avoided the shrewd curiosity of his eyes and went out again into the street; somewhere, it seemed clear, his knowledge touched hers, and of that contact it was neither necessary nor desirable to speak. Even a look might trespass did it endure too long. Better never to seek to know what he beheld in her, or what he thought he knew of her, that he should look a secret toward her. For this village kept its own secrets shut within, in the impenetrable recesses of the heart, and so would she.

By Firelight

Charles had spoken of him once, she remembered, as a local historian, and in his way something of a scholar. Was it from him that Charles had made inquiry when her gropings in the past had caused him anxiety? A long time ago it seemed, for she had taken good care since then that he should know nothing of them. Perhaps her name had passed; the inquisitive purchaser who smelled fire in the garden where they were so sure no such smoke or flame had ever blown. Her mind, turning back for a moment to the written word, grew dazzled at the autumnal sunshine and dizzy at the scudding clouds blown bustling before the wind. Then she slipped again into her spurious calm, half-joyous and half-numbed, easy with the world.

There was a young woman walking before her by a few yards as she came to the church, and the gait and carriage were familiar though for the moment the name eluded her. A Sunderne woman by her colouring and face, with large lustrous dark eyes and complexion of olive and bright rose; a strapping young creature as wholesome as a ripe apple, with a pace long and deliberate as a ploughboy's, and the same large grace of body. When she looked round in closing the lych-gate her eyes rested upon Claire with recognition but no other perceptible expression. She said: 'Good afternoon, Mrs. Falchion!' in a reluctant voice, and Claire could see her reflecting within herself that since they were going the same way they could hardly avoid each other's company, at least for the short walk through the churchyard and along the road to where School Lane wandered away into its deeper valley. Just in time her name came to mind again, and it was strange that it should ever have been forgotten. Another Frennet, this, Joan Frennet; the same sharp small pain went home in Claire's mind at this renewed echo. Ever the same names, the known faces, haunted her, in this bright outer world as in the secret world she bore within her heart. From Frennets and Kentons and Scholefields and Chittams there was no deliverance.

'Good afternoon!' she said, accepting the swing of the gate

from the girl's hand. They fell into step together, Joan curbing her long paces with the slight discomfort any constraint of body put upon her. Claire looked at her stealthily as they went, marking with a pleasurable envy the high, clear colour of her cheeks, the blown black hair lying in rounded curls along her temples, and the berry-fresh brightness of her mouth. So young, and so vigorous, and so gentle, why could not Jonathan love her and be happy? She could have supplied all the balance and placidity his nature lacked, and a little fondness for her would have made Sunderne a world of contentment to him. Perhaps it was not yet too late for that happy chance. Local opinion, of which Mrs. Greenleaf was the voice at Long Coppice, had had the pair of them married not so long ago.

'Lovely day for October isn't it?' said Joan, disliking the silence, for they were not so friendly that they could be together and silent and keep their peace of mind.

'I believe it will end in a storm,' said Claire, as formally. 'The wind's blowing up rather suddenly.'

'Still, we've been lucky this season, haven't we?'

'Oh, yes, very lucky!'

Silence again for a moment, but they could not let it endure. The grasses, yellowing and growing dry and sear toward the end of autumn, rustled past their ankles, and the moss-stained stones, leaning every way, nodded in the sun like drowsy ancients upon a bench on a summer evening; but it was growing cold. Somewhere in this place lay the bones of Master Nicholas, that likeable, quarrelsome, good-natured old autocrat who had died in innocence of the crime which was to be committed in his name. Somewhere in the garden at Long Coppice a few fragments of the body of Salathiel Drury lay unblessed, and the rest of him was where? Dispersed in ash upon the winds long ago from some refuse heap where the rubble of the pyre had been thrown. And yet he had the stuff of eternity in him for evil or for good. Claire could think of people who might conceivably be ended by a heaped fire and a winnowing wind; she herself, until this gravity entered in, might have proved lighter than chaff before the fan had any such gale broken upon her; but he was no such destructible creature, nor had he been destroyed.

Loneliness and pain and anger are also durable things; they too survive. The professional comforters, she thought, fail to tell us that. The after-life is not haloes nor hell-fire, but continuing struggle and weariness, hampered still by faults of nature though the nature be no longer human, isolated still by the inadequacy of tongue and hand and eye to express the heart's insatiable longing for companionship. Two people may walk together there as here, and grope towards each other as they go with outstretched hands, and never find hand to hold by, but always miss the touch they ache for by an inch misjudged or a step astray. To be walled up within oneself for ever, living and dead, must be the most desolate state man ever suffered; and how many suffer it! Perhaps heaven, she thought, is nothing but the loosing of the charm which shall make the inarticulate articulate, the awkward deft, and the constrained responsive for ever to an everlasting kindness. The crooked straight and the rough places plain!

'I suppose you're quite settled in at Long Coppice now,' said Joan Frennet. 'Becoming almost a native – by adoption, anyhow.'

'I'm afraid that may take more than one lifetime,' said Claire.

'I know we're hard to get to know,' admitted Joan with a shadowed smile, 'but it isn't as bad as all that. Are you intending to stay, then? You like it here well enough for that?'

'Oh, yes, I intend to stay. I can never be sure, of course, that something won't happen to pull me back to town, but I hope not, I think not. I want very much to settle down here.'

It sounded curiously artificial, all the more as it was true. Perhaps only the phrase 'settle down' was out of key.

'I'm glad you like Sunderne so much,' said Joan, with careful accuracy, for her voice made it involuntarily clear that she was not glad of the news that Claire meant to stay. If she had been absolutely frank she would have begged her to consider the damage she did by remaining, and uproot herself and go before it was too late. The quick, dubious glance along her shoulder said as much, though rather in accusation than pleading. How far was she right? It was so distant a problem that Claire could not get to grips with it, could not even believe in it. Jonathan for all his obstinacy and his helpless antagonism to his uncle was a rational young man at bottom, and could not fail to grow out of an unsuitable infatuation in good time. The girl would be there under his eyes when he came out of the ether, ready to be seen, ready to be desired again. Besides, thought Claire, I have not encouraged him, I've even gone a little out of my way to make him see sense. I never asked either of them to feel any attraction to me, and the only reason they did so was that I happened to look a little different from the women they lived among, and speak with another intonation; and when the novelty is worn off first one of them, and then the other, will notice that I am forty-one, and not more than superficially good-looking. Then perhaps we can settle down and be reasonably friendly without tormenting one another.

But close beside her she felt Joan Frennet doubting, grudging and fearing the issue, and vaguely her own confidence was shaken. Supposing there was really the material of tragedy here? Supposing the madness did not pass, and the triangle did not fall apart? What might she not be allowing those two troublous creatures to do to their own lives and each other's, and to Joan's, and to hers, and all for the want of her interest and energy to straighten out this crooked place? They were men, responsible for their own affairs, and she had no power over them; moreover they had as much right to be foolish as she had to be wise, and far more right to be foolish for themselves than she had to be wise for them. It is as often a crime to do as to leave undone. And yet she was answerable for her own part in the wretched business, and had it been well done? When she could scarcely hear what they said to her for another voice, and blown smoke between made their very faces dim as a dream to her?

And this girl who walked so quietly beside her, and would have liked to come at her openly for help but did not know how to begin, was she seriously to be considered as a forlorn maiden grieving for the loss of her lover? Was she to be one more dim reproach looming distractingly through realities, when it was so necessary the mind should be pointed fine as a needle, and the heart fixed and confident? 'I have done you no wrong,' Claire said to her silently. 'I owe you nothing. I never took anything of yours, and what you have lost was not lost to me. But you must not get in my way now, or it will be the worse for both of us.'

Aloud she said: 'This is beautiful country. I suppose the only reason it isn't overrun with visitors is because it's so inaccessible. Just one good main road could turn Sunderne into a holiday resort.'

'What an awful thought!' said Joan.

'Yes, isn't it? And yet I suppose occasionally people do find their way here, and fail ever to find their way out again. After all, that's more or less how I come to be here.'

'They've never stayed long,' said Joan, her head turned a little away so that the long swing of her black hair hid her face.

'Why not, I wonder?'

'Oh, I suppose it was too quiet for them after a while. Beautiful country is all very well in summer, but none of them ever stuck it through more than one winter.' Her voice was carefully indifferent, but her intention was childishly transparent. She stole one quick glance along her shoulder, and pursued in the same gentle voice: 'Not much use anyone staying in Sunderne if they need to have much communication with the outside world from November to March. I've known years when we've been snowed up most of that time.' They turned into the lane, the high wall sloping away behind them spidery with hair-thin roots of ivy cropped of their green. 'It drifts badly down Long Coppice,' said Joan thoughtfully. 'You couldn't have chosen a worse place for snow; it's the funnel the valley makes there that piles it up so. Have you got plenty of fuel and food laid in? I should think about it, if you haven't; though of course it isn't very easy to stock up as we used to before the war. What we shall do if we get cut off this winter I can't imagine.'

'It will be the same for us all, at any rate,' said Claire dryly.

'That can either make you feel better or worse about it. Personally I think it makes me feel worse.'

'I wonder you haven't left the place yourself before this,' said Claire with a sceptical smile.

'I wonder myself, but I'm still here.' She looked down into her basket, frowning and biting her lip, and the royal rose of her cheeks deepened angrily for a moment.

'It's true,' thought Claire, watching her, 'she's still in love with him. Only the consideration that he must come back here has kept her tied to Sunderne, and if she could break that she would go. But she can't. So I must go. If he stays and I go she may yet get her way.' Almost she regretted that she could not comply, but there was no sorrow of Joan Frennet's so important that she could care greatly for it. That severed splinter of her mind, dancing and scintillating in some fierce reflected light from a great way off in time or space, drew down upon her like a dropping hawk upon his hunting ground. The time of her peace was ending, burning out in that brightness. An intolerable sweet excitement sprang to life in her heart, and what was it now to her if all this village came to grief, every man and every woman of this cruel, shadowy-hearted, primitive valley which had murdered Salathiel Drury? They were none of her people. She owed them nothing, she had not sought to have any place in their thoughts, any influence upon their joys and sorrows, any part in their lives. What did she care if they were all damned? If she could have walked over their dead bodies to meet Salathiel she would have trodden them blithely and felt no grace of pity in her. She had done wrong to attempt to satisfy their demands of her, even by word or look shaped to their needs, for every spilt drop of energy was a crime against another and insatiable need which no one had ever yet assayed to satisfy. Never again would she spend upon any other creature the least coin of what was all Salathiel's due. There was nothing to spare. There was not enough. No human heart could contain enough to repay all that pain.

They came to the turn of the road, where School Lane wound away downhill.

'I leave you here,' said Joan, checking for a moment in mid-stride, with manifest gratitude.

'Yes, everyone always leaves me here. That's the worst of living in such a lost spot.' She smiled, but rather at the beckoning lane than at Joan. 'Good-bye, Miss Frennet.'

'Good-bye, Mrs. Falchion.'

They parted, and that encounter was over. No more need to feel and chafe at the reproof of a young unhappiness she could have spared only by abandoning the pursuit which was now her life and all her hope of immortality. Whether it was also his hope of comfort she could not know, but if it was not she might go, or die, or drift back into Charles's arms if he still found her worth wanting, for never again could it matter what she did or what befell her. She was no longer divided, even by a thought of kindness for any other creature living. Others might hold remedies for the sickness of others; if she could not medicine this one man she was forever useless. Everything was here, in the small enclosed garden and the crouching house to which she hastened. She felt the rushing of air in her ears, a great wind blowing past her, sourceless in the sheltered lane and the bright afternoon. The hour was close, as strictly timed as birth, as inevitable and as dangerous. Something tangible was what her heart ached for, something she could hold by and know she possessed. Yes, it was possession she wanted; not simply to heal and comfort and assuage, but to have and enjoy, after whatever fashion flesh can find with spirit. How rapidly it came upon her now, the tigerish beauty of truth! All the shams, even the involuntary ones, falling away from her nakedness, and she hastening towards the meeting-place to have him by storm and at all cost, to herself or the world. Unless this ferocious singleness were noble she knew herself utterly without nobility. The murderess had never so consumed for him, never with so little scruple sought to encompass him. Where was pity now, that strong root she had felt griping downward into her bowels and feeding upon her substance? She had marvelled at its vitality, and where was it now? Either dead, or burst suddenly into this monstrous, this unnatural flower, which had no place upon such a stem. Hard to recognise at sight a thing she had never seen in her life before, besides that it dazzled like the sun at midday and left itself unseen but as a flame-like whiteness, yet she knew it for what it was, and stood in awe of it.

This, then, was what it meant to love without hope of fruition, without expectation of pleasure, every sense rapt into the desire of any token, however brief and slight, by which the heart could live; all the world balanced upon the tone of a voice, the touch of a hand, the quality of a look. For if she achieved no miracle, dragged no talisman down to her out of his anguish, what was her life to her any more, divorced for ever from her pole? Panic alone remained after that, a prospect of appetite and energy running amok for want of an object, and flowing to waste in void upon void, lost rivers withering in a desert of inanity and emptiness. Worse by far than the decorous desert which lay behind her, because for a brief and blinding time she had seen herself delivered, and felt power and purpose flooding her being with tumultuous joy. But it would not come to that, for she felt time quickening to a climax, climbing to the hour for which she waited. What it would bring only God knew, but surely something, something would be drawn down to her; a breath of his voice would feed her hunger lifelong, a touch of his hand would keep her woman alive, and once to meet his eyes and be content with what she saw there was all she could ask of happiness. Possession itself was no more than that, to grasp a breath of wind, to lay hands upon a cry of anger and grief and hold it fast to her heart; and it would be enough, it would be everything.

By Firelight

She came to the triangle of the green, level and lush, with the barren outcrop of clay dead-white in it like a scar. The school on the left hand, the house on the right, long and low, couched from the wind that combed the ridge beyond; all was as it had been when first she came here, not so long ago, and the only change was that she was now in possession of the true translation, and could read the whole of it word by word. The dull sound of her own footsteps crossing that bare patch of ground struck echoes now, recollections of voices in shrill excitement and pleasure, cracklings of fire, and a sudden frightful cry tearing her imagination like a sword. Always that cry continued, somewhere within her hearing, near or afar; there were times when it was so distant that she scarcely heard it, but always it was there in the background of her mind, an awful protest against the last indignity inflicted upon him, the necessity of its own utterance. No one should ever be forgiven for dragging that cry out of his lips, never in this world or another. God would not forget it if she could not.

She let herself in by the front door, and closed it gently upon the world. Mrs. Greenleaf was gone, and in all the house and the garden there was no sound but emanated from herself, and these so light and soft that the effect was of silence. In this shrouding stillness she took the book of loose leaves to the window, and sat there for a long time re-reading what she had written. The wind freshened a little outside in the fine evening, and began to lift the scent of the herbs in clouds of drifting sweetness above the garden. There was a thin fragrant blue smoke moving upon it from a slow fire Whitton had left burning in the open close to the sundial, a neat beehive-shaped fire thatched with the trimmed turfs from the edgings of the paths. Once or twice as she lifted her eyes she saw the folds swaying and weaving against the dark of the trees beyond, a veil no thicker than tulle. Smoke and sweetness seemed to her senses to be one and indivisible, so gently and safely did the wind carry them; but the trees along the ridge were troubled, and whispered uneasily of autumnal storms to come before the month was dead and winter only a short journey distant on the rim of the valley. Between summer and winter her life, too, hovered hesitant, trying to hold time still that there might never again be the desolation of frost and cold. But it did not rest with her how the event fell, nor perhaps with God Himself. There were natural laws governing this as much as any other crisis of human affairs, currents of thought and feeling imperilling this as much as any other meeting. No, surely not as much as any other, for the dead should need no interpreters, but still there was room for misunderstanding, and where much is at stake, from sheer vehemence of longing the human intelligence may grow maladroit. She must be ready and at peace. She must do all things well this once though she died for it after; indeed, to do all things well it might be necessary that she should die.

She read the manuscript through, not in haste now, but with the deliberation of greed, fastening upon every new word of his as a hand to hold by and draw herself nearer. Here she who was all artifice had used no devices, and recognised no touch of her own hand; nor was it possible ever to set her name to the story, even had it been thinkable to publish it. She understood now what far-sighted instinct had made her, after that first false start, hide her work from Charles Kenton and all the world beside. It could never be offered to anyone; it would have been like cutting out her own heart to show it, like murdering Salathiel afresh.

And perhaps it was this very factor, this doubt of her own authorship, or of her single authorship, which brought the impact of the thing so fresh and awful upon her; for she sat there poring upon her own hand with slow tears gathering and overflowing from her eyes. Tears had never come easily to her because she had never felt the need of them; they burned like acid now, stinging her eyelids, and where they stood upon her cheeks a bitter heat branded her. No written word of hers could ever before, she supposed, have wrung a solitary tear out of anyone, and it was exquisitely just that she should begin with herself, as enthusiastic experimenters have sometimes injected untested serums into their own bodies.

She read it all, the narrative of the Sunderne witch-trial from beginning to end; and when it was done she sat quite still with the book in her lap, and the King's exclamation sounding grievously in her mind: 'Alas, I fear we have done a frightful wrong!' For over three hundred years that complaint had waited for its echo, until now the thunder of her heart took it up in passionate reverberation: 'We have done a frightful wrong!'

It was finished; was that the sign of the time? Could he not lean down to her until she had the whole of it in her knowledge? For there had never been any doubt that this was knowledge, whatever others might surmise from the scanty documents in the case, or the common laws of the land. They supposed, but she knew, for she had lived through the whole ordeal; beside Salathiel, within Salathiel, did it matter how? Nothing remained now but to wait, and even upon this pinnacle of desire she could surely do that with a good grace, she who had waited all her life simply for the hope of something to wait for. In this unpeopled silence the first sound of his step would reach her, a mere breath of his voice would bring her to his side. Yet for the ache within her she could not be at rest. She got up from her chair and began to go from room to room through the house, the book still held to her heart; but everywhere the silent air of early evening stirred to her own step, and brought her no other reminder of life. Well, she could wait, as surely, as tranquilly as for nightfall or daybreak, or any of the times and seasons which do not fail; and while she waited she walked the house where he had walked, holding his book in her arms, touching with wonder where his hands had rested, passing her fingertips over the worn surface of the table where he had sat at work, taking into herself with every nerve the conviction that he had been here and left something of his essence for her to find. This, to hold off thirst by moistening her lips until she could drink deep and be filled.

From an upstairs window she looked out in the dusk over the front garden with its half-cleared patterns of box, and the green beyond; and the quiet colours all dimming to iris made of the world without only another drifting veil of smoke. To the left, at the edge of the garden where the trees began, someone was standing motionless, looking up at the house; she found him by the very stillness of his body, and the poise of his head, reared intent to show her among the tree shadows a paler though swarthy face. No tremor shook her at the sight of him, for it was not yet so dark that at this distance she did not know Jonathan Kenton.

It did not matter; to her at this moment it meant nothing at all that he should suffer, nothing that he should avoid her company for more than a week only to stand watch at her gate by night when she could not be supposed to know he was by. No part of her mind detached itself to worry at the problem of what he was doing there, frozen under the trees and staring upon Long Coppice. He was a wrong which must right itself, a folly which must outlive madness and come down sooner or later into a world of reality, where no cheating lovers conspired against him with traps and lies, and no hope attended either his fondness or his jealousy. Let him stand at the door and spy upon her until his foot struck root, let him brood and smoulder until the dusk took fire from him, he would never see the lightnings of this love go by.

She passed on, and down the darkening stairs again, and went out into the garden. Walled in here with the herbs and the sundial she was secure from remembering the boy outside. In the freshness and the cold of night she drew breath with quickening exultation, as if a wind had blown upon her from the void where the lonely are, and brought her the first quivering of communion in something which was not speech, but some freer and more fluent manner of intercourse, loosed from the limitations of language. Why, after all, should the dead speak unless they please, having in them some measure at least of the quickened understanding which ends at last in the comprehension of God? But he would have the trick of the tongue still when he met with her, for that sense which supersedes the human senses must have love to keep it living, and he had never encountered love. From God he had not thought it his part to ask for it, and from men he had despised it. Unpractised still in the perfect articulation of silence, he would remember also her helplessness, and speak with her speech. Of his kindness she was utterly assured, though he had passed for a hard and violent, even a cruel man; and of God's grief for him, though he had never claimed it, and she had not been wont to dwell upon the possibility of it, she had poignant knowledge. 'Soon,' she said to the twilight, never realising that she spoke aloud, 'it will all be resolved, and we shall be at peace.'

It was cold, but this she did not even notice for her own heat. She walked among the mingled fragrance of herbs and turf-smoke, between the sundial and the fire, and sat down upon the stone seat where she had often sat in the sunlight writing, in the days before she became aware that she was writing her own story. How long she sat there was never known to her; it could have been only a moment, or an eternity of listening and waiting, for all she knew of it was that she sprang awake suddenly into a garden perceptibly darker than she had entered, and that the bonfire had burst one side of its thatch and was spitting bright red sparks into the air in a fountain, and spilling them down the changed and freshened wind away from where she sat. It was the crackling of the brushwood in the fire that startled her senses back to time and place, so linking past and present together that her mind heard again the answering cry which had so long haunted her from the distance. Not distant now, but clear and wounding and terrible, unless she had dreamed it. What was the truth from within, and what the dream from without, she could not in that moment be sure, but real or imagined this was a man's voice piercing the night and her heart with astonished pain. She sprang to her feet, the book leaping from her lap unnoticed, her senses reaching out at strain for what should follow. She felt all her being flooded with power and grace, translated from her own nature. She waited smiling, waited in the briefest, most exquisite anguish of expectation she was ever to know, while the new-sprung wind whirled about her, and her loosened hair was torn erect upon her head, and the comet flight of sparks went streaming down the darkness. She leaned forward against the impetus of time, spreading her arms to hold the hour as it came to birth, and so embrace it that she must be absorbed into it and pass with it, wherever time goes when it is spent and the dead when they are lost to living.

And then she heard her name called within the house. At first once only, faintly but wildly: 'Claire!' Then in horror and helplessness, very clearly, with the hollow ring of an echo following it close 'Claire! Claire, where are you? For God's sake, Claire!'

'I'm here!' she cried. 'I'm coming!' and sprang to meet him.

XV

'IT PASSES AWAY'

After the scream had stopped short it was desperately quiet.
He stood there under the trees with the revolver still levelled
in his hand, staring stupidly at the sprawled body upon the
garden path. He was slow to realise that it had lain there for
some seconds without further sound or any motion. The shot
had to some extent shaken the fog that clouded his mind, the
scream had thinned it, but it was the stillness that blew upon
it like a great wind and tore it to shreds. He knew what he
had done. He knew he had set out to do it. It only remained
to discover the necessary command of his mind and muscles,
and do the next thing as promptly; but the difficulty was to
believe sufficiently in what was already done. It wasn't
possible; such things didn't really happen. What if he had
put the gun in his pocket with some brooding idea of murder,
and taken station here in the shadow to make very sure
Charles should not enter the house unseen? Still it could not
be true that he had actually gone through with it. Something
operates to stop the hand, surely, even when the mind is
keyed near to insanity. Good God, he couldn't have shot
Charles! It wasn't possible! And if he had, it must be no more
than a superficial wound, not beyond treatment. Why, he'd
pulled the gun out of his pocket and let fly with it in the same
movement, by an uncertain light, and with a hand none too
steady. Maybe he had in his time been good with a revolver,
but not so good as all that. Besides, he'd acted on an impulse,
as blindly and angrily as the wind blowing, only his instincts
and not his wits directing the deed; and angry men's blows
never get home effectively. Or do they? By some devilish

gesture of luck, do they? It would be like him to do the job too thoroughly, just when he was within reach of seeing it must never be done at all.

The body did not move, but with intensity of staring he believed for a moment he saw its outlines shift. One hand lay in the bushy tatters of the fringe of box, the other was doubled under him to fend him off from the ground. The impact had taken him in the back; at this distance it was impossible to tell exactly where, but fairly high, surely, at a guess well up in the shoulder, with little or no damage. By the way he'd fallen, too, it must have been so. Why didn't he get up? Why didn't he even move, or groan, or curse, or show any sign of life? He'd come down pretty heavily, and the path was paved; maybe he'd stunned himself. That might be it, by the way the yell had snapped off short. But he couldn't be as dead out as he seemed, not from a fall at any rate partially broken by one arm. This was no good, thought Jonathan, swallowing his rising sickness, in the end he'd have to go and look.

It was an effort to make the first move, but once uprooted he could bear to go. He walked forward shakily and stood over Charles, peering at him doubtfully but hesitating to touch. Still no sound nor motion. He hardly dared look closer, but because he knew he must he fell on his knees and searched for the mark of his shot. There, low in the left side of the broad back, was a darker spot upon the coat, and his fingers found a sticky, warm dampness round it. He couldn't believe it. Things couldn't turn out like this, not here in Sunderne, not between him and Charles. By all the rules of chance he should have missed, but chance was breaking all its own rules. He sat back on his heels, staring a long time at the arrogant square back turned up to him from the path. Its stillness was out of character, but its vigour remained. Something about the cut of it, the swing of the big shoulders, the easy straight gait, had maddened him past bearing; but what wouldn't he have given now to see that same blunted view of it thrusting through the gate of Long Coppice as if the house and the woman were so much property in a pocket of the rough tweed coat. Maybe they were; what did it matter? Why had he ever let himself imagine it mattered so much? But they shouldn't have tried to get rid of him. They shouldn't have put their heads together to decoy him away to Australia and leave them a clear field. How could he endure it that Claire should lend herself to such a conspiracy? How could he stand by and watch Charles going in and out like a proprietor, and not want to kill him for it? And the careless thrust of the shoulder to open her gate, the flick of the hand swinging it to again, had caused something to break inside him, and he had done what he wanted to do.

He found himself trembling, and was shocked at the discovery, and trembled all the more. He put the gun down, very carefully because of the quivering of his hand, under the miniature hedge of box, and lifted Charles over in his arms. The body was so much dead weight; the face, bruised and soiled about the left cheek, was fixed in pained astonishment. There was no blood that he could see, but neither could his shaking fingers find any heartbeat, or his straining ear any sighing of breath. But he was being a fool. Charles was stunned, that was all. The pounding of his own blood in his ears prevented him from detecting any other pulsation. Presently Charles would open his eyes and stare gradual recognition, and curse him off in furious indignation to bring some more congenial assistance. On her very doorstep, too! He might as well have pushed her into his arms. Besides the other penalties to which he'd laid himself open. What was it, the charge they made? Unlawful wounding? Or attempted murder?

Oh, God, this was awful! His nerve was giving way. If he could have brought himself to pitch the gun in the pool and make a bolt for it, then it might not have been so frightening; but he knew he couldn't. Charles might lie here and quietly bleed to death for want of attention if he left him. Not that he cared if Charles died, not that he wouldn't still be glad of it;

but it mustn't happen that way. No, he couldn't run. He had to find out how bad it was, and he had to get help. Whatever he'd done, he must stand to it.

His fingers shook so, and were so clumsy even when he forced them into steadiness, that it took him a full half-minute to get a button or two of Charles's shirt undone, and his hand inside feeling for the heart. He found no heat of blood, no moisture, and no beat. A moment he crouched there trying to believe he detected a faint, capricious pulsation, deep in the big body; then a sudden dew of horror broke and crawled upon his spine, chilling him like a scud of rain. He lifted the inert weight wildly in his arm, shaking it so that the heavy head rolled against his shoulder.

'Charles!' he said urgently. 'Charles! Come on, snap out of it! Charles, do you hear me?'

But Charles couldn't hear him. It was too late for that.

Terror came on him that he was seen. The road was unfrequented, but the night was fine, and some courting couple might easily choose to walk this way. If he couldn't bolt, neither could he bear to be surprised like this. He got a purchase on one of the big wrists, and drew Charles's arm round his neck, and so heaved him up to his shoulder. The front door of the house was barely ten yards away, but it was all he could do to reach it. Some of his physical strength had gone with his sense; only the stimulus of horror enabled him to sustain the unwieldy weight as far as the deep doorway, and drag it labouring into the house. The sound of the door closing behind him should have made him feel more secure, but instead it loosed all the tumult of panic in him as if it had echoed the shot his own over-skilful hand had fired. He tumbled the body from him on to the long cushions of the settle in the hall, and fled from it without another look, stumbling and skidding on the rugs, crying out desperately for company.

'Claire!'

Where was she? Not in the room where he usually found her, for there was no light burning. Not upstairs, for the lamp on the landing was not yet lit. He wanted her suddenly with an appalling longing.

'Claire! Claire, where are you? For God's sake, Claire!'

An answering voice cried from the garden: 'I'm here! I'm coming!' At the very note of it a gush of gratitude and weakness sprang up in him, so prompt it was, so reassuring. As if she knew the need, and had been waiting for nothing else; as if she had the power to make all right again, even death, even murder. He heard her running along the path, fleet steps as confident and comforting as midday, running to answer the alarm in his voice and soothe away whatever terror had him captive. He had known she could be like this when she was moved, but how could he guess she was so ready to respond to the first appeal? And what was that quality in her voice and in her running so far beyond his expectation or understanding? Was it joy? What should she be doing with joy, here alone in the cold of the garden?

He saw her appear like a wreath of blown mist outside the window, a sudden stormy pallor, with bright white face and erected hair. The door was thrown open wide before her, and she sprang into the edge of the circle of light from the one shaded lamp, a gust of sweet air trembling about her, and scent of rosemary spilling from the swirl of her skirts. Even in his own extremity he could not choose but halt before the brilliance of her eyes, and stand aghast at her as at changeling or fairy. Her motion was like flight, and her sudden stillness, poised in the doorway, was like the lighting of a bird, skirts and arms and shoulders and hair settling and folding downward, nestling to her slenderness with the speed of passion and the grace of deliberation, smoothing every line into a marvellous repose. The outlines of her throat and face, where the light clung, were like candle-flames, so smooth, so long and so steadily soaring in their brightness that it was rather as if some artist in illusions had drawn a luminous woman upon the air. Her eyes which had curtained themselves languidly from his looks of late, were wide and brilliant now, shadow of lid and lash rolled back from them so that they drew to their deeps all the light in the room, and gave it back in a glitter of emerald and topaz. She was smiling. He had never seen such a smile, like rose-coloured lightning charmed into stillness. She stood there for a moment dazzling and daunting him with her strangeness before he realised that she was looking clean through him, and a long moment more before her searching eyes relinquished the hope of finding what they sought.

The change which passed over her was not gradual, but instant, the quenching of a star. The softness of her lips, which had promised utterance of unimagined kindness, took wing in a breath. The light which had made her incandescent was put out, and without a movement, without a tremor, she became white and firm as marble. Until then he had scarcely been sure if she knew him, but now she was as he remembered her, human almost to weariness, within the reach of acquaintanceship, misgiving and alarm, and she looked at him with the frightful awareness of a creature startled out of sleep into immediate danger. She drew a sharp but quiet breath, and asked in a whisper:

'What's the matter? What's happened?'

'It's Charles!' he said. 'I shot Charles! Oh, God, Claire, what am I going to do?' In the relief, however vain and however ephemeral, of having another person share his knowledge he began to shake uncontrollably, and clung to the wall to keep himself upright; but his voice was low, even secret, shocked into quietness. He saw her nostrils dilate, and the skin over her cheek-bones tighten whitely, but no rage of personal grief or anxiety visited her eyes. She came forward into the room and took him by the shoulders, holding him hard with fingers whose strength he had never suspected.

'You *what*? Do you know what you're saying?'

'I know what I'm saying, and what I've done! I tell you I shot him. We've got to get a doctor to him, Claire. He may be still alive. Help me, Claire!' he said piteously. 'Tell me what to do!'

Claire said: 'Where is he?' and putting Jonathan from her

with no gentleness strode into the middle of the hall, and looking round in one whirling glance, saw the body of Charles lolling along the settle. She plunged to her knees beside him, and felt at his heart.

'Not here? It wasn't done here?'

'I carried him in,' said Jonathan at her shoulder.

'In the garden, then? But why, why? What had he done? What had he said to you?' He tried to begin to answer her, through his sickness and lassitude, but as quickly she put his lame attempt by, with the least sudden gesture of her hand. 'Never mind! Wait!' She held her breath, frowning down upon her halted fingers.

'Is he dead?' asked Jonathan, the breath labouring in his throat with a slight but horrid noise.

'I don't know. I can't be sure.' She leaped to her feet again, and ran for a mirror to put to the astonished lips, and leaned over him again for a long moment straining for the least cloud upon its brightness. The convex surface continued clear. Slowly she sat back upon her heels, and put up a hand to her head as if to smooth away the confusion within, but let it fall again in her lap with the gesture only half completed. Something had happened to upset the synthesis of her heart and mind and spirit. She was aware of horror, of desperation, but had no means to feel them. She was broken into two contradictory halves, at once pitiful and scornful, fevered and cold. The only significance this cast body held for her was the material one of police, inquests and trials, the total invasion of her precarious peace. Yet this boy at her side still made his preposterous claim upon her, just by running to her, just by being in need; and which way was she to go? It is possible to be loyal where you do not acknowledge you have a debt to pay.

'He's dead,' said Jonathan.

She turned, raising herself hastily, and again took him by the arms, shaking him a little as emphasis to her words.

'What happened? I must know how this came about. Did he meet you outside? Did he speak to you? How did it begin?'

'I don't know – I was crazy. I came down here with the gun in my pocket, and waited among the trees—'

'I know,' she said sharply, 'I saw you there. Did you come with this in mind, then?'

'I suppose I did. I suppose I must have done. Oh, my God, Claire, it can't be true. He's only stunned, isn't he?'

'Go on,' she said peremptorily. 'You were there with the gun in your pocket. Was it loaded? Did you load it before you came out?'

'Yes. I knew he was going out, and I was sure it would be here. I wanted to kill him. But I never thought I could! I suppose I was getting some satisfaction out of going through the motions, but that doesn't mean I planned it this way.'

'Yet you knew what you were doing when you fired,' she said.

'No, I swear I didn't. Oh, I knew the next minute, but it was too late then. I – it was the way he walked, the way he came in at the gate there – I couldn't stand it. If he'd been only a bit later I might have cooled off and got the sense to go home, but he had to come then, while it was bad. And when he swung in here as if he had a lease on you – and I knew you were here waiting for him—'

'You mean he didn't even speak a word to you? He didn't even know you were there?' she panted, shutting her hands on his flesh fiercely.

'He went clean by me, never looking left or right – you know him. I told you he always went straight out for what he wanted. I just pulled out the revolver and shot him—'

'In the back,' moaned Claire, 'in the back!'

He said: 'Oh, my God, Claire!' in a shattering voice, and dropped his head into his hands, shrinking from her touch, but she kept her hold upon him, taking his bowed body into her arms. It was not by this road he had meant to find his way there, nor did the gesture mean more to him now than any other creature's exasperated kindness.

'It's all right,' she said firmly, 'it's all right! I know how it happened. Don't expect me to be complacent about it, but I do realise it wasn't quite an ambush from behind a tree. Here, sit down here!' She drew him to a chair, and thrust him into it bodily. 'I'll get you a drink.'

She went and came again with the demoniac energy he had never seen in her until this night and poured whisky into him, keeping her hand shut over his as he gulped it down, for the glass rattled against his teeth. He drew breath hard, and sat bracing himself by the arms of the chair, and for a moment they stared at each other in silence.

'He's dead. Isn't he?'

'Yes,' said Claire, 'you made a job of it; he's dead.'

'I was trying to kid myself I might be wrong. That makes it murder. For God's sake, what am I going to do?'

That part of her which was alive to the reality of the tragedy relinquished here all disdain of him and all impatience with his weakness. Did she know what it was like to have killed? What it did to the mind and the will? She put down the glass and came back to him.

'No one else knows anything about it? No one can possibly have seen you?'

'No, there was nobody about. I've got to get away,' he said, searching her face with his frantic eyes, 'there's nothing else for it. I've got to get out of this before anyone starts making enquiries about either of us.'

'And leave me to do your explaining for you?' she said, with a sweep of her arm towards the body on the settle. 'Am I immune from suspicion, do you suppose?'

'Oh, God, Claire, I didn't mean that! I'm sorry,' he said, abjectly. 'I'm sorry! I can't even think straight. Help me to think! What *am* I to do? What *can* I do, if I can't run for it? Even if I – got rid of him – there'd soon be a hue and cry. But it might give me a little time – and you'd be clear of it.'

'Don't be a fool!' she said brusquely. 'You wouldn't get ten miles before they'd lay hands on you. You advertised your feud too well to be safe for an hour after they know he's missing.'

'But they need a body to prove murder. Bodies can be disposed of.'

'You'd have to dispose of me, too,' said Claire. 'Do you think I shall be such a fool as to tell a pack of lies for you? Charles has as much right to justice as you have to mercy.'

'Do you think I'm going to hang for him?' cried Jonathan, clutching at her arm in a frenzy of suspicion that she meant he should.

'Yes, if you do anything so crazy as running away or trying to destroy the evidence. Oh, don't look at me like that, I'm not planning your death. All I want now is to keep you from making it a certainty. You know as well as I do you'd be in custody within a day. The first reaction to his disappearance would be: 'Where's the nephew?' Get hold of yourself now, and listen to me! Where's the gun? What have you done with it?'

He remembered it for the first time with the shock of desperation.

'I forgot the damned thing. Oh, God I must get it. I put it down in the garden when I lifted him.' He dragged himself to his feet in haste, but she took him by the sleeve and pulled him round to face her.

'There'll be no foolery of throwing it down a pit, or in the river. I won't let you throw your life after his.'

'I'll do what I damn well please!'

'Then it won't continue to please you for long. Can't you see the only hope you have is to go to the police yourself?'

'Give myself up? Are you mad? What a fool I should be!'

She kept her hold of him, her eyes in the narrow flame of her face green as a cat's in the dark. 'What a fool you'll be to do anything else. I tell you I won't lie for you. Whatever murders you've done I'll have no hand in yours. So either kill me, too, or do as I say. Go and tell the whole truth of your own will, and the truth will work for you. Let them ferret it out with every sort of hindrance from you, and it will hang you. Can't you see that?'

'I can see you'd want to hang whoever killed Charles,' he

said viciously. 'I suppose that's what you're after.'

'Fool, fool!' she cried, shaking him vehemently in her thin, long hands. 'Are you quite past reason? I wish I'd never set eyes on either of you. What have you been to me but a continual trouble? God knows why I should even try to help you, but I am trying. Don't you see that if you go to the police yourself, and do everything you can to make their job easy, it will count in your favour? There's a hope of a reduced charge, at the least. If you truly fired at him as you say you did, in such a rage that for the moment you were hardly sane, and if you come out with the whole story of your own free will, they may make it manslaughter, not murder. That's the only chance you have. A murderer doesn't carry his victim into the nearest house and call for help, as you have, or run for a doctor and the police, as you're going to do. Do you suppose they're incapable of drawing a simple conclusion?'

'You expect me to take a risk like that?' said Jonathan in a suffocating voice.

'It's the least risk that offers, and you must take it. Can you seriously hope to be at large for a day, whether you give yourself up or put them to the trouble of finding you? Then give yourself the benefit of circumstances. Lie if you like. Say the gun went off in your hand. I daresay he'd lie for you if he could, being a Kenton. If you must lie, for God's sake do it properly and stick to it, and if there's any doubt in your mind that you can make a good job of it leave it alone. Only don't run! It would be suicide to run.'

He said, suddenly collapsing together between her palms: 'I know you must be right, Claire. You always have been right.'

'Then go, quickly. Take the gun and give it up. Send the doctor down to me here, and then go to the police. Don't lose any more time. Every minute you save is in your favour, and every one you lose is against you.'

He straightened himself with an effort. 'I hate leaving you here alone with him.'

'What, still, Jonathan? Oh I'm not afraid of him, if that's

what you mean. Why should I be?'

'Will you help me to go through with it, Claire? It isn't so damned easy.' She felt him trembling. 'Yes, it's all right, I am going. I know I've no choice, or precious little. But will you – just stand by? It makes a difference.'

'I'll help you, now and always, as well as I can. Whatever happens, I'll not be far away, I promise you that, Jonty.'

'God bless you, Claire!' he said, and shut his arms about her for one fleeting second before he put her away from him and moved with very fairly firm steps towards the door. The walk was not his walk as she knew it, but as rigid as the gait of a mechanical doll; yet he went steadily, and she did not doubt that he would survive the lonely walk to the village with still enough strength of purpose to complete his errand. And after that it was out of his hands and hers.

What had she promised him? More than she could make good? More than she owed him. Yet she would not go back from it, neither in will nor in heart, neither now in silence nor at any later time in the turmoil she dreaded for herself and him. Not even when her vision divided, and she could wonder and rage at her own folly, and in the same breath pity him with a steady and radiant reflection from another pity, too gigantic and too painful ever to be seen whole except in a mirror image. She watched the door close after Jonathan's going, and stood for a moment still looking after him when the sound of his steps had faded from her hearing; then she crossed the floor to the dead man's side. Poor Charles! The living take up so much of one's time; who has leisure to regard the dead?

Now it was very silent, and the one shaded lamp only coloured a small corner of the obscurity. Outside was the night in its impersonal vastness, and here only an illusion of light which served to make clear how dark was the world. In the outer fringes of her consciousness there was the sound of the rising wind circling the house steadily, soaring and crying, crying its hunger upon a thin sad note that never rose or fell from its desolate monotone; but within she was aware only of the strangeness of silence where for the moment no voice called, no hand moved, and no heart felt desire of anything. She stood staring down upon the body of Charles, the startled face upturned to her now so indifferently, the arrogant eyes shut from taking any further pleasure in her, the single heart and resolute mind loosed for ever from the slavery of coveting her, even as a prize of war. To love is to give up half your personality, and to hate is to cripple what remains; but Charles was free of both tyrannies. Seeing so much vitality and energy brought to so sudden a stillness she had thought at first: 'Poor Charles!' as if he had been cheated of what was his by right, but now she saw that he had only just been made free of it. Jonathan had not intended that, but perhaps the power which had given Jonathan his nature had intended it. When she lifted one chilling hand and laid it more easily upon the cushions it returned her no touch, nor did one line of his slumbering body grow taut at her nearness. He had left life with astonishment, but his repose was no less complete for that. How admirable is death, she thought, which restores to lovers and all other prisoners this majestic indifference. Hedged about as she was by the nightmare future and the sterile past, for a moment she could almost conceive that this superhuman calm extended to her own heart, so still was everything within.

And then like lightning-stroke, the pain, the pain! This quietness was not hers, but only something at which she could look on and wonder for a moment while her stunned mind groped about blindly to reorientate itself in the darkness of a world shaken from its equipoise. There was no gradual recovery, no cramp of returning consciousness. Suddenly this dazed and darkened creature within her reared itself upright and turned its face towards its true pole, and sense and sight came back upon her full with the onset of fire and storm. Confusions burned away from her as the clothes had flared into tinder from Salathiel Drury's body, and a sadder wind than the outer evening knew folded about her spirit and drew round her an ascending spiral of flame. She sprang erect from leaning over the body, reaching upward for air until almost she seemed to lift herself from the ground; and she cried out for vehemence of desire and terror with a weird, wild cry which cast its echoes about the lofty roof like sparks struck from the steel of her pain. What was it to her if Charles was dead and Jonathan was in danger of death? Why had she let them deflect her with these unexpected weapons from the end she passionately desired? Why had she let any disaster of theirs shake her eyes from her star? So short a time of looking away, and where was the light now, and how was she to follow it, being blind and benighted? So short a time of comforting Jonathan, and where was Salathiel gone? Out or reach, out of hope, passed by like the crying wind and the plunging autumnal stars while she fumbled with the little pestering stupidities of men, where was now the moment of meeting? Nothing had happened, no voice from without or within had cried out to her in warning, but while her face was turned away the purpose of her life had approached and passed by. Had he wondered, had he mourned, that she reached no hand to him? Had he receded from her with backward-turned face and desolate eyes, or gone with even breath and unreluctant tread, since she had failed of her tryst, and go he must? And was there left of him nothing within her reawakened reach?

What had she done? To what had she condemned herself? Into what an emptiness had she suffered herself to be betrayed? A dizzy sickness sprang up in her like a gush of bitter water, whirling about and about in her brain. It was as if she span madly in the unwinding of the broken coil of time, only this wild diminishing flight left to her before her spirit subsided into a stony stillness. She put out her hands to fend herself off from obstructions she could not be troubled to see, and clawed her way out by the garden door into the fragrant and mournful night.

With the cold touch of the wind some last despairing strength visited her limbs. She ran down the slope of grass, and stood a moment to free her face from the veiling softness of her blown hair. Stars between the tumultuous clouds stood beautiful in calm, unaware of time and insensible to pain. But God must know, if God can see beyond the nebulæ. She ran on down the narrow path between the cushions of thyme and sage, her face raised to the unresting wind, her breast full and heavy with imprisoned fear. There was nothing here, nowhere touch or sense or breath of him between the garden and the sky. Had he smoothed away utterly in passing even the prints of his feet? Or had she made for herself out of the malleable stuff of her own obsession the tremor of his approach, the conviction of his nearness, the sure knowledge of time's ascent to her zenith? For it was gone, and this place was empty and sweet and untroubled. He was not here. He had not come, or he was come in her absence and in her absence departed. And which of these was truth she was not ever to know, never, never to know.

The sundial stood a column of pallor in the dark, and beyond it burned in a scarred and fitful brightness the heaped fire of turf, its smoke streaming away from her down the wind. She halted beside the stone bench, and looked about her with a sudden arrested wonder to find herself still sensitive to sound and sight where there could never again be anything worth hearing or seeing. For what she heard was the withdrawal of all music from the world in which she must still move and speak and seem to be alive; and what she saw was the recession of beauty and radiance from the garden, from the stars, and from her own late-blossoming mind. Nothing was left, nothing had been vouchsafed where the least sign, no greater than a dropped leaf, could have saved her. The dead leave no gentle remembrancers behind; nor does time halt long enough to shed one flower out of season, or gather up a longing and satisfy it even with one kiss before hushing it to sleep. She knew herself spent; she felt herself forlorn.

Past her stirring skirts there went a rustling whiteness, and the smoky red of the bonfire flared up for a moment, and again faded into dullness. She looked down, and saw her manuscript book lying open upon the bench where she had cast it from her. The clasps had sprung apart with the light but glancing fall, and the wind as she watched was peeling off the leaves one by one with a sad, deliberate motion, and feeding them into the pyre; as though a lover, with great heaviness, sat alone by night committing to tenderest memory before he burned them the letters of the dead.

A RARE BENEDICTINE

THE ADVENT OF BROTHER CADFAEL

Ellis Peters

'Brother Cadfael sprang to life suddenly and unexpectedly when he was already approaching sixty, mature, experienced, fully armed and seventeen years tonsured.' So writes Ellis Peters in her introduction to *A Rare Benedictine* – three vintage tales of intrigue and treachery, featuring the monastic sleuth who has become such a cult figure of crime fiction. The story of Cadfael's entry into the monastery at Shrewsbury has been known hitherto only to a few readers; now his myriad fans can discover the chain of events that led him into the Benedictine Order.

Lavishly adorned with Clifford Harper's beautiful illustrations, these three tales show Cadfael at the height of his sleuthing form, with all the complexities of plot, vividly evoked Shropshire backgrounds and warm understanding of the frailties of human nature that have made Ellis Peters an international bestseller.

'A must for Cadfael enthusiasts – quite magical' *Best*
'A beautifully illustrated gift book' *Daily Express*
'A book for all Cadfael fans to treasure' *Good Book Guide*
'Brother Cadfael has made Ellis Peters' historical whodunnits a cult series' *Daily Mail*

Other Ellis Peters bestsellers from Headline: MOURNING RAGA, DEATH TO THE LANDLORDS, PIPER ON THE MOUNTAIN, CITY OF GOLD AND SHADOWS, DEATH MASK, FUNERAL OF FIGARO, THE POTTER'S FIELD

HISTORICAL FICTION/CRIME   0 7472 3420 5

HARRIET SMART
— A —
GARLAND
OF VOWS

**A MOVING AND PASSIONATE
EDWARDIAN LOVE STORY**

Lady Kitty Valentine is the daughter of an Earl. Raised in luxury,
trained in the arts and social graces, she is expected to make the right
marriage. But Kitty chafes against the confines of her class, and when
she meets Philip Winterfield, she falls in love with a man her parents
can never approve of. Everything conspires to keep them apart, and
she has to give him up even as she gives up his child.

Philip is the younger son of John Winterfield of Winterfield Works in
Birmingham. His father is a stern and rigid Catholic, whose religious
moralising disguises a frightening brutality. Apprenticed to his uncle,
architect Sebastian de Troyes, Philip is inspired by his uncle's genius
but forced into subterfuge by the spectre of Sebastian's drunkenness.
After a final confrontation, he escapes to London, leaving behind his
only chance of happiness.

Years later, newly widowed after a desperately unhappy marriage to
Lord Randolph Glastonbury, Kitty is reunited with Philip. But the
blissful reunion is not all that it promises to be...

'Extremely promising first historical novel...precisely and lovingly
observed...excellent' *Sunday Times*

FICTION/SAGA   0 7472 3781 6

A selection of bestsellers
from Headline